Linda Fairstein is a former prosecutor and one of America's foremost legal experts on crimes of violence against women and children. For three decades she served in the office of the New York County District Attorney, where she was Chief of the Sex Crimes Prosecution Unit. In 2010 she was the recipient of the Silver Bullet Award from the International Thriller Writers association. Her Alexandra Cooper novels have been translated into more than a dozen languages and have debuted on the *Sunday Times* and the *New York Times* bestseller lists, among others. She lives in Manhattan and on Martha's Vineyard.

Also by Linda Fairstein

The Alexandra Cooper Novels

Final Jeopardy
Likely to Die
Cold Hit
The Deadhouse
The Bone Vault
The Kills
Entombed
Death Dance
Bad Blood
Killer Heat
Lethal Legacy
Hell Gate
Silent Mercy
Night Watch
Death Angel
Terminal City
Devil's Bridge

Non-Fiction

Sexual Violence: Our War Against Rape

LINDA
FAIRSTEIN

Killer Look

sphere

SPHERE

First published in the United States in 2016 by Dutton,
an imprint of Penguin Group (USA) Inc.

First published in Great Britain in 2016 by Little, Brown
This paperback edition published in 2017 by Sphere

1 3 5 7 9 10 8 6 4 2

Map by David Cain

All characters and events in this publication, other than those clearly in the public domain, are fictitious and any resemblance to real persons, living or dead, is purely coincidental.

A CIP catalogue record for this book
is available from the British Library.

ISBN 978-0-7515-6039-8

Typeset by Palimpsest Book Production Ltd, Falkirk, Stirlingshire

Printed and bound in Great Britain by Clays Ltd, St Ives plc

Papers used by Sphere are from well-managed forests
and other responsible sources.

Sphere
An imprint of
Little, Brown Book Group
Carmelite House
50 Victoria Embankment
London EC4Y 0DZ

An Hachette UK Company
www.hachette.co.uk

www.littlebrown.co.uk

For

Lisa and Alex

Marc and Suzy

Through tattered clothes great vices do appear;
Robes and furred gowns hide all.

King Lear, WILLIAM SHAKESPEARE

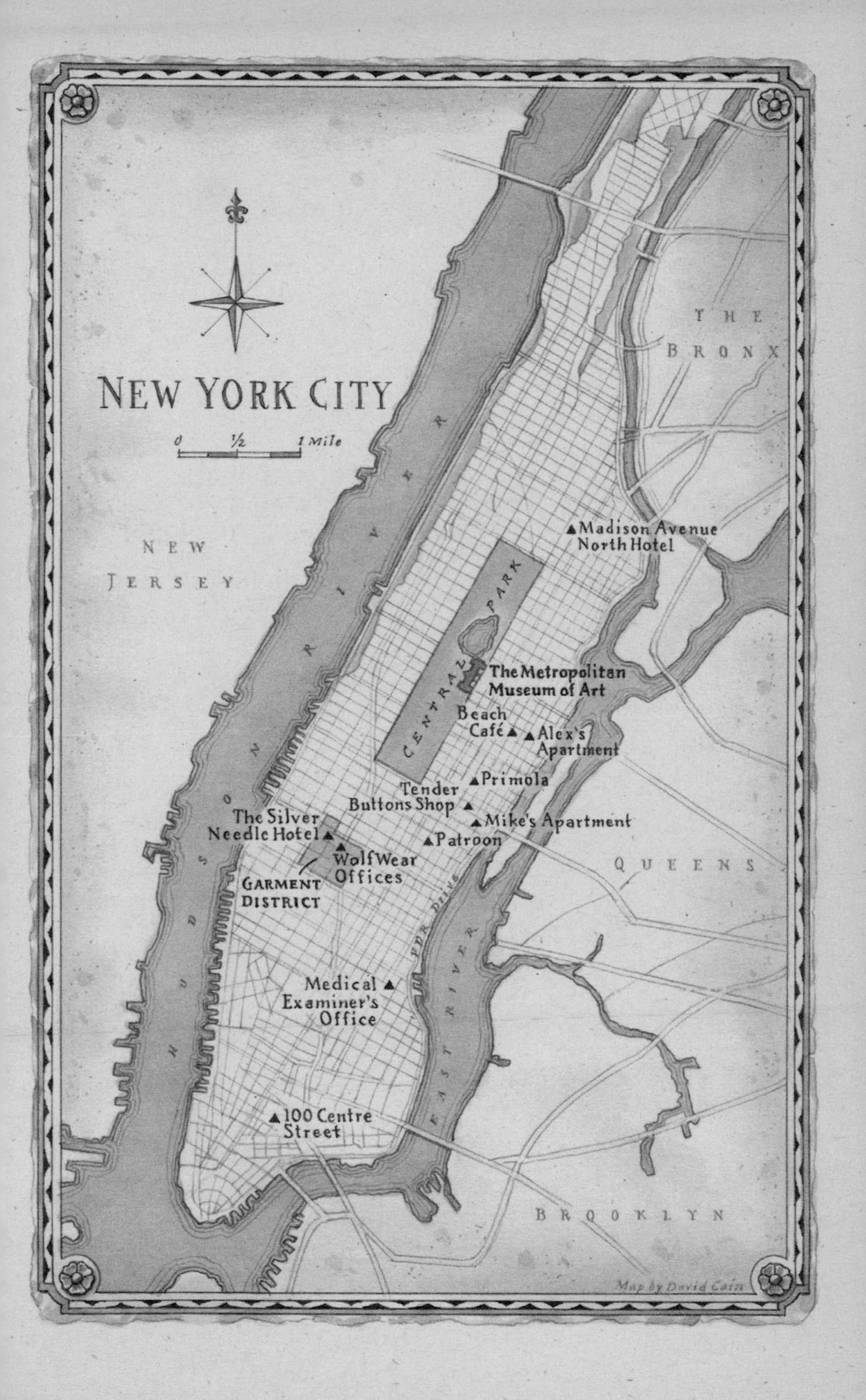
NEW YORK CITY
0 1/2 1 Mile
NEW JERSEY
HUDSON RIVER
THE BRONX
QUEENS
BROOKLYN
EAST RIVER
CENTRAL PARK
FDR Drive
Madison Avenue North Hotel
The Metropolitan Museum of Art
Beach Café
Alex's Apartment
Primola
Tender Buttons Shop
Mike's Apartment
Patroon
The Silver Needle Hotel
Wolf Wear Offices
GARMENT DISTRICT
Medical Examiner's Office
100 Centre Street
Map by David Cain

One

'Murder trumps everything.'

Mike Chapman turned his back and stared out the window, talking to me but unwilling to make eye contact.

'What do you mean?' I asked.

Darkness had enveloped my Vineyard landscape a bit earlier each evening as November crept up on us. The late fall also brought a bone-deep chill and the threat of a serious frost.

'Like you don't know, Coop?'

'Of course I do, in general. But why did you say that now, Mike? Before we have dinner. Before we get into bed.'

It was six fifteen and I was standing at the bar, refilling my glass with ice cubes and a couple of inches of scotch. It had been three weeks since I'd been kidnapped and held by murderous thugs, out to exercise their revenge for an old grudge.

'That was the lieutenant who called,' he said, turning at the sound of the cubes dropping into place. 'He's ordered me back to the city on a case. Besides, I don't seem to be doing much here for your post-traumatic stress.'

I sat the glass down and let the scotch trickle over the ice to reach a good sipping temperature while I walked over to Mike, wrapping my arms around his neck. 'You're doing everything for me that I need. You know that.'

'Really? And all this time I thought it was the alcohol getting you through the night,' he said. 'I'm beginning to believe your view of things is that PTSD stands for Pour That Sweet Dewar's.'

I let go of him and retreated to the bar. 'A smack in the face instead of a kiss on my lips. Got that one loud and clear.'

'Then do something about it, Coop. Put the brakes on your extended cocktail hour.'

'Why? You've just announced that you'll be leaving in the morning,' I said. 'Did I get the message right? Murder trumps *me*, that's for sure. My safety, my well-being, my comfort level, my—'

'"My, my, my". Sounding totally self-centered now, aren't you?' Mike said. 'The *New York Post* and the other tabloids are going to miss that I-can-nibble-on-barbed-wire-and-dance-barefoot-on-burning-coals-while-I'm-sending-those-predators-up-the-river-forever crusader for justice. That image gets benched in favor of a whining sex-crimes prosecutor who trades in her silk blouses for a straitjacket. You'll have the sympathy of every juror in the box.'

'I'm not looking for sympathy from anyone.'

'Alexandra Cooper, for the People,' Mike said, banging

his fist on the dining-room table like his hand was a gavel and he was a criminal-court judge. 'Tall and tough, sleek and shiny, loopy grin on her face when she ventures to smile, but she's afraid of her own shadow now. Ladies and gentlemen of the jury, I'd advise you not to make any sudden moves, 'cause she might freak out, and never, never frown in her direction, because she takes everything very personally.'

'Cut it out, Mike.' I took another hit of the cool scotch.

'Self-pity doesn't become you.' He walked toward me, took the glass from me, and held my face between his hands. 'And you can lose that look in your eyes, too.'

'Fear? You've always told me that fear is healthy.'

'True, when you've got something to be afraid of. That's all over, Coop.' He pulled me against his chest and stroked my hair with his right hand. 'Maybe you need to come back to New York with me. Come home.'

'This is my home.'

I'd bought this old farmhouse in the town of Chilmark on Martha's Vineyard more than a dozen years ago, with my fiancé – a young doctor named Adam Nyman. When he died in a car accident on his way to our wedding week-end here, it became my refuge. The remote location and the serenity of this hidden hilltop made it a sanctuary from the stress of my high-profile work in the Manhattan District Attorney's Office.

'You think you're ready to go it alone?' Mike asked, rocking me gently from side to side in his long arms.

'Sooner or later I have to, don't I? Tomorrow's as good as any other day.'

I had been taken hostage by a stone-cold killer and his accomplices a month earlier, kept bound and sedated for several days, fed only oranges and bottles of water.

'You haven't spent a night by yourself since—'

'I know exactly when.'

'Snap at me? Kind of like a dog biting the hand that feeds it,' Mike said. 'A mad dog.'

Once I was rescued from my abductors, the docs had kept me in the hospital for four days to examine and observe me. I flew up to the Vineyard the afternoon after my release with Nina Baum – my college roommate and one of my two closest friends – who had left her husband and young son in Los Angeles to be with me for a week. When she had to go back, my other best pal, Joan Stafford, had come up from DC to keep watch over me. I had no secrets from either of them, and it had been so easy to confide my every thought and feeling while they tended to my fragile emotional state.

I broke away and reached my arm out to grab the glass.

Mike beat me to it and dumped the drink down the drain. 'I've got a nice Sauvignon Blanc for dinner,' he said. 'Take a break from the booze and let's enjoy the fire for an hour.'

'Then what?' I asked. 'You'll ration me?'

'Yeah. I'll serve you out of a thimble,' he said. 'That way you won't be as likely to pass out on me as you did last night.'

There wasn't a better homicide detective than Mike Chapman. We had partnered on cases from the time I'd been a rookie in the DA's Office. He had covered my back more times than I could count throughout the past decade, and he teased me mercilessly, to the point at which protesting was hopeless. Since late summer, we'd been lovers, neither one of us certain that we could make this new dynamic work for us because of the tension in the intervening weeks.

Paul Battaglia, the district attorney, had told me to take off as many months as I needed to restore my sense of security. I knew, when he said it to me, that my safety wasn't an issue. He was referring to my sanity. Everyone seemed to think I'd become unbalanced by my victimization.

'I didn't pass out, Mike. I just fell asleep.'

'In the middle of my best moves? Better for my ego if you go with passing out.'

I walked into the living room and stretched out on the floor, on the white rug that fronted the fireplace. Mike followed me in, placed two more logs on the fire, then lay down beside me. After Joan's tour of duty as my keeper, the lieutenant had given Mike five days off to spend with me. I didn't want it to end.

'So what's the case that's taking you back to the city?' I asked while he rubbed my bare legs. I was wearing one of his shirts, which practically covered me down to my knees.

'No reason to talk about it. Nothing special.'

'There's a dead human being involved. Unnaturally dead. Of course it's special.'

'You're off-duty, Coop,' Mike said. 'And until tomorrow, so am I.'

'So I can't talk about murder. I'm not allowed to drink. I'm useless in bed. What's left?' I said, trying to make Mike laugh.

'Oysters first. Then lobster. Three-pounder for me and the smaller one for you.'

'That's my surprise? Sounds delicious.'

Unlike my girlfriends, Mike had tried to leave me alone in the house for a few hours each afternoon. I knew he was testing me, and it turned out I wasn't as nervous as I feared I might be.

'I've got to put some meat on your bones, babe.'

After Columbus Day, all the stores and restaurants on my end of the island shut down for the winter season. The year-round population wasn't enough to support their businesses. We always bought our chowder and fried clams at the Bite, our cooked and split lobster and shucked oysters from Larsen's Fish Market, burgers and ice cream at the Galley. But they were closed till April.

'I can help you cook.'

'Not your best skill set, Coop. When I start the water boiling, you can bring out the dishes and silver, and light the candles,' Mike said. 'Then all you've got to do is eat.'

I hadn't regained much of an appetite since leaving the hospital. Waves of nausea would sweep over me from time to time for no reason at all.

I rolled over to get on top of Mike and shimmied my way up his chest so that I could put my mouth on his. I kissed him deep and long, then slid down onto the rug, on my back.

'Glad you can still chow down, Coop. You should save some of that for the lobster tail.'

An hour later, after some fireplace foreplay, I spread a towel a few feet away from the hearth while Mike shucked the oysters that were fresh out of Katama Bay.

'Appetizers in here,' I said. 'It's much more romantic.'

We both inhaled the briny oysters to a mix of Sam Smith, John Legend, and Frank Sinatra. I was saving Smokey for the bedroom.

I kind of lost my way again while Mike was cooking. Not so much a function of the darkness and the wind that was picking up around the perimeter of the house and howling a bit, but the thought that the next day he'd be gone and I would be alone to wrestle with my demons.

My mind wasn't on the great-looking feast that Mike had prepared but on the bottle of wine that he opened while I plated the lobster.

'Cheers, Coop,' he said, clinking his glass against mine. 'You're in much better shape than you were when I put you and Nina on the plane to come up here.'

I nodded. If that's what it looked like to him, then so be it.

'And don't be a hero. The minute you're ready to come back to the city, I'll be in charge.'

'I don't want Battaglia to know, Mike. I'm not ready to go back to work.'

'Screw him, kid. No need for him to know your business.'

I held out my wineglass.

'Let me see you take a whack out of one of those claws first.'

'Hardball, is it? How about giving me a straw for the vino?'

We were both subdued throughout dinner. The great thing about lobster was that I could hide the parts I didn't eat in the shells that would be discarded. I just wasn't hungry.

By the time I did the dishes – seizing the chance to pour myself a nightcap – Mike was in the bedroom suite, showering. I stripped off my clothes and stepped in beside him, under the giant rain-shower head. I lathered up and shampooed my hair, eager to get the day's anxiety washed away.

I crawled into bed next to Mike. He was on his back, one hand behind his head, staring up at the ceiling.

'Don't worry about me,' I said. 'About tomorrow.'

'That's not where I was, Coop.'

'Your victim, then?'

'Yeah.'

'Who was he?'

'She.'

'She? Do I know the case?'

'It's not exactly a bedtime story.'

'Try me,' I said.

'You're doing well enough with your own nightmares, kid.'

'I'm mostly over that, Mike.'

'Bullshit,' he said. 'You were thrashing around like a dervish the night before last.'

'That was then, Detective. Maybe I can help. What case?'

'You don't know it. The body was found two weeks ago, while you were up here.'

'I read the newspapers every day.'

'Some vics don't make the headlines, Coop. They just lie on a slab at the morgue, waiting for someone to come along and claim them.'

'How'd she die?'

'Blunt-force trauma, we think.'

'How come you don't know?'

'The body was pulled out of the East River, south of the Triborough Bridge.'

'Who was she?'

'I heard you the first time you asked,' Mike said. 'We didn't have a clue at the time. There was no ID on her, and the sea creatures had done a pretty good job gnawing on her face and fingers. But that's why I'm going back to work.'

'You mean you don't even know her name?'

'Lieutenant Peterson just got a confirmation on that at three this afternoon.'

'Thank God someone finally claimed her. I hate to think of—'

'Nobody's claimed her yet.'

'So how was she identified?'

'The broad had silicone breast implants, Coop. Seems

that one of them survived intact during her submersion in that floating cesspool they call a river.'

'What did that give you?'

'Every implant has a manufacturer's serial number on it, so it can be tracked for quality assurance or defects.'

'Seriously?'

'Yeah. An implant is a medical device, kid, just like a pacemaker or defibrillator. So Tanya Root – that's the broad's name – had her breasts enhanced last year at a clinic in Rio. Now all I have to do is find out who wanted her dead.'

Two

Morning fog, a common occurrence on the Vineyard, delayed Mike's seven-thirty flight to White Plains. The major airlines didn't run this time of year, so he was on a single-engine nine-seater Tradewind flight to a small airport just north of the city.

'So what will you do to figure out who Tanya Root is?'

We were on our third cup of joe in the Plane View coffee shop, in the terminal at the edge of the airfield. I was trying to distract Mike, whose cloud gazing was a hopeless attempt to gauge the turbulence of his flight off the island. He had an intense fear of flying – just about the only thing I knew, other than commitment to a personal relationship, that scared him.

'The usual,' Mike said. 'The lieutenant put Jimmy North on the case with me.'

'He's that new kid in the squad who worked with you to – well, to find me, isn't he?'

'Yeah. Whip-smart. Great cop.'

'He must know something by now,' I said.

'Ran a background check on the name and came up with one hundred thirty-seven African American Tanya Roots in the USA.'

'But there must be more specifics in the medical record from the clinic. Date of birth? Home address?'

Mike checked the email on his iPhone – the last case convinced him that his vintage flip had obvious drawbacks – and read from it. 'The address Miss Formerly Flat-Chested gave was a flophouse hotel in Rio near the clinic.'

'No help there,' I said.

'The medical history lists her as saying she was from the States, but nobody cared about the GPS coordinates as long as she was paying cash. And the doc noted that he guessed her DOB was phony. She used one that made her twenty-three, but he figures she was closer to thirty.'

'Weird that he would make a note about that.'

'Not so much,' Mike said. 'He did it in the context of encouraging her to come back for work on her eyes, and to think about a first facelift before she was forty. So he did his own professional estimate of when she might plan those events.'

Instinctively I reached for my chin. I was thirty-eight, and not the plastic-surgery type. I liked what nature did to the faces of those who lived interesting lives. But I checked to make sure my jawline was still firm. I couldn't imagine a facelift at this age.

'Don't worry, Coop. You flap your mouth too much to develop any flab under there.'

I could hear the engines of the small plane before I saw

its white fuselage break through the low clouds. Its wings were tilting left to right, fighting the wind and weather as the pilot struggled to set it down on the runway.

'So why all the talk of work on her face and body?' I asked.

'Because she told the good doc that she was a model.'

'A model?'

'That's what we've got to go on. A name that may or may not be legit. A phony date of birth. No address. And we know that somebody crushed her skull and threw her into the drink from somewhere in East Harlem.'

'Was there enough detail for a facial reconstruction?'

'Forensic anthropology at the ME's Office is working on that now. From what I saw of the remains, it will be rough to do one,' Mike said. 'But we've got to get some kind of image into the papers and out in public. The tabs would probably rather put close-ups of her breasts on page one, and the doc has plenty of those.'

'It would be great if they can't get their hands on that stuff.'

'This investigation is going to be worked more like a grand-larceny auto than a homicide.'

'That's cold,' I said.

'Every car has a VIN number, Coop. Find a stolen car, an abandoned one – whether it's a '95 Chevy or a 2015 Jag – the VIN will trace you back to the owner. Just a fact. Tanya's breasts have unique digits. Sooner or later we'll put them together with the right broad.'

The prescreening announcement for Mike's flight came

over the loudspeaker. He picked up his duffel bag and left money for the bill and tip.

'Thing is about models,' I said, standing up to walk with Mike to the security check-in, 'is that they've sort of made it by seventeen, or twenty-one at the latest. If Tanya Root has any kind of career, someone should call in with info the minute you go live with the story.'

'Hoping so, kid.'

'But a late twentysomething trying to make a change in her professional life by enhancing her bra size doesn't sound like top runway material to me.'

'That's why I expect my day will be knocking on doors and coming up empty till we get some kind of lucky break,' Mike said.

'There's a huge fashion show at the Metropolitan Museum next week,' I said. 'I'm sure lots of models are in town and around for that. Might be people involved there you could talk to about your victim. I feel so totally useless to you these days.'

Mike dropped his duffel to embrace me and deliver a last pep talk. 'It's all behind us, Coop. You've got no one looking to do you any harm, there's no bogeyman hiding under your bed, and you've got a bigger and better support system than anyone I can think of.'

I had flashbacks, whether my eyes were open or closed. Before I got out of bed every morning, I had relived the moment of my abduction a dozen times. The smallest exercise that required no thought – brushing my teeth or putting on lipstick – gave me the chance to revisit hours spent with my captors. The videotape in my brain was on a loop that kept replaying itself constantly.

'I know you're right,' I said to Mike.

And he knew I was lying.

'You going straight back to the house?' he asked.

'I am.'

He kissed me on the forehead. 'I'll call you when I land.'

'That's if your white knuckles haven't embedded themselves in the armrests on the plane.'

'Glad you haven't lost your sense of humor entirely, Coop,' Mike said. 'I've got my big-boy pants on though. I'll be fine.'

There were only two other passengers traveling with Mike. I watched them load up, and waited until the plane taxied out to the runway, revved up its engine, and took off into the dark clouds overhead.

I was back up in Chilmark by the time Mike touched down forty-five minutes later. He had business to do, and I needed to adjust to life alone. I locked the front door of the house – unheard-of to do on the Vineyard, but lately every precaution I took seemed reasonable to me.

The first clap of thunder nearly bounced me out of the chair in my office. It was an odd time of year to have an electrical storm. I didn't need the fury of a sound-and-light show to unsettle me.

It caused the house power to go and my internet service to crash, but only nineteen seconds later the generator kicked in and rebooted everything.

I tried to distract myself with a good book, but most

of the things on my shelf were crime novels or nineteenth-century British literature, the latter an interest that had absorbed me since my days majoring in English at Wellesley College. I'd lost my taste for both the hard-boiled and the dense storytelling – temporarily, I hoped.

I phoned in to some of my team at the DA's Office, but everyone seemed to be in the courtroom or at the morgue or the Special Victims Squad, handling their own cases as well as doubling down to cover my load of investigations and trials, too.

The turkey sandwich I made was dry and tasteless. I played with half of it and threw away the rest.

The rain had stopped by early afternoon. I was reclining on a sofa in the living room – feeling too lethargic to do anything – making my third or fourth attempt to re-create the steps I had taken last month when I left celebrating colleagues at Primola Restaurant to slip off to meet an ex-boyfriend. I was looking for a safer route than the one I had chosen then.

I heard the car's tires crunching on the broken clamshells that decorated the long drive up to my property line before I saw its black silhouette.

I went to the window to check out my visitor. I was shaking uncontrollably as I tapped in the password on my iPhone.

It looked as though there was a driver in front and two heads in the backseat.

I scrolled my contacts to get to the Chilmark Police Station, two miles away. They would have a quicker response time than the down-island officers who manned the 911 calls.

The rear door on the driver's side of the car opened, and I saw a man's leg kick out and plant itself on the wet path. Then, just as quickly, the man pulled his leg back inside and the idling car lurched into reverse.

'Chilmark Police. How can I help you?'

'This is Alexandra Cooper,' I said, blurting out my address, too. 'There's just been an intruder at my house and I need an officer up here immediately.'

'Alex? This is Wally Flanders. Someone broke into your house?'

'Wally! So glad it's you,' I said. I'd known him for years and didn't have to explain my background and why I might be in danger. 'Not a break-in, no, but—'

'What do you mean by "intruder"? Have you had a burglary?' he asked. 'Mike Chapman dropped in the other day. Sort of told me about things. He's with you now, isn't he?'

'No. Mike just flew off this morning,' I said. Of course he stopped at the police station on one of his outings so the locals wouldn't think I was crazy if I called for help. 'Not a burglary, no.'

'What then?' Wally asked. 'I can be up there in ten minutes.'

'A car. A car with strangers in it just drove up to the house. A guy started to get out and then they must have seen me in the window and backed off,' I said. 'Backed off for now.'

'Drove up to your front door, Alex?'

'Not exactly. But whoever it was trespassed on my property.'

I could hear myself talking but couldn't stop. I had fielded this kind of call from unhinged witnesses – solid people who'd had screws shaken loose by a close call with crime, as well as total wackjobs who had never been grounded in the first place. I didn't want to be the crackpot caller, but I was doing a damned good imitation of one.

'So you're not hurt, Alex, are you?' Wally asked. 'And there's been no forced entry at your home?'

'Not yet.'

'To be clear then, we've got a trespass. Unauthorized car drove up to your front door and—'

'Actually, Wally, the car stopped before coming onto my lawn.'

'You mean he was on the path that leads to you from State Road?'

I knew what was coming next. I didn't own that path. It was the common property of the three other neighbors – none of them winter residents – who lived on my deserted dead-end hilltop.

I tried to modulate my voice as my nerves continued to fray. 'Still, Wally, there's no one here this week. I'm all alone. There's no legitimate reason for anyone to drive in here.'

'Alex? I'll come up there if you'd like. I can be there in a flash,' Wally said. 'But you do know that Fern's house has been on the market for four years, don't you?'

I knew that as well as I knew my name. 'Sure.'

'There are real-estate people in and out of there all the time since the price came down over Labor Day. Could be just an honest mistake, Alex, but I'll come up and check it out right away.'

I didn't do my usual and tell him not to bother. I wanted to see a cop on my turf, and I wanted to see him before darkness fell.

'That would be great. I'd really appreciate it,' I said. 'Do we have Uber on the island yet?'

I was still confused about why the Uber car I had called the night of my kidnapping hadn't seen what the perps did to me. Everyone was still a suspect in my overworked mind.

'Uber? You mean the car service?' Wally said. 'None of that bullshit here yet. Just Patti's Taxi and Aquinnah Cabs. You need a lift?'

'Just asking.'

'I'll be right up, Alex.'

'Thanks so much, Wally. See you shortly.'

I was throwing my clothes and toiletries into my tote when my phone rang.

'Hey, kid, what's keeping you busy?'

'Just trying to relax, Mike. You know. Reading a bit. Thinking about having a massage delivered to me at home,' I tried to joke. 'Sweet to hear your voice.'

'You okay, babe? You sound kind of tense,' he said. 'Did I forget to put that child-proof safety lock on the Dewar's?'

'Not funny.'

'Look, Coop, Wally just gave me a call.'

'What? Whatever happened to privileged conversations?' I had gone from unbalanced to angry in a flash. 'I'm livid that he told you about it.'

'Wally Flanders is neither your lawyer nor your doctor. And he's certainly not a priest or rabbi,' Mike said. 'He's looking out for you. How's that? He's doing what I asked him to do in case I had to leave. I just didn't know if the phantom of the black sedan was a real thing or a scotch-induced vision.'

'I haven't had a thing to drink, Mike. That car was – well, okay, this is what you want to hear, right? I'm hallucinating. Does that make you happy?'

'Whoa. The rabid-dog mood is back. Gotta love that pooch.'

'We're about to be disconnected, Detective Chapman. Wally's knocking on the front door.'

And I needed a drink more than I needed oxygen.

'Record time, Wally,' I said. 'I think it's only been eight minutes since we hung up. I can't thank you enough.'

'Newspapers made it sound like you've been to hell and back. I don't blame you for being jumpy.'

'I know I'm perfectly safe here.'

'That black car is next door, Alex. Real-estate broker showing the place to some folks from DC. Comfortable with that?'

'It's still here? How long is it going to take them?'

I didn't figure being alone on this road with people I didn't know.

'I'll walk back there and find out, Alex.'

I hesitated for a minute and then decided to ask anyway. 'Wally, there's no direct flight to New York after the morning one that Mike was on, right? Is there still a five-P.M. Cape Air to Boston this time of year?'

'Yeah. It's the only late-afternoon flight out of here now.'

That would take just thirty-three minutes, and then I could grab the shuttle to LaGuardia.

'Are things quiet enough – I mean, except for me,' I said, with a forced laugh, 'that I might impose on you to run me to the airport?'

'I don't see why not, Alex. I'll walk next door,' he said. 'Can you be ready in ten minutes?'

'You bet.'

He backed out of my doorway, left his car in place, and walked up the drive toward my neighbor's home.

I dialed Cape Air, booked myself into one of the three remaining seats, and poured a short nip of scotch while I finished gathering my papers and clothes.

The bumpy flight was right on time. I'd been through worse things than air pockets lately. I dragged my suitcase to the Delta terminal, submitted myself to the metal detector, and boarded the 7:30 shuttle to LaGuardia.

I didn't make the choice of my destination until the cabdriver had crossed the bridge and headed south on the FDR, passing the spot, no doubt, where Tanya Root's body had been dumped in the river. If I went home, I risked the possible rejection of Mike not coming over to me when his tour ended.

I gave the driver the address of Mike's apartment – a tiny walk-up near York Avenue on East Sixty-Fourth Street that was so small and dark he had nicknamed it 'the coffin.'

We'd had keys to each other's homes for more years than I could remember, for an assortment of good reasons. I climbed the stairs and let myself in.

I didn't bother to unpack, but I took a steaming hot shower before I tossed Mike's dirty underwear and socks off the bed and settled myself under the covers.

It was after eleven P.M. when I heard the door close behind him and looked up at his face as he stood over me. His fingers were combing through his thick black hair as his puzzled expression turned into a smile.

'What happened, Coop?'

'I needed you, Mike. Murder trumped everything but that.'

Three

'Did you vote, Alexandra?' Stephane asked me.

I was waiting for Mike and our friends Mercer and Vickee in the bar at Ken Aretsky's Patroon, another restaurant in my comfort zone of places with great food where I also felt totally at home. Stephane, the handsome maître d' with the most divine French accent, had helped me to a glass of my favorite Chardonnay.

'*Mais oui, mon ami,*' I said. Somehow I had lifted myself out of my state of emotional paralysis to get things done after Mike had left for work. 'I always vote.'

It was the first Tuesday in November.

'Your boss, he is up for reelection today?'

'Next year, Stephane.'

I had been crushed by what I had recently learned about Paul Battaglia's political involvement with a shyster minister, the Rev. Hal Shipley. Though Battaglia had a two-decade hold on the job of district attorney, I found myself wishing he would find a graceful way to step down. I had no desire to support him any longer.

'I'll have whatever she's having,' Vickee Eaton said to Stephane as she sidled up next to me at the bar. 'Been way too long, girl.'

I reached over to give her a hug and probably clasped on to her a little harder and longer than I meant to do.

'I wasn't sure you would come tonight,' I said. 'I'm mortified. I didn't want to see you and Mercer before I found a way to express how very grateful I am to you for—'

'Stop that, will you?' Vickee said. 'Did it ever occur to you that I was just doing my job?'

'And breaking every rule in the book while you did? I don't imagine that was the case.'

Vickee Eaton was also a detective, assigned by the police commissioner himself, Keith Scully, to the Office of the Deputy Commissioner for Public Information. Mike told me that it was Vickee who kept him one step ahead of the PC's plans in the manhunt for the demented perps who had taken me.

'How are you, Alex?' Vickee asked, one hand on my arm as she tried to get me to square off and look at her. 'Really. The truth.'

'Let me give you ladies your privacy,' Stephane said, pouring wine for Vickee.

'Would you please top me off?' I asked, tapping the side of my glass.

'Certainly, Alexandra.'

'We'll be four, Stephane,' I said as he headed toward the main dining room.

'*Oui, Mademoiselle.* Detective Chapman already called to reserve.'

'Are you feeling any better for a few weeks on the Vineyard?' Vickee said.

I knew the answer people wanted when they asked how you felt after an ordeal or a tragedy. The questioner meant well, whether you just buried a relative or had your third round of chemo or were the survivor of a sexual assault. They rarely wanted to know about the dysfunction or disarray in your life caused by the traumatic event. They wanted the short answer. They wanted, 'I'm okay' or 'I'm over it'.

'So much better, Vickee. I think I'm back on my feet again.'

Her reaction would tell me whether Mike was spreading the news that I was hanging on to my marbles by a thread.

'What did you do today, Alex?'

She met my stare with a poker face. But that's how good a friend she was, too. Good enough to ask me to be godmother to her son, Logan, when he was born four years ago. Good enough not to judge me by one of Mike's reports on my condition.

'Voted. Shopped for groceries. Took some things to the dry cleaner. Started to sort out one of my closets.'

Best to leave out the hour or two I spent in a fetal position on my bed, and the uncontrollable tremors that started when my cell phone beeped with an AMBER Alert about the kidnapping of a Brooklyn toddler.

'That's the way, Alex. Take it slow. Nobody's expecting

you to be slaying dragons in the courthouse anytime soon,' Vickee said. 'The guys will be here any minute.'

'Mike and Mercer are together?'

'Yes. The commissioner figured he ought to put a Special Victims detective on the Tanya Root matter till they get a handle on how and why she died.'

Mercer Wallace – Vickee's husband – was one of a handful of first-grade African American detectives in the NYPD. He was a rock-solid investigator, four years older than Mike, and the person with whom I had worked more rape cases than any man in the department.

My professional antennae stood up at attention. 'Why? Does Scully think she was raped?' I said. 'I'd better get someone assigned from the office to team with them.'

'Slow down, girl. You're on leave, remember?' Vickee said. 'Catherine Dashfer is handing out the assignments for you. She's on it herself.'

No wonder I hadn't been able to reach her yesterday. She was my trusted deputy and close pal, but I suspected she had orders from Battaglia to shut me out of the trail of information.

'There are some things I ought to tell her,' I said to Vickee. 'I've had some ideas since I heard about this last night. Like next week's big fashion show at the Met.'

'Tell Mike,' she said. 'Tell Mercer.'

'You don't think Catherine will talk to me about it?'

I was beginning to sound paranoid now, which was bound to make all my buddies take note. There didn't seem to be a PTSD symptom that was passing me by.

'Of course she'll talk to you, Alex. It's just that you're going to see the guys in a few minutes,' Vickee said. 'What other ideas have you had?'

I didn't answer. I took a slug of my wine, looking around for Stephane to fill my glass before Mike arrived.

'What? You don't trust me anymore?' Vickee said, rubbing my back.

'You don't seem to think my Met suggestion is the way to go. I mean, I know very few supermodels ever have big breasts,' I said. 'Kind of ridiculous this woman wanted to enhance them at this point.'

'Kate Upton,' Vickee said. 'She's got a chest, Alex.'

'But she was discovered when she was sixteen.'

'Maybe the girl wanted to be like Tyra Banks. Huge ones.'

'But Tyra was even younger,' I said, nodding at the bartender, who had taken his place opposite us in time for the evening crowd. 'Fifteen when she was picked up to hit the runway and the cover of *Vogue*.'

'Whatever your point is, Alex, I don't think the current wisdom in the department is that Tanya Root is a supermodel, by any stretch.'

'I get what you're saying. But if the guys have no way to jumpstart this, they might at least talk to people in the fashion community,' I said. 'Or do you already know something that Mike didn't tell me?'

'Don't be silly, Alex,' Vickee said. 'I have no idea what the guys found out today. I'm just talking common sense. The woman's age, the surgery to increase her breast size, the fact that if a top model has gone missing there'd be someone – an agency head, a boyfriend, a designer – someone to blow the whistle on her disappearance.'

I didn't have anything else to offer about Tanya Root. I knew that before I opened my mouth. But I didn't like the feeling of being out of the game. Mike, Mercer, and I had worked scores of these cases as a team, feeding ideas off one another's insights and experience.

'Keep an eye on my glass,' I said, smiling at the bartender. 'If you see me getting low, just add some more and put it on my house tab.'

I could go a lot longer on wine for an evening than I could on whisky.

'Sure thing, Ms Cooper.'

'Logan would love you to come for an overnight at our place,' Vickee said, changing the subject entirely. 'You could spend a few days with us. Readjust to city life.'

'I'm dying to see him,' I said. 'Maybe after I get settled in back at home.'

I saw Mercer coming to join us while Vickee was doing her best to offer me another safe haven. He was much taller than Mike – almost six-foot-six – and had his arms spread wide to embrace me.

'You look a hell of a lot better, Alexandra, than the last time I saw you,' Mercer said.

'That's a good thing,' I said. 'My psych-ward pallor was off-putting to everyone.'

'It wasn't a psych ward. It—'

'Might as well have been,' I said. 'Everybody poking

and prodding me like I was an alien creature, just set down on Earth for a short visit.'

Mike followed Mercer into the small wood-paneled room and stepped behind me, planting a kiss on my neck.

'Got that one right, Coop,' he said. '*Klaatu barada nikto.*'

Mike was quoting from his favorite movie about aliens: *The Day the Earth Stood Still.* I had watched the original and the remake with him more times than I could count.

'Coop believes she was saucered in from another planet to save all the Earthlings, just like Gort,' he said to Vickee. 'Why don't you convince her that other people have the situation under control?'

'I'm trying to do that, Mike,' Vickee said.

'She's got this messianic complex, like the world will really come to a stop if she isn't solving sex crimes twenty-four/seven.'

'Don't be ridiculous. Tomorrow is manicure and pedicure, then haircut and color. Relaxed enough for you, Detective Chapman?' I doubted that I could sit still long enough to be pampered, but I so desperately wanted to give it a try.

'Sounds perfect to me,' Vickee said.

'Sparkling water all around,' Mike said to the bartender.

'Don't do that on my behalf,' I said. 'Not-drinking, I mean. I'm off the scotch.'

'Why would you think that's the reason, kid? Mercer and I have worked up a real thirst today. Might be that something we stirred up by snooping around will have us going back at it later on.'

That was pure bullshit. Mike could throw down vodka all night and, with a few cups of espresso, be back on the job with no sign of overimbibing. Besides, nothing was going to heat up on Tanya Root's case tonight.

'Progress?' Vickee asked.

'Nothing to speak of,' Mercer said.

'Anyone come up with something helpful on Tanya Root?' I had already perked up at the prospect of talking about a real investigation.

'Not yet,' Mike said. 'There should be a sketch ready to go public by tomorrow or Thursday.'

'No missing persons?'

'Always. Calls galore, but nothing that fits,' Mike said.

'The model angle?' I asked.

'More likely a hooker. Model wannabe,' he said, turning to the bartender. 'You mind switching on that TV, m'man?'

The bartender picked up the remote and clicked the power on. The small set was hung in the corner, above the rows of bottles of aged liquors that had such rich color and, I imagined, soothing taste.

Mike took the remote from the bartender and began searching for *Jeopardy!*. He had an unerring sense of timing and had rarely missed the last question of the show, whether at a crime scene or the Medical Examiner's Office or a dinner with friends. For as long as I could remember, Mike and Mercer and I had bet on Final Jeopardy!, passing twenty-dollar bills back and forth throughout any given week as though they were Monopoly money.

'Were there any signs of sexual assault on the vic's body?'

I asked Mercer as Mike found the channel and upped the volume.

'Didn't Mike tell you there wasn't much of anything left for the ME to study?'

'Well, how about the interior vaginal vault?'

'Ms Root was in the water for days,' Mercer said. 'Sort of washed out any evidence there might have been.'

'How stupid of me. I should have known that,' I said.

'Saved me from insulting you, Coop. Right on the money. Stupid it is,' Mike said. 'Now, pay close attention.'

Trebek revealed the giant blue board with the category: MAJOR LEAGUE BASEBALL.

I groaned. Things were definitely not going my way.

'Put your money on the bar, kid,' Mike said. 'One twenty for us, and another for the bartender, who seems to think you're the glass-half-full, not half-empty, kind of person.'

'You know as much about baseball as we do,' Mercer said.

'Yankees,' I said, pulling the money from my tote. 'Just Yankees.'

'The Final Jeopardy! answer is: HE IS THE ONLY PLAYER TO WIN THE AMERICAN LEAGUE BATTING TITLE WITHOUT HITTING A HOME RUN.'

The timer ticked on while the three contestants seemed as baffled as I was.

'Child's play,' Mike said. 'Okay if we go to our table?'

'I'll send the Pellegrino over,' the bartender said.

'And my Chardonnay, please?'

'Ixnay on that, kid,' Mike said. 'You stay sober and I'll let you play detective with me this week. Break you back in, if you're up to it.'

None of the contestants had come up with the correct question. Trebek apologized to them before he got ready to ask the winning question.

'You got this?' Mike asked Mercer.

'Indeed I do.'

They both spoke at the same time. Mercer said, 'Who is Rod Carew?' while Mike said, 'Who is Sir Rodney, one of the great Zonians?'

The two friends high-fived each other as we walked to the front of the dining room. I looked longingly at the dregs of my drink, left behind us on the bar, while they tossed around statistics about the Twins star who had been born in the Panama Canal Zone.

Mike tried to get me to eat some of his grilled thirty-five-day dry-aged sirloin and sides of onion rings and fries – usually my favorite dinner – but I could barely manage a Caesar salad, which Stephane whipped up at the side of the table.

Vickee chattered on about the social gossip of the last three weeks, trying to keep the conversation away from crime and violence. Keith Scully sent his regards – which signaled to me that Vickee had told him she was on her way to see me tonight – and one of the other women at DCPI was pregnant again and one of the guys from Major Case who'd given me a hard time over the years had been flopped back to a lesser command.

'You can do better than this,' I said. 'Something more interesting must have happened while I've been in PTSD land. Give me some of the real dope.'

'Why is it always all about you, Coop?' Mike said, leaning back against the smooth leather surface of the booth encircling our table. 'Why can't the four of us just chill for the evening?'

This time I had reason to think it was about me. I couldn't shake the feeling that everything in my life had been turned upside down – maybe never to be righted – just a few short weeks ago.

I pushed the salad around my dinner plate, like a six-year-old playing with her food.

'I'm going to go home tonight,' I said. 'To my own apartment.'

Vickee flashed a quizzical look in Mike's direction. 'Why don't you – ?'

'I think that's a great idea,' Mike said.

'Mind your business, Vickee,' Mercer said. 'Home is where Alex should be, actually. It's where she lives, for God's sake. And there are two doormen on duty 'round the clock.'

I was testing Mike, but he didn't seem to mind the pushback at all.

I lived in a pricey high-rise close to Park Avenue in the seventies. The trust fund my father had set up for my brothers and me, after he and another doctor he partnered with invented a tiny plastic device used in practically all open-heart surgical procedures, allowed me a lifestyle that public service couldn't support. The Cooper-Hoffman valve had sent me through Wellesley and the University of Virginia School of Law, and made it possible for me to do the work that I found so deeply rewarding.

Mike's cell phone vibrated, and he stood up at the side of the booth to take the call. He turned his back to us, listened for close to a minute, then talked for twice as long before rejoining our table.

Mercer and Vickee knew better than to ask him what the call was about. I, on the other hand, felt no need for boundaries at this particular moment.

'Tanya Root?' I asked.

'Since when have I been a one-case wonder, Coop?' Mike asked. 'All quiet on that front.'

'None of you are talking about your other work. Rape, murder, the load of cases you've been handling. You all obviously think it will upset me.'

Mercer and Vickee shifted in their seats, deferring to Mike's judgment.

'It was Lieutenant Peterson, kid. Picking what's left of my brain.'

'On what?' I asked, leaning in toward him.

'A suicide in the south.'

Mike's command was Manhattan North Homicide, which picked up all the murder cases north of Fifty-Ninth Street, to the tip of Manhattan bordered by the Harlem River. The Manhattan South Squad covered the southern half of the island. Both were elite units made up of skilled detectives – mostly men, even at this point in time – who combined classic investigative talents with evolving forensic techniques.

I sat back. The NYPD was required to respond to suicide scenes. They were, after all, unnatural deaths.

'Why you?' I asked. I wanted Mike to come home with me. He hadn't yet said that he would, so the last thing I needed was a case to take him away.

'It's a helium inhalation suicide,' he said. 'Hotshot businessman in his hotel room.'

'They're growing in the "right to die" movement, aren't they?' Mercer said.

'Yeah. We've had two of them in the north this year, and one was mine. The south lieutenant called Peterson to see if we had any pointers for the scene investigation.'

'You're going too fast for me, guys,' I said. 'What's growing? What's the manner of death?'

'Exit bag over the head, Coop,' Mike said. 'Asphyxiation by gas.'

Four

Mike drove me home after dinner. He stopped the car in the porte cochere that ran in front of my building like a driveway.

Vinny and Oscar were the doormen on duty. Vinny was at the passenger's side door as soon as he saw Mike pull in. He opened it for me and waited while I turned back to Mike.

'Coming up?' I swallowed hard – pride too – as I asked the question.

'I've got an early morning. You try to get some real sleep,' he said, flashing his trademark grin to reassure me that things between us were okay. 'Tomorrow night, for sure. After all, you'll be blonder by then.'

I leaned over and kissed him on the cheek. 'Don't give up on me yet, okay? I'm coming back, I promise.'

Vinny walked me inside, where Oscar had already pushed the button for the twentieth floor. There were security cameras in the elevators, and I knew they would be watching me all the way up.

I turned my key in the lock and pushed open the door. I'd left the lights on when I went out for dinner, preferring to come home to familiar things that I could see.

It was only nine thirty. I poured a sensible amount of Dewar's and took it into the bathroom with me to sip while I soaked in a hot whirlpool tub.

I climbed into bed with a stack of magazines, ignored the doctor's advice about taking Ativan with my liquor, and started flipping through pages till sometime close to three A.M., when the drugs overcame my insomnia and I fell soundly asleep.

When I woke up it was almost eleven A.M. Mike had left me three voicemails, among others from friends. He had started his day witnessing the autopsy of a young mother caught in the crosshairs of a gang shooting in Washington Heights. From the morgue, he had stopped at the boutique hotel where the suicide had occurred, and the final call was his attempt to express his concern for me.

I slipped into my robe and walked to the front door to pick up the newspapers.

The *Post* was on top of the others. Its entire front page was devoted to the man who had chosen a stark hotel room in which to end his life. The photograph was a headshot of a face familiar to fashionistas and socialites, as well as to entrepreneurs who had followed – and tried to emulate – his rags-to-riches story.

Wolf Savage, the seventy-two-year-old clothing designer who had built an empire that rivaled those of Ralph Lauren and Oscar de la Renta, had carted two helium canisters to his hotel room, undressed himself, lain down on the bed, and put a plastic bag over his head.

Mike hadn't mentioned the name of the dead man to me. I was stunned. The well-known designer was the one who had broken away from his competitors months ago and announced he'd be holding his own fashion show – out of season – at the Metropolitan Museum.

LONE WOLF. That was the headline that appeared over the picture of Savage, which was side-by-side with an image of the logo that branded his work and was recognized worldwide. WW – for WolfWear, with the head of the animal inserted in the space between the double letters – had become almost as ubiquitous as Lauren's polo pony.

I turned to the page-two story. 'Billionaire businessman Wolf Savage, who was as well known for the string of wives he left behind as he was for his eponymous clothing brand, died alone yesterday in a suite at the Silver Needle Hotel. Estranged from his fifth wife, forty-one years his junior, Savage chose to end it all by himself in a rented room in the Garment District, instead of at one of his posh homes in Connecticut, Palm Beach, London, or Milan.'

I brewed a cup of coffee and sat down at my dining table. Wolf Savage was front page in the *Times* and *Journal* as well, where both the articles focused on the serious business accomplishments of the Brooklyn-born executive, who in four decades had transformed his small, inexpensive line of sportswear into an international trend-setting phenomenon. He was a couturier as admired in Paris as in New York, and a retrospective of his greatest work was being held at the Costume Institute in the Metropolitan Museum simultaneously to the fashion show Wolf had planned to move to the Temple of Dendur, also at the Met.

I dialed Mike's phone.

'About time you woke up, kid. Everything okay?'

'So far, so good,' I said. 'I'm just reading the papers. Why didn't you tell me the suicide you were talking about was Wolf Savage?'

'What difference does that make, Coop? You know him?'

'I don't know him from Adam,' I said. 'But sometimes I wear him.'

'You like that shit, with some beady-eyed animal crawling up the front of your clothes?'

'It's good stuff, WolfWear,' I said. 'And this is a huge story. Anything unusual at the scene?'

'Same old, same old,' Mike said. 'What time is your appointment at Elsa's?'

'Hair's at four. Mani-pedi at one.'

'That's the life, kid. You better get a move on.'

'How are you spending the rest of your day?' I asked.

'The girl who was autopsied this morning. We got some leads on the gang members who were involved. Going back uptown to check them out.'

'Mike?'

'Yeah?'

'It feels good to be back in the city,' I said. 'And I really liked the message you left for me. You know, the last one.'

'Nice,' he said. 'Nice on both fronts. You stay busy, Coop. I'll see you later.'

I skimmed the Wolf Savage stories. There hadn't been time for a full obit, but there were a bunch of features culled from clips about him over the years.

The Garment District – a rectangular patch of Manhattan that spreads from Fifth to Ninth Avenues, West Thirty-Fifth to West Forty-Second Street – had once been the heart of this entire country's clothing design and manufacturing industry. As technology and cheap foreign outsourcing picked away at this long, local supremacy, Wolf Savage – according to the *Times* – was one of the power players fighting to maintain the character of this historic one square mile of city real estate.

Sort of ironic, I thought, that he chose to end his life in a new hotel, the name of which paid homage to an essential tool of the trade – the Silver Needle – on West Thirty-Eighth Street, in the very heart of what had been, for more than a century, the Garment District.

My phone pinged to announce an incoming text. It was Joan Stafford. 'How about that Savage Soiree gown you wore to my wedding? Save it for the Costume Institute at the Metropolitan Museum. Value just went up.'

'Your WolfWestern suede jacket from last year when fringe was so hot? I should never have made fun of it,' I replied with both thumbs. 'You can have your own room at the Met, Joanie.'

It pinged again. I laughed to myself, thinking of all our shopping expeditions together and what other Wolf creations hung in our closets. But this time the texter was Laura Wilkie, my longtime secretary.

'I hope all is well, Alex. Just wondering – a young woman called a few minutes ago. Says she went to high school with you. Lily, from your swim team in Harrison. She seems desperate to talk to you. May I give her the Vineyard number?'

So Laura didn't know I was back in town. That was a good thing. Maybe the level of gossip about me had settled down. I racked my brain to pull up a mental image of Lily. I thought of a scrawny brunette with sad eyes, a year behind my grade, who did backstroke on the relay team I anchored with freestyle.

'All good with me, Laura. Miss you. Miss everyone. Best to give Lily my cell, thanks. Talk to you soon.'

'Can't wait to have you back,' Laura texted. 'Will do.'

In less than a minute, my phone rang. 'Hello,' I said. 'This is Alex Cooper.'

'Alex? It's Lily Savitsky. I didn't know whether you'd remember me, so thanks for taking my call.'

'Not a problem,' I said. 'Harrison High. The Dolphins. You did an awesome backstroke.'

It was a pretty common occurrence, actually, for people from my past to reach out to me, because my career was such a public one. Friends of friends who'd been sexually abused, relatives of relatives who needed a therapist or a divorce lawyer, acquaintances of folks I'd met only once or twice who wanted free legal advice. I was used to these calls.

'Yeah. I guess it's been twenty years,' Lily said. 'Look, I know you're out of town, but I have a pretty urgent situation, Alex. I'm hoping you can put me in the right hands.'

'I can try, Lily,' I said. 'What's it about?'

'I don't know where you're traveling and what kind of news you get, but it's the lead story here in the city that a designer named Wolf Savage killed himself yesterday.'

My back stiffened. 'I've seen the papers, Lily. It's the top story everywhere.'

'Then I need your help,' she said. 'The police and the medical examiner won't listen to me.'

'Go on.'

'Wolf Savage was my father,' Lily said. 'He didn't kill himself, Alex. I'll bet everything I have that he was murdered.'

Five

I told Lily that I was actually back in Manhattan and could meet her in forty-five minutes at PJ Bernstein Deli, a short distance from my apartment. Two months earlier I would have offered to make Lily Savitsky comfortable in my home, but my trust level had eroded. The guys at PJ's had known me forever, and aside from the great food, they'd be looking out for me if she were anything other than a grieving daughter.

I showered and dressed in jeans and a cashmere turtleneck. After I canceled my hair and nail appointments, I threw on a ski jacket and walked out of my building, up to the corner.

As hard as I tried to conjure memories of Lily, all I came up with was her flutter kick, her shyness, and large brown eyes like those of a spaniel that had been left alone for too many hours every day.

Her mother was tall, like mine, and carpooled to most of the swim meets, like mine, evincing a keen interest in Lily's accomplishments. I couldn't remember ever seeing her father. I think I had worried about my teammate then because I thought her father was either a total deadbeat – missing in action – or dead. Thinking back, I must have figured it's what gave Lily such a sad look.

If I had ever connected her with Wolf Savage in those days, the memories had been buried in the intervening years.

I sat in the rear of the restaurant and positioned myself so that I could see Lily when she came through the door. She was easy to spot – still lanky, with dark-brown hair that capped her thin face and surrounded it with ringlets. I waved at her and she came toward me, pulling out the chair opposite me.

'I'm so very sorry for your loss, Lily,' I said. 'I simply had no idea that Wolf Savage was related to—'

'You had no reason to know, Alex. I never talked about him to anyone but my mother. I carried such a sense of shame about being abandoned. He left us – he left my mother and me – when I was six.'

The waitress came over to take our order.

Lily said she wasn't hungry while I asked for a Diet Coke.

'You've got to eat something,' I said, trying out the lines people had used on me the last few weeks. 'You'll need the strength.'

'Just some tea, please,' she said. 'And maybe a bowl of your soup of the day.'

'Make that two,' I said.

'Look, Alex, I know this isn't exactly your line of work, but you're the only person in law enforcement I know.'

'If there's any way I can help, you can be sure that I will.'

'Where do you want me to start?' Lily asked.

'Give me a quick update,' I said. 'What are you doing these days? Have you had any relationship with your father recently, and especially what makes you think this isn't a – well, his own doing?'

I thought that Lily's description of her life and her reasons for thinking the responding detectives – and even Mike – had missed something at the death scene would help me measure her stability.

'I'm still in Harrison, Alex,' Lily said, referring to the affluent neighborhood in Westchester County where my family had moved when I was ten, after my father's invention, the Cooper-Hoffman valve, had become such a game changer in the medical community. 'Married a guy I met in grad school. Got my MBA at Columbia. Had three kids in pretty quick order, so I've never used my degree.'

'Your husband?' I asked, opening my iPad to take some notes.

'Really good guy. David Kingsley. He's a partner at a private equity firm in Greenwich,' Lily said. 'Is it true you've never been married, Alex? And no kids? In twelfth grade, I would have pegged you as a future full-on soccer mom, not a hard-ass prosecutor.'

'Life's full of surprises, Lily,' I said, thinking that was more civilized than replying, *None of your business*. 'Let's concentrate on you right now. Tell me the personal side of your history with your father.'

'Condensed version, right?'

'For now, right. All I'm after is how to help you get in the right hands, if I can do that.'

'Of course,' she said, thanking the waitress for the hot tea as she set our drinks in front of us. 'So my mother was the second Mrs Savitsky. Once my father moved to Europe and changed his name, my mother refused to speak about him to almost anyone. I actually never knew there had been a first Mrs Savitsky until I was about eight years old. That one was from the Brooklyn Savitsky era.'

'Sorry?'

'My father was born in Brooklyn, Alex. My grandparents emigrated from Russia in the late '30s. I never knew either of them. My grandmother had two miscarriages before my father was born.'

'Was he an only child?' I wanted a full sense of the family dynamic before I bought into Lily's suspicions.

'No, there's a younger brother, too. My uncle Hersh – well, Hal – who runs the business end of things for my dad.'

'Is he a Savage or a Savitsky?' I asked.

'My father stayed Savitsky till the business started to take off. Then he got rid of my mother, and after that, his name. Hal wanted to take the ride with him, so they became the Savage brothers. It was such an embarrassment to my mother and to me.'

'How about wife number one?'

'She died. Early on. That's when I found out I had an older brother, Reed.'

I gave up my iPad for a paper napkin. This one called for a diagram of the family tree.

'He wasn't part of my life until the last few years,' Lily said. 'Born Reed Savitsky, but he goes by Reed Savage. He's forty-one now, four years older than I am. When his mom died, he went to London to live with my father and his third bride. Little Lord Savage, to the manner born.'

'What does he do now?'

'He's in charge of the international part of my father's operation.'

'Do you have any part of the business interest in the company?'

'How I wish I did. It's really the reason I went to graduate school. I thought I could get beyond the estrangement from my father by showing him how much I wanted to play a role in his life.'

'Sounds like a great idea.'

'Worked my ass off in B-school after college, but got the double-whammy from my uncle and half-brother.'

'How so?'

'They planted the seed in my father's mind that I was only after a share of his fortune.'

The waitress put bowls in front of each of us and I waited while Lily blew on the steaming-hot soup.

'I mean, there was a bit of truth in that, Alex. I would have loved to have worked my way into the business empire – worked for it, not just enjoyed a sense of entitlement – but I wanted a father out of this whole thing, too. He was adored by everyone around him, according to the social columns I read day in and day out. I wanted a taste of that.'

I understood that part completely. I couldn't imagine life without the love and support of parents I adored and respected.

'So your uncle Hal and Reed are pretty tight with each other?'

'Best I can tell.'

'Have you spoken with either of them since your – since yesterday's news?'

'Yes,' Lily said, nodding at me. 'I had dinner with Hal last night. He's always had a soft spot for me, for my kids.'

'And Reed?'

'He was flying in from Heathrow. Chartered a plane when he got the news yesterday afternoon. I'm supposed to meet with both of them shortly,' Lily said. 'That's why it was so urgent that I see you.'

'So your relationship with your father,' I said. 'It's obviously complicated and we'll get to all that if it's necessary – if I can be helpful here. Recently, was there contact?'

'Yes, things had been getting much better between us lately.'

'Why do you think that's so?'

'It's a combination of factors, I guess. My husband, who's a prince of a guy, went to see my dad without telling me. He thinks he's the one who talked Wolf into getting to know his grandchildren – as well as me – and having them as a sort of a living legacy for him. My view? I think it helped that David makes a really good living. I'm sure my father checked out his background and financials, and was beginning to understand that we aren't gold diggers. Maybe it's a little bit of both.'

I wondered whether Lily knew if she was in her father's will, and what the effect of suicide would be on all the sharks circling the body.

'It helped, of course,' she said as we both took a few swallows of the soup, 'that Wolf had split from wife number five last year. She really hated me.'

'Why so?'

'I guess it got back to her that I was peeved that my father had broken the rule.'

'What rule?' I asked. I had to admit that it felt good to put something nourishing in my stomach.

Lily cracked a smile. 'Supposed to be that rich old guys have a formula: They shouldn't marry women younger than their kids,' she said. 'It's meant to be half the guy's age plus seven, as a minimum. So my father was sixty-eight when he married the bitch, and she was twenty-eight.'

I jotted down the math.

'I was thirty-four at the time. Sort of "ouch!" to have a stepmother so young.'

'I bet it was,' I said. 'And wives three, four, and five – where are they today?'

'It's a bit like Henry the Eighth, though a little out of order,' Lily said. 'Died, divorced, beheaded, div—'

'Beheaded? Was number three killed?'

'She might as well have been, according to Uncle Hal. Just hung out to dry.'

'Look, Lily, I guess the most important question is why you think you knew your father well enough to claim he didn't want to end his own life.'

She pushed the soup bowl away.

'Wolf Savage was at the top of his game, Alex,' she said, ticking off reasons on her fingers. 'For the last year he's been in negotiations to sell his business to some billionaire who wanted him to stay in charge – continue to be the front man and face of the company, to keep dazzling the fashion world – but to have this fantastic backer with a huge infusion of cash. Then my father came up with this ingenious idea to launch his own solo show – break apart from the eighty or so mash-ups that Fashion Week in New York has become.'

The phenomenon that was the city's Fashion Week was staged two times a year – in February and September. Wolf Savage's radical plan to split from that tradition had made major headlines throughout the summer.

'It's a very controversial idea,' I said, 'from what I've read in the papers.'

'Part inspiration, and part a consequence of my father's big falling-out with the powers that be who run the September week.'

'I didn't know about that.'

'It was overshadowed by the bigger news. The Costume Institute at the Met is installing its first WolfWear retrospective to coincide with the show – can you imagine that? Wolf Savage at the Metropolitan Museum of Art? He was at an all-time high about it – heart and soul.'

She paused for a couple of seconds.

'Maybe he was ill, Lily. Maybe there was something wrong with him that he didn't tell you about,' I said.

'Oh, there was a lot wrong with him, Alex. I'm the first one to say that. But he was healthy as a horse, unless there's something called Viagra poisoning,' she said. 'Wolf was the kind of man who would never put a bag over his head if he suffered from that. He preferred to brag about his conquests, even to me, as unhealthy as that is.'

So this was a young woman who had gone from being the abandoned daughter of one of the world's most prominent self-made entrepreneurs, to one of the players jockeying for his fortune. She was already setting up her brother as a villain in what was undoubtedly a family feud, and maybe even her uncle, too. This conversation was giving me a headache.

'Look, Lily. I've got some good friends in the Homicide Squad, but I'd have to tell them that you've got more than just a recent hunch that Wolf Savage was too content with his life to end it himself.'

She made a fist around her soup spoon and banged the end of it on the table. 'This man, Alex Cooper, was my father.'

'I know that, but—'

'Maybe I didn't have the relationship with him that you had with your dad as a kid – and by the way? You seem to have reaped the rewards of your father's smarts, haven't you?' she said rather snidely. 'That's not what this is about.'

I understood the strain she was under, but how could she possibly pretend to know whether Savage had been despondent at all, or whether the details of his sexual entanglements had brought him low?

'I apologize, Lily, if I seemed insensitive. Let me call one of the guys and see if he can sit down with you one day this week.'

'"One day this week"?' she said, mimicking me. 'I told you there was an urgency to this.'

'Okay,' I said, knowing the last thing Mike would want today was me sticking my nose into anything he had a role in. 'I'll phone right now. Are you available tonight, when he's done with his shift?'

'At three o'clock today, just a couple of hours from now, Reed and Hal have a meeting with the chief medical examiner,' she said, pounding the spoon's handle onto the tabletop again. 'You want urgency, Alex? They want my father's body released to them this afternoon for burial. They want it released without an autopsy.'

Six

Mike beat us to the Office of the Chief Medical Examiner on First Avenue and Thirtieth Street. He came down the steps in front of the blue-brick facade of the building when the cab Lily and I rode in pulled up at two forty-five.

'Thanks for taking the time to do this, Mike,' I said, introducing him to Lily.

'Niceties to follow, ladies,' he said. 'Two of the Wolf-pack members are already inside, ready to take Mr Savage away with them.'

'Has the meeting started?' Lily asked.

'No,' Mike said. 'They're just waiting on the ME's lawyer in the conference room.'

'Did you have a chance to check out anything I told you about Lily's intuitions yet?'

'Bottle it for now, Coop.' He wasn't going to answer my question in front of a potential witness. My bad.

I jogged up the steps, signed Lily and me into the visitors' log, then asked the security guard at the desk to buzz us in to the corridor that led to the conference room.

The two men inside stood up as we entered. Lily walked toward them and kissed each of them on the cheek. All three were appropriately somber.

'Alex, Detective Chapman, I'd like you to meet my uncle, Hal Savage, and my brother, Reed.'

The nattily attired brother of the deceased, who appeared to be a very fit seventy-year-old, held out his hand to Mike. 'Good to meet you, Detective. Although I'm not quite sure why you're here. I'm Hershel – Hershel Savitsky, in fact.'

Lily rolled her eyes in my direction.

'Reed Savitsky,' Lily's half-brother said, not moving away from his chair.

'I can see the direction this is taking,' Lily said. 'I'm not sure why you're reclaiming the Savitsky name, gentlemen. Is it just for the purpose of convincing the ME that your motive is really a holy one?'

'They are the names on our birth certificates, Lily,' her uncle said. 'Mind your place here. You're fortunate that we've included you.'

'You know my father was not a religious man.'

'Shows what you get for keeping him at arm's length all these years, Lily,' Reed said. '*My* father, the man I lived with, was really devout. It went all the way back to his roots. But then you never knew our grandparents, as I did.'

There was a knock on the door and Jeremy Mayers entered. 'Am I interrupting something?'

'Nothing at all,' Hal Savitsky-Savage said, starting a new round of introductions.

Mike and I had known Jeremy for years and relied on his good counsel to the city's chief medical examiner.

'I understand that you asked for this meeting, Mr Savitsky, to discuss the release of your brother's body today.'

'That's correct,' Hal said. 'I'm just wondering why this particular detective and this young lady are—'

'I'm with the District Attorney's Office, sir.'

'NYPD,' Mike said.

Jeremy was unconcerned with our presence at the moment. 'Is it correct that you have a religious objection to the autopsy, which we've scheduled for tomorrow morning?'

'We have exactly that,' Hal said. 'And you, Mr Chapman, you're not the detective on the case. I met with him yesterday, at the hotel. He didn't seem to think there'd be a problem.'

'This will be a legal decision, sir, made by my office,' Jeremy said, trying to gain control of the meeting. 'The NYPD doesn't get a vote on it.'

'Very well, then,' Hal said from his post at the head of the table. 'I'm not sure what you know about Jewish law, Mr Mayers, but it's a well-established principle among Orthodox Jews that one cannot desecrate a corpse.'

'I'm familiar with this issue, of course. We've encountered it here many times, and I'm quite respectful of it.'

'Good. That's good to know.'

'I was just reminding my uncle,' Lily said, 'before you came into the room, that my father was not a practicing Jew, Mr Mayers. Jewish? Culturally and socially, yes. But he didn't believe in organized religion, and he's the kind of man who would move heaven and earth to make sure there had not been any injustice that brought his life to an end.'

'Lily's my half-sister,' Reed said, clearly ready to open the bag with all the dirty laundry in it. 'We've never been much involved in each other's lives, so she's – well, ignorant's a harsh word – but she's not so much aware of my father's beliefs as my uncle and I are. Lily and my dad were estranged for decades, to put it mildly.'

'About his religious beliefs, then,' Jeremy Mayers said. 'What can you tell me?'

'My grandparents emigrated from Russia. They were Orthodox in the old country, despite all the repressive efforts against Jews.'

'And they were Reform by the time I was born,' Lily said.

'We were very observant, my brother and I,' Hal said. 'As kids and all throughout our lives. You ought to hold your tongue, dear.'

'It didn't seem to bother anyone that my mother was a lapsed Catholic,' Lily said. 'I wasn't there for the wedding, of course, but I've seen the pictures. Grandma and Grandpa threw a pretty swell party, and the guy who performed the wedding was a judge. Judge Donnelly, if I'm not mistaken.'

'My father belonged to a synagogue in London,' Reed said, talking over her. 'Central Synagogue, one of the most historic in the city.'

'And to Park Avenue Synagogue here in New York.'

From the expression on Lily's face, these facts looked like news to her.

'That must have been for entirely social reasons, Reed. If Wolf joined two fancy synagogues, it was simply a gesture of belonging to the community that supported his business ventures. Membership is one thing, showing up and believing in the purpose of being there is quite another,' she said. 'He must have ponied up for Park Avenue in case his next child-bride needed a good pre-K for their future offspring.'

'Do you have proof of his membership?' Mayers asked. 'Any indication of whether and when he attended services? Some way to get in touch with one of his rabbis?'

Hal Savage put his hands on the table, palms down. 'I think both Reed and Lily will agree that I have had the closest relationship with my brother – the longest and closest of anyone on this Earth. We grew up in the same home, with respect for the traditions and values our parents brought with them to America. I went to work with him almost every day of our adult lives.'

Reed nodded. Lily stared her uncle down.

'We talked about this kind of thing quite often, Mr Mayers, my brother and I,' Hal went on. 'Jews believe, you know, that our bodies are sacred, that they belong to God, and not for mere mortals to do with what they wish. That's why the corpse can't be violated after death.'

Lily turned her head and whispered to me. 'Hal's talking the talk, but this is just mumbo-jumbo. The only bodies my father believed were sacred were those of the young babes he lusted after. And they belonged to him, he thought. Not to any higher spirit.'

'Lily?' Reed asked. 'You have something you want to say to all of us?'

'You know, the first time I ever heard the word "autopsy", I can remember how creeped-out I was about it. I was just a kid, Reed, and one of the relatives – it might even have been you, Uncle Hal – called to tell my mom that your mother had died. She was so young – maybe only thirty-one or -two, right?'

Lily paused for a few seconds, perhaps just for effect, or because the memory had such a profound impact.

'I heard the word "autopsy" during that phone conversation, so I went and looked it up in the dictionary. That's what my mother had taught me to do when I came across words I didn't understand. Kind of ironic, isn't it? I'll never forget what I read that day, Reed. "A dissection performed on a cadaver". Powerful image to a young kid. But I don't recall hearing that Wolf registered a religious objection to that procedure then. So, why now?'

Reed didn't speak.

Hal, on the other hand, jumped right in. 'You know, Lily – or perhaps you don't – that there are a couple of exceptions to Jewish law.'

'I'm ready to learn.'

'When a doctor thinks there's knowledge to be gained from doing an autopsy – something that might contribute to saving the lives of other patients,' he said calmly to her, 'then it's permissible to do one.'

'I didn't know you were a Talmudic scholar, Uncle Hal,' she said. 'I'm surprised you don't have a line of yarmulkes yet. Maybe sequined – or fringed, if that's still this season's trend. Or tie-dyed. I hear that's big for spring.'

'Reed's mother died of a very rare kind of cancer. There was a good reason to perform an autopsy. My brother would never have objected, despite his faith.'

'There's another good reason to do one,' Mike said, tossing his notepad on the table in front of him, 'with no disrespect meant to your religion. And that's when a criminal investigation into the circumstances of the death is pending.'

All eyes turned to Mike.

'Where's the detective who had this case yesterday?' Hal asked. 'I want to talk to him. I want Mr Mayers to hear from him.'

'That dude is taking orders from me now,' Mike said. 'I sent him back to the hotel for some more information. He needs a refresher in Crime Scene Investigation 101.'

'What sort of information don't you have?' Hal asked. 'I can give you anything you need to know. I just want Wolf's body to be handled properly, according to Jewish tradition, and I want him to be buried tomorrow.'

'Your brother died in a suite on the tenth floor, registered in his name – Wolf Savage.'

'I know that, Mr Chapman. I went to that room to identify his body.'

Mike must have been onto something. He'd obviously made some phone calls after I told him about Lily's appeal to me. I didn't think he'd tell me what had made him flip until after we were apart from Hal and Reed – and Lily – but he was sniffing around.

'The first guys on the scene did a pretty thorough search.'

'Indeed they did,' Hal said. 'Everything from examining and photographing the objects in the room to taking my brother's clothing to grabbing his cell phone, and so on. They even found a suicide note, Detective. I haven't been allowed to see it, but I know they found one there. They checked video cameras that proved no one else had come and gone from that suite – not even the hotel maid or room service.'

'What they didn't stop to find out – till I sent them back today – is that every room on that floor is registered to someone from your company,' Mike said. 'To a single person, who would have had access to each suite on the tenth floor.'

'Nothing sinister in that, Mr Chapman.'

'We'll be the judges of that,' Mike said. 'I know you guys are switching back and forth between your names today – Hershel and Hal, Savitsky and Savage, but why don't you tell me who this character is?'

Mike opened his notepad and read the name. 'Velvel Savitsky. You got a Velvel I don't know about? Somebody I can talk to? A missing relative?'

Hal just shook his head back and forth, with a totally dismissive glance at Mike.

'He's not a missing relative at all, Mr Chapman. He's the dead one,' Lily said. 'Velvel Savitsky was my father.'

'Velvel is the Yiddish word for "wolf", Detective,' Hal said. 'Add that to a long list of things you don't know.'

Mike looked down at the table.

'Velvel Savitsky,' he went on, 'was Wolf Savage.'

Seven

'Are we starting with what you know, Chapman, or what you don't know?' Jeremy Mayers asked, after escorting the three Savitskys out of the conference room. 'Which list is longer?'

'Like it's my fault for not putting Velvel together with the Wolfman?' Mike asked. 'I have trouble with my English, and now you expect me to interpret Yiddish for you?'

'Are you really taking this case over, Mike,' Jeremy said, 'even though you're Manhattan North?'

'The police commissioner wants all hands on deck. The deceased has a huge profile, and I'm the guy who has experience with this kind of case. Scully's also afraid the first crew might have missed something at the scene,' Mike said. 'The press is going to be all over this sucker.'

'Tell us about the scene,' I said. 'Explain the significance of the whole tenth floor being registered to Savage himself.'

'You, Ms Cooper, are here on background only,' Mike said.

'Yeah, Alex, why are you here at all?' Jeremy asked. 'Nobody was raped.'

He obviously didn't know that everyone sane in the criminal justice system was holding me at arm's length.

'Mike wouldn't be doing this either if I hadn't stuck my nose in,' I said. 'Lily was an acquaintance of mine when we were in high school. She called the office this morning. I had no idea Wolf Savage was her father.'

'Here's the deal,' Mike said. 'During Mayor Bloomberg's administration, a whole bunch of boutique hotels were built in the Garment District. Part of the movement to preserve some part of the business where it's always been.'

'What do you mean?' Jeremy said.

'There was a time not that long ago that ninety-five percent of the clothing made in the USA was produced in that little swatch of Midtown Manhattan,' Mike said. 'Now it's down to three percent. That's what the manager of the Silver Needle Hotel told me this morning. So in order to keep the high-end executives staying in this area, instead of elsewhere in town – because all the rest of the stuff from buttons to trimmings is still done right there – the mayor had the idea to use some of the land to build these fancy little hotels.'

'But where did Wolf Savage live?' Jeremy asked.

'Suburban mansion in Greenwich. Penthouse loft in Tribeca. Big properties in cities around the world. What's the diff?'

'Well, because why a whole floor full of rooms in a Garment District hotel?'

'According to the manager, almost all the big fashion

houses keep a block of suites like this,' Mike said. 'They're constantly entertaining their backers from overseas, buyers from stores around the country, models and stylists working the big shows or late hours, and no matter how many homes they have it seems to be an emergency place for the executives to rest their heads rather than take a car service to the burbs.'

'I guess,' Jeremy said.

'The manager added that Wolf Savage was a player – no surprise – and always liked to have a suite at the ready. Kept a few suits and shirts and socks in this room, which were all there yesterday.'

'So what did the first guys on the scene miss?' I asked.

'It was one of the housekeepers who found the body,' Mike said. 'She had standing orders never to go into the Savage suite till after one P.M. Seems some of the ladies who frequented the tenth floor were late risers.'

'She screams,' I said.

'Security and the manager arrive. He's the guy who calls 911. It takes the first cops a while to remember that suicide falls under our umbrella,' Mike said. 'The south gets there and combs the place pretty thoroughly.'

'What did they miss?' I asked.

'I'll go over everything that was at the scene with you later, Coop.'

'What did the note say?' Jeremy jumped in.

'Something like, "I'm sick",' Mike said. 'You guys want to know about the tenth-floor rooms or what?'

'Yeah,' I said. 'The rooms.'

'Hold on,' Jeremy said. 'Sick with what? None of the relatives mentioned he was ill.'

'Maybe no one knew,' I said.

'Focus on the rooms, will you? I'll be doubling back on all the rest of that stuff,' Mike said.

'Fast enough so that I can make my decision on the autopsy?' Jeremy asked.

'Stat,' Mike said.

'That will help. So about the rooms?'

'The hotel has security cameras, of course. They're on a twenty-four-hour reel. The guys got on it right away and watched the videos from the time Wolf Savage slipped his card into the lock for 1008 on Monday night, about ten P.M., till the time the housekeeper went in and let out enough shrieks to wake the dead. Well, except for the guy in the room. About two fifteen in the afternoon.'

'So?' Jeremy said.

'Solo. Nobody dancing with the Wolf. Nobody else in or out of the room the entire night and morning,' Mike said. 'The cops see the bag over his head and the color of his skin. They get the hookup to the helium canisters and spot a two- or three-word note on the dining-room table. An empty vial of oxy, which would have made him more mellow to turn on the gas. They watch a little closed-circuit TV. That's all cops do now, by the way. There are more surveillance cameras on the street and inside buildings than there are perps. Done. Suicide. No overtime. Off-duty and headed for cocktails.'

'Not unreasonable,' I said.

'You've been in more hotel rooms, Coop, than Gideon's Bible,' Mike said. 'You know those extra doors, they're usually like on the side wall in the living-room suite?'

'The kind I'm always hoping is another closet?' I said. 'Then you open it and it simply faces another room. Locked from your side.'

'Exactly what I mean.'

'Yeah. I'm always afraid that door is going to be how Norman Bates slips into the room while I'm out and about and gets into my shower to wait for me,' I said.

'See?' Mike said. 'And some people think your paranoia is a new thing.'

'I wouldn't leave home without it,' I said, smiling at Mike.

'So the purpose of those doors, as you might guess, is in case the guest wants to expand his suite. Buy a few rooms for the family and unlock all those doors.'

'And the tenth floor at the Silver Needle?' Jeremy asked.

'The entire floor belonged to Wolf Savage, rented in his doppelgänger name for a year at a time. Turns out that he only locked the ones adjacent to 1008 when he was entertaining someone. When he was having a slumber party.'

'So it's possible that someone could have slipped in or out of his room after he entered it?' I asked. 'And back out again, after he was dead?'

'Someone could even have been waiting for him when he got there,' Mike said.

'And you're saying the cops never checked the video

feed for the other rooms on the tenth floor, in or out? Before or after?'

'The whole strip is interconnected – and internally unlocked – from 1000 to 1012. The only camera they interrogated was the one to 1008.'

'And now the other films have all been rerecorded,' Jeremy said. 'Just looped over and over again.'

'I got detectives double-checking them now,' Mike said, 'but I expect that all they're going to see on what's left of the tape are cops from the precinct and the Crime Scene Unit and the Homicide Squad stumbling over other cops going in and out of the room.'

'So you believe Lily? That her father's death might be a homicide?' I asked.

'This is a damn near perfect way to kill somebody, Coop. I found that out four months ago, in a case I had on the Upper West Side.'

'What do you mean?'

'Pick the gentlest means of committing suicide, so everybody feels sorry for the dead man. It only takes one person – this time it could be Lily – to tell you he had everything to live for, while the rest of the family is rushing to put him six feet under,' Mike said. 'That's when I start looking for someone with a motive to murder him.'

'You got to give me something more than this, Chapman,' Jeremy said.

'Keep Wolf on ice for forty-eight hours,' Mike said. 'Don't slice and dice yet, okay? The commissioner has made this case his top priority. You find out what doc was treating him and what kind of disease caused him to do this to himself, if there's any truth to that theory. In the meantime, I'll find out why the other housekeeper who works that floor thinks there was a guest in Room 1010 who never registered at the front desk.'

Eight

'Uncle Hal is demanding to see my boss,' Jeremy Mayers said, returning after stepping out to tell the family members that the decision about releasing Wolf Savage's body would be delayed for two days. 'So she wants to talk to you first.'

Emma Parker followed Jeremy into the conference room. She greeted Mike and me and apologized for the stained lab coat she was wearing, which carried the pungent odor of formalin into our windowless space from the autopsy theater she had apparently just left.

'Have you missed me that much, Chapman?' she said. 'Or do you really think we have a second case of murder by staged suicide?'

'Both true, Dr P,' Mike said. 'That's what I'm thinking right now. Only, the first job was done by total amateurs. I think we're up against a real pro here.'

She was a handsome woman, in her mid-fifties, who looked more like a corporate executive than a pathologist spending her days teasing the truth out of the bodies of the dead.

'Sounds like there's a lot more at stake in this instance,' she said.

'Big-time.'

'Set it up for me,' Emma said. Then she turned her attention to me. 'Aren't you supposed to be on leave?'

Jeremy raised his eyebrows.

'This is way more interesting than how I've been passing my time, Emma. Don't shoot me down, please?'

She smiled at me and pointed at Mike to begin.

'I'm nowhere on this, Doc,' he said. 'I got called in late, and to be honest with you, I've got some catching up to do.'

'You know an autopsy isn't going to tell you very much in this kind of death.'

'I'm well aware of that,' Mike said. 'But you let this body go and we've got no chance to get any of the tox screening that might prove valuable down the line.'

'What do you two mean?' I asked.

'A lot of the right-to-die organizations have been promoting this method of euthanasia in their writings in books and all over the Internet,' Emma said. 'It's not just the terminally ill who have been committing suicide this particular way. We've seen a significant number of cases in this office of individuals with psychiatric disorders – you know, people with auditory hallucinations and histories of repeated suicide attempts – as well as some who were substance abusers, who choose this manner of death.'

'When you say "this way", Emma – ?'

'So the hardline suicides are just what you'd expect

them to be, Alex. Gunshot wounds, which occasionally miss the mark, as you know. Hangings – painful and run the risk of being sloppy and slow. And overdoses. Also not always a successful method,' Emma said. 'When the suicide-interest groups first got into this, their recommendations often included the use of a plastic bag over the head. Sometimes sleeping pills first, but then a bag.'

'An "exit bag",' I said, repeating Mike's words.

'Exactly.'

'What kind of bag?'

'Thanksgiving's only a few weeks away,' Mike said. 'You know those turkey-sized oven bags?'

'Tell me you're just making a bad joke,' I said.

'He's not, Alex,' the doctor kicked in.

'Or a thirty-gallon trash bag,' Mike said.

'The problem is,' Emma said, uncrossing her arms and sitting down at the table, 'is that the bigger the bag, the longer it takes for the carbon dioxide to build up and the oxygen to run out. Panic sets in, and if the guy – or girl – hasn't fallen asleep with pills, he's usually ripping at the bag to breathe.'

'Because the will to live is so great,' I said.

'Or the dying is so uncomfortable. That's why the inert-gas method became popular, especially in countries where suicide is legal.'

'I don't get the difference,' I said. 'I don't know what the gas does. In fact, I don't even know what an inert gas is.'

'Too much English lit and not enough science,' Mike said.

'Inert gases are things like nitrogen, argon, methane,' Emma said, 'and helium. They don't have any toxic effect – they're also free of odor and taste – but what they do is dilute the body's oxygen when they're breathed in, especially with the head confined in a bag, usually closed with a Velcro kind of tape.'

'There's no traumatic feeling of suffocation, Coop. And it's wicked fast. The oxygen level in the blood drops dangerously low in a few seconds. Am I right, Doc?'

'Dead on. It only takes a few breaths of the gas, and I say your subject – call him your victim – would be gone in less than one minute.'

'But how would you know that?' I asked. 'Somebody actually watches?'

'Yes. Yes, they've been observed,' Emma said. 'There have been studies out of places like Switzerland, where assisted suicides are legal if they're not done for what the law there calls "selfish motives".'

'Yeah,' Mike said, 'like if one of your relatives had a fortune and was planning to cut you out of his will, then you wouldn't be allowed to kill him.'

'In two of the reported cases of observed deaths using helium and a plastic bag over the head,' Emma said, 'the time from inhalation of the gas to loss of consciousness was ten to twelve seconds. And no attempts at self-rescue, either. Not the half-hour of thrashing around in a trash bag.'

'Both speedy and reliable,' I said.

'So much so that last year the governor of Oklahoma

signed a bill allowing nitrogen asphyxiation – which works the same way as helium inhalation – as an alternative execution method in capital cases.'

Mike did a thumbs-up. 'Gotta love me a trendy way to knock out the bad guys. Kill them with kindness.'

'That's part of the reason Mike's so on top of this. Helium inhalation suicides have shown a striking increase in the last few years,' Emma said. 'It's a brilliant – almost foolproof – way to conceal a homicide.'

I nodded in Mike's direction.

'There's an absence of specific findings at autopsy, though,' she said. 'That's why Mike has to do the heavy lifting here.'

'How so?' I asked.

'There are no visible signs on Wolf Savage's body that anything violent happened or any kind of struggle occurred,' Emma said. 'I've done an external, head to toe, and there aren't even the self-scratches of someone trying to get the bag off his head and neck. That's completely consistent with this method of suicide, so it wouldn't signal anything to me.'

'But normally you'd do an autopsy, wouldn't you?'

'Required by law, Madame Prosecutor.'

'Would one be useful?'

'Could be,' Emma said in a noncommittal manner. 'Oxycontin on the bedside table.'

'There!' I said. 'Isn't there a doctor's name on the prescription?'

'You're behind the times, Coop,' Mike said. 'The good,

old Oxy isn't made in the States anymore. That bottle in the room was mail order from Canada. No way to trace it back.'

'What's the difference between Canadian Oxy and ours?'

'The reason that there was such an epidemic of abuse when Oxy was first introduced is that its active ingredient – oxycodone – was such a powerful painkiller that it was made for slow-acting release, to keep a patient sedated overnight,' Emma said. 'But it was such a fine powder that addicts just crushed it and got all the effects, along with a swift high, in just minutes.'

'So the FDA changed the composition of the drug,' Mike said. 'Now, it simply turns to a gummy mush if you try to crush it up to avoid the slow time-release. That's why the addicts have dropped Oxy in favor of a return to heroin. The other case the doc and I had was traditional horse as the sedating drug. The vic was an addict, so it was easy to cover up the homicide after he got himself high. Then they bagged him.'

'But you'll find Oxy in the tox study,' I said. 'If Wolf ingested that first.'

'We will,' Emma said.

'And disease. The autopsy will tell you what he thought was going to kill him, if someone didn't help him find his own way to the grave.'

'Look, Alex. If Savage had an internist who called me tonight and told me that there was a diagnosis given to the man a month ago, or a week ago, that he was facing down a terminal cancer or heart disease that's on the verge of killing him – and if the same physician had the scans and images to support the diagnosis – I might bend to the request of relatives on a religious basis to just let the body go.'

'So how do you help Emma resolve this, Mike?' I asked.

'She doesn't have any info from a doctor yet about Wolf's health, for one thing,' Mike said. 'I'm not the only one looking for a guy to have a reason to kill himself. And I get to go back to the Silver Needle. Everything's still in place, except for the body. I get to study the scene.'

'How did you break the other case you two had that was like this?'

'One witness too many, Coop. The dead guy's girlfriend betrayed him. The kid was a student at NYU, but a full-on heroin addict. He was into the dealer for thousands of dollars, and sleeping with the dealer's girl. She snitched on him and set him up.'

'Ugly.'

'She thought she could handle watching him die after she got him high for the last time, but she was the weakest link,' Mike said. 'We broke her on the second interview.'

'That was luck, having a witness to the murder.'

'This time, I know the helium got into Wolf's hotel room concealed in the bottom of a hand truck that came right out of 520 Seventh Avenue, where his main office is.'

'You mean those carts that have clothes hanging on them – the ones that are all over the streets and sidewalks throughout the Garment District?'

'Yeah. There were dresses hanging from the rack, so it looked like every other cart. The canisters were in the well on the bottom. That was one of the first things the cops checked out yesterday. But nobody bothered to track the helium – or the hand truck – back to its source within the office building.'

'Someone must have seen who delivered the cart,' I said.

'All I got, Coop, is that it was two young men. One tall, one medium height. Nothing remarkable about them,' Mike said.

'Just so we're clear,' Emma Parker said, pushing back from the table. 'I'll stay in touch with you, Mike. The minute the family comes up with medical information, I'll give you a call.'

'I'll let you know if I get lucky at the hotel,' Mike said. 'And tomorrow I'll knock on doors at the Savage offices.'

'Forty-eight hours, right? Is that a deal?'

'Deal,' Mike said.

'Stay close to him this time, Alex,' Emma said, winking at me as she headed for the door. 'We don't need you disappearing again.'

'I think she's had her outing for the day, Doc. Might be time to put her back in her cage,' Mike said, tousling my hair as he walked behind me.

I didn't like that image. I flashed back to the dark, dank space in which I'd been held. But I was learning to keep my reactions – or as Mike would call them, *over*reactions – to myself.

'She knows more about the fashion world than you do,

Mike. Alex might come in handy while you try to sort this out,' Emma said. 'She asks good questions.'

'Yeah, like I'm supposed to be the answer man?'

'Seems to be working for you just fine, Detective Chapman.'

'Here's a question for you, Emma,' I said. 'Has it ever happened, in your experience, that somebody walks in here to actually try to prevent you from doing an autopsy of the deceased, and then turns out to be the murderer? I mean, it just seems so over-the-top obvious.'

'Actually, Alex, it's been done. Maybe not the smartest tack to take, but perhaps these two relatives didn't know Wolf's daughter – what's her name? Lily? – was back in the picture,' Emma said. 'Maybe they didn't think they would meet with any resistance here.'

'Slow down, you two,' Mike said. 'You don't even know who's driving this bus. Is it Uncle Hal alone? Or is it Reed? Or are they just stooges doing what someone else has suggested? I'm not saying either one of them is the killer. It's just that once you let the body go, we've lost any chance of getting what we get on the autopsy table.'

'Nobody's even heard what's in Wolf Savage's will yet, have they?' Jeremy asked.

'Tomorrow afternoon,' Mike said. 'That should tell us something.'

'How do you know about that?' I asked.

'That's what the lieutenant from Manhattan South told Peterson.'

'To your point, Alex, it's not only against Jewish law

to perform autopsies,' Emma said. 'It's forbidden in Islam, too. And Christian Scientists prefer they aren't done. But it always gives me pause when people come in to oppose the procedure and are looking to fly the body out of the country the next day.'

'We've had this scenario scores of times,' Jeremy said. 'I've got to say the objections are usually legit, but we've had our share of bodies spirited out of here, only to have exhumations ordered by a court later on. Pretty hard to enforce when they're overseas.'

I thought of a case that Mike and I had worked together, which involved the exhumation of a teenage girl for an autopsy in a room right down the hall, years after her death. Nothing that I ever wanted to see again.

I put my elbows on the table and pressed my fingers against my forehead, rubbing it to ease the headache that was coming on. 'I wish I had never taken Lily's call,' I said. 'Maybe she's the bad guy in all this. Maybe she's just using me as the way to get back at her father. Maybe she's—'

'Let's not rush to judgment, kid. These days you're good at seeing ghosts where there aren't any.'

Nine

Mike and I left the Medical Examiner's Office shortly before five P.M.

'I'll shoot you home,' he said. 'I'll just be a few hours and then we can grab some dinner.'

'Doctor's orders, Mike. You heard Emma tell you to keep me close,' I said. 'Aren't you going to the hotel?'

'Yeah.'

'One more look around? Check out the suite the house-keeper said someone had used?' I asked. 'C'mon. It's the kind of thing I'm useful for. An extra pair of trained eyes is always good.'

'Got my extras, Coop,' Mike said. 'Mercer's meeting me there.'

'It's not his case either. Not even in the same ballpark.'

'Yeah, but he's the man on the job I trust more than anyone. He's got the bones for this kind of detail work.'

Mercer and Mike had partnered together in the elite Homicide Squad about a decade ago. Both of them loved working painstaking investigations, but while Mike especially enjoyed the fact that homicide victims didn't need hand-holding, Mercer craved supportive human interaction. So he transferred to the Special Victims Squad, where he savored the emotionally charged work and the task of restoring dignity to a surviving crime victim as much as I did.

'I thought you said that if I stayed sober, I could hang with you.'

Mike looked at his watch. 'I guess two extra pairs of eyes don't hurt.'

We were in Mike's car for only a minute before I got a text from Lily Savitsky and read it to him. '"Thanks for taking me seriously. I really need to talk to you as soon as possible."'

'Tell her you're done. The only conversation she's having is with me.'

I texted that message back to her, along with Mike's cell number.

It's you I need to talk to, Lily responded, and I repeated it aloud. 'And I need the name of a good lawyer.'

Mike threw the car into park and asked me for Lily's number. 'Ms Savitsky? Mike Chapman here. It's my case now, do you understand that?'

He paused and waited for an answer.

'Alex Cooper is off-limits. Understand that? She's not allowed to recommend lawyers for you and she's not authorized to take information about this investigation if that's what you've got. She's not anchoring your swim team any longer, okay?' Mike said. 'You call her or text her again and I'll consider that to be harassment.'

'Thanks for dealing with her for me,' I said. 'You think she's looking for a lawyer on the estate issue, about Wolf's will? Or a criminal lawyer?'

'That's one of your not-so-good questions, Coop, in case Dr Parker is interested. There's no angle of Lily Savitsky's life that should be of interest to you now, okay?'

I couldn't help thinking about Lily – how she had reconnected with me though there was only the slimmest thread that linked our lives twenty years back, that she had come to get to know her father, or think she had, only recently, and that now she was tangled in the unhappiness of how he came to die.

It was a short drive across Thirty-Fourth Street, then north to get to Thirty-Ninth Street, halfway down the block between Seventh and Eighth Avenues. We parked across from the Silver Needle Hotel. The small shops that lined the sidewalk were closing for the evening.

Even though the manufacturing of fine garments had been driven offshore, all the businesses on these blocks still reflected the long history of a neighborhood that was centered on that trade. These were the storefronts where all the trimmings and notions, buttons and zippers, lace veils and ribbons that gave each outfit a unique look were concentrated and sold.

'Window-shopping?' Mike asked as I waited for him in front of one of the stores while he reported in to the lieutenant about our conversation at the ME's Office.

'I can't count the number of times I used to come into the city with my grandmother,' I said, 'taking the train to Grand Central Terminal from the suburbs, to walk over here to the Garment District so she could get the special things she needed to make my clothes.'

'Give me a break,' Mike said. 'You and homemade dresses?'

My mother was the child of Finnish immigrants who had come to America in the early part of the twentieth century and settled on a farm in New England, which mimicked the landscape of their Scandinavian home. I remembered everything about it from visits – the two-seater outhouse wallpapered in old *LIFE* magazine covers, the rich aromas of the wood-burning fireplace, the sauna that was heated up on Saturday nights only – and ended with a running jump into the frigid waters of Billy Ward Pond.

'You know the story, Mike. Long before my father became successful, my maternal grandmother moved in with us when she was widowed. She brought a lifetime of her practices with her,' I said, pointing at the colorful spools of thread that lined the shelves inside the front door, 'and making clothes for my mother and for me was one of them. She'd get her silver needles and thread from a shop like this, then grosgrain ribbon down the street to trim my holiday outfits, and lace from around the corner to make collars for my party dresses.'

'Sweet thought,' Mike said, turning around to cross the street. 'You should take up a craft like that. Calm your nerves.'

The young man at the front desk of the Silver Needle

called the manager, who was expecting Mike. They had met the night before.

Charles Wetherly asked Mike where he wanted to begin. The answer was the room in which Wolf Savage had died.

'Mercer will be here any minute,' Mike said to me as we stepped off the elevator on the tenth floor.

Crime-scene tape dangled from the doorknob of Suite 1008. Wetherly unlocked the door and we all entered the suite.

'Detectives came back early this afternoon,' Wetherly said, looking around the large sitting-room area. 'They dusted for fingerprints, just like you ordered.'

We avoided objects and arm rests with black dust and each found a place to sit.

'Have you had a chance to look more closely at the hotel register, Mr Wetherly?' Mike asked him.

'I told the officers who came first thing yesterday that there had been no other guests checked in to rooms on this floor. Not for days. No reservations, no guests.'

'But you didn't mention that every room on this floor was registered to Wolf Savage.'

'Excuse me, Detective. They're all registered to Velvel Savitsky, like I told you,' Wetherly said. 'And I have no idea who that is. Or had none, I should say. Not until your men informed me.'

'Don't you think it's unusual that one guy had an entire floor?'

'Not at all.' Charles Wetherly was flushed, clearly nervous about being questioned. 'It's very common in this business, Detective. We're half a block from Fashion Avenue.'

The 'Fashion Avenue' name had been added to lampposts as signage in the Garment District all up and down Seventh Avenue back in the 1970s. That's how the thousands of people who worked in the industry knew the street.

'When Oscar de la Renta was alive, he kept the top two floors for his design staff when they worked late and for his models – they often came here to relax, be made up, and have their hair done for events. Most of them didn't even stay in the rooms overnight.'

Charles Wetherly listed a who's who of prominent designers who kept blocks of rooms in the Silver Needle and neighboring hotels. Each floor of this one was named for a fashion magazine. There were VOGUE, GLAMOUR, and ELLE suites, while others were ESQUIRE, VOGUE HOMME, and GENTLEMAN'S QUARTERLY. The walls of the lobby and the hallways were covered in a blue pinstripe fabric, like an elegant suit.

'Do you have a practice?' Mike asked. 'Do you require these companies to make reservations, or to give you the names of the people who'll occupy the suites?'

'Of course we do. First of all, we have to let housekeeping know what to prepare for and clean up after. We have to restock the minibars, change the key cards, replace the flower arrangements, let security know what's happening on every floor,' Wetherly said. 'Every department has to be notified – day and night – about who's under our roof.'

'Who's ultimately in charge of all that?'

Charles Wetherly cleared his throat. 'It's my responsibility, of course. I share it with the head of security, who happens to be a retired detective.'

Mike put on a pair of vinyl gloves and pushed back the door to the next room. He was studying it from the threshold, and knowing his style, he was scrutinizing the death scene for any details the men might have missed the day before.

'Did Savage use this suite often?' he asked.

'Quite a lot, Detective. Usually his secretary would call ahead to ask us to get the room ready, if it was for an evening. Peonies were his favorite flowers, no matter what the season. We knew what wines he preferred, and that he liked small-batch bourbons.'

'That's for evenings,' Mike said. 'Did he use it during the day?'

'That, too,' Wetherly said. 'In those instances, the secretary never called. Never. It was Mr Savage himself who phoned the desk.'

'Those were business appointments, or sexual assignations, would you guess? The nooners, I mean.'

'I can't answer that, Detective. We wouldn't be in business very long if we traded in that kind of gossip.'

'It's not gossip anymore, Mr Wetherly. It's actually evidence now.'

'Evidence of what, Mr Chapman? The man killed himself. You might consider letting him rest in peace.'

'You must have known him fairly well,' Mike said. 'You sound very – well – protective of him.'

'I became acquainted with him over the years,' Wetherly said. 'He was a good customer. Very gracious to me.'

'He was a player, too, am I right?'

'I wasn't supposed to be quoted on that,' Wetherly said, looking to me to intervene.

'It seems pretty obvious from a glance through the pages of the *New York Social Diary*, even beyond just counting the number of failed marriages,' I said. 'Look, how many of the other major designers who kept suites here used them in the afternoon?'

Charles Wetherly was the soul of discretion. Or trying to be. He wouldn't name names.

'Oscar de la Renta?' I asked.

'I never had the honor of meeting Mr de la Renta, ma'am. He was generous to his staff and his guests, putting them up here, but he never set foot in this hotel.'

'Donna Karan?'

'A lot of her models stay here during Fashion Week twice a year. But no, she doesn't use the hotel.'

We threw back as many names at him as he had listed to us, but none seemed to have used the Silver Needle for afternoon affairs.

Mike backed away from the bedroom without going in. He turned and walked over to the door on the opposite side of the room.

'Where does this lead?' Mike asked.

We both knew the answer. He was testing Wetherly.

'This suite, where Mr Savage died, is 1008,' the manager said. 'That door would open into 1009.'

Mike turned the knob with his gloved hand, but it didn't budge.

'They are individual units, detective. Mr Savage liked to have the entire floor at his disposal. Twelve rooms. Two of them are one-bedroom suites, like this, and the rest are singles,' Wetherly said. 'We're a small hotel. A sliver building, if you will.'

'I gotta say I'd be at a loss to know what a man would do with so many rooms, Mr Wetherly,' Mike said. 'My whole apartment would fit in that marble bathroom inside. And I like my women one at a time, when I can even get that action going. Twelve bedrooms? That's a big slumber party.'

'I'm sure I can't give you a good reason either, Mr Chapman. And I'm no more interested in your social life than I was in his,' Wetherly said, frowning at Mike's last remark. 'Housekeeping said the other rooms on this floor were rarely disturbed, even on the occasions that Mr Savage used this suite. They were dusted regularly and freshened up, but there was no sign of occupancy.'

'So what did you make of that?' I asked.

'I think Wolf Savage liked his privacy respected, Miss Cooper. He didn't want anyone else sharing the space with him. He told me that once when I tried to buy back two rooms at the end of this hallway for a week during the height of the fall buying season. He wouldn't hear of it, no matter how high the price the prospective guests offered.'

'By "the space" you mean the entire tenth floor?'

'Exactly. It was a luxury Mr Savage could obviously afford.'

'Now, if I remember correctly,' Mike said, twisting the knob again, 'this wasn't locked yesterday.'

'That's right, Detective,' Wetherly said.

'But Mr Savage liked them all open, you said.'

'Entirely his decision, Mr Chapman. Sometimes when he was entertaining in this suite, he locked the doors from inside here with his key card. Mr Savage had a master card that worked on all the locks on this floor. Usually, they were open.'

'You responded when the housekeeper found the body, am I right?'

'With my head of security, yes, I did.'

'And the doors to the two adjacent rooms, were they locked, or unlocked?'

'I believe they were unlocked, Detective. Mr Savage was here alone, as you know.'

Mike glanced at me. 'I don't know, Wetherly. I can't think of any point in time I'd consider more private than when someone's about to end his life. Might have been a good moment for Savage to engage the locks, right? Make sure no one entered accidentally.'

'I'm not an investigator, sir. I don't know what someone in that position would be thinking,' Wetherly said. 'I hope never to know.'

'But this one is locked now,' Mike said. 'How about the one in the bedroom that leads out the other way?'

'They are all locked, Detective. On both sides of this

suite and to the ends of the hallway,' he said. 'Mr Savage's secretary called this morning. The company no longer wishes to keep this suite of rooms.'

'What?'

'The rental agreement was canceled today. Mr Savage's office has made arrangements somewhere else for the big show,' Wetherly said. 'We haven't touched this room, of course, at the direction of the NYPD. But the others are back on the market.'

'On whose authority?' Mike asked.

'I didn't ask that, sir. I'm quite familiar with the woman who called.'

'Let me have your master key.'

'Sorry?' Wetherly said. 'I can't do that, Detective.'

'You'll have to do it, and you'll have to keep this entire area, including the adjacent rooms, off-limits till I tell you we're done with our work,' Mike said. 'Now, dip the card in the hole and open this door for me.'

Charles Wetherly took a few steps toward Mike. He removed the key card from his suit pocket and slipped it into the lock. Mike turned the knob and the door opened.

The room was a mirror image of the one we were standing in. Wetherly went through the doorway, followed by Mike and then me. Mike passed the manager by and crossed into the bedroom, walking toward the door that connected to 1010.

That was the room the housekeeper believed had showed signs of occupancy on the night that Wolf Savage died.

'Dip it,' Mike said again to Charles Wetherly.

'I tell you there's nothing to see, Detective. A new code has been entered and the cards that Mr Savage had will be useless now. No one could have accessed these rooms since the detectives were last in here, because the old code is invalid.'

The man hesitated for a few moments, then inserted the card into the hole. Mike twisted the knob and the door swung open.

Charles Wetherly gasped and stood still. There was a tall man with skin the color of ebony standing in the middle of the room, his arms folded across his broad chest.

'Who are you and how did you get in here?' Wetherly asked.

'Mercer Wallace. NYPD,' he said, flashing his blue-and-gold detective shield at the startled manager. 'Housekeeping found this key card at the bottom of the laundry chute in your basement.'

Mercer passed the card to Mike with his gloved hand.

'If nobody rubbed them off,' Mercer said, 'the card might still be good for prints.'

'Room 1010,' Mike said. 'Better check your security system, Mr Wetherly. Seems the old card still works like a charm. Now all we need to figure out is which one of the three bears was sleeping in *this* bed.'

Ten

'I didn't want Wetherly to see me talking to the housekeeper who spilled the beans,' Mercer said after we sent the manager back downstairs with instructions to ask each of the people who serviced the tenth floor to be sent upstairs one at a time. 'That's why I let myself in up here.'

'She found this key card?' I asked.

'She went looking for it,' Mercer said. 'She actually went looking for the dirty linens off the bed, like Mike told her to, but there was no way to separate them out by this time. When she shook the bundle of sheets from this corridor, it fell out of them.'

'Why would someone go to all the trouble to actually stage a murder that plays as a suicide, and leave his or her room key behind?'

'Better than getting caught with it out on the street, or at your desk,' Mike said. 'Besides, you don't know whether it was inadvertently covered by the bed clothes or intentionally tossed in with the laundry. These things get thrown out all the time, and the desk just cuts a new key.'

'Yeah,' I said, 'but Wetherly claimed he had all the locks on this floor changed, so why was Mercer still able to get in with an old one?'

'Now, that's what Dr Parker would call a good question, Coop,' Mike said. 'It could simply be incompetence, or that nobody at the front desk followed Wetherly's orders yet.'

'So Wanda is the housekeeper who found Savage's body, right?'

'Yeah. She's on her way over to talk to us right now. Took a few days off to settle her nerves,' Mike said, 'but security called her in for us.'

'We can start with your buddy,' Mike said to Mercer. 'What's her name?'

'Josie. Josie LaPorte,' Mercer said. 'I told Wetherly to send her up first.'

Within minutes there was a knock on the door. A heavyset woman in her mid-forties, dressed in a collared T-shirt and slacks, forced a smile to greet Mercer when he opened the door for her.

'Don't look so nervous, Josie,' Mercer said. 'These are my friends Mike and Alex.'

'Pleased to meet you,' she said.

In answer to Mercer's questions, Josie told us that she had worked at the hotel for four years, and for the last two had been assigned to floors ten through twelve, five days a week from Tuesday through Saturday.

'I'd like you to come back to the suite that Wolf Savage used,' Mike said. 'We can get started in there.'

He turned and walked toward the connecting interior door, but Josie didn't move.

'I can't do that,' she said.

'It's all right now. The body isn't there.'

'I don't care. It's still bad juju,' Josie said, shaking a finger in Mercer's face.

'This will only take a few minutes, Josie,' Mike said.

'I didn't work that room.'

'But I'd like you to explain how they connect to each other and what your interaction was with Wanda – who found Mr Savage – not only on Tuesday but other times before that.'

'When Josie say the juju is no good, you won't get me in there no way, mister.'

Mike wanted to understand her adamant objection.

'There's nothing to be afraid of, Josie,' he said. 'You did a really good thing by telling the cops that you think someone was in here the other night, and by looking for the room key. You did a great thing.'

She was trembling the way I did when I got nervous lately. I knew Mike hadn't counted on any hotel voodoo getting in the way of his investigation. He tossed the conversation back to Mercer. 'Help me with this, bro.'

'Is it something religious, Josie?' Mercer asked.

'Part that,' she said, taking backward steps toward the hall door. 'But only part.'

'Mr Savage – well, you understand that he's at the morgue now,' Mercer said. 'Is the juju because you believe his spirit is still in this hotel, Josie?'

'His people don't believe the same as mine,' she said. 'They maybe don't know that his *ti bon ange* has to be put to rest.'

'His good little angel,' Mercer said. 'You believe in the Nine Nights, Josie? Haitian voodoo?'

'Yes, I do,' she said. 'I do.'

'I don't mean to be rude, but can you explain to me what that is?' I asked. 'The little angel, I mean.'

She clasped her big hands together and looked at me. 'My people know the soul of a man – le *ti bon ange* – leaves the body, like when Mr Wolf died. We gotta pray for nine nights, so his soul gets a good place to rest until after a year and a day, when body and soul get reunited.'

'So these nine days are important?'

'Very important, *madame*,' Josie said, pointing a finger at me. 'If Mr Wolf soul don't get prayed over and saved, then he wanders the world.'

'That's better than having him hang out here,' Mike said, trying to encourage her to come with us.

'No, no, no. Then if it don't get taken care, his spirit brings misfortune to us,' she said, making a big circle in the air with her right arm. 'To all of us.'

'You want him here, on the tenth floor with you,' Mike asked, 'or you don't?'

'Last place I want Mr Wolf is here,' Josie said. 'That's why I won't go in the room, 'case his soul waiting there to trick me.'

'Can I help to calm you down?' I asked. 'You said that's

only part of why you won't go into Mr Wolf's room. We'll help you if we can. What else is it?'

'Ask Wanda that.'

'She's not Haitian,' Mike said, his impatience sounding in his voice. 'I've met Wanda. She's not afraid of any juju in that room.'

'Mr Wolf gonna bring me down with him. I can't go in that room with you because maybe he left his spirit there to watch what I do,' Josie said, pausing before she added, 'and because he didn't never let me go into his room.'

'That's two different things,' I said. 'Why didn't he let you go into his room?'

Josie looked me up and down, not disapprovingly, but as though she were exploring our differences. 'Because he think I'm old and I'm fat.'

I shouldn't have been smiling when I told her that was a ridiculous idea.

'Not an idea at all, *madame*,' she said. 'It is exactly what Mr Wolf told me.'

'I apologize, Josie,' I said. 'I wasn't laughing about it. I can't believe he talked like that.'

It looked like we were going to get another side of Wolf Savage from some of the staff at the Silver Needle Hotel.

'I had this hallway when I started cleaning here, before Mr Wetherly assigned some of the rooms to Wanda,' she said, her eyes widening as she got more and more upset. 'And he did that because Mr Wolf complained about me.'

'About your work?'

'I do very good work. No complaints about my work,' Josie said. 'He didn't like me. He told me he liked young women, younger than me, and skinny ones. Mr Wolf told the manager to keep me out of his room.'

In this day and age of lawsuits brought for every kind of employment discrimination, I couldn't imagine that Savage would open himself up as such an easy target.

'We'll talk to Mr Wetherly about that,' Mike said. 'Don't you belong to a union? Couldn't you fight that kind of prejudice?'

'You seen Wanda?' Josie said, her eyes darting from my face to Mike's to Mercer's. 'I didn't tell anyone about it. Not my union rep, not my manager. Nobody. Mr Wolf, he likes them like Wanda. Pretty girls and skinny, too. Besides, people call me crazy if I repeat what he says.'

She was giving off a distinct vibe of crazy – something that struck close to home with me. I was beginning to think Mike couldn't go to bat at the ME's Office with Josie as his star witness. I wondered whether there was any truth to her story that the key card she had passed along had been found with the dirty laundry. Maybe it had opened the door to this room for Mercer because Josie, who had handed it to him, was using the newly issued card.

'I haven't met Wanda,' I said, 'so why don't you just stay right in this room and tell us what you saw yesterday, when you got to work?'

'You gonna make trouble for me too?' Josie asked. 'Your detective friend talked to Wanda. He seen her.'

'Let's get this straight, Josie,' Mike said. 'You came to us. You said something to the cops when you got back to work this morning, right? Something you didn't tell Mr Wetherly yesterday. We just want to know what you saw.'

Mercer and Mike kept coaxing her to open up until she finally spoke.

'First thing I saw is tracks,' she said, walking toward the window, understanding that she was not supposed to touch any of the furniture in the room.

'What kind of tracks?' I asked.

'Tuesday – yesterday morning – I come in this room about eight fifteen. I started at this end of the hallway and check each room. They was empty and I just dusted around,' Josie said. 'Then I see the track marks on the carpet, and I know I'm gonna get blamed because the Monday cleaning girl, she didn't write about it in her report.'

She leaned over and put her dark finger against the pale yellow wool of the carpet.

'Grease,' Josie said. 'That's grease.'

Mike leaned down and separated the carpet fibers with his gloved hand. 'What about it?'

'You roll things in from off the streets and it bring grease on the wheels,' she said.

'Could be somebody's luggage,' Mike said, 'with wheels on it. They pick up grease from the pavement and from rolling around the airport.'

'I was in this room every day last week,' Josie said, crossing her arms as though she were holding up her ample chest. 'No guests. No occupancy. No grease.'

'Then the weekend housekeeper was here?' I asked.

'Yes. But her report was the same as mine. She have to tell me,' Josie said, 'if she turned over the bed linens or find any kind of stain that she couldn't remove.'

'You're saying someone came in here Monday night or Tuesday morning,' I said.

'And you want us to think it was with the hand truck that carried – well, that brought the rack of dresses in?' Mike said.

'I just think someone was in this room and made those tracks,' Josie said. 'Too big to be from suitcases.'

She didn't seem to know anything about the helium canisters that had been found on the cart in the dead man's room, so I didn't intend to mention them. 'The tracks weren't darker than this when you first saw them, were they?' I asked instead, crouching down to look.

'Certainly they were,' she said defiantly. 'Before I knew the man was dead, I cleaned them best I could. Is my job to do that.'

I looked up at Mike and frowned. That was a lost opportunity to get an image of the treads from the rubber wheels, which most likely were from the hand truck that brought in the gas that killed Wolf Savage.

'Not to worry, Coop,' Mike said. 'The truck is still here.'

He would be able to check the condition of the wheels. He walked into the room that connected this one to the Savage suite. I'm sure he was examining the floor for any signs that the truck crossed through that way.

'Cleaned the floor of that room, too, Mr Detective,' Josie called out after him. 'Same spots.'

Mercer and I followed Mike into the adjoining room, which looked completely undisturbed.

'Thanks, Ms LaPorte,' Mike said. 'You get some rest now, okay?'

She nodded to him and backed out of the room.

'So there's no video of the hand truck coming into the hotel?' Mercer asked.

'None by the time the detectives started checking video,' Mike said. 'The twenty-four-hour loop had recorded over Monday's comings and goings. Besides, it's a common occurrence. The manufacturers send garments over here every day for buyers and the sales force to vet.'

'Savage didn't bring it himself, then?' I asked.

'Nope,' Mike said. 'The first responders told me all deliveries like this come through the service entrance on the side of the building.'

'So that's on tomorrow's list,' Mercer said. 'Find the dude who brought the truck over from Seventh Avenue.'

'Yeah, I'll be making a real nuisance of myself at WolfWear. Hal's probably busy circling the wagons so nobody gives anything up to the cops, and it's unlikely that anyone lets me stick my nose in the books while I'm there either,' Mike said. 'Get off your knees, Coop. What the hell are you doing down there?'

'I saw a glint of something on the carpet.'

'C'mon, kid. Let's find out if Josie has credibility with

anyone else in the joint,' Mike said. 'Breaking news, babe. Grease don't glint.'

I ran my fingers over the short nubby wool until a tiny metal object scratched my thumb. I pried the gold-toned circular piece, a bit larger than a nailhead, out of the carpet hairs and held it up.

'When you're looking for the hand-truck dudes tomorrow, make sure one of them has gold buttons – tiny ones – on his suit or shirt,' I said.

'What have you got?' Mike said, stepping in my direction.

'It's a tiny piece of gilded metal. The kind of detail item that decorates a piece of women's clothing,' I said. 'Looks like a tiny gold button to me.'

Eleven

Mike interviewed three other employees after Josie. They were from the saw-nothing, heard-nothing, knew-nothing school of witnesses. They had black holes where their memories should have lived.

Charles Wetherly came back upstairs to see how things were going. It wasn't that he was interested in our well-being, but hopeful that we would let him know whatever it was that we were finding out.

'Tell me about Josie,' Mike said.

'Nothing special to tell. She's been here longer than I have,' he said.

'But she wasn't allowed to deal with Wolf Savage? To clean his room?'

'Nonsense. Did she tell you that?'

'Well, that's not her assignment, was it?'

'Frankly, Mr Chapman, Mr Savage was put off by her ramblings,' Wetherly said. 'He thought Josie was a bit unhinged.'

'In what way?'

Charles Wetherly could barely conceal his annoyance. He didn't want to give any more information to us – having no idea the direction in which we were going – but rather wanted us to tell him what was going on.

'I think it's fair to say that Josie has some idiosyncrasies, Detective. She talks to herself a lot, she makes up stories—'

'You calling her a liar?' Mike asked.

'Not my choice of words at all,' Wetherly said. 'She's not malicious. She just likes to tell tales.'

Not what any of us wanted to hear. How could we trust the story about finding the key card to the room, or any of her other observations?

'Her ramblings,' Mercer said, 'are you talking generally or about her religious beliefs?'

'We all know Josie takes her voodoo very seriously. I think that was very off-putting to Mr Savage. All the talk about spirits, with the occasional zombie thrown in.'

'Zombie?' I asked.

'I'm surprised Josie didn't tell you herself,' Wetherly said. 'She hounds the rest of the staff with her views.'

'Try me,' Mike said.

'When one dies an unnatural death, like a suicide—'

'Or a murder . . .'

'Yes, Detective, or a murder – then his or her soul is vulnerable to the voodoo priests, who control them. Josie calls them the undead,' the manager said, as though wishing to wash out his mouth when he said the words. 'Or zombies.'

'So zombies and Wolf Savage?' I asked.

'He was a businessman, Ms Cooper. He surrounded himself with professionals, all first-caliber,' Wetherly said. 'Savage didn't brook fools or incompetence or, for the most part, people who disrespected him.'

'Are you talking about Josie?'

'For one, yes.'

'How did she disrespect him?'

'There was a young model, a Russian girl,' Wetherly said. 'Quite beautiful. She did some work for Mr Savage, which nailed him the cover of *Vogue* two years ago. She was staying here at the time, down the hall in one of Josie's rooms. Then she was let go from WolfWear, but was lucky to land on her feet, for Vera Wang no less.'

'And she fell out of a ninth-story window in her apartment in the Financial District,' I said. 'Front-page news.'

'Sure,' Mike said. 'Manhattan South had the investigation. No signs of foul play, if I'm right. They ruled it a suicide.'

'Then you know the story,' Wetherly said.

'Wait,' I said. 'Was Savage involved in that in any way? Seeing her? Angry with her?'

'Not at all,' Wetherly said. 'He had no concern for the girl once he stopped using her. The last person to see her alive was her boyfriend, but the police cleared him. All of us who knew her followed the case quite closely, as you might imagine.'

'And Josie?'

'Josie was very fond of the girl, so naturally, when she had such a tragic end to her life, Josie told everyone who'd become acquainted with the model while she stayed here that she was – I know, it sounds like one of those ridiculous TV shows – that she was undead. A zombie.'

'And Wolf Savage didn't like that,' Mike said.

'Josie has this thing – she says it's the moral code of Haitian voodoo, but that's not my expertise, Detective – that greed and dishonor are the two great sins. Unfortunately, she felt the need to stop Mr Savage in the hallway one day and accuse him of both.'

'Ballsy move, for a housekeeper,' Mike said. 'The greed I can understand if the rumors of his net worth are true. Dishonor?'

'I've told you, I don't like being the source of this kind of thing, but in this instance it was reported at the time on *Page Six*,' Wetherly said. 'The Russian girl.'

'What? Savage had an affair with her?'

'I have no personal knowledge of that. It was Josie's theory, and it was certainly true that Mr Savage sort of discarded the young woman rather precipitously.'

'So she accused him of turning the girl into a zombie?' Mercer asked.

'Yes, she did. And she convinced everyone that the dead girl's spirit was trapped on the tenth-floor hallway, because of the way Mr Savage dishonored her.'

Mike shook his head. 'Is it true that he once complained about Josie's physical appearance?'

Wetherly looked puzzled. 'I'm not sure he ever took notice of that. What do you mean?'

'Well, that she was fat, or she was old. That he wanted a more attractive type to service his room.'

'That, Detective, sounds just like Josie trying to stir things up. She thrives on that, and she's extremely jealous of Wanda, who covers the main suite. Wolf Savage never had that kind of conversation with me. I wouldn't stand for that anyway,' Wetherly said. 'For a male guest to be so interested in his housekeeper that he comments on her body or looks? I'd remember that distinctly. The last thing I'm looking for at the Silver Needle is a Dominique Strauss-Kahn sort of situation.'

'So here's what I don't get, Mr Wetherly,' I said. I didn't know what to make of Josie at this point. 'Savage was one of your best customers, right? I mean he ensured you full payment on all these rooms, year-round. How come he didn't demand that an employee who talked to him so rudely that way be fired?'

'That, Ms Cooper, is a secret that died with Wolf Savage, I'm afraid.'

'What do you mean?'

There was a knock on the door that startled both of us.

'I actually told Mr Savage that I would get rid of Josie. That I would place her at another hotel, if the union wouldn't let me dismiss her,' Wetherly said. 'He was furious with me for suggesting it. He told me he was willing to tolerate all the hocus-pocus of her voodoo, all her in-his-face gibberish, and that I was to leave her alone.'

'But why?' I asked. 'Didn't you ask him why?'

'Do you ask the district attorney "why?" when he directs you to do something?'

I'd tried it once not too long ago and the results were disastrous. 'No sir,' I said.

'Josie had some kind of hold on Wolf Savage,' Wetherly said. 'Ask *her* about that, not me. It was he who had the hotel hire her – before I came along.'

'You mean, Wolf Savage knew Josie before she started working here?' Mike asked.

'He's responsible for getting her this job.'

'What was their connection?'

'I assume you would have asked her that question, Mr Chapman, or that she would have brought it up with you,' Wetherly said. 'Her employment file is silent on the issue, except that Wolf Savage is listed on her original application as a reference.'

'Let's get her back up here right now,' Mike said. 'I dropped the ball on this one.'

'She's gone for the evening, Detective. Her shift was over by the time you'd finished questioning her.'

'Where does she live?'

'Little Haiti,' Wetherly said. 'In Crown Heights.'

'What time does she come in tomorrow morning?'

'She won't be in for the next few days, Mr Chapman. She wants some time off, actually,' Wetherly said. 'Blames you for it, in fact.'

'Blames *me?* What the—'

'Josie said you tried to force her into the dead man's room, Detective. That it was against her religious beliefs, and that you mocked her for that. I doubt you'll be seeing Josie LaPorte again anytime soon.'

Twelve

'Get a car out to Crown Heights, Loo,' Mike said to Peterson. He described Josie LaPorte and gave the lieutenant the address that was in her personnel file. 'I'll still be here at the hotel when the guys find her. Bring her back so I can finish what I started, and be sure to tell her we'll meet in the manager's office, not on the tenth floor.'

The person who had knocked on the door moments earlier was Wanda Beston, who entered as Charles Wetherly left.

She was a twenty-eight-year-old New Yorker who had worked at the hotel for about one year. She was petite and slim, with a pretty face and an engaging smile.

Mike's experience with Josie led him to start at the basics with Wanda before getting to the previous morning's discovery of the body.

She was a high-school graduate who had dropped out of community college and taken a job at the hotel to earn enough money to get her own apartment and go back to school by the time she was thirty.

Wanda had never met Wolf Savage before she started working at the hotel; never seen or been with him anywhere away from the Silver Needle; and kept her distance from Josie LaPorte, who was meddlesome, nosy, and accusatory.

Yes, Wanda had cleaned the Savage suite regularly and was aware that the man had frequently entertained women in his room overnight. No, she didn't know the names of any of the women. No, he had never come on to her or done anything inappropriate in her presence. No, she wasn't aware that he had any health issues.

Yes, she met one of his wives on several occasions, but had no idea whether the woman was number four or five. No, she had no idea whether he was a religious man, but the fact that she heard him swear on so many of his phone calls – added to the number of sexual partners she cleaned up after – led her to believe that he was not.

'Do you mind coming back into the suite with us, to describe exactly what you saw yesterday morning?'

'Whatever you need, Detective.'

Wanda was open and cooperative. Mike walked through the doors that led to the suite that Savage occupied. She didn't hesitate to follow him in, and Mercer and I brought up the rear.

'This is the living room, as you can tell,' Wanda said. 'It's usually much neater than this, of course.'

The Crime Scene Unit detectives had traipsed through the room several times, lugging their equipment. Crime-scene tape was wrapped around several chairs and the sofa, which were all covered in the same chintz fabric.

'This is where Mr Savage met with his designers sometimes, and the buyers from the out-of-town stores,' Wanda said. 'He often kept a laptop on that desk, although he wasn't very savvy about technical things. Sometimes he'd ask me to Google a company and then he'd forget I was working around him while he'd study the photographs.'

'I don't remember seeing a laptop when I got here last night,' Mike said. 'Did the cops take it with them?'

'I straightened up in here the other morning, before I opened the bedroom door,' Wanda said, holding her forefinger against her lips as she thought about the question. 'I don't recall seeing it. But then, sometimes he had one of the guys take it back to the office for him – you know, to upload new images from his own system. I just don't remember anything clearly after I saw him on the bed.'

'I get that,' Mike said, making a note on his phone, which I'm sure was a reminder to follow up on the whereabouts of the laptop.

'Did his brother spend time with him here at the hotel?' I asked.

'Do you mean Mr Hal?' Wanda said.

'Yes.'

'I guess I met him two or three times in the last year – always at meetings of four or five people – but I wouldn't say that he spent any time here.'

'How about his son, Reed?'

'I've met him also. A few more times than Mr Hal,' Wanda said. 'I think the son lives in England. But he never stays here at the Silver Needle when he's in town. He told me once that the Surrey was his favorite hotel, 'cause he preferred the Upper East Side to the Garment District.'

Mike was leading the way through the threshold to the lavishly appointed bedroom.

Before Wanda could step through, I asked, 'How about his daughter? Have you ever met her?'

For the first time, I saw Wanda smile. 'Yes, just after I started working here last year. In fact, I babysat for her several times when Mr Savage and her mother went out. She's an adorable little girl.'

'Babysat? I must be confused. I was talking about his grown daughter, Lily Savitsky.'

Wanda's smile disappeared as quickly as it had surfaced. 'No, I don't know Lily, or anything about her. Perhaps I'm mistaken about the child,' she said. 'I shouldn't have spoken about them.'

Mike had turned in our direction to listen.

'We need to know everything you know, Wanda,' Mike said. 'Please.'

She had lowered her eyes. 'It's so long ago at this point. I was new to the hotel, and this very attractive woman – about my age – was in the suite with her child, who must have been five or six. She introduced herself as Mrs Savage – that's all I can tell you.'

Both Lily and the news reports mentioned the five failed marriages of Wolf Savage, but the only child in the papers was Reed Savage – not even a mention yet of Lily. We had some research to do, for sure, although the reading of the will might solve some of those issues for us.

'How many times did you meet her?' I asked.

'Three, maybe four. And there were two evenings that Mr Wetherly allowed me to stay on with the child while Mr Savage took his wife – well, that woman – to dinner.'

'What else do you remember about the child? Do you know where she and her mother lived?'

'Somewhere out of the country,' Wanda said. 'Because the child had never been to New York before – or to the States – and she was so enthusiastic about seeing everything in the city. I know that her name was Coco. That stood out to me, too.'

'Coco?' Mike said, sidetracked from his purpose for this conversation.

'Yes, her mother told me she'd been named for Coco Chanel.'

'What do they call that, Coop? Fashion-forward, right? Coco Savitsky? Coco Savage?' Mike said, moving to the center of the bedroom. 'I love a guy who can reinvent himself. Me? I'll be walking a beat for the rest of my life.'

The king-size bed had been stripped of its four-hundred-thread-count linens, which had accompanied Wolf Savage on his trip to the morgue. They would be analyzed for bloodstains, bodily fluids, and trace evidence of any kind, even if the ME ruled the death a suicide.

Wanda Beston took a few steps into the room, keeping her calm. 'Mr Savage – well, his body – was the first thing I saw when I walked in here,' she said. 'I was expecting the room to be empty. Sometimes his guests were late to get up, but he was always out of the hotel to his office pretty early.'

She paused for a few seconds.

'As soon as I opened the door, I could see him on the bed, with that awful plastic bag over his head. I ran toward him – that was just a natural instinct – to pull it off, but when I reached his side, it was obviously way too late to help him.'

'What did you do?' Mike asked.

'I'm not sure I know what I did, I was so shocked to see him like that – his color and all. I've never seen a dead person before, outside of a funeral home.'

When the mortician-magicians, as Mike liked to call them, were finished, the body in the casket bore little resemblance to the corpse of someone who'd met an unnatural death.

'Our chief of security told me I screamed really loud. I mean, loud enough that guests in the room below called him before I even picked up the phone to dial the desk,' Wanda said. 'But I don't remember screaming at all.'

'That's not unusual,' I said, piling my emotions on top of hers, 'when you experience something so traumatic.'

'Did you touch anything, Wanda?' Mike asked. 'Did you touch the mask, or the gas canister?'

She pursed her lips and tried to think. 'His arm – Mr Savage's right arm – was hanging off the side of the bed. I reached for it, to see if there was a pulse. I know that for sure because I remember how cold it was to the touch.'

I turned away while Mike asked her more questions

about the feel of the arm and hand. He was interested in rigor and whether he could time the death against Wanda's arrival on the scene.

'Was it unusual to see a hand truck in the suite?' Mercer asked.

'Not at all. The racks full of clothes would be hauled over here by young employees at every hour of the day and night,' she said. 'Sometimes just for Mr Savage's approval, and sometimes for meetings he held here with other people.'

'They must make a mess for you, coming through the streets, tracking all that dirt and debris?'

'I get paid to clean up other folks' messes, Detective.' Wanda smiled at Mercer as she answered him. 'Two things were different about this though.'

'What?'

'The clothing racks are always kept in the living room,' she said. 'There was no need to bring them in here. They're just samples for people to look at. Nothing at all to do with the man's personal life.'

'What else?' Mercer said.

'There's a piece of canvas tarp that we keep in the closet in that room. The guys that move the hand trucks over get let in by one of the bellmen – that is, unless Mr Savage himself has given them the key – and one of them spreads out the tarp so all the trash from Seventh Avenue doesn't roll out on this nice yellow carpet.'

'Makes sense,' Mercer said as Mike tried to retrace the tire treads out of the bedroom, to see which way they went.

'The note?' Mike said, reentering the bedroom. 'Are you the one who found that?'

'No sir. I just ran straight for the phone and asked the operator to connect me to the front desk. I couldn't even think which extension that was.'

'When you cleaned the bathroom, Wanda,' I said, 'you must have seen his toiletries all the time?'

'Yes, Miss Cooper. The police officers took everything with them after they photographed the room, though. I'm supposed to be interviewed at their offices tomorrow. Routine, they told me, because I was too upset to be useful when they first met me.'

'The local precinct or the homicide detectives?' Mike asked.

'The precinct, sir. No one said anything about a homicide. Are you – ?' Wanda's eyes widened and she froze in place.

'No need to panic all over again. We always investigate suicides,' Mike said. 'I think what Alex wanted to know is whether you saw any medications that Mr Savage kept in his room. Pill bottles? Liquids?'

'Nothing like that, Detective,' she said, shaking her head. 'That man always looked healthy as an ox. He had more energy than anyone I've ever met. Real positive energy.'

I hated it when two units were cross-checking each other on an investigation. Mike would have to see what personal effects, and whether any were medications, the precinct cops had removed from the room. They wouldn't want to be second-guessed by a homicide honcho about foul play once they had declared the death to be a straightforward suicide.

'Besides, Mr Savage had everything to look forward to,' Wanda said. 'Some huge company was going to buy WolfWear, he told me, and he was going to add to his fortune.'

I thought of Josie LaPorte and her concern about greed. Why did Wolf Savage need to increase his fortune?

'And he had this special show happening at the Metropolitan Museum next week,' she said, withdrawing a small envelope from her pocket and handing it to Mike. 'He even gave me two tickets, so that I could take my mother to a big-time fashion show. You might as well have them back. Give them to Mr Hal or Mr Reed.'

Mike looked in my direction and nodded at me.

'There's a question I'd like to ask you, Wanda,' I said, 'and I'm happy to talk with you privately, if that's easier.'

'I'm fine right here,' she said, eyeing me as though she were suspicious of my motives.

'Are you sure Mr Savage never came on to you? Did anything physically inappropriate?'

'Miss Cooper, I answered that already,' Wanda said. 'He didn't give me these tickets because I'd done him any favors. He never tried anything with me, and he knows I'm not the kind of woman who was looking for business on the side. Is that clear?'

'I wasn't suggesting that—'

'In fact, he offered me a job in the company,' she said, doing everything except wag a finger in my face. 'He set up interviews for me, week after next, so that I could get work as a receptionist in the office, if Human Resources agreed to hire me.'

'I apologize to you, Miss Beston,' I said. 'I'm glad he took an interest in you. That's a really nice thing to hear.'

'He was a good man, Mr Savage,' Wanda said. She was angry at me and I didn't blame her. 'He told me he wanted me out of this uniform, okay? Out of this maid's uniform.'

'You talked to him often,' Mike said. 'At least, that's what it sounds like.'

'If he came back to the room while I was still working on it, yeah, I talked to him, Detective. And more important than that is the way he listened to me,' Wanda said. 'In some ways I knew more about the Garment District than he did, and he liked to hear my point of view.'

'How does that go?' Mike asked.

'My mother worked as a seamstress for a clothing company right around the corner from here from the time she was fifteen, and her mother before that. Their people came up from South Carolina, in the first wave of the Great Migration.'

'That's when mine came, too,' Mercer said. He was across the room, leaning against a large armoire, watching Wanda Beston. 'From Mississippi, in our case. The move from the rural South – from the remains of plantations – to the urban North.'

'Mr Savage didn't know the first thing about that,' Wanda said. 'He didn't even know how this one square mile of New York City real estate got its start as the Garment District.'

'Alex here knows everything about the city's history,' Mike said.

'No, I think Wanda's got me beat this time.'

'How about you, Mr Wallace? You ought to know.'

He shook his head. 'You got me there, Wanda.'

'It's one of the great ironies of history. By the 1850s, when the first sewing machines had been patented, this little patch of the city began to manufacture textiles for the whole country,' she said, staring straight at Mercer. 'Your ancestors and mine? They were raising cotton and baling it to send up here – right around the corner to what became Seventh Avenue.

'And men like Wolf Savage,' Wanda went on, 'made their money by producing the uniforms our people wore in the fields and in the plantation houses and shipping them back south. What established this place as the center of the garment-producing world is the very clothing that marked our folks as slaves.'

Wanda Beston turned in a circle till she came face-to-face with Mike. 'Who's going to get me out of this uniform now?'

Thirteen

I walked Wanda Beston to the elevator and thanked her for coming in to help us. Mercer and Mike were sweeping the death suite one more time when I reentered the room.

The hand truck with a rack full of pastel summer sundresses from the WolfWear line were a bright spot in the cheerless room. The dresses had been pushed apart after the first photographs had been taken so that the two metal canisters that had been hidden below them could be removed and taken to the crime lab for analysis of their remains.

'That's a sobering thought,' I said, closing the door behind me. 'That clothing for the slave trade was what put the Garment District in business.'

'Yeah,' Mike said. 'I was ready to open my mouth and hazard a guess that it was Civil War soldiers' uniforms that were the first mass-produced clothing. But Wanda had me beat with her nugget of history.'

'Where did they find the note that Wolf wrote?' I asked.

'Right there,' Mike said, 'on the night table.'

'Anything else?' I asked. 'Any signs of a struggle?'

'Nothing. Not a thing out of place.'

'Did you give any thought to whether it looked like someone had straightened up the room?' Mercer asked. 'Like the scene was too staged?'

'Glad to know you remember your days in homicide, buddy. You think I'm still an amateur dick?'

Mike had come on the job three years after Mercer.

Mercer laughed. 'You know how it is when you want to put your own hands on an investigation. Start with a total redo.'

'I bought into the suicide theory,' Mike said. 'Everything fit.'

'We don't know enough about the man himself,' I said. 'We've got to talk to the people who knew him best, at the office. The family members have too much at stake to rely on their truth-telling, don't you think?'

'*We?*' Mike said. 'I'm still stuck on the "we" bit, blondie.'

Mike was opening dresser drawers and looking in the desk for anything he and the first responders might have missed.

'Isn't it better to have my keen sartorial eye helping you on this case?' I said. 'Especially since you seem to think that "home alone" is bad for my health.'

'Consider today my favor to you,' Mike said, walking over the threshold to the living-room area. I followed him in.

'You owe it to me and the Harrison Dolphins, Detective. That's what brought Lily Savitsky to your attention.'

'I've got a short window before Dr Parker lets the dearly departed depart from the morgue. I got places to go, Coop. People to see.'

'What's tomorrow?' Mercer asked.

'Starting my day bright and early at the Savage offices. Meet and greet with some of the staff. The CFO, Wolf's executive assistant, the marketing guru,' Mike said. 'Make sure the business part of the business was on solid ground.'

'You think you can trust Josie – the housekeeper who had the key to the other room?'

'Not from here to the corner. Not that she's sinister, but because I can't quite figure her out,' Mike said, checking his watch. 'I'm waiting for the guys to pick her up, right? I'm more than curious about how Wolf came to be her reference for this job.'

Mike picked up the remote and turned on the television. He had a better sense of timing than anyone except Jack Reacher. He really didn't need to wear a watch. He hit the Final Jeopardy! question on the mark, just like he did every weekday.

'Do you know the difference between ready-to-wear and haute couture?' I asked.

Mike ignored me.

'What's an atelier, Detective? And how do they set the pecking order for seating at next week's fashion show?'

'You have a distinctive advantage, kid. You learned your French on your back, in a bedroom on the Riviera.'

'Oooooh. Low blow, Mike,' I said. He was referring to a former lover of mine, whom he disliked intensely. Luc was a restaurateur in the South of France. 'It's not your language skills I was referring to. It's the fact that there's a lot about this business that you don't know.'

'Here's what I do know about: murder, Coop. Greed, jealousy, lust, revenge. That sort of covers the main motives. I don't get a whiff of one of those in the next day and a half, it doesn't matter what language the fashionistas speak and what the spring colors are.'

Alex Trebek had just revealed the screen to show that the category was EXPLORERS.

'Pony up the cash, you two,' Mike said.

The topic was perfect for both of them. Mike had majored in history, with an emphasis on all things military, from the breed of Napoleon's warhorse to the number of ships that sailed in the Spanish Armada. Mercer's father had been a Delta Airlines mechanic, complete with travel perks for his family. My dear friend had papered the walls of his childhood room with maps of the world and knew almost as much about the geography of places he had not been as those to which he had traveled.

'I'm good for it,' I said.

'The Final Jeopardy! answer is: HENRY HUDSON'S *half moon* CREW MEMBER JOHN COLMAN WAS THE FIRST THIS IN 1609,' Trebek said, repeating the explorer's name and the year of his arrival in New York Harbor.

'We're on a roll, Mercer,' Mike said. 'Double or nothing?'

'Double at least,' Mercer said. 'I'm feeling lucky.'

'My historical knowledge isn't entirely shabby,' I said. I hoped they couldn't hear the tremor in my voice. The

Hudson River, named for the great explorer, was ground zero for my all-too-recent period of captivity.

The first contestant was wrong. 'Who was the first man to claim the land for the British?' Trebek said, reading from her slate. 'No, madam. That would be wrong. Hudson was English, of course, but working for the Dutch East India Company when he sailed into the harbor.'

The second contestant shook his head. Like me, he had gotten no further than 'What was the first – ?'

Trebek laughed. 'Well, you're not even as close as a wrong answer, sir. Sorry you didn't take a stab at it.'

The third contestant and current show champion didn't even venture a guess.

'You guys think you know?' I said.

'Oldest cold case in our homicide files,' Mike said. 'Who was the first murder victim in New York's recorded history?'

'I'm surprised you don't know that, Alex,' Mercer said. 'They've been teaching it in the Academy for years. Applying modern forensics to a four-hundred-year-old case. Seems John Colman took an arrow to his throat.'

I clutched my neck with my hand.

'Local Indians were none too happy to see a boatload of white men with muskets,' Mike said, as Trebek confirmed that was the winning factoid.

Mike clicked off the remote just as his cell phone rang. He took the call, turning his back to Mercer and me, then pocketed it and faced us.

'How's your voodoo, Coop?' he asked. 'Can you cast a spell or do any black magic?'

'Not so good lately,' I said. 'Why?'

'The cops from the Seven-Seven just called the lieutenant. They'll sit in front of her building all night if that's what it takes, but another tenant in Josie LaPorte's house says she came in after work today and left twenty minutes later with a suitcase.'

'Maybe she's tracking the spirit of Wolf Savage,' I said.

'We don't even know what their connection is, or why he recommended her for this job.'

'And now,' Mercer said, 'Josie LaPorte is in the wind.'

Fourteen

The three of us stopped in at Primola for dinner. Giuliano, the owner, was glad to see us and sent over a round of cocktails to welcome me back. Press reports of my abduction moments after leaving the chic restaurant on the Upper East Side had done nothing to hurt his business. It probably increased demand by curiosity seekers, not that it would be easy for them to get reservations or prime seating.

The ice-cold scotch was as soothing to me as a double dose of tranquilizers would have been. I drank it too quickly and was glad that Mike stepped outside to call his boss so I could slip in a second serving. He noticed it as soon as he sat back down, pursing his lips as he looked at me.

'Where will you be tomorrow?' Mike asked Mercer after we paid the bill and stood up to get our coats and leave.

'We got a great hit in the databank from an old rape evidence kit that was part of the backlog of cases in Ohio that had never been tested,' he said.

'No one told me—'

'Easy, girl,' Mercer said, putting his hand on my arm. 'Everything's under control. Your team's on it.'

The perp was already in prison on a conviction my unit got two years ago, Mercer explained to us, and he was driving upstate to interview the man.

'He knows you're coming?'

'Knows that. Just doesn't know his DNA linked him to five victims in Cleveland, dating way back before he saw fit to move to Manhattan.'

'That dude got some 'splaining to do,' Mike said, slapping Mercer on his back. 'Leaving his jism all over town like that. No wonder DNA are Coop's three favorite letters of the alphabet.'

'No wonder at all,' Mercer said, kissing me good night. 'Stay in touch with me, Mike.'

'Roger that,' Mike said. He took my hand and walked me to his car, which was parked around the corner. 'Do you want me to—'

'Yes. Yes, of course I do.'

He laughed. 'Don't jump the gun, babe. Maybe I was going to ask if you wanted me to suck your toes or drop you at the nearest all-night spin class.'

'I don't care how the question ended, Mike. I'd like you to be with me.'

'All in,' he said, opening the car door for me. 'As long as there's no shop talk.'

'Deal.'

I showered first and slipped under the covers. Mike

followed. I was still getting used to the feel of his hard body against mine, his strong arms wrapping around my torso to hold me close to him. He made me feel safe, and I liked that as much as I enjoyed being loved.

The combination of making love and a powerful sleeping pill got me through the night. I didn't even feel the mattress move when Mike slipped out of bed in the morning to run over to Central Park for his jog around the reservoir.

I was dressed and on to my second cup of coffee by the time he returned. I had my culinary specialty – a perfectly toasted, lightly buttered English muffin – ready to serve when Mike finished grooming for the day.

'Where to?' I asked.

'You're a spoiled girl, Alexandra Cooper,' he said, 'You're only getting your way because you're likely to find some kind of mischief if I leave you alone, and because maybe you do know something about the fashion world that I don't.'

I was dressed for Seventh Avenue, with a little more attention to style than my ordinary attire for the DA's Office. My mother had given me a black Armani sweater for my birthday, which complemented the slim-fit Escada slacks that hugged my hips. I tied a classic cashmere Hermès scarf around my shoulders, cinching my waist with the signature gold *H* belt.

'Are you giving me up to Lieutenant Peterson?' I asked. 'Does he know I'm going to be shadowing you today?'

'You're lucky he likes you.'

'But he won't tell Battaglia?'

'You're lucky he really dislikes the DA,' Mike said. 'Let's go.'

I stood on tiptoe and kissed Mike at the nape of his neck, lifting his thick, dark hair to make contact. He brushed me away, but with a smile, ready to get to work.

It took only fifteen minutes to get to Midtown. Mike parked on West Thirty-Sixth Street, just off Seventh Avenue. It was still too early for most offices to be open for business, so we bought another cup of coffee at a street cart and walked north on the east side of the broad avenue.

Every few feet for the next five blocks, embedded in the sidewalk below us, was a huge circular disk. Each one carried the name of a famous designer – Bill Blass, Diane von Furstenberg, Calvin Klein, and two dozen others – and a sketch of the person next to his or her name.

'What's this about?' Mike asked.

'It's the Fashion Walk of Fame,' I said. 'It's sort of fun to see. It's the equivalent of the Hollywood Stars for the great designers who've worked here.'

'You spend much time here lately?'

'Sample sales. Personal shoppers take clients like Joan and me into the showrooms of the fancy houses, if you can wear a sample size,' I said. 'You can get stuff wholesale.'

'So there's a frugal side of you after all?'

'Nothing beats a bargain.'

'Who's that guy?' Mike asked.

We were about to cross the street, stopped in front of an eight-foot-tall bronze sculpture of a man wearing a yarmulke, his shirtsleeves rolled up. He was seated, bending over a table guiding a piece of clothing that he was working on a sewing machine, pumping the pedal with his foot.

'That statue is called *The Garment Worker*,' I said. It was iconic, designed by a woman whose father – an immigrant from Russia, like my father's family – had been a tailor in the district. 'My dad used to tell me that this area, this industry, was really a unique part of New York. No matter where people came from, if they were willing to do mind-numbing physical labor – sewing garments or working in a cutting room or crowded into a sweatshop – in exchange for a regular paycheck, they could find work.'

'But now that's all gone overseas,' Mike said.

'Most of the manufacturing has, for sure,' I said. 'I think a few of the old-timers are still trying to make the district work.'

We crossed the street and entered the lobby of 530 Seventh Avenue. We signed the security log and were directed to the WolfWear offices on the twenty-eighth floor.

We stepped off the elevator into the main reception area. It looked more like a funeral parlor than an upscale design house. There were enormous baskets of flowers, as though each florist had tried to out-stuff the arrangements of his competitors. The largest ones, their cards displayed on the petals of a large rose or the stem of a bird of paradise, were signed with a single name, which was all you needed to know about the top echelon of this business: Anna, Donna, Marc, Giorgio, Carolina. The aggregated cost of the flowers I could see would have fed a small village in Africa for a month.

The receptionist was coming out of the hallway to settle in at her desk. 'Good morning,' she said. 'We're not yet open, but how may I direct you?'

'I'd like to see Mr Savage's personal assistant,' Mike said.

'I assume you've heard about his death,' she said. 'I'm afraid we're not entertaining any of our clients for another week or so.'

Mike took his shiny gold-and-cobalt-blue badge out of his pocket and flashed it at her. 'I'm not here to be entertained, ma'am. I'd like to see his assistant.'

The woman jumped out of her chair like she'd been stung by a scorpion.

'I'm so sorry,' she said. 'It's just that we're not expecting you. The police were here yesterday to look at some items in Mr Savage's office. I'll go back and see whether—'

'I'd prefer you sit down and use your intercom,' Mike said. He always favored the element of surprise. 'Tell her there's a Mr Chapman to see her.'

'Certainly, sir,' she said. She pressed a few buttons on her telephone console and then said exactly what Mike had asked her to.

'What do you think the cops took from his office?' I asked Mike. He was standing in front of a large poster of one of the supermodels, who was decked out in WolfWear from head to toe.

'I know they needed a handwriting exemplar to compare to the suicide note. Pretty routine to get one for the case file. I can't imagine they took anything else of consequence if they didn't go begging your office for a search warrant.'

The WolfWear logo was everywhere. It was spelled out in gold letters a foot tall on the wall above the head of the receptionist. There were framed photos from the covers of all the fashion magazines – American and international – and pictures of movie stars on red carpets at every awards show dressed in Savage style. Coffee mugs were stacked on a side table, and ballpoint pens were neatly arrayed on top of notepads that bore the faint outline of a wolf's head on the paper.

I heard the intercom buzz and watched the receptionist pick up the receiver and turn to the side, covering her mouth to whisper into it.

'Mr Chapman? I'm afraid Mr Savage's assistant isn't in yet. Perhaps you can come back this afternoon?'

'That wouldn't be too convenient for me,' Mike said, walking past the receptionist's desk before she could get to her feet again. 'You stay put. Water the flowers, why don't you?'

She tried to block my path as I followed Mike into the hallway, but I sidestepped her and caught up with him.

Most of the offices had glass windows that fronted the corridor – offering the transparency that had become the modern corporate buzzword – and few of them were occupied.

The third door down the row on my right-hand side had a sign reading HAL SAVAGE and below it the word PRESIDENT, but no one was inside. The other names we passed by were meaningless to me, but I made a mental note of them as I tried to keep up with Mike. There was a long room with a conference table in its center, and on each end was a rack of dresses – all evening wear, all black with various degrees of glitzy trim.

More offices, smaller ones, led us down the hallway. The place seemed deserted, and quiet as a tomb. We were headed toward a dead end, with a solid wood door smack in the middle of our path.

Just before we reached it, a tall woman in a chic charcoal-gray suit and three-inch heels stepped out of her cubicle to the left side of that door.

'Excuse me, Mr Chapman. I am – I was – the assistant to Mr Savage. I'm afraid I'll have to stop you right here.'

'You must have come in the back door,' Mike said. 'The girl at the desk told me you weren't in yet.'

'I was in the restroom, but I just got the message from her,' she said, dabbing at her heavily mascaraed lids with a handkerchief. Her smile was as artificial as her Botoxed lips and gelled fingernails. 'We're all so upset about our great loss. How may I help you?'

'Who's in charge today?' Mike asked.

The ubiquitous logo was plastered on the wooden door in front of us, and below the fierce-looking animal image was the single word: SAVAGE. I knew Mike would have loved the opportunity to snoop around the dead man's office, but it was the one room that seemed not to invite transparency.

'I'll wait,' Mike said.

'That's not acceptable, Detective. I'll show you out.'

She took a step toward him but Mike didn't budge.

'I'm not looking to lock horns, lady. I just need to speak to one of the company's officers. A few simple questions about your boss's business so we can get out of your hair and put this matter to rest.'

'I know exactly what your angle is, Mr Chapman, and you're not letting anything rest,' she said. 'Including my late employer. But there's nobody home here.'

'Then I guess it will just be you and me, won't it? And this is Detective Cooper,' Mike said. 'Let's just sit down in that office you're guarding and get the lay of the land.'

She stretched out her long arm across the doorway. 'Some other time, Detective. And by the way? I read the newspapers. I know exactly who Ms Cooper is,' she said, turning to me. 'We have absolutely no need for your services here, dear.'

I hated it when people called me dear. I was about to tell her that when I heard a man's voice shouting from behind the wooden door.

'It's done, Savage. Play hardball with me and I'll have this all over the media before you can bury your brother.'

Mike got to the door, pounded on it twice, and turned the handle. I was looking over his shoulder, and everyone in the large room was staring back at us.

'I'm sorry,' the assistant called out to Hal Savage, who was sitting at the head of a large table in the office space. 'I couldn't stop him.'

He got up and charged toward Mike while I tried to scope out the characters around the table.

'Get your ass out of here, Chapman,' Hal said. 'Take the dame and get out of here.'

Reed Savage was seated at his uncle's left hand. The other four men at the table were probably the executives whose faces matched the names on the doors in the hallway.

The man doing the shouting was standing in front of the window, apart from the startled group of businessmen. He was Asian, medium height and broad-shouldered, in his forties, speaking with the clipped British accent of those Chinese educated in English schools in Hong Kong.

'A prayer meeting?' Mike asked, tossing the envelope with Wanda Beston's tickets onto the table. 'Or business as usual, now that the lone wolf has opened up some room at the top?'

Hal thought better of putting his hands on Mike. 'Get security up here,' he barked at the assistant, who was frozen behind my back.

'What's your name, pal?' Mike said, pointing at the angry Asian man.

He got no answer.

'Tight-knit little family, aren't you?' Mike said. 'Let me guess. You must have flown in from Beijing – the Chinese branch of the Savitsky clan – to pay your respects and collect your share of the pot.'

Hal Savage took a swing at Mike – an awkward older man's jab – missing his jaw by inches and landing on the bookshelf next to my head. Two of the WolfWear crystal trophies crashed to the floor at Mike's feet, shattering into thousands of tiny pieces.

Fifteen

'What was wrong with that?' Mike asked. 'The guy's Oriental.'

'Rugs are Oriental,' I said. 'People are Asian. And the Savitsky stuff is uncalled-for. You're so damn rude is what's wrong with that.'

Political correctness was not Mike Chapman's strong suit. I had cleaned up after several bloody noses and bandaged many scrapes over the years, all attacks provoked by Mike's unfiltered mouth.

'When I was growing up there were only three detectives I idolized,' Mike said. 'My old man, Philip Marlowe, and Charlie Chan. So don't get down on me about being PC, okay? I learned a lot from that Ch—'

'Do not say Chinaman, okay? Just hold your tongue, Detective.'

The assistant had ushered us back down the hallway to Reed Savage's office. He asked us to wait so that he could explain the situation to us.

Reed took only a minute to get to us, closing the door

behind him and taking his place behind his desk, inviting us to sit across from him.

'You want to hit Replay, Detective Chapman?' Reed said. 'You want to separate me out from my uncle?'

'Your call.'

'My name is Reed. Reed Savage. Legally changed to that after my mother died and my father took me to live with him.'

'And his third wife.'

'My stepmother.'

'Is she still alive?' I asked.

'Yes, she lives outside of London – half an hour from my place in town,' he said. 'Very reclusive, but my father took good care of her when they split.'

'Does she have any involvement in the business?'

'Nothing to do with it. Never did.'

'Back to you,' Mike said.

'My mother was Wolf's first wife. Short-lived marriage, and as you heard today, she died young,' Reed said. 'I'm forty-one years old. Divorced, no kids. I'm the VP for the international branch of WolfWear. I live in London and keep an apartment here, in Tribeca. What else do you need to know?'

'I want background about your father,' Mike said. 'More reliable than what we got at the morgue, and we can come back to that. But I want to start with what's going on in that room down the hall right now. Who's the guy threatening to take something to the media, and what's he taking?'

Reed's secretary opened the door, walked in, and handed

several telephone messages to him. 'I told Ms Wintour you'd get right back to her,' she said, referring to the all-powerful queen of the fashion world. 'She has some ideas for the show next week, and some issues to resolve about seating.'

'Hold everything till we're done in here. I can't be interrupted.'

The young woman pivoted on her stilettos, looking down to her nose to see what Mike might have brought to the table that was so important, and left the room.

'You mind if I call you Reed?' Mike asked. 'Too many Savages here to deal with.'

'Of course. That's how we all refer to each other. First names.'

'Who's the screamer? The Asian gent.'

Reed looked at the slips of paper rather than at either of us.

'We're not the press, Reed. If there's something you'd like us to hold in confidence,' I said, 'we're good at that.'

'You don't seem to believe my father killed himself.'

'Give us a reason. How sick was he?'

'Heartsick, Ms Cooper.'

'What? Another romance?'

'No, no, no,' Reed said, cracking a smile. 'It's the business that was my father's real baby. He was sick to death about what's been going on with the company. This can be off the record, right?'

'You ready to confess to committing a crime?' Mike asked. 'Otherwise, I have no reason to go public with what you've got to say.'

Reed Savage loosened his tie and leaned back. 'The man you're asking about is George Kwan. You've probably heard of him.'

I looked at Mike and we both shook our heads in the negative.

'No? Kwan Enterprises? George's father was one of the first Chinese billionaires, entirely self-made.'

'How did he make his money?' I asked, wondering if it was in some illegal market, like the opium trade that had once flourished in the Far East.

'George Senior runs the business. He's quite brilliant, actually,' Reed said. 'He customized and designed supply-chain solutions for the world's most successful retailers.'

'You're losing me,' Mike said. 'Break it down.'

'Okay, detective. Kwan Enterprises is an investment holding company that's headquartered in Hong Kong. It started as a trading business a century ago, when porcelain and jade and silk – oh, yeah, and fireworks, another great gift to us – were the products being exported from that part of the world to the US and Europe.'

'That worked until the sixties,' I said, 'when the UN enforced a trade embargo on China.'

'Right. A lot of Asian companies went under, but the Kwan family managed to roll with the changing times. They shifted their interest to the apparel industry more than twenty years ago, when American manufacturers began to outsource the production of their goods to India and China, because of the cheap labor.'

'Marking the decline of the Garment District,' I said.

'Yeah, and my father – Wolf – really hated that. He tried to resist it for a very long time, but the need to compete made it inevitable.'

'Enter the Kwans,' Mike said.

'Exactly. They figured out that there was big money in overseeing the whole broad picture,' Reed said. 'Think of the biggest name in fashion that you can, and assume you've got a CEO who's been the magician, mostly interested in creating the look that will seduce his audience.'

I guessed that was supposed to be Wolf Savage.

'You don't want to spend time or resources scouring the world for cheap labor, people you can't communicate with and can't watch every day in their workplace. Well, the Kwan model is to find the factories throughout Asia for the big designers and take away all the headache-inducing micromanagement. They hire the workers, oversee the quality control and compliance issues, procure the raw materials, then contract with the vendor base to produce and deliver the finished products. The whole point of them is to keep the lowest price possible for the manufacture of each product. That's what a trading group does. They've sort of taken over the whole fashion industry.'

'But the street – I mean, literally Seventh Avenue and those little shops on all the side streets,' Mike said, 'still looks pretty much the same, even though we hear it's a struggle to keep the work, keep the unique nature of this place. What goes on around here?'

'One of the reasons this district works,' Reed said, 'is that people in our business still use it all the time. We may produce garments overseas – no more Made in America tags on the clothes, no more insistence by our First Ladies that they only wear USA goods – but some things are just essential to this trade.'

'Like what?' Mike asked.

'Suppose I need a prototype for a high-end garment we've got in production,' Reed says. 'The Bergdorf Goodman buyer wants to see it tomorrow. Not next week, but tomorrow. FedEx can't get it to me overnight from the interior ass-end of China. But you've got a concentration of people here, right within this one square mile, with the most specialized skills imaginable that have been passed down from generation to generation and do this work better than anyone in the world.'

Reed stood up and reached for a dress that was draped across the shelf behind him. He seemed to be passionate about his work – or his father's fortune.

'See this zipper? How it starts in the center of the garment and zigzags around and down the side, all the way to the hem? Can you imagine how hard this is to produce, and what it would cost to do in large quantities here?' he asked. 'But we've got a zipper guy. There's a store on Thirty-Seventh Street and all they do is zippers.'

'Zippers?' Mike said. 'You're telling me some dude makes a living just doing zippers?'

'Nothing else. Plastic ones, metal ones, solid gold if you wanted that. Up and down, sideways, curled around your waist. My man will have that dress made up before the close of the day, while everyone in the factory in China is sound asleep.

'You want a belt covered in fake leopard skin or a ruffled collar trimmed with lace? Wolf had a belt guy around the corner and a store that sells lace – black, white, purple, pink, chartreuse – but only lace. That's why everyone in the industry keeps a toehold here. There's no place like this district in the entire world.'

'Go back to George Kwan,' Mike said. 'What was his relationship with Wolf like?'

Reed folded the dress and put it back on the shelf. 'Difficult. In a word, difficult.'

'Why's that?'

'Wolf is – was – a very independent man. Fiercely so. He liked to do everything on his own terms. So he watched with great trepidation as Kwan Enterprises began to take a bite out of all the competition.'

'What do you mean by a bite?' I asked.

'George Kwan – the son – started small. His first investment was the buyout of one of the older shoe brands in Europe, a French company that just couldn't compete in the marketplace any longer,' Reed said. 'Then he set his sights on a Belgian leather-goods business – gloves and small purses. Things like that. In just the last three years, he's begun to hit on fashion houses in Paris, Milan, and here at home. Names you would undoubtedly know, Ms Cooper, judging from the pieces you're wearing today.'

'Hitting on them how?' Mike asked.

'Kwan Enterprises delivers a hundred million units of

consumer products every day,' Reed said. 'Can you even conceive of that kind of operation? Then, after the products are made, they control distribution centers, transport, and every other management service.'

'Wolf didn't want any part of that, I guess,' I said. 'But what kind of leverage does George Kwan have to go after the big-name fashion houses?'

'The volume of their company's growth made them unstoppable,' Reed said. 'It gave them a bargaining power so enormous, pressuring suppliers to lower costs, that they just shrugged off all opposition to their modus operandi.'

'What didn't your father like about them, besides giving up control of his empire to someone else?'

'Obviously, the Kwan model depressed wages for workers in all their facilities,' Reed said. 'He didn't like the idea of slave labor, of a manner of doing business with governments that weren't in the habit of enforcing regulations.'

I thought immediately of Wanda Beston, the housekeeper who told us about the Garment District's start.

'And then there were the great risks because of safety violations inherent in the Kwan model. You might recall the two great tragedies in Bangladesh.'

'I'm sorry,' I said, 'but I don't.'

'Both were in garment factories,' Reed said. 'In Tazreen, one of the Kwan manufacturing centers went up in flames when fabric and yarn caught fire. There were iron grilles that prevented the workers from escaping the inferno, and more than a hundred of them died.'

I thought also of my history lessons about the horrific

Triangle Shirtwaist Factory fire of 1911 in Manhattan, in which 146 workers – mostly young girls, immigrants – were trapped inside at their sewing machines, dozens of them leaping to their deaths when escape paths were blocked. It prompted many of the reforms that made the Garment District safer.

'Rana Plaza was a few years after Tazreen. The factory managers ignored complaints about cracks in the building's structure,' Reed said. 'When the entire concrete structure collapsed days later, more than one thousand workers were killed.'

'Those numbers, the number of human lives,' I said, 'is just staggering. Wolf had good reason to want to keep arm's length from that kind of operation.'

'Now you've heard from the soft-touch member of my team, Reed,' Mike said. 'Given that recent history of negligent oversight by the Kwans, I don't even begin to get why your father was having any conversation with them.'

Reed looked away.

'C'mon. What's Georgie got on him that you don't want the media to know?'

'The WolfWear brand was started more than thirty years ago, Detective. As of today, it remains one of the very last wholly independent fashion houses in this country.'

'It's iconic,' I said.

Reed acknowledged me with a nod. 'My father hit the big-time with his off-the-rack clothing within ten years of starting out. His ready-to-wear line.'

'I assume all clothes come ready to wear,' Mike said. 'Open the box, put on the dress, and bingo, you're ready to step out the door.'

Mercer was right. I could be useful to Mike in this world. I let Reed Savage explain his business.

'Until a hundred years ago, Detective, women's fashion was really ornate,' Reed said. 'It depended on a precise fit to the body of each client. At the beginning of the twentieth century, the industry was revolutionized by modern manufacturing. Clothing was made for a range of standard sizes, meant to be worn without significant individual alteration. It became more affordable to women of all classes and income because it was mass-produced. Ready-to-wear is what we mean by clothes the customer can take right off the rack.'

'Okay, so Wolf wanted to keep his independence,' Mike said. 'I get that. What's the problem?'

Reed Savage pushed back from his desk and walked over to the window. 'My father thinks – thought – that I was the problem. Or at least part of it.'

Mike cocked his head. 'Couldn't have thought too ill of you if he put you in charge of the international side of things.'

'George Kwan sniffed out the weakness before Wolf figured out what it was,' Reed said, staring out at the top of the Empire State Building, just a few blocks away. 'We'd always been a strong brand, a unique identity, but we'd reached a point where we weren't growing at all. Kwan told my father the problem was me.'

'Coop – Ms Cooper told me you've got stores all over Europe. How bad can it be?'

'Yeah. I opened a huge boutique on the Boulevard Saint-Germain. We've been on Bond Street forever, and the Via Veneto. I even pushed us into Moscow when things loosened up there. But it hasn't been enough.'

'What does it look like on the books?' I asked.

Reed turned around to face us and dug his hands into his pants pockets. 'Two years ago, we had products in twenty countries. Our revenue was about two hundred fifty million dollars.'

Mike let out a low whistle. 'Not hurting there.'

'You don't understand, Detective. Last year it was up a fraction, but fell below that two-fifty figure by the end of the year. That number is nothing in our business.'

'Kwan blames you for that drop?' Mike said.

'Kwan told my father that we can no longer manage this as a family business. A luxury company, but not family-run,' Reed said. 'That we have to move to a second phase now, in order to develop a strong global brand.'

'But you're the global guy,' Mike said.

'I wasn't invited to those early meetings, Detective,' Reed said, his teeth clenched and his hands balled up in his pockets. 'No one told me about the plan.'

'What exactly was the plan?'

'Kwan Enterprises offered to buy up a percentage of WolfWear.' Reed's answer was short and clipped.

'How much?' I asked.

'I feel like I'm tripping over my tongue when I speak

the number,' he said. 'George Kwan wants eighty percent of my father's business. The family would keep twenty. And he was willing to let Wolf remain CEO.'

'That must have been a blow to your father,' I said.

'By the time I was let in on the negotiations, he was feeling crushed. His mood ranged from angry to despondent,' Reed said.

I thought Reed was making a subtle play for his father's suicide motive. But Lily had used a similar point to argue against the fact that Wolf took his own life.

'My uncle Hal and I?' he went on. 'We were the sacrificial lambs.'

'You mean you two were to be axed?' Mike asked. 'Why so?'

'George Kwan put the blame squarely on our shoulders. Said we had to go.'

'What blame?'

'Look, Wolf was the design genius. He was completely hands-on about the creative part of the business, confident about what women wanted and how much they would pay for it,' Reed said. 'We're strong in American and Europe, as you know. But we're completely unknown in the shopping districts of Beijing and Mumbai. We don't have the slightest footprint in Dubai.'

'Footprint in Dubai? Are you supposed to be making hijabs and abayas now?' Mike asked, referring to the traditional headscarves and cloaks.

'Yeah, Detective. Actually, we are. Arab women are the world's biggest buyers of high-fashion items,' Reed said.

'My father was slower to realize that than many other companies. That's one of the reasons we're stumbling.'

'So Kwan Enterprises will use its fortune and its experience in this industry to develop your company in new markets,' I said, still trying to figure under what circumstances the religious Arab women would use these expensive clothes.

'Yeah, the markets I missed, in particular.'

I was looking for the silver lining. 'But isn't there a good side to this? Won't it ensure the longevity of your brand, and maybe, with your father's death, that there will be a place for you in the business?'

'Ms Cooper,' Reed said, 'Hal and I are trying to claw our way into this deal with our fingernails. We love this brand. It's everything my father spent a lifetime building and expanding.'

'How much of your father's money do you have to put up for the buy-in?' Mike asked.

'Most of what's left, unfortunately.'

'"What's left"?' I asked, repeating Reed's words.

Reed practically collapsed back into his chair, glaring at me. 'You all seem to think that Hal and I are after Wolf's fortune. Like Lily does. Like everyone else who's been hanging off him like a remora on a shark, waiting for him to die.'

'I guess you'll know exactly how much after you meet with the lawyer this afternoon,' Mike said, getting up to leave.

'That's what George Kwan is threatening to go to the

media about, Mr Chapman,' Reed Savage said, elbows on his desk, holding his head in his hands. 'Wolf must have been doing some kind of disappearing act with his money, Detective. Or cooking the company's books. There's barely enough money to keep this place afloat.'

Sixteen

Hal Savage wasn't about to be put off by Reed's secretary. He opened the door and went directly toward Mike, holding out his hand.

'First thing I want to do is apologize, Detective,' Hal said. 'It's been a tough week.'

'Not a problem,' Mike said, wiggling his nose between his thumb and forefinger. 'No direct hit. No damage done.'

Then it was business as usual for Hal, the apology obviously just a way to move us out of the Savage offices.

'Reed, I know you want to talk about your dad with the detectives, but we've got a lot of catching up to do,' Hal said to his nephew. 'I'm shifting responsibility to you for the caterer, liquor, florist—'

'You're planning a memorial service for Wolf?' Mike asked.

'In time, Chapman. In time,' Hal said. 'We're behind the eight ball here. I need you to move on with your work and let Reed get on with his day.'

'These arrangements are for the big show next week, Detective,' Reed said, trying to shake off the last few minutes of our conversation. 'My father's effort to go one-up on Fashion Week.'

'The show goes on?' Mike asked. 'Despite Wolf's death?'

'What my brother planned is really a bold move,' Hal said. 'I think it's one of the things that overwhelmed him in the end, to tell you the truth. After all, he'd been working for almost a year on this break from Fashion Week, this big plunge to go to the Met. We would not only hurt the brand by canceling his plans, but we'd be out of pocket a small fortune.'

'Yeah, can we talk about that?' Mike asked.

'About the show?' Hal asked, halfway out the door, holding it open for us. 'What does that have to do with anything?'

'Not the show. That expression you used: "small fortune". I'm wondering—'

'Wonder on your own dime, Mr Chapman,' Hal said. He stormed back down the hallway, clapping his hands and shouting out to anyone who might have been in range, behind closed doors. 'Get to work, everybody. We've got a tight deadline. We've got to rock the runway for Wolf!'

'I think he's done with us,' I said, ready to head for the lobby.

'Hey, Hal,' Mike called out. 'What's the medical update on your brother?'

The man stopped in his tracks. 'I won't miss the second

time I swing at you, Detective. The answer to that is between me and the medical examiner, got it?'

'Can't we talk?' Mike said. 'About Wolf's death?'

Hal Savage slammed one hand against the wall. 'Out of the hallway, Chapman. You win. The whole staff doesn't have to hear this.'

Hal opened the door to Wolf's suite at the end of the long corridor and we traipsed down after him. This time, the room was empty. There was no sign of George Kwan or the other employees.

'Quite a disappearing act,' Mike said. 'What'd you do with Kwan?'

The glass-fronted offices should have made it obvious to us had he left while we were with Reed.

'Not so sinister as you might think, Detective. There's a private elevator behind that door,' he said pointing. 'The one that looks like a closet. My brother didn't like everything he did to be quite so transparent as the architects who designed the offices for him expected.'

I looked around the room. There were half a dozen life-size mannequins, some wearing the most casual styles and others dressed to the nines. One seemed perfect for a young woman working in a law office, trying to appear more stylish than her H&M-dressed colleagues, and another was a daring backless gown with just enough straps holding up the top to avoid a fashion mishap.

'Reed was telling us about some of the business problems you were up against,' Mike said. 'I'm thinking it helps explain why Wolf could have been so depressed.'

Hal Savage raised an eyebrow and looked at Mike quizzically. 'What? You're ready to admit that you're wrong? You'll let me – ?'

'I'm saying if I knew a little more, maybe—'

'You'll let me give my brother a proper burial before the hoopla starts next week? You know that's the decent thing to do.'

'Reed says—'

'Look, the kid told me he wanted to give you some background, help you understand my brother a little better. Didn't he?'

'Not so much background,' I said, 'as the current state of the business.'

'He wasn't supposed to do that,' Hal said. 'I know he's grieving, but he wanted to explain his father to you. I guess it's his own way of dealing with circumstances.'

There was some serious gaming going on. Unless something that Reed said to us flipped him 180 degrees, Mike was just playing at understanding the dead man's depressed state of mind. And I just as seriously doubted that Reed was sent in to deal with us on anything other than Hal's agenda.

'So, medically?' Mike asked.

'Like I said, that nice lady doc will deal with it. Wolf flew out to the Mayo Clinic every year to have a full exam. That's what they do out there. You check in like it's the Ritz and they do a full work-up,' Hal said. 'He got some tough news this time – kept it close to the vest, like he did with most personal things in his life.'

'Sorry to hear that. Everyone says he looked so healthy.'

Hal Savage shrugged. 'Looks can be deceiving, Detective. You ought to know that.'

'I've been fooled by the best of them,' Mike said.

The smile on his face was fake and forced. It might work on Hal Savage, but not on me.

'I'm kind of fascinated by the brother bit,' Mike said. 'Me, I've only got sisters. I can't imagine what it would be like to work with any one of them for more than a day, if you know what I mean.'

'Would it help you to understand us if I tell you what we came out of? What made Wolf so proud – well, vain's a better word for it – and why a fall would be so hard?'

'Yeah. You want to do that? Yeah.'

Hal Savage walked over to one of the trophy-filled cabinets, featuring awards from every corner of the design industry, and reached up to the top shelf. He came down holding a black fedora – a men's hat that looked like it had some age on it.

'Hold this, young lady, will you?' he said, passing the hat to me. 'Read the label inside it. Tell me what you see.'

I turned it over and noticed the black silk label with gold thread. 'Savitsky Hatters. Brooklyn, New York.'

'You mocked me, Detective, when I used the name of my father – and my grandfather – when we met yesterday, but this hat explains why I did that. It explains Wolf and me, whether you like it or not.'

'Try me again,' Mike said.

'What do you think that's made of, Ms Cooper?'

I stroked the soft fur of the brim. 'Velour?' I guessed. 'Rabbit? I'm not really sure.'

'Ah! The cheap hats of today are rabbit, I can tell you that. This one, the pride of my father's shop, was beaver. Real beaver.'

'My grandfather used to have one just like that,' I said.

'Are you Jewish, Ms Cooper?' Hal said, stepping closer and smiling at me.

'Yes, my father's family came from Russia,' I said. 'My mother converted to Judaism when she married.'

'Then you know, most likely, that religious Jews keep their heads covered as a sign of respect for God,' Hal said, pivoting to explain the rest to Mike. 'Observant Jews wear the traditional skullcaps, Mr Chapman, like you mentioned, and many even wear them under other headgear, like my father's favorite fedora here.'

He took the hat from me and rubbed his hand around the brim.

'The various styles go back hundreds of years, Detective, to Hasidic courts in Poland and Romania. And this is what my father did,' Hal said. 'He made hats for his people, okay. Three, maybe four hundred a year. That kept him in business.'

'Always the same hat?' Mike asked.

'No, sir. Not a chance. Maybe the brim and the crown look the same to you, but styles change, like with every other fashion. Some preferred hats with curled-up brims, or scaled-down sizes for bar mitzvah boys, higher crowns and even what Papa called the Lubavitch pinch – three dents in the crown, favored by the late Rebbe, you know?' Hal said, laughing at something, probably a memory that was associated with his father. 'A Lubavitcher might be good for several each year, the way they go through them.'

'So your old man made hats,' Mike said. 'And you and Wolf started in the business with him.'

'At his knee, Detective. Watching him break his back, competing against the Greenbaums and the Goldsteins. Listening to him go on about how he was building the foundation so that the two of us could take it over, follow in his footsteps. Today – right now, today – if you went to Williamsburg to buy one of the damn rabbit hats they sell? You'd pay a hundred dollars for one of them. So my father? Back when I was a kid? He was probably getting eight or ten dollars a hat for the real deal,' Hal said. 'Enough to give my brother and me a quarter each to go to the movies on a Sunday. Can you think of any better reason to get out of his business? You sweat all day to make someone else who lives down the street from you look good, and you get eight fucking dollars for it? Can you imagine that?'

Mike shook his head.

'I didn't mean to be vulgar, Ms Cooper. I'm just under a lot of stress here.'

'I'm trying my best to imagine it,' Mike said. 'My father started out walking a beat on a Brooklyn street – wouldn't have known a beaver fedora from Davy Crockett's coon-skin cap. Taught me how to slip past the ticket girl at the Loews Orpheum when he couldn't come up with the money to take me to the movies, but still I wanted to walk in his shoes from the moment I was old enough to know what he did and why he loved it so much. Getting rich was never part of the program.'

Hal Savage placed the hat in the middle of his brother's empty desk.

'I'm more like you,' Hal said, pointing a finger at Mike. 'I could have stayed with my old man forever, if it hadn't been for Wolf.'

Now he was winning the contest for most disingenuous, I thought as my eyes roamed from his wolf-head cufflinks with ruby eyes to his manicured nails to the lines of his bespoke Brioni suit.

'So this whole business start-up was his doing?' Mike asked.

'You've got to give him all the credit. I'm the older one, but he had the vision,' Hal said, lifting his arms up and waving his hands in the air. 'Hey, Wolf figured if it was good enough for Lifshitz, it was good enough for him.'

'Lifshitz? What do you mean?'

'You got to be kidding me, Detective. Just what I said. You've been living under a rock all these years?'

'Lifshitz,' I said to Mike. 'That's Ralph Lauren's real name. He was born in the Bronx as Ralph Lifshitz.'

'You're pulling my leg now, aren't you?' Mike said. 'Some guy named Lifshitz has all those lily-white models sporting polo ponies on their breasts? Has grown men wearing sports jackets with crests on their pockets? Sells flannel shirts, dungarees, and lumber jackets costing more than I make a week to look like they're auditioning for a John Wayne movie? You're making a bad joke, Coop.'

'She's making my point, Detective,' Hal said. 'You can sell furry fedoras till the cows come home if your name is Velvel Savitsky. But you've got a much better shot at couture if the world knows you as Wolf Savage. My brother figured that out by the time he was out of high school.'

'And you left your old man in the dust to follow Wolf?' Mike said.

'We were damn good to my father, Mr Chapman, to the end. I wouldn't go there if I were you,' Hal said, back to his snappish mood. 'Blood has always been thicker than water to Wolf.'

'Except for now, when he was ready to cut you and Reed out of the business.'

'*What?*'

'You're the Chief Financial Officer, Hal,' Mike said. 'Reed says you two got the blame for driving the company off a cliff. He told us that Wolf was ready to make the deal with Kwan Enterprises – the deal that took you two off the marquee.'

'What did that kid tell you?' Hal Savage looked as though his head might explode.

'C'mon, man. I may look stupid, but not so much as you think,' Mike said. 'You sent Reed out to us to deliver a message. That's what he did.'

'He could only spill as much as he knows. My nephew's a decent young man.'

'Decent enough to go with you to the medical examiner to give you some cover, wasn't he?'

'Truth is, he flat-out missed the mark in the international market. The Kwans are trying to turn this place around, Detective. They've got no use for him. I'm trying to hold on to him by the scruff of his neck.'

'How about you?' I asked. 'Reed says you two were in the same boat.'

'My brother was a genius, Ms Cooper. The fashion world – this entire business – is about fantasy. Fantasy and dreams. It's about a designer who can seduce you into thinking you need what he's selling. "If I had that dress," he said, pointing at the slinky bare-backed number on the mannequin, '"I could have gotten the guy who shot me down last week," or "If I wore that suit to a job interview, I know I'd get hired."'

Hal Savage sat down at his late brother's desk. 'Wolf knew better than anyone in this business how to romance a look. That's what he did, season after season.'

'No offense,' Mike said, 'but if he was such a genius, what exactly did he need you for?'

He leaned back and put his hands behind his head. 'From the time I was a kid, Detective, I used to keep my father's books. Did all his accounting for him from the age of ten. Wolf got all the creative talent, and I got the brains for business.'

'Well, maybe Reed leaked out a little bit more than he should have,' Mike said. 'If you're the brains behind the books, why don't you just show us the money?'

Seventeen

'I don't have to show you a damn thing, Chapman. I try to be a good guy and give you a window on my brother and his life, but you don't know what playing nice means, do you?' Hal Savage said. 'We'll all get the straight news from the lawyer when he lets us hear about the will this afternoon. If any of that's your business, I'm sure that Lily will be blowing smoke up your nose the minute the meeting ends. But if you want the company's books, get a subpoena.'

'May I try to be the voice of reason?' I said, looking back and forth between the two men. 'We didn't come here to make trouble for you or for Reed. We didn't know we'd walk into George Kwan or any of this mess this morning. But Mike and I are trying to do the right thing, if you can believe that.'

'Right thing? Really? For me?'

'No, actually. For your dead brother,' I said. 'And we're in the middle of a world that we don't quite understand.'

Hal sat up and gave me his fiercest stare.

'From the perspective of your niece, Lily, it looks like her father had everything to live for at the moment,' I said. 'So of course we're interested in the financials of the company. We have to be.'

'Then ask Reed how come he missed the news about the market in the Middle East. He's the one who put us in the shark tank, Ms Cooper.'

I moved to the edge of my seat, hoping to engage Hal Savage in a conversation about his expertise while keeping Mike out of his face.

'I'm really puzzled by this whole idea of Dubai and China and those emerging markets as such a big piece of the action. What's that about? Devout Muslim women have to dress in hijabs and abayas, don't they?' I asked.

'Sure, Ms Cooper. We get that. In our business we call it "modest fashion" – you know, like a euphemism that covers the needs of Orthodox Jews, Mormons, and even Muslims,' Hal said. 'Let me ask you. Do you know who owns Harrods?'

I remembered when Princess Diana was killed with her boyfriend, Dodi Fayed, in the car crash in Paris. It was his father that owned the famed London department store. 'The Fayed family, isn't it?'

'Got you there, didn't I?' Hal wagged his finger at me and smiled. 'The Harrods started the business in 1824. Grew it to the great store it is today with the best instincts in the business. They put in the first commercial moving staircase in the world in 1898. You know what I mean? An escalator. First one ever. Gave the nervous shoppers a brandy when they stepped off at the top. Very cool move, that one. A million square feet of retail space – one solid million.'

'The Fayeds sold the store?' I asked.

'Yes, to the Qatari royal family,' Hal said. 'Sort of a crossroad moment for Western fashion and Islam or other religions. On the top floor there's a shoe salon – Shoe Heaven, they call it. A thousand dollars gets a girl bejeweled sandals – just a touch of bling to stick out from under her sari or her abaya.'

'That touch, as you say, can't be what brought your nephew down.'

'You know what Reed missed? He may have seen the tip of the sandals and the handbags with solid gold clasps and the sunglasses with diamonds on the frames, but he lost the big picture. Just a couple of years ago, Muslim women worldwide spent more than two hundred and fifty billion dollars on clothing and footwear. That's billion with a capital *B*, Ms Cooper. And by next year that figure is supposed to double. Five hundred billion, how's that?'

'What do they do?' Mike asked. 'Just hang the stuff in their closets and stare at it?'

'You sound like Reed,' Hal said, shaking his head. 'You know how many women in the world buy haute couture? Do you have any idea?'

'C'mon, Coop,' Mike said. 'Earn your keep. What's it mean? Oat what?'

'I hope you're better at murder than at French, Mr Chapman,' Hal said. 'Haute couture translates into "high fashion", Detective. Exclusive custom-fitted clothing. Expensive fabrics, constructed by hand from start to finish, with the most perfect needlework. Not machine-made. No mass production. You take Ms Cooper here over to Paris and set her up at Dior or Chanel, they'll make her a one-of-a-kind-garment that's tailored to her body, every measurement done just for her. Then you can invite her to the policeman's ball.'

'If you weren't so condescending, you might almost be funny,' Mike said.

Hal Savage ignored him and turned back to me. 'The haute couture market only serves about two thousand customers worldwide. That's it. And Muslim women are about half of the market, although the hardest to identify. In public, they wear the black cloaks made by their own designers back home, but under those abayas or behind closed doors they're head to toe in Dolce & Gabbana.'

'Are you serious?' I asked.

'The smart houses picked up on the fact that rich Arab women – I call them the Royals and Oils who shop abroad, if you get my drift – have a real thing for expensive beading. The high-end dresses are beaded and sequined from their necklines to their ankles, beaded stockings and beaded gloves, beads where nobody saw beads before. The brands that make high-end lingerie? Their profits are going through the roof.'

'Before you blame Reed,' I said, 'didn't Wolf get any of this? Didn't he see it as a way to romance his look all the way to the Mall of the Emirates in Dubai?'

Hal got up from the chair and walked around the desk, sitting on the edge of it, just opposite to me. 'God bless my brother, and I hope he's resting in peace, but I have to tell you I think he was a bit prejudiced – not that he would ever admit it.'

'Prejudiced? In what way?'

'Listen, Ms Cooper. The European fashion houses were milking the Arabs mercilessly by the 1980s, like they were cash cows,' Hal said. 'Wolf? He was a little bit afraid of that. Afraid the Savitsky name would surface under the Savage label – that maybe he'd put too much into that Middle Eastern market and he'd fail miserably once they cottoned on to who he really was. Fear and prejudice – they beget each other.'

'But he's already huge,' Mike said.

'America? He's one of the kings. Europe? Wolf represented American style, just like Ralph and Donna. The desert? C'mon, he was afraid he'd wind up in quicksand.'

'But other big companies?' I asked. 'Have they bought into it?'

'Dubai's a luxury retail paradise. Gucci's there, Stella McCartney, D&G,' Hal said. 'Look, all the things this business worships – vanity, sensuality, materialism – they're the kiss of death in many religions, like Islam. My brother thought it was crass exploitation, and even if Chanel could get away with it, he'd be just the one to crash and burn.'

'Is what you're telling me that because he was Jewish, he'd be singled out for that?'

'There was a bit of that fear in his world view. Not to

mention the fact that we were hit with a big lawsuit a few years back.'

'To do with this issue?'

'Yeah,' Hal said. 'Directly this issue. Our sportswear line was competing head-to-head with Abercrombie & Fitch for that lower-price-point preppy look. One of our managers at a mall store we opened in the Hamptons refused to hire a young applicant because she wore a hijab. He told her it was against our "look policy".'

'That's pretty revolting,' Mike said. 'You've got a look policy?'

'You can be sure the schmuck who thought up that idea doesn't work here anymore, Detective,' Hal said. 'The case went all the way up to the Supreme Court. A discrimination suit, which scared the daylights out of all of us.'

'Which hopefully you lost,' I said. 'And that made your brother even more skittish?'

'Lately, everything made my brother jumpy. Like out-of-his-skin jumpy. I'm telling you he got some bad news at Mayo.'

The intercom buzzed and Hal Savage turned around to pick up the phone. 'I'll be with her in five minutes, okay? Just ask her to wait. Make nice. Give her an advance copy of the program for the show. And when you see the detectives leaving, bring in that white silk jumpsuit that I want JLaw to wear Monday night. I want it hanging in here for that meeting.'

Mike perked up at the mention of his favorite actress's name. I was allowed to swoon over Bradley Cooper and

Idris Elba while Mike fantasized about Jennifer Lawrence and Cate Blanchett.

'That's *Women's Wear Daily* coming in to interview me, Detective. It's the bible of our business, so let's cut this short.'

'This has been really helpful to me,' Mike said. 'I'm seeing another side of your brother that may explain his death. I'm trying to get a handle on this part of Wolf that was facing a failure, maybe for the first time in his career.'

'It wasn't so long ago, Detective, that American designers dressed people to go to work. Do you understand that?' Hal asked. 'You, Ms Cooper, you ever hear of Anne Klein?'

'No, sir. Afraid not.'

'You got a mother? Ask your mother,' he said. 'In the '60s, it was Anne Klein who changed the way American women dressed for the workplace. Got them out of shirt-waists and into separates. Moderate pricing. Revolutionized the look and made it possible for cheaper brands to knock it off for ladies all over the country. By the way? Anne was born Hannah Golofski – also in Brooklyn. I'm telling you, Russian Jews have done more to style American women than all the Chanels and their peers ever did. She eventually sold her company to a hot young designer named Donna Karan.'

I nodded.

'Now I'm talking, right? Everybody knows Donna Karan,' Hal said. 'Donna, Ralph, Oscar, Calvin, Wolf – pure American style. Pure class. Then what happens?'

'Got me,' Mike said.

'A bump in the road called casual Friday. The beginning of the end. Now we've got an entire generation that goes to work in hoodies and jeans. Hoodies and jeans, can you imagine? Tech kids wouldn't know a style from a stained T-shirt. It's been a nightmare to our business.'

I'd never thought about the drastic change in the workplace. My prosecutorial colleagues were still wearing suits for courtroom appearances and jury trials, but most of my other friends dressed down in almost every other line of work.

'The pressure in this business is enormous, Detective. Wolf not only had the bad news from the Mayo Clinic, but he had his creative life crashing down around him on every side.'

'But he also had this spectacular event launching just next week,' I said. 'That's what doesn't make sense to me.'

'What I really want to say to you, Missy, is that I'm so sick and tired of hearing your skepticism about what makes sense to you or not.' Hal was on his feet again, frustrated with our conversation. 'You ever hear of Alexander McQueen? A young Brit who was at the top of his game.'

'Yes, I have.'

'Forty years old, with early success and a bright future, so it seemed to me and the rest of the design world. Loaded up with pills and cocaine, and then he hanged himself, just days before his hot show at London's Fashion Week.'

Hal was making his point by stabbing his forefinger into the desktop on every fourth or fifth word.

'L'Wren Scott? How about her? Right nearby in Chelsea, probably on your watch, Detective,' he said, snapping at Mike. 'Did you give her people a hard time, too?'

Everyone in New York knew the story, which had made headlines a few years back. The glam model turned designer who was Mick Jagger's girlfriend at the time she died also hanged herself – from a doorknob in her apartment, with a silk scarf wrapped around her neck – at the age of forty-nine.

'Scott's luxury brand was in debt up to its eyeballs. She canceled her Fashion Week entry – the whole industry was in turmoil – shortly before the event,' Hal said. 'When this business tanks, it sucks all the life out of you. Trust me, Detective. I'm putting on a good face for the media so my brother goes out on top. I'm doing everything I can to keep this company alive.'

He was on his feet, waving his hands to shoo us out of his office. 'Now, if you two don't mind, I've got things to do. Time, tide, and Anna Wintour wait for no man, Detective. You're keeping *Women's Wear* out in the cold, and then a kid from *Vogue* has to interview me, and after that a group of runway models who are going to light up the sky for us on Monday night come in to get their marching orders.'

'Must help with the mourning process,' Mike said.

'You release Wolf's body and then I'll do the proper mourning. Meanwhile, I think we're done.'

As I approached the door, I could see the svelte secretary ready to come in as Hal had directed.

'Can you have someone show us around?' Mike asked. 'I'd like to see where the garment racks – you know, the hand trucks like the one that was in your brother's hotel room – are kept.'

'I've got no problem with that, Mr Chapman. The girl will get you someone to show you around.'

I winced at that old-fashioned reference to the secretarial assistant as 'the girl.'

'Thanks.'

'These offices upstairs and the basements. Chock-full of hand trucks. They're the workhorses of Seventh Avenue. Watch that you don't get run over by one on your way out,' Hal said. 'Now, are we quite done?'

'For today,' Mike said. 'Appreciate your time.'

Hal opened the door and took the slinky white garment from his secretary. He held the hook of the hanger up in the air and twirled the piece around, so that we could see all of it.

'You've really got Jennifer Lawrence coming to your extravaganza?' Mike asked.

'I'm an optimist, Detective. So far, she's not returning my calls. But my brother dressed her for her first Golden Globes, so hope springs eternal.'

'She'd be stunning in that,' I said.

'It's a killer look,' Hal said, lowering the jumpsuit and hanging it from a hook that extended out from the bookshelf behind the massive desk.

The sexy piece of clothing didn't fit with the word 'killer.' But I was still too full of suspicion to appreciate the phrase.

'That's what Wolf would call it when he nailed a style dead-on. He'd point his finger and thumb at the model like he had a pistol in his hand. Then he'd say, "Let me dress you for the red carpet, Jennifer. You got a killer look."'

Eighteen

'Did you hear what he said?' I asked.

'"Killer look"? It's just an expression, Coop.'

We'd spent more than an hour being toured through the Savage offices and the building's basement, including the loading dock, where all the hand trucks were stored. Nothing seemed to distinguish any of them from the others. All were dinged and dented, with wheels that had rolled over garbage and in fuel that dripped onto the busy street.

We were walking up the ramp to the sidewalk and it was the first time we'd been alone together since leaving Hal Savage.

'I wasn't worried about his turn of phrase, Mike. I mean the "sick" thing.'

'What?'

'Hal practically has me on the suicide motive. I mean, once you peel back the curtain, there are lots of reasons that Lily may not have known about what could have depressed her father, and that's before we even know anything about his screwed-up personal life,' I said. 'She probably didn't realize the bigger implications of the Kwan takeover plan.'

'I hear you,' Mike said. 'I'm on the same wavelength. What are you talking about? That he dissed his secretary by calling her "the girl"?'

'No, no. When he got really annoyed with me because I was skeptical about Wolf killing himself before the big launch, he said that he was "so sick and tired" of hearing me go on, basically.'

'Happens to the best of us, babe. What offended you?'

'Nothing. Think of the suicide note, okay? Didn't it read "I'm so sick"?'

'Yeah. Over and out. That was the whole note.'

'I know that "sick and tired" is a pretty common expression, but think about it. This one cuts both ways.'

'How?' Mike asked.

'Well, if you buy into the suicide theory, then you have to believe that all the man wanted to say is that he was ill. Pretty shorthanded way of announcing it. Nothing about physical pain. Nothing about how much he was suffering or how long he thought he had to live. And certainly nothing about his business setbacks.'

'Nobody said he was Shakespeare.'

'But suppose this is a murder, which is certainly where you were headed at the end of the day. Imagine that the whole scene was staged.'

'Got it.'

'Have you compared Wolf's handwriting to Hal's? To

his son's?' I asked. 'Or maybe the two brothers spent so much time together their speech patterns were similar.'

'You're going – where?'

'That at some point, Wolf Savage wrote a note complaining to someone that he was "so sick and tired" – of something,' I said. 'Let's assume that it had nothing to do with his impending death, since in this scenario, he doesn't know he's going to die. Is this how he talked? Was he complaining to someone?'

'Basically, was the piece of paper he wrote on altered? Or torn?' Mike said. 'I don't have the original. All I saw was a copy.'

He took his vibrating phone out of his pocket. 'Chapman here. Hello?'

'You've still got work to do,' I said, thinking about the note and walking down the avenue toward the car while Mike talked into his phone.

'Yeah. We're just across town. See you in fifteen minutes.'

'Who's that?' I asked.

'Emma Parker. She's got something to show us. Wants us pronto.'

We sped up our pace. 'You think she's getting any external pressure to make a decision on the release of the body?'

'She wouldn't say what it's about, but the commissioner's walking on eggshells till she tells him what she's doing.'

Mike squared the block and drove back to the East Side. It was noon by the time we were admitted to the ME's Office and seated at Dr Parker's conference table again.

'You want to know who we talked to?' Mike said. 'What we learned in Savage country?'

'Not till I've walked you through my morning,' Emma said. 'Kind of a roller coaster of a day so far.'

She leaned over the table, cued up her laptop, and projected an image on the large screen hanging on the wall.

'This is from the Mayo Clinic records, which came through a few hours ago,' she said. 'Wolf Savage had a thorough work-up. No sign of heart disease, nothing neurological. Colonoscopy normal. Just one sign of trouble, which could have set him off. See this?'

Emma used a pointer to tap on the screen, over the area of the right lung.

'That murky white stuff?' I asked.

'Yes. That's what the initial X-ray showed, which caused the docs to do a CT scan of his chest.'

'Are we looking at lung cancer?' Mike asked. 'I'll get off my high horse if that's how sick the guy was. We better get this body out of here now.'

'My first thought, too,' Emma said. 'But there are a lot of false positives with lung imaging. That's why they sent him for the scan, which also kept the question mark about a malignancy wide open.'

'C'mon, Doc. What diagnosis did they give him? What kind of treatment?'

'Slow and steady, Detective. I want you to get this information just the way that I did, okay? They wanted Mr Savage to stay another day, but he refused. He checked himself out. Told the team that he'd see his own internist at home.'

'Did they prescribe anything for his pain?' I asked. 'Oxy? Anything like that?'

'No meds. He was completely asymptomatic. No pain, no cough, no other indication of a malignancy. There was nothing to prescribe unless he stayed the extra day and finished the diagnostic process, but he told them he had too much going on at work to stay.'

'Do they know if he followed up back here?'

'No. Three phone calls to his office went unreturned.'

'So he was really sick after all,' Mike said.

'I walked this over to NYU Hospital,' Emma said. The great university medical center was just adjacent to the ME's Office. 'Talked to the top pulmonologist. He thinks it's not lung cancer at all – a false positive on the X-rays and CT scans. That what we see on the screen is a very mild aspiration pneumonia.'

'Meaning what?'

'That a piece of food – or even saliva – went into Savage's lungs instead of down the esophagus to his stomach. Common in older folks, more especially in men. It causes the irritation, the inflammatory lesions that are the infection you see in the images. They often masquerade as cancer.'

'No symptoms at all?' Mike asked.

'In a very mild case, he might have developed a fever – maybe not even for a day or two after he left Mayo. Had he not been so impatient, they would have caught it the next day. If we can find his local doctor here in town, Savage might have taken a short course of antibiotics, but that's about it.'

'So nothing that was going to kill him?' I asked.

'A good aspiration pneumonia can certainly do that, but by the time it did, Wolf Savage wouldn't have been walking around the city, going from work to his hotel. He'd have really been laid low, likely to have spiked a fever, maybe even become delirious and therefore oblivious to anyone around him.'

'But if he went to his doc here, when he got home from Mayo?'

'An antibiotic could knock it out in a normally healthy adult. Otherwise, it wouldn't be worth the trouble to set up an exit bag and all the drama that went with it just to do the job.'

'So you're right back on the fence about how Wolf died?' I said. 'We've actually got some facts that might have led him to suicide.'

'Did I say my morning ended with that diagnosis?' Emma said, digging her hands into the pockets of her lab coat. 'Or do you want to see what I asked you to come back here for?'

'Too hot to handle in a text?' Mike said.

'Boiling hot,' Emma said, reaching for her laptop and removing the image of Wolf Savage's lungs from the screen. 'Fasten your seat belts.'

'Ready to roll.'

'You know it's routine for us to enter the deceased's DNA in the crime-scene databank.'

'Of course,' I said. Since the 1990s, the creation of two vastly different systems of DNA analysis had revolutionized the criminal-justice system. The one most familiar to the public through newspaper accounts and television shows is the one in which the genetic profiles of convicted offenders are entered into the databank. This ever-growing pool of felons and predators – more than ten million of them now – allows law-enforcement agencies to compare evidence in unsolved cases to the known criminals.

The databank to which the ME's Office had access is for crime-scene evidence. They could input evidence from a variety of sources – whether unidentified remains or fluid on the clothing of a victim – to memorialize the evidence in hopes of an eventual match in the convicted offenders' databank. Eventually, they could upload the results to the national CODIS system as well.

'I decided it would be smart – no matter what my decision is – to have some of Wolf Savage's DNA in the system.'

'But you made a promise to the family not to autopsy yet,' I said, anxious about the conversations we'd just had with Reed and Hal.

'I've kept that promise, Alex. You know I would. But we had the plastic bag that was placed over the head of the deceased,' Emma said. 'It came in with the body, of course. And I figured if we analyzed the bag for trace evidence – skin cells and such – it might help us resolve whether the man hurt himself, or had some help shuffling off his mortal coil.'

'That makes good sense.'

'There were several sets of fingerprints on the bag that Savage used. I'd expect that to be the case, even if he acted solo, because we don't know where or from whom he got the bag. So I asked the lab to get me skin cells that had sloughed off onto it,' she said. 'As well as salivary amylase.'

'You mean DNA from the point inside the bag where his saliva hit the plastic?' I said.

'Exactly. They worked up a profile for me – several profiles, actually – and we entered them into the crime-scene databank last night.'

'Several profiles?' Mike asked.

'Yes. Like I said, Savage isn't likely to have been the only one who touched the bag, so we have a few other genetic prints to consider,' Emma said. 'But that doesn't mean we've got a known killer. It could just as easily be that someone handled the plastic before the day it came into the possession of the deceased.'

Mike sat back in his chair and put his feet up on the conference table.

'And here I thought you were going to declare this a homicide and solve it for me at the very same time,' he said. 'I feel like I'm on a seesaw.'

'I'm afraid I haven't solved anything at all,' Emma said. 'I came back in from NYU an hour ago and found this report waiting for me on my desk. The biologist who got the results doesn't even want to enter it into the computer system until we figure out the consequences.'

Emma Palmer came around behind Mike and me and put two pieces of paper side by side on the table between us. I had studied thousands of DNA analysis reports over the last decade when matching or excluding suspected sex offenders. I had learned the methodology so that I could present it to jurors clearly and withstand challenges by the most knowledgeable adversaries. I was familiar with the peaks and valleys, the alleles and chromosomes – every technical term that made this science so formidable, beyond any and all doubt.

'Who have we got here?' I said, looking from one page to the other. Most people thought DNA profiles printed out of a computer with passport photos attached, identifying the subjects of the search. That was a myth. All I could see were the loci – the points on each profile – that were identical to each other.

'Help me with this,' Mike said.

'It's not a match,' I said. 'Yes, you've got a lot of markers in common, but then you've got just as many more that don't line up.'

'That's Wolf Savage on the left,' Emma Parker said. 'No question about that.'

'Then whose profile is on the other piece of paper? It must be a relative of his, Emma,' I said, speeding through thoughts that a strong Y chromosome might prove a link to either Wolf's son, Reed, or his brother, Hal. 'Did you get this off the plastic bag?'

'That would almost make sense, Alex, wouldn't it?' she asked, picking up the paper and flapping it in the air, grimacing as she walked to the head of the table. 'But this is the genetic profile of the vic that was fished out of the East River two weeks ago. The young woman whose body has still not been claimed.'

Mike practically fell off his chair. 'Tanya Root? You're telling me there's some kind of genetic link between her and Wolf Savage?'

'I'm willing to bet you, Mike, that Wolf Savage is actually her father.'

Nineteen

'I could really use a cocktail,' I said to Mike, rubbing my forehead with my fingers.

We were all alone in the ME's conference room, trying to figure out whom to tell – and in what order. Commissioner Scully? Lieutenant Peterson? The district attorney?

'I'm not sure I'm ready to deal with the stress once the department declares this a homicide.'

'No point getting pickled now, Coop. This is a morgue, not a day spa,' Mike said. 'Think this through with me.'

'What's there to think about? If you tell the lieutenant first, then you can continue to go about your business like a total professional. If you're serious about letting Paul Battaglia in on this news right now, he'll play it to suit whatever angle pleases him, including which reporter he graces with the leak.'

I had spent a decade being loyal to Paul Battaglia, trusting his integrity and believing that his oft-used campaign slogan – 'You Can't Play Politics with People's Lives' – was actually a principle he embodied.

But I had learned some hard lessons about him not long before my abduction. Politics makes strange bedfellows, I know, but Battaglia should never have hooked up with the sleazy Harlem minister – the Rev. Hal Shipley – who was no better than a street thug.

The possibility that the DA could be bought or bribed loomed all too large in my mind.

'You just don't want me to call Battaglia because he'll be peeved that you've jumped into the middle of this mess while you're on leave from the office.'

'I don't care what you tell him, Mike. I think he's sold his soul to the devil – to Shipley. I don't know when I'll be ready to go back to that office.'

I was struggling with how to handle my suspicions about Battaglia. I didn't think I could face him without confronting him on his duplicity.

'C'mon, babe. Work with me,' Mike said, pacing up and down the long room. 'Somebody kills Tanya Root, okay? Female, black, close to thirty years old. Nobody seems to miss her, want her, or care about her. She winds up lying on ice in a refrigerator next to a seventy-year-old white guy – millionaire type – who seems to be her biological father. Start there.'

'Chapman's Rules of Homicide Investigations,' I said. 'Volume One, Rule One: There's no such thing as coincidence in a murder case.'

'Correct.'

'I'd start with the fact that whoever killed Tanya Root didn't expect her to be found. The East River is not a river, right? It's a tidal estuary. Tanya was supposed to sleep with the fishes forever, flushed out into the ocean beyond New York Harbor.'

'Check. The killer didn't know her breast implants were immortal.'

'How come neither her half-sister, Lily, or her half-brother, Reed, made any mention of her?' I asked.

'Half?'

'Same father. Black mother, Mike. Start with the obvious,' I said. 'Either they didn't know of her existence or they figured we wouldn't find out about her existence because she was permanently out of the picture.'

'Check that. Add Hal to the silent Savitskys.'

'Tanya's a rough ten years younger than Lily. So it's possible she's the child of wife three or wife four,' I said. 'You can't rely on the hastily drawn-up obits for accuracy.'

'You don't have to be married to have a kid, Coop.'

'Check that, too.' My mind was racing in a dozen different directions. 'Had he abandoned her, like Lily? Did he acknowledge paternity or even know of her existence? You've got to reinterview everyone involved.'

'Triple-check.'

'Tanya described herself to the Brazilian plastic surgeon as a model.'

'Wishful thinking.'

'But maybe she was a model, or trying to be one. Maybe she was in contact with her father all along.'

'Hey, maybe Wolf's the one who wanted her dead, Coop.

Throw that into the mix. She might have been blackmailing him about their relationship.'

'Way too many unknowns,' I said.

'Someone kills Tanya. And her death is likely to have something to do with her father. Once we nailed an ID on her – assuming he happened to have still been alive at the time – we'd know to give him a hard look. Her death has something to do directly with Wolf Savage. That's the trail I have to follow.'

He picked up his phone, checked the contact list, and pressed the number he was looking for.

'Who are you calling?' I asked.

'Jimmy North,' he said to me, then spoke into the phone. 'It's Chapman. We've got a development on Tanya Root. Can you meet me at the morgue?'

'Is he coming?'

'Yeah. And you're going.'

'Where? I'm with you, right?'

'You're going home, kid. Do not pass Go. Do not collect two hundred dollars. Do not stop in at the Beach Café and test drive an afternoon Bloody Mary, much as you'd like to. Just go directly home. Can I trust you to do that?'

'I can help with—'

'This investigation is going to take off now. The lieutenant won't want me babysitting the rest of the day, okay? I need to be at the offices of Savage's lawyer before the family comes out of the meeting about his estate. Jimmy and I have to separate the players and pin them each to the wall like they were butterflies stuck into Styrofoam.'

'You're mad at them now,' I said. 'That won't help, Mike.'

'They're a greedy bunch of self-serving liars. Then we've got the housekeeper who disappeared on us – and the other one who was hoping Wolf would help her. I'm back to square one.'

The door opened and Emma Parker came in, wearing her sternest Chief Medical Examiner face. 'I've just gone over those results with the two senior forensic biologists. No mistake about it.'

'Paternity confirmed?'

'Yes, Mike. You'd better get your ducks in a row. I've got to call the Savage family. I'm declaring Wolf Savage's death a homicide. There'll be an autopsy conducted tomorrow morning.'

Twenty

I walked up the steps to the main entrance of the Metropolitan Museum on Fifth Avenue at Eighty-Second Street. No matter how many times I had made the climb since my childhood, the elegance of the century-old building never failed to impress me. Its grand facade capped the setting on the edge of Central Park, long called the Gold Coast of Manhattan because of the mansions that had lined it in the city's gilded age.

I had stopped at the Beach Café on Second Avenue on my way home from the morgue. I'd promised Mike that I wouldn't do a Bloody Mary, but I needed a glass of wine with my chef's salad. The second glass relaxed me even more.

When I got to my apartment, I was restless and agitated. I couldn't focus on a book or newspaper, all my friends were either at work or with their kids, and I hated being ejected from the investigation.

It was that restlessness that propelled me to get out of the apartment and walk uptown to the museum. I wasn't the least bit interested in culture at the moment, but I figured someone had to be setting up the Wolf Savage exhibition.

My membership card got me in the front door. I passed through the enormous Great Hall and made my way down the staircase to the newly renovated Anna Wintour Costume Center.

It was four o'clock and the doors were wide open. Two men high up on ladders were just inside the foyer, draping a black bunting over the large sign that announced the special exhibit: SAVAGE STYLE.

'Sorry, miss, but we're closed at the moment. We're doing an install for the show that opens on Monday,' one of the men said to me.

'Thanks very much. I'm not here to see the exhibit. I'm a friend of the family, actually,' I said, playing on my long association with Lily. 'I live nearby. I just thought I might wander through and, you know – well – reflect a bit.'

'Not a problem. We clear all the galleries in an hour.'

'Understood.'

The rooms were darkened, with spots down-lighting the classic clothing, representing five continents over centuries of their manner of dress. I picked up a brochure from the front table, which described the 1946 merger of the once independent Museum of Costume Art with the Met, and its later elevation to an actual curatorial department.

The front gallery was exactly as I remembered it, with a permanent display of some of the 35,000 items and accessories that made up a historical record of fashionable lives since the fifteenth century.

There was no one at work as I strolled through the hall, past the 1850s British court dress crafted in exquisite blue silk with gold metallic-thread trim, the military uniform worn by a soldier in the Spanish–American War, and the sexy-looking pair of silk stockings from 1920.

I turned the corner to enter the second gallery and ran into two women fussing over a mannequin. This was definitely Wolf Savage's turf, as I glanced around at the other wooden figures in the space.

'Need help?' one of them asked.

'Just looking.'

'Didn't the guys out front tell you we're closed?'

'Yes, but I – well, it's an old family connection to Mr Savage and I—'

'Oh, that's all right then,' she said. 'We work for the museum, but someone from his staff is in the next gallery. Just keep going.'

I didn't see anyone in the third room. The lighting was dim and the space was tightly packed with decades of Wolf Savage designs.

You could trace the evolution of his work simply by looking at the level of sophistication and the more luxe fabrics that he began to use over time.

The sportswear that had first put WolfWear on the map was on show at the front of the room. It was playful and accessible, a very colorful mix of clothing that must have had a modest price point and broad appeal.

Mounted on a shelf on the wall to my right was his signature design WolfPak, a striking cross-body bag made first in denim, for $25, in the 1970s. Framed beside the prototype was the model of the bag featured last year on the cover of *W* magazine – in green alligator with a $5,000 price tag.

I stopped to admire an enlarged photograph of Savage himself, on the cover of *Paris Match* ten years ago, marking his triumph at Parisian Fashion Week. Beneath the smiling face of the designer, as he was exiting the Musée d'Orsay with a stunning woman on his arm, was the headline: COUP DE LOUP . . . the coup of the wolf.

'Are you lost, or didn't you get the message that these galleries aren't open?'

I heard the voice but didn't see the speaker.

'Excuse me?'

'Down here, luv,' she said. 'Try not to step on me, please.'

She was sitting cross-legged on the floor, pulling her head out from beneath the full skirt of a ball gown that she was adjusting in some way.

'No worries,' I said, smiling at her. 'I'm Alex. Alex Cooper.'

'Is that supposed to mean something to me?' she said. 'Because it doesn't.'

She was a very attractive young woman, a few years younger than me, I guessed. Very slender with long limbs, short spiky auburn hair, and a gamine look about her.

'Not at all. I'm just introducing myself because—'

'No need. I'm too busy for tea at the moment. You ought to move along,' she said, disappearing under the skirt again.

'I – well, I know some members of the Savage family. I just thought—'

Her head popped out again. 'Should have said so, luv. Then you're not a trespasser after all.'

'Still, I didn't mean to interrupt you.'

She uncrossed her long legs and stood up, brushing off her hands on her jeans. 'I'm Tiz. Tiziana Bolt. Very sorry for your loss.'

There was a trace of a British accent in her speech, but it sounded very put-on.

'I can't pretend to have been close to Mr Savage himself. It's actually been years since I saw him,' I said, remembering that Lily thought it very unlikely I'd met him at all. 'I'm planning to come to the exhibit next week, but it just felt right to see if I could pop in because of – well, what a difficult time it's been.'

'His spirit's here, that's for sure.'

'Do you – did you work with him?'

'More of a freelance thing,' Tiz said. 'Velly was a friend, really. A good friend.'

'Velly?'

She toyed with some wisps of her hair. 'Oh, just my name for him. He was born Velvel Savitsky. If you didn't know that, you can read the background in the brochure you've got in your hand. Drove him crazy that I called him Velly, but then he counted on me driving him crazy.'

Tiziana Bolt tucked her thumbs in her rear jeans pockets. I supposed her remark was meant to be provocative. I'd get back to the question of their relationship in time.

'Yes. Yes, I knew that was his name,' I said. 'I grew up with Lily, actually.'

'Lily? Who's that?' I couldn't see the expression on her face. Tiz had busied herself with smoothing the creases in the skirt of the navy-blue gown.

'Wolf's oldest daughter,' I said. 'Lily Savitsky.'

'Oh yeah. Heard about her, but I didn't realize she was in the picture. Velly treated Reed like he was an only child,' Tiz said.

So much for Tanya. That still didn't tell me whether this woman was close enough to anyone in the family – or the company – to have been in a position to know more.

'Strange,' I said, confident that the information about the connection between the two dead bodies in the morgue would be public by morning, 'Lily always hinted that there was another sibling. I don't know. Wives number three or four, I think. I should have paid more attention when she talked.'

'No shortage of wives was there?' Tiz said. 'Mind if I keep working?'

'Please. Don't let me get in the way.'

'Good to have company. Spooky in a big old museum when it's so empty down here,' she said. 'Would you hand me those gloves?'

I stooped to pick up a pair of elbow-length leather gloves from the floor and passed them to Tiz, who fitted them on to the fingers of the uncooperative mannequin.

'Did you say you worked for the company?' I asked.

'Once upon a time, but only for a nanosecond, when I first got out of school. Mostly I just freelance.'

'Wolf hired you to help with the exhibition?'

'You could say.'

'You must be very talented,' I said, trying another smile out on Tiziana to see whether I could loosen her tongue.

'Why's that, luv? Because I can dress up a wooden doll?'

'Well, to be selected to prepare a major retrospective at the most iconic museum in the country. Is your background in design?'

'My background is nobody's business, Alex,' Tiz said, looking me in the eye for the first time and laughing as she spoke. 'My degree is in drama.'

'Let me guess. The Royal Academy of Dramatic Arts. London.' I was jumping ahead, thinking she had met Wolf – or Reed – in England, where both had lived.

'Did I fool you with that accent? Pure Bronx it is,' Tiz said. 'But in this business, if you can't be a little bit exotic among all the garmentos, you might as well drive a truck. I can't speak a lick of French, so I throw in a "luv" every now and then and it's what's kept me employed for the last ten years or so. Downton Abbey is the new Versailles.'

'Pretty good deal. Doing what?'

'You're scaring me, girl. Are you in the business too? Spying on me for Calvin or Giorgio?'

'No way,' I said, laughing with her. 'It just interests me. I mean, fashion does.'

'Have a look around. You can see all the stages of Savage style.'

I circled several of the costumed mannequins, taking in their outfits but thinking of what I should be asking Tiziana Bolt.

'I can't believe women dressed like that in the '80s,' I said. 'Look at the size of those shoulder pads.'

'Velly said it was this power thing that working women had in those days. Pinched, wasp-waisted suits with enormous shoulders,' Tiz said. 'Looks like football players to me, but loads of ladies bought into it.'

'What does your company do?'

'My company? That's a stretch. You're looking at my company, Alex. Velly taught me to call myself a consultant, like everyone else who's unemployed.'

'But it's you who picked the clothing to make up the retrospective?'

She shook her head. 'He did it himself, months ago. He took enormous pride in this display. He knew all his rivals would be eating their hearts out. The Institute always features its permanent collections and only does two special exhibitions a year. This is totally his moment.'

'So interesting,' I said. 'But then so tragic with his death.'

'He'd be laughing at the irony,' Tiz said. 'Talk about going out on top. Do you think any reporters would take on criticizing Wolf Savage after Monday night's show? Nobody will dare speak ill of the dead.'

'It doesn't quite matter if he can't hear the praise.'

'Aren't you Debbie Downer, luv.'

'Well, it is depressing, Tiz. We didn't have a clue – I mean, according to Lily – that her father was ill.'

'Nobody did. He's a very private guy, as you must have been aware. So private he rarely even mentioned having a daughter named Lily,' she said, moving on to reposition a black-sequined long dress that had a plunging neckline and lace cut-outs on both sides of the waist.

I didn't know if the callous remark was Wolf's thinking or Tiz's interpretation.

'That's a beauty,' I said.

'One of a kind. I sort of wish he'd knocked it off for his retail line. Velly designed it for Julia Roberts to wear to the Oscars, but she chose that black-and-white Valentino instead, which was featured everywhere,' Tiz said. 'This one got lost with the also-nominated runner-ups. Pity, that.'

'I have to say your work sounds riveting to me.'

Tiz turned her head and gave me the once-over. 'You don't look exactly like a devotee of high style, Alex. Basic black head to toe with a splash of color around your face. Really? You can do better.'

'Anytime you want to give me a hand, I accept, Tiz.'

'You should have let Velly take you under his wing. That's how he helped me get started.'

'What was that like? It must have been an amazing opportunity.'

'Pick one,' Tiz said to me. 'Do you like this sheer white blouse – or the same one in silver lamé?'

She held the sheer one close to her body and threw back her head, striking a pose.

'You've clearly done some modeling, haven't you?' I asked.

'Till he rescued me, like I was saying.'

'From what?'

'That life, luv. I'm the type who never made the runway for the big shows. I was just what they call a fit model,' Tiz said. 'You know what that is?'

'I think so. Aren't they the ones who work in the top studios – the body on which a designer makes his clothes?'

'Exactly,' she said, buttoning the sheer white blouse in place without waiting for my answer.

Tiziana Bolt said the name of the man who spotted her when she was vacationing with her boyfriend in the Caribbean. She was seventeen at the time. 'Ever hear of him?'

'I don't recognize his name,' I said.

'Flash in the pan, luv. You think I'm thin now? This guy thought the starting point for his upscale clothing line should be a girl on the brink of hospitalization from starvation,' Tiz said. 'He basically limited my intake to diet sodas and unfiltered cigarettes. Sure, I had that young, coltish look. Almost six feet tall and built like a prepubescent boy, I was. The crew called me his in-house skeleton. And that was before he started me on cocaine.'

'The man you worked for – a known designer – started you on drugs?'

'And here I was worried you might be a journalist and I'm just shooting my mouth off to you.'

'No, no. I'm not a journalist.'

'I haven't been to confession in fifteen years, but it's very comfortable talking to you,' Tiz said. 'Must be the Savitsky connection.'

'Probably so.'

'You're shocked? You really have to be an outsider to this biz not to know that one of the ways models get through endless hours of shoots is being drugged,' Tiz said. 'Couldn't do it stone sober. Ever hear a model say she's hot?'

'I don't know any models, I don't think.'

'One of the classic signs of anorexia is that light fuzz – you know, hair – that begins to grow on your face and arms,' she said. 'It's a response to the body trying to keep itself warm when it doesn't have any fat on it. You could have dropped me in the middle of the Sahara Desert in those days, wearing a mink coat and combat boots, and I still wouldn't have felt the least bit hot.'

'Drugs and an eating disorder,' I said. 'That's a deadly combination.'

'At seventeen? I was truly the walking dead.'

'But you couldn't leave this guy?'

'Really, Alex. I guess you don't know much about addiction,' Tiz said. 'He had me totally hooked on coke, and equally handcuffed by the big salary. I had no education, no training to do anything else.'

'What stopped it? What got you sober?' I asked.

'My boss was a stoner, too,' she said, adjusting the wide-brimmed hat on the last mannequin, slanting it to give her a sexier air. 'One night after he debuted his spring line during Fashion Week, he was texting back and forth with his boyfriend. Sexting's the better word. This one was all over the tabs at the time. Ring a bell?'

'Not yet.'

'You must live a really secluded life, Alex. You'll have to tell me what you do,' Tiz said. 'Anyway, he took photos of his private parts, and instead of texting them to his lover, they wound up on his Twitter feed with the words "TOUCH ME!"'

'Of course I know who you're talking about. I do remember that. The *Post* had a field day with that story.'

'Well, it served to put that jackass out of business, and I wound up in rehab. Hazelden, in Center City, Minnesota – the butt end of nowhere.'

'It worked, didn't it?' I said.

'You bet it did. Nineteen years old and totally washed-up. All the money I hadn't spent on vintage designer clothes, I spent on six months of inpatient rehab.'

Tiz walked over to the rack of WolfWear that was standing against the far wall. She pulled a leather coat off its hanger and draped it over her slim shoulders, topping the look with a felt cloche hat and vogueing a bit as she walked toward me.

'I showed up at breakfast one morning, sporting a Balenciaga dress that I picked up at a thrift shop in SoHo for thirty-five bucks. Black silk, trimmed with hot-pink lace,' Tiz said. 'Over the top for rehab, but it gets so damn dull there by your third month in. I wore pretty outrageous stuff, just to keep myself sane, but nobody ever noticed.'

'I'm sure they noticed you.'

'That day, there's a new guy at the table. Older than my dad, but totally got my sense of style. Checks me out head to toe the minute I drag into the room, then points at me, kind of cocking his thumb and finger like it was a gun. "You got a killer look, girl. You got a real killer look."'

'Wolf Savage,' I said, recognizing the signature compliment that Hal told us about just that morning.

Tiziana Bolt smiled at me again. 'You *do* know him, Alex. You've heard that line before.'

'Wolf Savage was at Hazelden?' I said. 'You met him in rehab?'

'He went by Velvel Savitsky out there. Much more hush-hush that way,' Tiz said. 'Less likely to wind up in the newspapers. See my point? You're his daughter's friend and you didn't even know about it, did you?'

'Not a clue,' I said. There were endless layers that Mike and I would need to peel back to know more about Wolf Savage.

'That's when I nicknamed him Velly, 'cause I knew who he was from the moment I laid eyes on him. He'd have been busted out there if I called him Wolf – you know, if people in rehab actually knew who he was. Besides, the Velvel bit just cracked me up. Nothing he could do about it,' Tiz said, putting the coat back on the rack. 'That man had a wicked addiction to Oxycontin.'

Twenty-one

Tiziana Bolt and I were sitting at a table for two in the Members Dining Room on the fourth floor of the Metropolitan Museum. The staff was setting up for the evening service, but there was still enough daylight to see the spectacular vista of Central Park that the sloping wall of windows offered.

Tiz's work on the exhibition won her perks like entrance to the private dining room, and since I had proved my insider status to her by recognizing a typical Savage compliment, Tiz asked me to join her for a late-afternoon cup of tea.

'May I have some Earl Grey?' she said to the waitress.

'I'd like a glass of Chardonnay, please,' I said. 'Are you sure you won't join me, Tiz?'

'Nine years clean and sober, Alex. Thanks very much.'

I wanted to get back to the beginnings of her relationship with Wolf Savage. Tiz spoke of him with a hint of intimacy that I hoped to explore before turning her over to Mike.

But she was going on and on about the excitement of

opening the exhibition and helping to stage Wolf's alternative to a Fashion Week show on Monday night. She didn't seem the least bit interested in asking me any other questions about myself. She trusted me quickly, which made me feel a bit guilty – but not guilty enough to stop talking to her.

'What else does – did – Wolf have you working on?' I said.

'I'm coordinating the show. Monday night – the big one. Like totally coordinating everything,' she said, spreading both long arms in a wide circle over her head.

'What a huge responsibility.'

'You're telling me, luv.'

'I thought that would be all in the hands of Hal and Reed,' I said.

'Well, dear, if you know them then you know why Velly had a limited respect for their abilities.'

'I don't really know them,' I said. 'I mean, we've met briefly. You're in a much better position to understand all that.'

The waitress set down our drinks. I waited till Tiz squeezed her lemon and sugared her tea before taking a sip of my wine.

'Reed's a nice guy. Mind you, we're not close or anything, but he doesn't have a fraction of the eye for style his father did,' Tiz said. 'And Hal? He's got a jealous streak longer than a runway at Heathrow.'

'Jealous of his brother?'

'Of course he is. Same gene pool, but Hal isn't smart

enough to get out of his own way. If those two can keep WolfWear alive for another six months it will be a miracle.'

'I thought Hal and Wolf – Velly – were best friends.'

'That's the face they presented to the world, but if Velly hadn't killed himself first, Hal might have stuck a knife between his ribs before they were done,' Tiz said. 'Buy yourself a ticket for Monday night and watch Hal preen and prance. I promise you it will be revolting.'

'I wish I could buy a ticket to the show,' I said. 'But I know they're entirely closed to the public.'

'Don't you know why Velly got kicked out of Fashion Week after last season?' Tiz asked.

'Not exactly. Not the details, I mean.'

'God, Alex. You need to get out a little more. All the designers used to be in Bryant Park,' she said. 'For years and years. You know? They tent that whole area behind the New York Public Library. Those tents are where most of the shows are held.'

'I know. I follow the blogs,' I said, grinning at my new friend. 'It may not be apparent to you, but I'm a bit of a clotheshorse. Off the rack, though.'

'I thought as much,' she said. 'Mix-and-match approach.'

Drama school hadn't done much for her tact.

'Then some of the stars began breaking out. Out of the tents, I mean,' she said. 'Imagine how it is. They each want a venue that can top the others. Some of them feel they've outgrown the Bryant Park setup. Kanye West – not that he knows the first thing about fashion – took over Madison Square Garden last winter. Think of that, will you? Eighteen thousand seats in a huge arena – not folding chairs in a Midtown tent – and he put on a show as well as released a new album the same night. They've all gone frigging mad.'

'Didn't you say that Velly got kicked out?'

'Let me explain. Fashion Week's been around since the 1940s, Alex. Meant to showcase American designers as well as to attract attention away from French fashion during World War II. Then this brilliant fashionista, Fern Mallis, was running the CFDA – the Council of Fashion Designers of America. You've probably heard Velly talk about her?' Tiz asked, barely stopping to draw breath. 'In the '90s she had this amazing idea to consolidate all the New York City events into one calendar and put them under a tent in Bryant Park.'

'It was always very exclusive, wasn't it?' I asked.

'You bet. Always private. By invitation only. The entire focus was on the press and on the buyers. It became the biannual way the fashion industry did business, with fall shows for spring/summer lines and the February shows for fall/winter.'

'How many shows go on at a time?'

'Once designers started breaking out of Bryant Park, there were four or five different venues, maybe eighty shows in a single week. Last year they were spread out around town – over at Chelsea Piers and in the Meatpacking District, uptown and downtown – anywhere that could offer something special, or someplace shocking. Each one of them trying to outdo the other.'

'Does Anna Wintour go to all of them?' I asked. 'Is that even possible?'

'Not a chance. But everyone wants her to appear, because it really elevates the status of a show if she blesses it with her presence.'

'Then there are all the celebrities to account for.'

'Movie stars and such? Designers *pay* them.'

'To come to a Fashion Week event?' I asked.

'We dress them, luv, and on top of that we pay them to show up and applaud. Pure advertising. I mean, an Angelina Jolie or an Uma Thurman might be there because she actually wears the clothes of a particular designer, but otherwise the houses are scrambling to put their threads and their bling on anyone's back, because that's what star power is. That's what a photo on Instagram can do for a brand,' Tiz said. 'And that's the reason we never hear back from a lot of the headliners we reach out to, 'cause they just don't need our money.'

'Was it always that way?'

'No, luv. There was a time – before all that snow went up my nose – that the shows were great fun. Boy, do I remember those days. I mean, it was a blast. Supermodels who wouldn't get up off the sofa to pick up a telephone for less than ten grand a day would work the runway at Fashion Week for peanuts. Every one of them you ever heard of wanted in on the action. Things were fresh and designers were all about creating beauty, not becoming the next corporate brand-builder.'

Tiz ordered another cup of tea. I needed to slow down on the wine.

'So why did Velly get booted from the tent, right?' she asked. 'Is that what we were talking about?'

'Yes. I'd like to know.' I was curious about whether Wolf Savage had done anything to undermine the classic engine that drove his industry, making more enemies along the way.

'There's a big divide within the CFDA organization. Some of the old-timers like Velly wanted to change the whole concept of the week. Make it less exclusive and turn it into a consumer event.'

'Like the idea of selling tickets to the public?' I said.

Tiz Bolt leaned in over her teacup as though she had a state secret to give away. 'Truth to tell, Alex, there's so much corruption and so many kickbacks in this business, it's like an explosive waiting for someone to strike a match.'

'How do you mean?'

'You could go online tonight and find a cottage industry of brokers selling tickets to Monday's show. All of them obtained illegally, by the way,' Tiz said.

'You mean Velly didn't get his way?'

'Of course not. There goes the neighborhood, if you know what I mean.'

'I'm not sure that I do.'

'February was Velly's last time under the tents, the last time he was allowed to play in the sandbox with the other designers who fought to hold on to tradition. So he dreamed big, Alex. He set his sights on this museum as soon as the

Costume Institute came up with the idea of doing a retrospective on his work. The hell with Fashion Week,' she said. 'Wolf Savage wanted his own special moment in time.'

'Kanye West sold tickets, though,' I said.

'Face it, Alex. When it came down to being in Kanye West's camp, or Calvin Klein's, Velly did the right thing.'

'You mean he backed off his plan to make his show consumer-friendly? Broadcast it to the masses?'

'At least he tried to. But by the time he made up his mind to try to mend fences, the scalpers had already sniffed blood, so when Fashion Week started last February, one site listed accommodations at the Plaza Hotel, a VIP shopping trip at Saks, and two tickets to other shows in Bryant Park for $1,500, $2,500. For lesser designers than Velly, that is.'

'That's a real break with tradition.'

'The higher-ups blamed Velly for the idea of letting in the riffraff. I mean, no one expected better from Kanye West, did they? But Wolf Savage? On top of that, someone at Savage proper must have had sticky fingers. Swiped a few tickets, despite orders from the show runners not to. Check it out – I'm telling you that the Savage show in February went for something like $7,500. Stolen tickets – I swear to you. Totally illegal.'

'You're joking,' I said.

Maybe I could have the office investigate the scams once we were deeper into this. It might be a way for Tiz to overlook my deception.

'It's no joke,' she said. 'This whole concept has changed.

The younger guys just starting out in business – and Velly – they're the ones that don't do as much couture work. They don't need the closed doors and exclusivity. It's social media that destroyed the entire idea of what the shows worked to build for the industry for the last three decades.'

'Social media?'

'Sure, Alex. There used to be such incredible curiosity and interest before each event, when fashion editors were on the edge of their seats, waiting to see a new collection. Look, you go to the World Series and when the seventh game starts, you have no idea who's going to win, do you? You have no idea what will happen next,' Tiz said. 'Isn't that a large bit of the excitement, of the fun of the game? Now, with the first reveal, all the outfits are blasted out to the world on Instagram, like I said. There's an immediate return on investment.'

'So the couture houses really don't like the idea.'

'They hate it,' Tiz said. 'It used to take six months before the images would get out and could be copied for the masses by nameless brands who were hired by department stores. WolfWear could knock off a Givenchy day suit for the next season. Now? Guys with a whole range of lines – like Velly – can go into production in China, for peanuts, within a week.'

'And that pleases the companies that are buying up the designer names? Backing them?'

'Of course it does. Cheap copies they can flood the market with, Alex. Not to mention how the pressure has gone up so many notches. It used to be spring and fall collections. Now there's pre-fall, then fall and winter. Then resort, and pre-spring before spring,' Tiz said. 'These guys have to do accessories and shoes and handbags. Some of these big names are even dressing flight attendants with a separate label. You don't think the global goons care about the designer – about the creative end of the business – as long as there's something to sell?'

She must have known about the George Kwan deal. 'Kwan Enterprises?' I said. 'I've heard rumors about some kind of hostile takeover. I guess that Velly didn't want that to happen.'

'Heaven forbid,' Tiz said, putting the back of her hand to her forehead and pretending to be faint. 'That was entirely a Hal Savage proposition. He and Velly were fighting cats and dogs over George Kwan.'

'So here I was,' I said, adopting Lily Savitsky's point of view for the purpose of fishing for information, 'thinking Wolf Savage was on top of the world. I couldn't understand why he'd take his own life. This exhibition – an honor so few designers have had. Monday's big show. A son to follow in his footsteps. A daughter who was trying to reestablish herself with him. I just didn't get it. Now you make it sound like it was all doom and gloom around the man.'

'This glittery fashion world is completely smoke and mirrors, Alex. The stakes are enormously high, and I think Velly knew he was about to have his legs cut out from underneath him,' Tiz said. 'He wanted to go out on top is what I think.'

'By putting a plastic bag over his head?'

'Painless way to go is what they tell me.'

Harsh words for a friend.

'Who told you that?' I asked. 'That his death was painless.'

'Oh,' Tiz said, sounding surprised. 'Word on the street is all I know. What I read in the papers. Like that.'

'Have you spoken with Reed? Or with Hal?'

'No. Neither one. I just left messages with my condolences. I get my working orders from the assistants who handle the front office.'

'Okay, so Velly rocks the boat by trying to open Fashion Week to the consumer market, and that gets him booted from Bryant Park earlier this year.'

'Yeah. Kiss of death, I guess. I mean not literally, but I think his whole operation was tanking.' Tiz leaned back and gestured with a thumbs-down motion.

'I get so much more emotional about these things than you do,' I said, waving to the waitress and asking for a refill. 'I admire your sangfroid.'

'Don't know what that is, luv.'

'Sorry. Keeping calm under stressful situations,' I said, thinking of the literal French meaning of the word – cold blood. 'Another tea?'

'Two and through for me.'

'Is there anything that made Velly plan his revenge at the Met, besides the retrospective of his work?' I asked.

'There's no bigger stage in this city, Alex. The Metropolitan Museum of Art? What's more highbrow than this joint?'

'Nothing, I guess.'

'A few years back, the House of Chanel took over the Palais-Royal in Paris, turned it into a French chateau. Spent five million on re-creating the space and the look. If you want to talk over-the-top, there it was,' Tiz said. 'Then it began to happen in New York. One of the major fur houses leased the Park Avenue Armory and re-created St Petersburg in the days of the tsars. Brought in ice carved from Alaskan glaciers to make everyone feel the chill, develop a yearning for sable.'

'Ridiculous.'

'Maybe to you, Alex, but this industry thrives on outrage. Outrage. Wolf Savage – Velly Savitsky – in the Temple of Dendur at the Met? C'mon. It's a stroke of genius.'

The ancient Egyptian temple, created during the reign of Emperor Augustus Caesar in 10 BCE, had been given to the United States in 1965. It was one of the most magnificent structures built in its time – Aeolian sandstone – and saved from destruction in the building of the Aswan Dam by American dollars.

'It sounds more like an exercise in ego to me,' I said.

'Don't you see Velly was trying to go global? He set his show in this fabulous temple from the Roman period in Egypt, in a totally elite venue that can only fit about three hundred seats, in the city's center of all things high-brow cultural – but it gives him the ability to live-stream an event at the very same time to everyone who wants the grand look but can't afford the ticket. Flipping the bird to everyone who counted him down and out.'

'But the temple itself represents—'

'Yeah, luv. I know. The pharaoh's offering to the gods,' Tiz said. 'Sounds completely appropriate to me. And damn if it didn't make Velly laugh. The idea of him launching his line to the new global gods of style. What an offering that's going to be.'

There's no accounting for taste, as my mother liked to remind me frequently when I was a kid.

'I'm just curious, Tiz, but what does it cost to rent the temple – that entire wing of the museum – for Monday night?'

'I didn't see the contract myself, but I know it's upwards of one million dollars.'

'One million? That's a staggering number.'

'That's just the price for the space, Alex. That's before you throw in the gobs of flowers and the liquor and the security costs and all that,' Tiz said. 'Plus the salaries of the models.'

'How many are there?'

'Sixty. Six-oh. In most shows they use twenty girls and make them change two or three times,' Tiz said. 'Velly was following the Calvin Klein method. One outfit, one girl. No sweating the quick-change routine backstage.'

'So where's the money for that coming from?'

Tiz held up her hands and pursed her lips. 'Don't know.'

'It has to be Kwan Enterprises,' I said. 'From what I've been hearing about the Savage business dealings, there wasn't the money to bankroll something at this level.'

'I can assure you George Kwan is not the one underwriting

this show,' Tiz said, standing up and signaling for the check.

'Who, then?' I asked. 'Who's paying the bill for all this?'

'I haven't a clue, Alex,' Tiz said. 'I thought I could wheedle anything I wanted to know out of Velly, but that's a mystery I just couldn't solve.'

Twenty-two

'I've got to go now,' Tiziana Bolt said. 'It's almost six. Taking the elevator down?'

'Yes,' I said. 'How can I contact you if I want to stay in touch?'

'I'd really like to meet this Lily chick. See why Velly never talked about her.'

'She'll be curious to meet you, too.' The Columbia MBA with husband and kids was not what I'd call a chick, but the language fit Tiz's persona to a *T*.

'Got a card on you?'

'No. I'm on leave from my job, actually.'

'What do you do, anyway?'

'I'm a lawyer.'

'Lawyer? Awesome,' Tiz said. 'No wonder you ask so many questions.'

'I'll give you my cell,' I said, taking out my phone to enter her contact information. 'Mind giving me yours?'

We exchanged numbers and while doing so, I realized that I had forgotten to press the lobby floor. We wound up back on the lower level, where the exhibition was.

'I just need to pick up my tote and my jacket,' Tiz said. 'I'll walk out with you.'

As we wove our way through the posed mannequins, I was reminded of her remark that, like the up-and-coming young designers, Wolf Savage wasn't known for his couture line.

But there were at least a dozen formal gowns on display, and Joan Stafford and I each owned a couple that boasted a couture label.

'Hasn't Velly's formalwear been a successful part of the division?' I asked.

'You seem to know your French, luv – like with that "sangfroid" line,' Tiz said, imitating the way I talked. 'Don't you know about haute couture?'

'I thought I did.'

'You being a lawyer and all, I'm surprised. In France, there's a commission that regulates which design houses can use the haute couture label,' Tiz said. 'It's all firmly written into the laws.'

Sometimes a bit of the Bronx seeped through the fake British accent, especially when she was trying to speak French. I could see why that put-on had failed her.

'You mean, you can't just be a great stylist, do made-to-order work with expensive fabrics, and call it couture?'

'No way. There are specific rules in France. Government legislation about haute couture,' she said, stuffing her papers into a worn-looking Vuitton Neverfull bag. 'Special fittings are required, and an atelier – you know, what that is, Alex?'

'Yes. A workshop,' I said. 'A studio.'

'That workshop has to have at least fifteen staff members and twenty full-time tech people. And the label has to present at least fifty original designs twice a year – evening-wear and daytime. On and on like that, and well, Velly never made the cut, despite the fact that he sucked up to the French like it was the way to go.'

'I'm so surprised.'

'Let me tell you, the man didn't deal with rejection well. The likes of Chanel, Dior, Gaultier, Armani, Valentino, Versace – they're legitimate French couture houses, designated by the government. It isn't a club that wanted Velly Savitsky.'

'Is it different in America?' I asked.

'Sure. Here you just sketch out a pretty design, limit the numbers of it that you produce, and slap on a label that says the word "couture".'

'I'm pretty sure I have a couple of old WolfWear gowns in the back of my closet,' I said. 'I know the label had a fancier name, but certainly no fittings and no studio.'

Joan and I had bought them together at a sample sale for some charity benefit. They'd been remaindered at some upscale department store and we got bargains, we knew, while the money went to a good cause.

'Haute Sauvage?' Tiz said, laughing. 'You? Really? Let me guess. Something with long sleeves and a high neck. Very lady lawyer-like.'

'What you see is not always what you get, Tiz.'

'What style? I know most of the lines.'

'It was a toga. Sort of a Roman toga – white chiffon with a long scarf of the same fabric that kind of draped over the shoulder.'

'Hail, Caesar,' Tiz said, grabbing me by both elbows. 'I know the dress! It was from the collection about five years ago, right? Strapless, with a band of gold trim around the top and a gold rope belt that looped at the waist. Do I have the one? A slit on the left leg up to the thigh. Right?'

We were both laughing.

'That's the one I own. My friend made me buy it.'

'Did you wear it to an orgy? Please say you did.'

'To a Halloween party, I think. Bad mistake, that one.'

'Damn. I wish I could get you a pass into the show on Monday. You've got to wear it, Alex. I think we've got one of those – in aqua – on the runway. What a hoot,' Tiz said. 'All those Park Avenue social X-rays always come in their old favorites. Let me snoop around and ask for a freebie. You'll fit right in.'

'Don't ask, Tiz. I'm not going to be there, and I will never wear that dress again.'

She was too open, too nice. A free spirit with a big personality. I didn't want her head to roll if she mentioned my name to Hal or Reed Savage. Not to mention anyone finding out that a prosecutor had taken a comped ticket to get into a top-price event.

She was sashaying down the hallway, zigzagging between the mannequins, pretending that she was swishing a chiffon skirt to either side of her legs.

'Will you indulge me in a silly question, Tiz?'

'You're a lawyer. They're mostly silly, aren't they?'

'Got me there,' I said. 'In all your time modeling and around fashion houses, how many of the women had breast implants?'

'You're a little late to get into the game, Alex,' she said, turning to size up my body.

'I'm serious, Tiz. Is it done?'

'The girls who work Victoria's Secret catalogues and swimsuit covers, they might,' she said. 'But high-fashion models? The runway? The more androgynous the better. Tall, thin, and flat-chested like me. If diet doesn't get rid of the breasts, then reduction surgery will do it.'

I was thinking of how Tanya Root and her Brazilian implants might have fit into the picture of the Savitsky–Savage odyssey.

'Look at this,' she said. 'Dammit.'

'What?'

'Just mumbling to myself.'

She had stopped in front of a figure dressed in a Chinese silk gown tight-fitted to the dummy, with golden-threaded birds and flowers embroidered onto a bright-red ground. The bottom was tapered and the neck was closed with a mandarin collar.

'See? This happens even when the garments are maintained under the most perfect circumstances,' Tiz said, adjusting the camera app on her phone to take a picture of something she noticed on the garment. 'Mrs Thurston Higgledy-Piggledy the Fourth or Fifth loaned this to us for the exhibition, and I thought we went over it with a fine-tooth comb. I was certain she stores her vintage stuff in the same cryogenic freezer with Ted Williams's head, and that it was in pristine condition.'

'Looks pretty swell to me,' I said.

'The frigging frog is missing.'

'What?'

'You must know what a frog is.'

'Sure.' Frogs were the ornamental braiding for garment closures that consisted of a button and the loop through which it passes. 'I just didn't get what you were talking about at first.'

'This was supposed to be a key detail of the dress,' Tiz said. 'One closure at the neck and four down the side of the piece. Hand-stitched frogging in the self-fabric, which cost an arm and a leg per yard.'

The large pearl button was in place, but the loop was frayed and hanging away from the button instead of around it.

'Can it be fixed?' I asked.

'This broad probably eats pizza with a knife and fork, and a napkin tucked in under her chin,' Tiz said, losing her cool. 'Everything we took from her was just perfect, except this one spot, and nobody noticed it – not even me – till this moment.'

'You've got the weekend to have it repaired.'

'Find me the fabric, Alex. Think you can? It's from 1998, Velly's Chinese Wall line. I dare you to find another piece of it.'

'There's a zipper maven and a lace store and a sequined trim shop,' I said, trying to calm her down. 'Isn't there a frog maker in the Garment District?'

'Sure I can find a frog maker. But it's the damn material,' Tiz said, dropping to her knees and flipping the hem of the dress to see whether there was enough extra fabric to craft a new loop. 'And we don't dare snip an inch from this one without clearance from Her Ladyship.'

Tiz got back on her feet and typed in a message to herself, adding a photograph of the dress – its collar, hem, and mangled frog.

'Oh, Velly,' she said, talking to herself. 'You'd take someone's head off for missing that little froggy.'

I didn't have much to lose by getting more personal at this point.

'I've just got to ask, Tiz – I mean, I hope you don't think it's out of line – but it sounds like you knew the man better than anyone else, at least in this last decade of his life.'

We were walking through the last room, with the life-size magazine covers of supermodels and the reproductions of headline stories featuring Wolf Savage.

'Probably as well as anyone. That's true,' she said.

'You're smart,' I said. 'And you're terrifically attractive. You've got a great sense of humor and a lot of style.'

'You want to know if I f—?'

I interrupted her. 'Were you lovers?' I asked.

She laughed. 'Not for his lack of trying, you understand. I'm just not into men who are as old as my dad.'

Lily had commented on her father's infatuation with young women.

Tiz stopped in front of the photograph I had paused in front of earlier. It was the shot of Wolf leaving the Musée d'Orsay after his brilliant coup at the shows in Paris – a handsome man with a spectacular beauty on his arm.

'Do you know who she is?' Tiz asked.

'No.'

'Don't you remember the name Samira?'

'I don't.'

'One of those first-name-only supermodels. An Ethiopian girl who prowled the catwalk from the time she was seventeen like she was the only star in the galaxy.'

'Looking at this photograph, I can understand that.'

'Velly found her in a refugee camp on some bullshit humanitarian trip he made to Africa, after some kind of famine or plague. I can't remember which one.'

'Why are you making fun of that?'

'The man made the trip for the publicity, Alex. Not because his heart was in the cause, but to have the cameras focused on him all the time,' Tiz said. 'He saved Samira's life, I'm sure, and then he launched her on a career most girls would sell their souls for.'

'He was her mentor, then? Like he tried to be with you?'

'Yes, he was her mentor, and yes, she sold her soul to him, too.'

'They had an affair?' I asked.

'Velly Savitsky liked his women young, and except when he was forced into an early marriage by his parents or stuck in rehab, in the heartland of white America with me, he preferred them dark-skinned,' Tiz said. 'He had an affair with Samira, and then he ended her career by impregnating her.'

My head was spinning, wondering if Wolf Savage's predilection for black women could lead us to his blood connection to Tanya Root. Before I could form a question, Tiz finished her story.

'Samira's spirit was broken when she lost all her modeling jobs because of the pregnancy. She went home to Africa, to her village, to have the baby,' Tiz said, letting her emotion show for the first time since we'd met hours earlier. 'But she died there. Both Samira and her son died in childbirth.'

I had no words to speak.

'It's one of the things that haunted Velly to the very end of his life.'

Twenty-three

I tried to press Tiz Bolt for more information as we walked upstairs and through the grand hall to the museum exit.

She had never heard of Tanya Root, didn't know of any woman in Velly's orbit with that surname, and wouldn't give up – if she knew – the names of any of the other women in his life.

Tiz was surprised that I wasn't aware that the third, fourth, and fifth wives of Wolf Savage were black women.

'African American?' I asked.

'I would have said that, but none of them were American, Alex. I have no idea where they were from, but they were foreign.'

I thought of what the housekeeper who'd found the body had told Mike, Mercer, and me, about babysitting for a woman who'd come from abroad to stay in the suite several times, with a young child she'd assumed was his daughter.

'I have so many things I want to ask you,' I said, certain that Tiz Bolt would have every good reason to turn on me when she found out who I was.

'Another time for that,' she said, skipping down the last few steps to the sidewalk. 'I've got a dinner date. Have to dress up and put on my face. *Ciao*, Alex.'

She waved goodbye and walked north on Fifth Avenue. It was dark, and I lost her in the bright headlights of the cars and buses as she crossed the street a block away.

I started to walk south, toward my apartment. I dialed Mike's cell but it went straight to voicemail.

'It's me. Call me as soon as you can,' I said. 'I'm on my way home. I mean, I went home when you told me to, but I went back out. I walked up to the museum and I ran into this young woman who knew Savage really well. You've got to call me. It was a total coincidence – well, almost a coincidence.'

I stayed on Fifth, using all my willpower to avoid any of the other avenues that were lined with restaurants and bars. Mike would be annoyed that I had worked an angle of his investigation alone – even though I had gotten an enviable load of information from Tiz. He didn't need to find me intoxicated as well.

My nerves were jangly. Mike was probably still debriefing some of the family members about the contents of Wolf Savage's will, and I was anxious to see how Lily had been treated. The evening's breaking news was likely to lead with the fact that the famous designer's death had been declared a homicide, and possibly even include his connection to another murder victim – Tanya Root. And I had just spent a couple of hours misleading a perfectly nice young woman about the reasons for my questions on the Met exhibition. I felt like I was unraveling all over again.

I thought about hailing a cab, but the cold fresh air was helping to clear my head. I went straight down the avenue, turning east on Seventieth Street, passing the Frick Collection building – once the family mansion – and the handsome wrought-iron gates that protected its serene gardens from passersby.

At the corner of Third Avenue, I stopped into PJ Bernstein Deli. I ordered salads and sandwiches for Mike and me in case he came home hungry later, and called Vickee Eaton while I waited on a stool at the counter. Her mailbox was full and not accepting messages.

I took a cup of hot coffee with me, collected the bag of food, and paid the bill.

I was on the short downhill to the driveway that led to the front door of my building. I put up my collar against the wind, balancing the coffee so it didn't spill onto my hands.

A dog walker with three of my neighbors' large pets was hugging the side of my apartment, cleaning up after the trio.

I was on the outer edge of the sidewalk, trying to avoid the mess.

The door of a large black SUV with tinted windows swung open and a man shouted my name. 'Alex! Alexandra Cooper!'

The hot coffee sloshed around, scorching my hand as it came over the lip of the cardboard container. I dropped the cup and bag of food, trembling as I flashed back to the night of my abduction.

The car was the same make and model, but this time the voice was familiar to me. I started to run anyway, too startled to put the picture together.

A man stepped into my path and smiled at me. 'You'd better turn around, Alex. The boss needs to talk to you.'

Twenty-four

The detective who had the bodyguard assignment for Paul Battaglia led me back to the SUV. The rear passenger door was open, and the district attorney slid over to allow me to get onto the seat beside him.

'Give us five minutes,' he said to the detective.

'Sure thing, boss.' He slammed the door shut and walked away from the car.

'Sorry to sneak up on you, Alex. The doorman told us you weren't at home, so I figured I'd wait half an hour or so.'

I stared straight forward, at the headrest above the driver's seat. I was struggling to catch my breath.

'Alex? Are you all right?'

'What's your best guess, Paul?' I couldn't look at him. 'You couldn't have given me a call? Waited for me in the comfort of my lobby? Or did you simply decide that the terrorist tactic of having someone sandbag me on the sidewalk close to home would be a pleasant reminder of my kidnapping?'

'Let's not be too dramatic, Alexandra. It's not as though you wouldn't recognize my voice. I never thought I'd put a scare into you.'

'I scare pretty easily these days,' I said.

'Does that explain why you're drinking so much?'

My head snapped toward him. 'What's your source for that crap, Paul?'

I used to have so much respect for him. I worked my tail off for him, day and night, trusting in both his judgment and integrity. I represented him in front of the community – at churches and synagogues, schools and precinct houses. Now I could barely recognize my own voice talking back to him.

'I don't need a source, Alex. I can smell it on your breath.'

'Over the stink of that cigar? I doubt it very much.'

He put the Cohiba back in his mouth and continued to talk around it. 'I thought you were on the Vineyard. Stabilizing yourself to get back to your desk.'

'I'm on leave, Paul. I'm not required to keep a GPS in my pocket.'

'You've turned on me, Alex. I need to know what that's about.'

I put my hand on my chest, hoping to stop it from heaving.

'Sooner or later we're going to have to talk about this,' he said. 'Before you come back to work.'

'Plenty of time to go, then. As you can see, I'm not at my best.' I was lightly patting the raw skin of my left hand.

'You're not possibly feeling I didn't do enough for you during your ordeal? My wife thinks that perhaps—'

'What your wife thinks is of so little interest to me that I'd put it back in the bottle, Paul,' I said. 'In fact, you were the first person – though many have followed – to suggest to me that your wife is a fool.'

Battaglia's wife – who considered herself to be an artist, though she couldn't paint her way out of a paper bag – had embarrassed him recently by writing an article for some blog. She described having intercourse with him in the bathroom of his hospital suite when he was in-patient for a gallstone procedure. It was too much information for all of my colleagues, and few could call up the image of the dignified barrister after the piece went viral in the office computer system.

'Some thoughts are best kept to yourself, Alex.'

'Then leave your wife out of our conversation.' She was despised by his secretary and was an object of ridicule to the legal staff. I knew he wouldn't do much to defend her.

For so long, I had admired his professional ideals, despite rumors of his sordid personal life. Paul Battaglia had a reputation for sleeping his way through half of the journalists who had covered his rise to political power thirty years ago, and others who curried favor with him by stroking his private parts.

'I don't like the way you're talking to me,' Battaglia said, cracking the window to tip the ashes off his cigar.

'For once, you might be the one between a rock and a

hard place, boss. The worst you can do – that is, the worst thing for *you* – would be to fire me. You're the one who created this monster – you've put me in the media spotlight so many times that now I'd get a huge audience to listen to my version of the story,' I said. 'Best-case scenario is that when I'm ready to have this conversation with you, you have the answers to calm me down again.'

'I must have been crazy to give you so much latitude, Alex,' he said, the cigar firmly planted between his front teeth. 'There are even rumors you might make a primary run against me next year.'

We were side by side, but neither turned to face the other.

'Are you afraid to comment on that one, Alex?'

'You know I have no interest in politics,' I said. 'I have one passion, and it's my work with crime victims – women and children. That's what drives me, Paul. I think you know that.' I paused. 'Oh, and then there's the awful risk of STDs in your job, isn't there?'

'What are you talking about?' Battaglia asked, trying to control his vicious temper. He was the king of petty-revenge points. He'd find a way to carry the heaviest grudge for as many years as it took to think of a payback.

'You want to talk rumors? It's all over town you got a sexually transmitted disease from Reverend Hal Shipley. That you bent over to please him one time too many and he—'

'You've lost your mind, Alex. Next time I talk to you, you'd better clean up—'

'Next time you talk to me, please give me enough notice to have a lawyer with me, Paul,' I said. 'I know why you didn't call me to ask whether you could drop by. 'Cause then there'd be a phone record of the call. And you waited outside the lobby so not even the doorman could say we were together.'

'So this is all about Hal Shipley, is it?'

'No, no, no. This is all about you, Mr District Attorney. I saw the letter you sent to Shipley, telling him you could make the case I was working on go away,' I said. 'I saw it with my own eyes. I hadn't even met the victim yet or determined her credibility, but you were sending her up the river.'

The smoke seemed to be coming out of his mouth, where he'd clenched his cigar into place. I was sure it was also coming out of his ears.

'You can make whatever deal you want with the devil,' I said. 'But just leave me out of your planning.'

Battaglia opened the car door on his right and yelled the detective's name. The man came dashing back to the SUV and opened the driver's door. 'Yeah, boss?'

'Alex has to go. Let's get out of here.'

I opened the door and started to get out of the car.

'By the way, Alex, the ME called me this afternoon. She's declaring the Wolf Savage death a homicide,' Battaglia said. 'There's a presser at One Police Plaza right now.'

That explained why Mike hadn't returned my call.

'Dr Parker told me you made a cameo appearance at the morgue, Alex. I was actually coming by to talk with you about that,' the district attorney said, tossing his cigar over my head. 'Better to cut out that extracurricular activity while you're still nursing your wounds.'

'Or what, Paul?' I asked. 'Or what?'

'It's just an expression of my concern for your well-being.' Paul Battaglia said, ready to drop me and move on. 'Don't think of it for a minute as a threat.'

Twenty-five

The experience of being held by captors for days had made me hypervigilant since the rescue. Despite my exhaustion, hunger, and unhappiness, I heard Mike's key turn in the lock at ten fifteen.

I ran to the door to greet him with a short terry robe wrapped around me.

'Man on the hall,' Mercer said, coming in behind Mike.

'Twofers? How lucky am I,' I said. 'Give me a minute.'

I went back to my bedroom to pull on sweats and a fleece jacket. When I returned, the guys were at my bar, calling to me to bring a full ice bucket to them.

'I had this dreadful encounter with Paul Battaglia,' I said, setting the ice on the bar. 'I was way out of line, Mike. I know that, but he caught me off guard, lying in wait for me near the driveway and scaring me half to death.'

'Calm down, babe.' He turned to me and put his arms around me. 'You're shaking like a leaf.'

'I may have just thrown away my job.' I buried my head into Mike's shoulder.

'Hell, you always wanted to be a ballet dancer, didn't you? You're a little long in the tooth for that now, but—'

'As I recall,' Mercer said, 'you've got the district attorney by the short hairs, Alex. He's not about to do anything.'

'Yet,' I said. 'You meant to add "yet", didn't you?'

Mike pushed me back and lifted my chin. 'Smile for me.'

'I've forgotten how to do that.'

'Practice,' Mike said, picking up the half-gallon bottle of Dewar's. 'I'll let you have a drink with us. You've shown remarkable self-restraint.'

'You mean you trust me?'

'Not exactly. But I marked the bottle before we left the house this morning,' he said. 'And you got through this little crisis without dipping in. Good for you.'

I didn't need to confess to my interlude at the Beach Café and the wine at the Met dining room. By the time I'd had my confrontation with Paul Battaglia, I needed a steaming-hot bath more than a cocktail.

'You're tracking my pours? I can't believe it.'

'That's the least of it, Coop. You're going to start running with me in the mornings, too. Boot camp begins tomorrow.'

Mercer was pouring the drinks.

'I actually bought food for Mike and me, but I dropped the bag on the street when Battaglia shouted my name. I have nothing for you guys to eat.'

'I ordered a pizza on our way up. It'll be here in half an hour,' Mike said.

'We've got a lot to catch up on,' I said. 'Tell me what you did after I left.'

'First of all, we missed *Jeopardy!* because of the presser about the ME's findings,' Mike said. 'My mother taped it for me.'

'Seriously, Mike.'

'Okay, okay. So Jimmy North met me at the morgue, to go back over to the Savage offices. By the time we got there, Hal and Reed had left for lunch, and were going directly from there to the lawyer's office for the reading of the will. That's all we were able to get out of the secretary – she wouldn't budge on who or where the lawyer is – so it shut us down for a while.'

'I got called in because of the Tanya Root piece of the case,' Mercer said. 'We're starting all over on that investigation, now that we know Wolf Savage was her father. We're linked in with Mike and Jimmy, of course.'

'Murder begets murder,' Mike said. 'We just need the "why" and the "who".'

'Catherine will give you warrants for anything you want,' I said.

'Done. She's way out in front of this. You lose your job? She'll step right into your shoes. Nothing to worry about.'

'I'm not worried about Catherine or the unit for a minute, Mike. I'm worried about *me*.'

'We're going for Wolf's phones – business and cell, incoming and outgoing – for the last six months. Reed Savage and Uncle Hal, too. And Lily Savitsky.'

'But she's just—' I blurted out, not sure why I would leap to defend a woman I hadn't seen for twenty years.

'She's Tanya's half-sister, Coop. And the dead man's daughter. Think big-picture. Everybody's got a motive till they don't.'

'Sorry. You're right, of course,' I said. 'Were you able to grab any of the family members after they met with the trusts and estate lawyer?'

'Nope. I don't know how long the meeting took. But nobody came back to the office. That's on tap for tomorrow morning, after the autopsy of Wolf Savage,' Mike said. 'Mercer and me.'

'I figured that. Battaglia spoke to the commissioner, right? He told me that Dr Parker let it slip that I was at the morgue with you, and that he doesn't want me doing any more of that.'

'Don't inhale that scotch, kid. It's your one and only, so sip it slow,' Mike said. 'Yeah, we went straight from Seventh Avenue to headquarters. Scully knew it was important enough to do a stand-up conference on this one. Did you catch it?'

'I saw a rerun. A clip of it anyway. How much did he give out?'

'Bare bones. That news reports of Savage's suicide were premature. That his death has been reclassified as a homicide, pending autopsy and an investigation,' Mike said. 'Then he had a blow-up of the anthropologist's reconstruction of Tanya Root's face, and said that she has been identified as the daughter of Wolf Savage.'

'So far, Alex,' Mercer said, 'none of the hundred-plus women in America with that name fits the 'scrip of our

Tanya Root. We're hoping that because this story will get international play, especially coming from Commissioner Scully, that someone who knows her, somewhere in the world, will come forward.'

'Do you have a phone number for her? Any way to retrace her steps here?'

'You know anybody who goes swimming in the East River with a phone, Coop?' Mike said. 'We don't even know that the name she gave the plastic surgeon is her real one.'

'So maybe I got some information today that will move you forward.'

'Let's hear about your little escapade,' Mike said. 'It's always interesting when the patients get out of their strait-jackets for a few hours.'

'Yeah, quite refreshing for me, actually. Off my meds. No keeper,' I said. 'I just got lucky, is all it is. I didn't have any reason to know what I was going to walk into.'

I started to detail my conversation with Tiziana Bolt while Mercer took notes.

My information was coming out in bits and pieces. 'We need to know more than what the gossip columnists have printed about his third, fourth, and fifth wives over the years,' I said.

'We're on that,' Mercer said.

'You already knew about them? That they were – ?'

'"Women of color" is what Scully called them. He made Vickee research the guy's bio from decades of press clips about him,' Mercer said. 'That's one thing that benefits us from his living such a public life.'

'So Reed's mother was his first wife, and she's long dead,' I said. 'Then he married Lily's mother.'

'Then the third wife is the Brit who raised Reed,' Mercer said. 'Alive and well – the recluse who lives outside of London.'

'She's not supposed to be an issue in this,' Mike said. 'Reed told us his father took good care of her when they split, and local police in her village say she hasn't set foot out of town in ten years.'

I was sketching a family tree as I sat on the sofa with a legal pad.

'Did she figure out four and five?'

'You know Vickee. She's a relentless researcher,' Mercer said. 'The fourth wife is from the Caribbean originally. Nevis. She lives in New Orleans now. She met Wolf when she was trying to break into modeling here in the city as a teenager. Married him when she was twenty-one, and the only job she could land was in a showroom of a glove manufacturer.'

'Great hands, I guess,' Mike said. 'Not a total bust.'

'Short marriage. No kids,' Mercer said. 'I talked to her on the phone. She's remarried, to a former Saint.'

'A saint?' I asked.

'Think football, Coop. New Orleans Saints.'

'Happy and healthy, and very comfortable answering my questions,' Mercer said. 'Holds no grudge for Wolf. The man treated her like a queen.'

'Did she know about Reed?' I asked. 'And Lily?'

'Met Reed. Heard about Lily but never met her. And

no, she never knew anything about an illegitimate child. Never heard of Tanya Root.'

'The woman had to come from somewhere,' I said.

'She's going to stay in touch with me. She remembers that Wolf Savage was very familiar with New Orleans, and told her he'd spent time there in a relationship with another woman,' Mercer said. 'She's going to see if she can find that woman's name in one of her old journals or diaries.'

'That would be great,' I said. 'If my math is correct, Tanya was conceived sometime between the third and fourth marriages, right?'

'Seems to be so.'

'Did Vickee come up with anything on the fifth wife?'

'An African woman.'

'Ethiopian?' I asked, telling them the story of Samira.

'No,' Mercer said. 'This one was from Ghana. A young businesswoman, actually. We haven't been able to reach her by phone. Thirtysomething when Wolf married her, according to the tabloids. She stole a bundle of money from him. Got nothing in the divorce and went back to Ghana a year later, where she started her own company. Vickee can't find her name in any of the newspapers since she left the States.'

'You guys really have your hands full,' I said, holding the chilled glass against my forehead. 'Does Dr Parker know what killed Tanya?'

'Blunt-force trauma confirmed,' Mercer said. 'Her skull was crushed in the rear.'

'Which is nothing like Wolf's death,' I said.

'Right. I take his autopsy at nine, then Mercer and I try a new approach to the brother and the uncle,' Mike said. 'Track Lily down to see how she fared in the will.'

'You need to get the two hotel housekeepers,' I said. 'Wolf recommended Josie – the one who took off – for the job. We've got to find out where in life their paths originally crossed. Then there's Wanda. The one who found the body. She told us she babysat for a child whose mother was going out with Wolf. She assumed it was his wife and child, from somewhere abroad.'

'Not a wife,' Mike said. 'A lover, maybe. But there's no evidence of another marriage.'

'Even so,' I said, 'Wanda can give you a better description. Maybe a way to figure out who they are.'

Mike barely acknowledged my ideas, while Mercer wrote everything down. I knew Mike wanted me to keep my nose out of this entire affair.

'Then there's the business side of things. You're going to have to talk to Tiziana.' I looked in my contacts and gave Mercer the number. 'She probably has more reason to give you the real story than the brother and son.'

'Good work, Alex,' Mercer said, clinking his glass against mine.

'You should both be at the Savage show at the Met on Monday night,' I said. 'It will be a chance for all the interested parties to be under the same roof.'

The intercom rang. 'There's your pizza,' I said.

Mike went to answer it while I grabbed some plates and napkins.

'I agree with you, Alex,' Mercer said. 'The outfit that does security for Fashion Week is run by a guy who used to be a detective in the Nineteenth. I told Scully I'd call him and see if I can fake my way onto his staff.'

'If you're going in undercover, Detective Wallace, then I'm going to be your date.'

'You know how I feel about you, Alexandra, but Commissioner Scully would have my head for that. Think of yourself as a wallflower, Alex. This may be one ball you just have to sit out.'

Twenty-six

'How are you going to keep yourself busy today, blondie?' Mike asked.

We had jogged the one-and-a-half-mile trail around the Jacqueline Onassis Reservoir – the Central Park landmark that had been renamed in the First Lady's honor for her many contributions to the city.

'You are a tough taskmaster,' I said, wiping my neck with a towel as we walked back to the apartment. 'Shopping. I think I'll go shopping. Totally stress-free.'

'Next week, I'd like you to do a favor for me.'

'What kind of favor?'

'No, no, no. It doesn't go like that,' Mike said. 'Somebody who loves you asks you to do something for him, the answer is an unconditional yes.'

'Does it involve a case?'

'Nope.'

'I'd rather it did,' I said.

'Are you in or not?'

'What do you want? Just some vapid broad who jumps every time you tell her to?'

'Exactly what I've always wanted,' Mike said. 'I seem to remember that's how you responded to everything Luc used to ask.'

I slapped the back of his thighs with my towel. 'Move on, buddy. Sure, I'll give you an unconditional yes.'

'I'd like you to see my shrink – the one the department made me talk to when—'

'No! Not happening,' I shouted, breaking into a run to cross the avenue before the light changed.

During my days of captivity, Keith Scully had insisted that Mike meet with a psychiatrist. He'd been furious at first, thinking she'd been called in to deal with his anger management at the thought of my abduction. Instead, she had tried to find out as much as she could about me – from the man who was closest to me – to help find a reason for someone to have victimized me.

Mike caught up with me a block away.

'There's nothing wrong with me that your beloved shrink can help, Mike,' I said. 'I'm just thoroughly strung out. Can you deal with that?'

'Everything that happens triggers some kind of flashback for you.'

'She told you to expect that I'd have flashbacks. I told you the same thing – most of my victims have had them. It's part of the process, Mike. I want it to stop as much as you do.'

'Then talk to her, Coop. Maybe she can help you with some of your anxiety.'

'I want *you* to help me. That's what I want.'

'I'm doing everything I can for you. I can't stop working and be with you twenty-four/seven.'

'Why not? We can go back up to the Vineyard and just stay there for a month or two. I promise you I can work through this.'

'I need a paycheck, babe. And I do what I do because I like it, because I'm good at it. I'd be a lousy nanny, I really would.'

I knew better than to tell him I could support us – a trustifarian is how he referred to spoiled rich kids – so I just walked beside him silently.

'You're mad because I mouthed off to the district attorney,' I said.

'I would have punched him in his huge-beaked nose, babe. That doesn't bother me at all,' Mike said. 'Once. Will you just go talk to her one time?'

'It's the drinking, then. You drink a whole lot more than I do.'

'I hold it better than you, too. And I don't start quite as early in the day.'

'Once,' I said, jogging off ahead of Mike as I called back to him. 'I'll go talk to her once.'

He caught up with me and took me in his arms, kissing me on top of my head.

'You know how I hate public displays of affection,' I said, grinning back at him. 'Give me the phone number and I'll make an appointment with her for next week.'

'Made my day, Coop. I'll let you take me to dinner anywhere you'd like to go. Now you're being sensible.'

Mike showered and shaved, stayed with me for a second cup of coffee, then called his mother to ask her about the Final Jeopardy! question from the night before.

'Yes, Mom, I'm with Alex. This one's for her?' he said into the phone. 'The category is literature?'

'Tell her thank you for me,' I said. 'Double or nothing.'

'No way,' Mike said before repeating his mother's words. 'The answer is: "This person is the author of a 1914 book of essays called *Tender Buttons*."'

'Who's Gertrude Stein?' I said.

'She's right?' Mike asked his mother. 'Too smart for my blood. The nuns didn't let me read Gertrude Stein. Going to work now, Mom. See you on Sunday.'

Mike hung up and reached for the coffee mug. 'So she wrote a book about buttons?'

'No. But she lived in Paris, and the expression has a couple of meanings in French. One is a name for tiny mushrooms and the other—'

'Why does everything with you come back to French?' he asked, playfully pulling on my jogging ponytail. 'I'd rather watch an autopsy.'

'Well, today you get your wish, darling.'

I walked him to the door and kissed him goodbye, cleaned up and dressed, made a few calls to friends, and tried to think of ways to amuse myself.

I hadn't been shopping in ages. Maybe it would cheer me up to buy a new scarf or pair of snow boots in anticipation of predictions for a stormy winter ahead.

My usual route to my favorite stores was walking down

Third Avenue and cutting over to Madison somewhere in the sixties. I stopped at the cash machine, wandered into my local independent bookstore for a browse, and stopped to admire a cashmere sweater in the window of a new shop on Lexington.

I couldn't get the case out of my mind, probably even more so because I had been ordered to stay out of it.

Some of the details of the investigation continued to nag at me, and I kept going back over them again and again. One of them, which I was reminded of when I thought of the greasy tire tracks in the rooms adjacent to Wolf Savage's suite, was the gold-tone button I had found in the nappy carpet. I opened my phone to look at the photograph I had taken of it before handing it to Mike to voucher.

I didn't need to satisfy my curiosity by going to the Garment District and risking a scolding. The most unusual little shop I could think of was on East Sixty-Second Street, right on the path to my favorite shoe salon. My visit was triggered by Mike's call to his mother. The store had been a Manhattan institution since the '60s. It was called Tender Buttons.

It took me only ten minutes to reach my destination, a narrow brownstone building, recognizable as I approached it by the giant-sized gold button – a trade sign – that was suspended from the balcony above the shop entrance.

There were two saleswomen and one other customer there when I entered. The walls on both sides of the room, from front to back, were covered floor to ceiling with very small boxes. Each box held a different size and style of button – literally hundreds of thousands of them – from antique to modern designs. It was like a library of buttons, and all I needed was someone to tell me whether the one I had picked up from the carpet in the Silver Needle Hotel was in their card catalog.

I approached one of the saleswomen and told her my name, asking for her assistance in matching a button off a garment.

'All I can do is try,' she said, smiling at me as she put on her reading glasses. 'If there's anything distinctive about it, we may be able to help. May I see it, please?'

'Great. I have a photo of it on my cell.'

I pulled it up to show her. She took my phone and spread the image with her fingers to enlarge it.

'To start with,' she said, 'it's gold-toned. That gets us down from the hundreds to the tens of thousands, doesn't it?'

'That's a good thing, isn't it?'

'Just to give you an idea, Ms Cooper, we have four hundred different styles of buttons for men's blazers. We have seventeenth-century silver buttons that come from uniforms of British soldiers and coins of the realm. I can show you a little box of fossilized ivory buttons, if that's what you're looking for – so, yes, anything that tightens the search is a good thing.'

The woman picked up a jeweler's loupe to study the image. 'Is there any way you can bring this actual piece in?' she asked. 'It appears to be broken off on one edge at the top, and again almost in half. It's always so much easier to see if I have the actual object.'

'Maybe next week,' I said, hoping there would be a way to convince Mike to un-voucher the small piece of metal. 'I can try to get it next week.'

'I can't tell if it's real gold – like fourteen or eighteen karat – which would put it in an even smaller category. But it would also make it less likely to break in half.

'Okay. Yes, it almost looks like I've got half a heart here. That the whole button once was the shape of a small heart. Do you notice what I'm talking about?' she said, extending the photo and loupe to me. 'There's a sharp edge on this piece, where something snapped off. Two places, actually.'

'I'll take your word for it,' I said. 'You see these things every day, and I'm just a shopper. Is there anything else you can tell me about it?'

She took the items back from me and studied the photograph again. 'There's an indentation in the middle of this remaining side. It's possible there was once a stone – like a semiprecious stone or even a fake sparkle.'

'That's interesting. I can see the indentation. I just didn't know what to make of it.'

'Are you trying to match this to a particular garment, Ms Cooper?'

'Yes. I'm not very into this kind of thing, but I'm trying to do a favor for a friend.'

'Nice of you to do,' she said. 'Let me ask my coworker if she's seen anything like it.'

There was a series of antique wooden tables down the center of the shop. The other customer had left, seemingly content with a six-piece set of miniature enameled playing cards – buttons for a shirt for her husband's poker tournament.

'What do you think?' my saleswoman asked her colleague. 'Half a heart? Have you seen anything like this?'

'Well, it's not a heart at all,' the second woman said.

'That's the power of suggestion,' I said. 'We both agreed it looked like one.'

'In fact, I've seen one like it just a couple of days ago. We might have two more of them, if you're looking to complete an outfit,' she said, striding with great confidence toward a ladder on a track against the wall.

'You have seen this?' I said. 'You might have another?'

'Do you know the designer, young lady? It's off a vintage piece.'

'My friend told me it's Savage. Wolf Savage. That man who just died,' I said.

'More likely was killed, if you see today's paper,' the first saleswoman said. 'It's a pity.'

'Vintage Savage,' the second woman said, climbing up the ladder to the top step, just below the ceiling. She pulled a small cardboard box out from its place and balanced it with one hand as she carefully stepped down. 'You may be too young to remember some of the fashions from 1991, but it was all about animal prints on the runway that year.'

'I wasn't that into clothes so much as a teenager,' I said, more interested in why she had been asked about the same button just two days ago. Why, and by whom?

'It was the fashion industry's response to the anti-fur activists,' she said, holding up the photo of the broken button against the actual piece that was taped to the front end of the box. The word 'WolfWild' was printed under the button logo. 'Leopard-print dresses. Zebras. Giraffes. The fashion shows looked like a day at the zoo. I'm surprised some of them didn't eat each other alive.'

'Is that the button?' I asked. 'The exact one?'

'We don't like to disappoint, young lady,' she said, removing a pristine piece of metal from a tiny plastic envelope. 'You see, you were mistaken when you two called it a heart. Tried to fool me.'

'I see it now,' the first saleswoman said.

They each had their heads leaned in over the button.

'What makes it unique,' the second woman said, 'is that it was a variation on the usual WolfWear button. And we like unique in our shop. We remember unique.'

'May I see too?' I asked.

'In his lower-price collections,' the button maven said, 'Mr Savage used plastic buttons. Ordinary white or black, or color-coordinated to the outfit.'

'But in his couture?'

'You want couture? I'll show you buttons with diamonds or buttons carved from ancient pieces of lapis. They're French, all of them. Rarer than hens' teeth, and we sell them for a fortune. But that's real couture, Ms Cooper. House of Worth and Chanel and the like.'

'And the Savage line?'

'Well,' the woman in control of the button said, 'American couture. Nothing like the Europeans. Savage didn't do buttons with real gems or anything that grand.'

'But you said this one is distinctive,' I said.

'In all his higher-priced collections – call them couture if you insist – his buttons were always made in the shape of the animal's head, like his logo. He worked that feature into all his clothing, which in my view cheapened a high-fashion statement.'

'How foolish of me not to recognize it. It's not half a heart, it's half of the wolf's face.'

'Sort of like a Rorschach test, isn't it? Half a face and that notch where the little ear chipped off, too,' she said to me. 'Anyway, the animal's eyes were always made of plastic in Savage pieces. That's what's missing from that small hole in the metal. A plastic eye that matched the color of the design – red, blue, green. And an ear.'

The first saleswoman spoke up again. 'Yes, the missing ear threw me off, too. That's why I thought it might have been a heart. This little critter must have been in some kind of fight, and he was certainly the loser.'

Perhaps there had been a fight – a struggle in Wolf's hotel room.

I thought of Hal Savage's cufflinks with the ruby-red eyes. 'What color eye does this button have?' I asked, reaching for it.

'Black eyes, Ms Cooper,' the second saleswoman said. 'All the animal prints had some black in their designs – leopards, zebras, tigers. So Mr Savage used black plastic

– it was supposed to look like crystal – for the eyes on this one collection. And he had a series of reverse buttons made, too.'

'Reverse?'

'Yes, if the cuffs of the silk blouses had gold-tone buttons on the cuffs, with black eyes, Savage sprung for black onyx buttons for the opening of the garment, with little gold dots for eyes.'

She reached into the cardboard box and came out with the black onyx buttons. 'Big splurge for WolfWear,' she joked.

'I'd certainly like to take two of these gold ones, that match my broken button,' I said. 'And two of the onyx, please.'

'The metal ones with black eyes are forty dollars each.'

'Forty? They're useless old buttons.'

She laughed. 'You're the second one in this week. Must be a rush on old Mr Savage because of the show at the Costume Institute.'

'So you've gone and raised the price on me, haven't you?' I said, laughing along with her.

'Just a bit. You can have them for thirty. But the onyx are seventy-five dollars apiece. I can't do any better for you on those.'

'Very, very tender buttons, indeed.'

I gave the woman my credit card and waited while she wrapped the onyx fastenings in a little cloth bag, separate from the metal ones.

'Tell me, who's my competition?' I asked. 'Who else

has a broken button on her wild animal? My friend might be wearing her blouse next week.'

'She won't want to see herself coming and going, will she?'

'Certainly not. Maybe your other customer – the woman who bought the other button – she works at the Savage company?'

'Your first mistake is it's not a "she", Ms Cooper. I sold the button – just one of the gold-tone ones – to a man. A very polite man who came in the other day.'

'A man? Did he say why he wanted it?'

'A sale is a sale. I don't ask questions. And he paid cash for it, so I can't even help you with a credit-card receipt.'

'Older than I am?' I asked, thinking of Hal Savage.

'More or less your age. Could be younger.'

'Can you describe him at all?'

'Nice-looking fellow. He was wearing a navy-blue jacket – sort of a ski jacket – with the collar up against the weather. Sunglasses and a baseball cap snug on his head. Nothing unusual, but then I couldn't see much of him.'

Reed Savage? Or someone else who worked for the company?

'Do you happen to know what day it was?'

She thought for a minute. 'I was off yesterday. Let me see. It must have been Wednesday morning. First thing, shortly after the shop opened.'

I don't think Reed Savage had even arrived from London then. But it was certainly after Wolf Savage had died.

'You should know the same man also bought a dozen

gold military-style buttons from the Ralph Lauren collection of that same year,' she said. 'Could be a collector, Ms Cooper. You just never know.'

'I guess it could be as simple an explanation as that.' I didn't believe it for a minute.

'I mean, it's not like that little piece of metal – with an ear, without an ear – it's not like it's going to help Wolf Savage one iota now that he's dead.'

Twenty-seven

It was ten thirty when I tried to call Mike. I thought the autopsy would have been wrapped up by this time.

I hailed a taxi and directed the driver to Seventh Avenue, then I dialed Joan Stafford's home number in DC.

'Can you talk?' I asked.

'Back up a minute. How are you, my friend? Have you readjusted to city life?'

'Depends on who you ask.'

'What does Mike think?'

'Let's just say it's delicate, okay?'

'Aha! Then Mike might be back on the open market soon.'

Joan was as clever and funny as she was smart. She could make me laugh at everything about myself, and about most other situations. She was an accomplished playwright, but longed more than anything else to help Mike solve a case.

'Dish with me,' she said. 'Wolf Savage was *murdered*?'

'Looks that way.'

'Don't you know? I saw Mike's picture in the paper at the press conference,' Joan said. 'Don't hold out on me.'

'I've got nothing to tell yet. Remember, I'm on leave?'

'But you share a bed with the world's hottest detective, Alex. You must have your ways.'

'I may be slipping, Joanie. I have no information for you.'

'When my first play debuted in London ages ago,' Joan said, 'Reed Savage came to the opening-night party. He's divine. I could have gone for him but he had the cutest wife in tow. Then I heard he split from her. I think he sort of liked me.'

'Every man alive likes you,' I said. 'Most especially your husband.'

As deep as Joan's literary knowledge was, she also had an encyclopedic memory for anyone who had ever been in the society columns. She had attended their balls, dated their brothers, been at their premieres, knew their net worths, remembered their sins, and rarely forgave them.

'Think Savage,' I said. 'Think of the time we were at that benefit and some of his gowns were being auctioned.'

'We must have been tipsy. You bought one and I remember buying two. I swear the tags are still on them.'

'Blood oath. You cannot tell this to Mike or he'll have my head, Joanie.'

'Go on.'

'I think I can wangle my way into the Savage fashion show on Monday night.'

'At the Met? Temple of Dendur? You must take me with you. I'll fly up—'

'Joanie, Joanie. Big fat *no*. I'm talking about sneaking in somehow. There is so much intrigue within the family, within the company, that I just think it pays to be under that roof with all the drama inherent in the situation.'

'I thought you didn't know anything about the case.'

'I don't. But what a great way to try to find out,' I said. 'The problem is I only have one fancy Savage gown.'

The ladies who graced the rows of seats at the big shows always wore their best looks of the designers' past seasons. Saint Laurent and Versace and Michael Kors boasted a lineup of high-end customers who pulled out all their classics. I couldn't go to a Savage extravaganza wearing de la Renta. It just isn't done.

'Wear it, Alexandra. You have to wear it.'

'Do you remember the one I bought?'

'I'm thinking white and flowy, right? Am I close?'

'It's a toga, Joanie. That long white gown with the gold braiding.'

'*Stop!* Don't even think about it. It was almost comical when you tried it on, Alex. You looked like the handmaiden to Elizabeth Taylor when she gave Cleopatra the asp in that endless movie,' Joan said. 'Bad idea. Fashion mistake in the first degree. Not your look.'

'Damn. That's why I was calling. I have to wear Savage.'

'But not a white toga, and not in the middle of November. The fashion police will arrest you,' Joan said. 'You'll have to wear one of mine.'

'Are they in DC with you?'

'No, they're at my mother's, in the guest-room closet.

She'll be so happy to see you. I bet she'll lend you her pearls, too. She's got a fortune in eight-millimeter pearls that you can wrap around your neck two or three times. No one will notice the dress.'

'What are they like?' I asked. 'I'm tempted.'

'One is too summery, too floral. The one I have in mind is Wolf's take on the *Downton Abbey* period. I just never had the occasion to wear it.'

'Tell me, am I an upstairs member of the family or a downstairs kitchen maid?'

'Upstairs. Very racy. Kind of flapperish. It's black silk with a dropped waist. Short and sexy. Think about it, Alex. If you stop at that store on Second Avenue and pick up one of those Lady Mary Crawley black, cropped wigs and put on a glittery headband, no one – I mean no one – will recognize you.'

I laughed. 'You are so melodramatic, Joan.'

'But I'm not wrong. You'll be deeply undercover. You could even fool Mike if you wear some dress style that's against type, and with dark hair. To him, you'll always be "blondie".'

'This has real possibilities, Joan. I may drop in on your mother tomorrow.'

'I should come to town to help you dress.'

'Stay put.'

'But if you solve the crime, do I get credit?'

'An honorary gold shield, I promise,' I said. 'Gotta go.'

The cab stopped in front of 530 Seventh Avenue. I paid the fare and jumped out, dodging the usual foot traffic of men wheeling hand trucks and assistants dashing up and down the avenue with patterns and samples and fabrics of every kind.

I stood in the lobby and tried Mike's phone again. This time it went to voicemail. 'Call me. I've got an idea.'

I thought about waiting till he returned the call, but I always preferred the element of surprise. It was after eleven A.M. and I knew the autopsy wouldn't have taken this long.

I pressed the elevator to go to the WolfWear offices on the twenty-eighth floor. I was anxious to see if Mike and Mercer were already at interviews with Reed and Hal.

The reception area was packed with even more flower arrangements than the day before. I could barely see the top of the head of the woman behind the desk.

'Good morning,' I said. 'I'm looking for two gentlemen who are supposed to be meeting here this morning.'

'Who are they?'

'Mr Chapman and Mr Wallace,' I said.

'Oh, the detectives,' she said, getting up from her desk to walk me to the hallway door. 'They're in Miss Lily's office.'

'Lily Savitsky? She didn't have an office here yesterday.'

The receptionist smiled at me and opened the door. 'Well, she certainly does now.'

Twenty-eight

'Alex,' Lily said, 'I didn't know you were coming. You didn't miss much – we're just getting started.'

Mike was out of his chair and into my face. 'What's the part of "stay home" that you don't understand?'

'I honestly have to thank you,' Lily said. 'It's because of you that my father's body was autopsied this morning.'

'It's really these guys—' I started to say.

'Could you please give us five minutes in here, Lily?' Mike said. 'I need a little time with Alex.'

'Sure.' Lily squeezed my hand as she walked past me and left the three of us alone.

There was nothing to mark the office as her own. It was an empty room with an empty desk and equally empty shelves. It looked like it was her first day on the job.

'If you don't care about protecting your own reputation,' Mike said, 'the least you can do is show a little respect for mine. Who do you think you are? Miss Marple? Stumbling over poisonous mushrooms in the vicarage?

Just nosing around in other people's business like you're going to solve a crime?'

'Whoa, Detective Chapman. Would there have been any autopsy if not for me? You could have been so embarrassed if Wolf Savage had been cremated by his relatives and *then* you got DNA results matching him to his daughter.'

'Give her some props, Chapman,' Mercer said.

'I tried calling but you didn't answer me,' I said.

'What have you got?'

I took the small pouch holding two envelopes out of my pocket. 'Buttons.'

'Swell. Now what?'

I turned my back to Mike and talked to Mercer. 'Remember when we were in the Silver Needle Hotel the other night, and I found a glittery little piece of metal in the carpet?'

'Yeah.'

'A button. Or at least a piece of a button.'

'Could have been there for ages,' Mike said.

'But it wasn't,' I said. 'So I took it to a button store today to see if I could match it to anything.'

'And I take it you did,' Mercer said.

'Here's what I got,' I said, placing the two different pieces on the desk. 'The broken piece is from a Wolf Savage garment. That's for certain.'

'It was in Wolf Savage's row of suites,' Mike said, behind my back but clued into the conversation. 'I'd expect it to be from his line.'

'Do you have the list of the clothes that were on the hand truck when his body was found?' I asked.

'Sure, there's an inventory. And I've also got a photograph.'

'Look through them both and see whether there's any item of clothing that's got an animal pattern on it.'

'I've got the photo right here,' Mike said, opening the app on his phone. 'Like cats and dogs? Is that what I'm looking for?'

'Like jungle. Wild animals.'

'Not that I can see. Everything on the rack is in light colors. No sign of a safari.'

'I didn't think so. The clothes I saw when we were there were all pastel. A spring palette.'

'What does that tell you?' Mike asked.

'That the button you vouchered was broken in a struggle,' I said. 'And that it didn't fall off something from the hand truck. Someone must have been wearing it.

I pulled up the photo of the gold-tone object I had spotted in the carpet. I put it on the desktop beside one of the buttons I had just purchased.

Mercer leaned in. 'Good possibility, Alex. The devil's in the details,' he said. 'It's a woman's blouse you're looking for, right?'

'WolfWear from the nineties.'

'That puts a woman at the death scene,' he said. 'Or a cross-dresser.'

'Or someone trying to frame a woman,' I said.

'What if there was a struggle when someone – or more

than one person – tried to put the bag over Wolf's head?' Mercer asked. 'Could be he grabbed a sleeve or an arm.'

Mike picked up the new button and twisted it with his fingers.

'Be gentle – that little devil cost me thirty bucks,' I said. 'And just in case you think it isn't relevant, the morning after Wolf Savage was killed, some guy walked into the same shop and bought another one of these.'

Mike looked at me and winked. 'Now you're talking. Mind if I take this pouch along for safekeeping?'

'All yours, Detective,' I said. 'Okay, will you please tell me why Lily Savitsky is here this morning, and what the autopsy proved?'

'The postmortem was just what Dr Parker expected with a helium inhalation death. Nothing remarkable to observe,' Mike said. 'But just as importantly, there was absolutely no sign of disease. That alone justifies the procedure.'

'The lungs?'

'Clean as a whistle. The blotches that presented as aspiration pneumonia when Savage was at the Mayo Clinic were completely resolved. Probably a short course of antibiotics.'

'So as far as the man's medical prognosis,' I said, 'Wolf Savage had no terminal illness? Lily was right about that?'

'She was right. Maybe he was sick and tired of the relatives around him, pawing at him all the time,' Mercer said, 'but he certainly was not sick.'

'The toxicology will also be a useful piece of this, won't it?' I asked.

'Of course it will,' Mike said. 'But you know that can take four to six weeks.'

Television shows had such inaccurate portrayals of post-mortem tox results, making the reports available to the medical examiner at lightning speed. But the real-life examinations were painstaking and complicated. It was expected that Savage's blood would have traces of oxycodone in it, based on the pill bottle that was found at the scene, and the news of his prior addiction that Tiz Bolt had provided to me. But the lab would also look to see whether the concentration of the drug was in the toxic or lethal range, and, as usual, check to determine whether any other substances were mixed with it. For toxicologists, there is always a new drug of choice.

'What brought Lily to her father's office today?' I asked. 'I thought she hadn't been able to penetrate the glass ceilings and doors.'

'Looks like the family members regrouped after meeting with the lawyer yesterday,' Mike said.

'Why? What did the will say?'

'We were just getting into that with her,' Mercer said.

'Did her father include her in his estate?'

'He did,' Mike said. 'She doesn't get as much as Reed, but she's very relieved.'

'I'm happy for her. Maybe it'll help her find a way to participate in the business,' I said. 'I guess that's why she's here today.'

'The reason Lily's here today, Coop, is because each one of these Savages is trying to keep an eye on the others.'

'Why?'

'Wolf Savage certainly knew he had a daughter named Tanya Root, even if no one else in the family did.'

'How do you know?'

'Because he went the distance and disinherited her.'

'Damn. He had to name her in order to do that,' I said.

'Well, he did,' Mike said. 'Is that what it takes?'

I was trying to remember my law-school course in trusts and estates. Just the omission of a child in a will isn't enough to cut her out of the estate.

'To hold up in court, the child must be specifically named in the document. The man had to state that it was his intention to disinherit her,' I said. 'Otherwise, she could have come along and make a claim for a portion of the estate after her father's death, arguing that it was just an accidental oversight.'

'That figures,' Mike said. 'Well, Tanya Root is most specifically disinherited in this document. And none of these relatives even knew she existed.'

'Are you bringing Lily back in to continue your conversation with her?' I asked.

'Just as soon as you hit the road.'

'Oh, I'll go,' I said, with one hand on the doorknob, 'the moment you assure me you're up to snuff on your Surrogate's Court trivia.'

'Look, Coop,' Mike said. 'Don't play games with me.'

'Is the name Wolf Savage anywhere in the will?' I asked.

'Lily doesn't have a copy yet. I figure I can get one when it's filed with the Surrogate's Court,' Mike said.

'When David Jones died earlier this year – leaving a one-hundred-million-dollar estate – the media went crazy trying to get their hands on the document, with no success,' I said. 'As I'm sure they'll do in this case – maybe before you get there.'

'Why did the media care? Who was Jones?'

'We all knew him better as David Bowie, but he never changed his birth name – Jones – legally. Little legal factoids like that you might need to know.'

'You mean this will could be drafted in the name Velvel Savitsky?' Mike asked.

'If he was as sentimental about his family and his upbringing as Hal suggests, he probably never made the legal change,' I said. 'We all laughed at the morgue when Hal introduced himself as Hershel Savitsky, but the fact is they might never have gone to court to have the actual change made.'

Mike grimaced. He didn't want to get smacked down again by Keith Scully for having me around, but he knew nothing about the legal issues surrounding the estate.

'Just call if you need me,' I said.

'Get your hand off the doorknob, Coop,' Mike said. 'You know I need you.'

I swiveled and rested my back against the door. 'Were there any other specific disinheritances?' I asked.

'Lily said no, but we're not done with her.'

'I'm thinking of Wanda, the housekeeper who found the body. Maybe that child that Wanda babysat for wasn't Wolf's kid,' I said. 'But things could get complicated if he had this history of fathering children with casual lovers.'

'They've already gotten complicated,' Mike said. 'You might as well take a seat.'

'How so?'

Mike looked to Mercer and got a confirmatory nod before speaking to me. 'Lily claims that her father has a more recent will than this one.'

'What?' I was shocked. 'How long ago did Wolf create this will? It's only been a couple of years since Lily and her father have been getting along, so it must be fairly current.'

'Lily told us that her father had mentioned that he had retained a new lawyer just two months ago, for the purpose of changing some of his bequests.'

'Doesn't she know the lawyer's name?' I asked. 'There's no suggestion that anyone has come forward to the family, even with all this publicity.'

'Could be it's just wishful thinking on her part,' Mercer said.

'You think the only reason she's in this office this morning is because Uncle Hal and her brother Reed want to keep her from mouthing off about some other will that's floating around?' I said. 'You think they're just trying to keep her from fishing in dark waters?'

'Everybody's on tenterhooks,' Mike said. 'They can't possibly know whether Wolf got far enough with a superseding will to make it stand up in court – and whether they do better or worse in the new version. I think they want to keep Lily under their control.'

I was trying to remember everything she told us the first day I met with her.

'They're sure using the right buzzwords,' Mercer said. 'Anything drafted more recently than this, her brother told her, could be tied up in Surrogate's Court for years.'

'For what reason?' I asked.

'She said Hal was throwing around words like fraud,' Mike said. 'That if Wolf changed his will again so shortly after working out all the mechanics of this one because of pressure from a particular individual, they might be able to prove – what's the expression?'

'Undue influence,' I said. 'They'd argue undue influence.'

'That's it.'

'But *who*? Who does she claim – or do they claim – was the person exerting the bad influence?'

Neither Mike nor Mercer answered.

'Wolf would have to have been vulnerable in some way for a person to be successfully charged with undue influence. There are thousands of court cases with examples of that,' I said. 'Now we know after the autopsy that Wolf Savage wasn't even ill. What would have made him so vulnerable – even if he had some business problems – that would convince him to change his will?'

'How's this for vulnerable?' Mike said. 'Lily hasn't mentioned it to the rest of the family, but she thinks her father was being blackmailed.'

Twenty-nine

'By whom? For what reason? Why?' The questions came out of my mouth faster than I could think.

'You keep quiet and sit in the corner,' Mike said. 'My story to the commissioner, should he ask, is that you were just paying a sympathy call on your old backstroking buddy when we walked in the door.'

'I hear you.'

I took a chair in the far corner. Mike opened the door and signaled to Lily to come back into the room.

'It makes me so much more comfortable to have Alex in on our conversations,' Lily said. 'You must know how it is, when it's your first experience with the police. I'm overwhelmed by everything that's happened this week.'

Mike had parked himself on a corner of the desk, opposite Lily, forcing her to look up at him. He liked being in control.

'I was just telling Alex that you have a suspicion about some kind of blackmail,' he said. 'What brought that on?'

'I was right about the homicide theory,' Lily said. 'Wasn't I?'

'Do you mind starting with what happened at the lawyer's office yesterday?' Mike asked. 'We were interrupted before you finished. Work up to your idea about blackmail.'

'Like I said, I was just beginning to spend more time with my father in the last year. He had divorced his fifth wife – thank God – and we were trying for a reconciliation of some sort,' Lily said.

'How did you approach him?'

'I think I mentioned this to Alex the other day. My husband, David, thought it had a better chance coming from him, so he called my father to invite him to lunch. He did it the smart way,' Lily said. 'David took photographs of our kids with him. I think it touched something deep inside my dad that there was actually another generation that could be part of his legacy.'

'He must have liked that,' Mike said. 'Tell me about David.'

'We met at business school. Columbia. He's a partner at a private equity firm in Connecticut.'

'I suppose that means he makes money.'

Lily nodded. 'He's been very successful. He knew my father would appreciate that he didn't come here with his hand out, expecting financial aid.'

'But you were looking for a job here,' Mike said.

Lily sat back as though Mike had slapped her. 'I would have liked that, yes. I've got all the qualifications to make an impact on this business, Detective.'

'You and your husband, are you two solid?' Mike nipped at her again.

'I should hope so. What a mean question to ask,' Lily said. 'Do I have to answer all this, Alex?'

'It would help them, Lily,' I said. 'This is a really unusual situation, even for a homicide investigation. They need to know everything.'

'I'm going to ask you again, are you and David solid?'

There was something about her reaction to the question that kept Mike on her.

'We are now. Our older kids are nine and seven. We separated for a while five years ago. But we're really good. We've got a two-year-old.'

'The make-up kid,' Mike said.

Lily angled her head and forced a smile. 'We named him Wolf. That seemed to please my father enormously.'

'I'll bet it did. Your brother has no children?'

'No, he doesn't.'

'Would you mind telling us how your father's estate was split?'

'In a word,' Lily said, 'unfairly.'

'Where were we before Alex came in?' Mercer asked, trying to get Lily and Mike back on the same page.

'I was trying to explain what we've learned so far. First of all, there's the real estate,' she said. 'A loft downtown and a house in the country. They're both worth a lot of money, but Dad's lawyer suggested that they're mortgaged to the hilt. I don't know why, really, but it's a hint of the fact that Dad's finances weren't quite what he wanted us

– wanted the world, and the gossip columnists – to think.'

'Aren't there homes abroad too?' Mike asked.

'Several, but I believe they're owned by the corporation. So nothing coming to any of us from that.'

'I don't mean to be crass,' Mercer said, 'but how much money is there in the estate?'

'The lawyer doesn't have any idea of the current values,' Lily said. 'They'll start to marshal the assets now. According to the will, sixty percent of everything my father had goes to my brother, Reed.'

She had on her best poker face. That still left a large chunk for her, I thought. I'm not sure why she would have expected more, since she and her father had not enjoyed a long, close relationship.

'Then,' she went on, 'there were percentages for his favorite charities, of course, and smaller amounts for some of his longtime employees. He made sure to take good care of them. For me? Ten percent of his estate. That's for me personally, and the country house is in a real-estate trust for my children.'

'That's pretty damn good,' Mike said. 'Ten percent, I mean.'

'It might seem that way to you,' Lily said. 'It's not what he told me he was planning to do.'

'But he'd been estranged from you for most of your life,' Mike said.

'You'll forgive me if I'm not as pleased as you think I should be, Detective. I'm still his flesh and blood, and worked hard at getting back in his good graces.'

'How about Hal?'

'The business is a major asset of course,' Lily said, biting one of her fingernails. 'That's split between Reed and my uncle Hal. So my father shut that door on me, too.'

'It sounds like there are some financial concerns about the health of WolfWear,' Mercer said. 'Do you know anything about that?'

'Not enough, apparently.'

'Can you help us with that?'

'You'll have to talk to my husband. To David.'

'Why would he be the one to know?' Mike asked.

Lily hesitated, looking over to me before she answered. 'My father trusted David. He was looking to him for an outside perspective on the company.'

'What's this about the possibility of a newer will?'

'Have you mentioned it to Alex?' Lily asked. 'No offense, but she's a lawyer.'

I stood up and came closer to the desk. 'What makes you think there's another will? That could change everything.'

Lily threw back her head and chewed on her lip. 'Well, it would certainly create a shit storm down the hallway here. You never saw two grown men – my brother and my uncle – try to adopt anyone so quickly.'

'Tell me about it,' I said.

'You'll have to talk to David,' Lily said. 'He's the one my father told.'

'The detectives will of course interview David. But every second counts in this investigation,' I said. 'Give them the general strokes.'

Lily stared up at the ceiling for a full minute before speaking. 'It was about two months ago, early in September. David got a call from my father, who asked him to stay in town for dinner to discuss a project with him.'

'Which one?' Mike asked.

'The project was next week's show at the Met. Not the Costume Institute, but Monday night's launch of the new collection.'

'The big one.'

'Exactly,' Lily said. 'My father was thrilled about next week. That's one of the reasons I told Alex I was suspicious about his suicide.'

'What did your father tell David?' Mike said.

'I knew from the time I'd been spending with my dad that he was under all this pressure to sell the lion's share of the business to a Chinese entrepreneur.'

'George Kwan?'

'Yes. Kwan Enterprises,' Lily said. 'He didn't let on to me how troubled he was about it. That he feared losing control altogether, so he was trying to put off finalizing anything till after next week.'

'Why did he suddenly pick this point in time to choose David as a confidant?' I asked.

'You'll meet David,' Lily said. 'He's such a great guy, and my father was obviously trying to get out from under the competing forces of my brother, Reed, and my uncle Hal. He had come to trust David.'

'What did he want from your husband?' Mike said.

'My father wanted David to put together a consortium

or a group to make a counteroffer to the Kwans. He figured that was the kind of thing a private equity firm could do,' Lily said. She sighed and then looked straight at Mike. 'My father asked David to stake him the money. A lot of money.'

'How come you didn't tell me this when we met the other day?' I asked.

'Money wasn't the first thing on my mind, Alex. I'd just learned my father was dead,' Lily said. 'And David didn't give me the full story until last night – after the medical examiner told us he had been killed. Murdered.'

Mike held up his hand toward my face to stop me from interrupting his questioning of Lily Savitsky.

'How much money did your father ask David for?'

She had started in biting another nail. 'Two million dollars.'

'Sweet Jesus,' Mike said. 'What the hell for?'

I knew why. Tiziana Bolt had told me that Kwan Enterprises would never underwrite a fashion show for that much money. I suspected that was true – certainly not without a signed deal with Wolf Savage. They wanted him to front the money himself.

'Because that's what it is going to cost to put on a show like this at the Temple of Dendur,' Lily said. 'One million just to rent the space, another half a million for the gowns and the models. Then you start with the kickbacks.'

'Kickbacks?' Mike asked.

'David says that in this business, everyone alive gets a kickback for doing what they do, from the promoters to the caterers. It's the nature of the beast.'

'When did David become an expert in the fashion industry?'

Lily tried to conceal her sneer. 'His firm has worked in this area before. They've done turnarounds on some of the smaller brands. Nothing as big as WolfWear, but all names you – well, maybe Alex – would recognize.'

'That lack of high-fashion experience didn't stop him from being long on advice, did it?' Mike asked.

'No, it didn't. Not when my father needed help.'

'Did David come up with the two million?'

'He wasn't planning on withdrawing it from his bank account, Detective. We're not in that league,' Lily said. 'He raised it with his partners.'

I was beginning to see the light. 'David was willing to raise the money because he wanted his company's fund to do exactly what Kwan Enterprises wanted to do. Buy the business up – but at a greater discount – and let your father keep his dignity. Then David and his partners would still find some third-world operation to do the supply-chain work to make cheaper clothes.'

Mike's hands were on his hips – a sure sign that he was annoyed – but he didn't stop me.

'I – I don't know exactly,' Lily said. 'That's why I told you to talk to him.'

'I can see what was in it for your father,' I said. 'Truly, I can. A more favorable offer with someone he had every reason to trust. But what else was in it for David?'

Lily was down to her hangnails now.

'Is that where the conversation about the new will came

in?' Mercer asked. 'Was that whole thing your husband's idea?'

'David only wanted what was best for me, best for our children.'

'Does he know whether your father ever had a new will drafted?' Mike asked. 'Does he know the name of the lawyer?'

She shook her head, fighting back tears. 'No. But my father promised David that he would get it done before – well, before next week.'

'And in exchange, David's firm coughed up the two million,' Mike said.

'Why did you come here today?' I asked. 'What if Reed and Hal figure out that there was a quid pro quo for the big show to go on? They'll have every reason to turn on you.'

'I'd rather hide in plain sight, Alex.'

'They'll know every step you take,' I said.

'And I'll keep my eyes on them, too.'

'What's David up to today?' Mike asked. 'Where's he?'

'Look, before you go making David seem like the bad guy,' she said, turning to Mike, 'I didn't know about this Tanya Root woman. I didn't know I had a sister – well, a half-sister from one of my father's serial affairs – until yesterday. It's quite a shock.'

'But Tanya was disinherited by Wolf,' Mike said. 'He specifically cut her out of the will. What does she have to do with any of this business between you and your father? Why are you pointing a finger at her?'

'Just suppose for a minute that Tanya was also trying to get my father to change his will. Not because she wanted to help him, not because she wanted to be involved in his life and his business – but just to get money out of him.'

'That assumes,' I said, 'that they were still in touch with each other. That she knew – or found out – he was her father and that she had been in communication with him.'

'Then suppose she was the one who was blackmailing him, pressuring him to change his will?' she asked.

'We don't have to suppose anything, Lily,' Mike said, leaning both his hands on the desk to get closer to her. 'That "blackmail" word you're using – it's just a guess? Because if you've got the patience to wait this out, we'll have a subpoena for every phone call and email and text that ever went out from your father to any one of you in the last year. It'll get worse before it ever gets better.'

'You think I'm holding something back from you?' Lily asked. 'This Tanya Root person is a complete mystery to David and me. Whether there's a new will that surfaces and proves to be valid makes no difference to me. My father had already included me in this will.'

'Really? The one you just finished telling us was unfair?' Mike said. 'Can't have it both ways.'

Lily Savitsky snapped. She clenched her fists and pounded them on the desktop. 'Are you satisfied, Detective Chapman? Can you tell that I'm scared?'

'That's the first thing you've said that I understand one

hundred percent. Somebody killed your sister, and quite possibly your father, too, right?' Mike said. 'Most likely their murders are connected. You should be scared.'

'That's rough, Mike,' I said, stepping between Mike and the desk. 'Let's all take it down a notch.'

'You think I could be next, don't you?' Lily asked.

'Me?' Mike said. 'I think you're safe, actually. You're safe for as long as you're a suspect in those two murders.'

Thirty

'What did you mean by that?' I asked Mike.

Once Lily pulled herself together, she left the room to freshen up.

'Just what I said, Coop. You can't tell me the two crimes aren't connected.'

'I'm with you on that.'

'Maybe the killer is different in each case, but this is a family affair – either way, it's a father and his daughter who were murdered, whether for personal or business reasons. And as long as the killer, or killers, if Lily is not involved, think that she is a likely suspect – for financial gain and a bigger piece of the will – then she isn't going to be in danger,' Mike said. 'That's because the killer is likely figuring that Lily might take the fall.'

'Phew. That's an ugly thought.'

'But a real one.'

'Different killers?' I asked.

'I'm keeping an open mind. I'm willing to consider – I'm just saying consider – that Tanya Root was looking for something from Wolf Savage. Something that he wasn't willing or able to do.'

'Give her money,' Mercer said.

'Could be that. Could be she wanted into the family business, which also meant money. We won't know that until we find out more about her.'

'But it makes you think she could have gotten in the old man's way,' Mercer said, 'at a very inopportune moment.'

'Right. His day in the sun, with both the Costume Institute exhibition and the Met fashion show. The last thing he needed was someone threatening to upend his life.'

'Enough to kill her?' I asked.

'I doubt this was a hands-on job, Coop. But if Wolf Savage was desperate, he had the means to make someone disappear.'

'If that's your theory, then someone else killed him,' Mercer said. 'That's your "different killers" scenario.'

'But then you've got Reed and Hal and Lily,' Mike said, 'all three of them in precarious positions vis-à-vis Wolf. Now there are three people who each have a motive to get rid of Tanya, if she was pressuring him to change his will in her favor. And the same three people who have reasons to do him in, too.'

Mike was pacing around the room. He stopped at the door, which was closed. Taped to it was a list – enlarged, bolded, and in all caps. He began reading aloud.

RUNWAY PERFORMANCE RULES – WOLF SAYS:

NO SMILING
NO DANCING
NO EYE CONTACT WITH AUDIENCE
NO FAST MOVEMENTS
NO SLOW MOVEMENTS
DO NOT BE STIFF
DO NOT BE CASUAL
BE NEUTRAL
BE CALM
BE STOICAL
STOP AT THE END OF RUNWAY FOR THE CAMERA
DO NOT LOOK AT THE CAMERA

'Is this what I think it is?' Mike asked.

'Yes,' I said, looking over his shoulder at the list that contained at least twenty additional instructions. 'Runway rules for his models.'

'That's a crazy lot of rules for those broads. Makes me think—'

Mike's thought was interrupted as the door opened, striking him in the shoulder. Hal Savage barged in.

'We're trying to run a business here,' he said as Mike stepped back. 'What is it now? Why don't you people call and make appointments?'

'Actually, I tried to find you yesterday afternoon,' Mike said. 'Didn't your secretary tell you?'

'That was yesterday,' Hal said. 'Can you put this off

for a week? Give us time to honor my brother on Monday?'

'Some of what we need to know will wait. I'm sure you must be grateful we got in your way at the morgue,' Mike said.

'Grateful?' Hal said, missing the obvious sarcasm in Mike's tone. 'The one I'm grateful to is Lily. Murder was never part of the picture, in my mind. I owe her a lot for alerting you people to the possibility.'

'Would you have twenty minutes for us right now? Then we'll get out of your hair,' Mike said. 'Why don't we go down to your office? There's more room, and we don't need Lily to be in on this.'

'We can get this done here,' Hal said, crossing his arms and standing his ground.

'Twenty minutes. C'mon. There are things you wouldn't want me to go into in front of Lily,' Mike said. 'Things about the business. Kwan Enterprises and – well, her husband, David.'

'Okay, okay. I'm throwing you out after that,' he said, tapping on his watch face.

We followed him down the corridor, our small parade attracting the attention of all the worker bees in their glass-enclosed hives. In the short space of the last two days, the Wolf Savage sign on the door had been replaced with Hal's nameplate.

The room was now cluttered with racks of clothes – some of them appeared to be the new line ready to launch – and some looked like vintage WolfWear. They were probably arrayed for the final selection for Monday night's show.

Mercer, Mike, and I sat down across from Hal Savage.

'I'm shocked,' he said, sitting down and holding his fingers against his forehead. 'Did I say that yet? I'm just shocked by the medical examiner's news.'

There was nothing about the man that sounded sincere. It was as though he realized he had missed a stage cue to express to us the impact of yesterday's news.

'What shocked you?' Mike asked.

'That Wolf was murdered, of course. I'm reeling from that. I'll do anything to help you find the killer.'

'I'm counting on you for that,' Mike said. 'How about the rest of the story? Any surprises there?'

He looked up and put his hands down. 'The dead girl? Tanya Root?'

'Yeah.'

'I knew about Tanya. I've known about her since she was born,' Hal said. 'I didn't realize she was back in my brother's life. I swear it. I was sure he'd paid her off to disappear years ago.'

'Tell me the story.'

Hal Savage glanced in my direction.

'She's heard it all,' Mike said. 'Go on.'

'My brother had a problem his whole life. The kind of guy who couldn't keep it in his pants,' Hal said. 'Reed's mother – that was a marriage that was expected of him by the family. By the time the boy was conceived, Wolf was on the prowl. She found out about it and cut him off. Never let him back in their bedroom.'

'He left her for Lily's mother?'

'Yes. He was making a good living, although why he pretended he could be monogamous was beyond me. I liked Lily's mother,' he said, shaking his head. 'I have a real fondness for my niece, too. But Wolf was out of there while she was still a toddler. He never treated the kid right.'

'You had no way to influence that?' I asked. 'I mean, you're the CFO. It sounds like Lily had great credentials, with her business-school degree, to work with both of you. You didn't ever go to bat for her, did you?'

'My brother didn't want to hear about it,' he said, waving his hand at me. 'She's here now, isn't she? What's the complaint?'

'Yeah,' Mike said. 'Why *is* she here now? What's that about?'

'Mending fences, maybe. Making up for my brother's sins.'

'You okay with Lily's husband?'

'David?' Hal said. 'Ambitious kid. But not a problem for me.'

'Who's your vote for now?' Mike asked. 'I mean, if the company needs a bailout. George Kwan, or David Kingsley and his firm?'

'You're wasting precious minutes, Detective. I'm walking a tightrope this week,' Hal said. 'Give me a while to sort this out. David put up the money for the show. That was Wolf's idea. Now I'm left with my brother's bad decisions and Kwan Enterprises breathing down my neck. I can't answer you on that one today.'

'I think we sidetracked you from Tanya Root,' Mercer said. 'Go back to her.'

'Sure. Sure, I will,' Hal said. 'Wolf married a third time, to the woman who raised Reed. It was during the period when he lived in London, trying to get his business started in Europe. Nice lady. She put up with a lot. He parked Reed over there with her, and came back to New York.

'This was the right business for a guy who's basically a hound, Detective,' Hal went on. 'I hope you'll excuse me, Ms Cooper.'

I nodded at him.

'It's one thing to work in Brooklyn making black hats for Hasidic men. Kind of limits your exposure to temptation. But once my brother got onto Seventh Avenue, he was like a kid in a candy store.'

'Women?'

'Young women, especially. Models, wannabe models, designers, design students. He had an eye for the girls, and with his third wife and kid tucked away across the ocean, he indulged himself. Good-looking ladies, drugs like you wouldn't believe – and then – boom! The mega-success that provided the money to enjoy it all.'

'Is that when he met Tanya's mother?'

'I can't tell you that exactly,' Hal said. 'I'd figure Tanya to be around thirty years old. Go far enough back in the newspaper archives and there are probably photographs of Wolf with her mother.'

'Was she a model?'

'For a nanosecond. Yeah.'

'African?'

'Here's the thing, Detective. For whatever reason, Wolf was usually attracted to women of color.' Hal was looking over at Mercer now, as though seeking his approval. 'Whatever it was, he's one of the people most responsible for putting black women on the high-fashion runway. Sure, a few of the big-name designers did it with super-models like Iman and Beverly Johnson, but Wolf started more young women of color in their careers than any ten hotshots you can name.'

'But he was taking advantage of them at the same time?' I asked.

Hal Savage didn't pretend to hide his annoyance with me. 'You call that taking advantage of them? He wasn't forcing any of them to do things they weren't willing to do. Everybody benefitted from it, seems to me.'

Sexist? Racist? A throwback to another cultural norm? Hal Savage seemed to be all those things. I thought of bringing up the sad story of Samira – the Ethiopian woman Wolf had impregnated – who died in childbirth with his baby. How many like her were there?

Mercer reached over and put his hand on my shoulder.

'Anyway, to answer your question, Tanya's mother was about twenty when she came to New York. I don't remember what her name was – it was all the vogue to do the one-word name thing at the time. My brother was crazy about her. Treated her real good. She screwed it up by becoming pregnant.'

'Sorry,' I said, holding my temper in check, 'but I was

always under the impression you needed a guy to help with that.'

'You've got a sharp tongue, sweetheart.'

I put that in the memory bank right next to the men who called me 'dear.'

'That was it with Wolf,' Hal said. 'He wasn't a good father to his first two kids. What made these women think it would make a difference with them, I'll never know. At least this was the straw that broke the camel's back. I talked him into having a vasectomy.'

Hal chuckled over his own amusement at that thought.

'What about Coco?' I asked. 'The child of the woman who stayed in the hotel with him a few times.'

Hal leaned forward and wagged a finger at me. 'That, Ms Cooper, is a perfectly good question. You want to know who was taken advantage of? My brother, that's who. That wasn't his child, but the damn bitch tried to shake him down by claiming she was. Put the poor kid in the middle of it. She'd had an affair with him, like way too many women did – and then wanted to squeeze him for a payoff.'

'He didn't pay?' Mike asked.

'As a result of the vasectomy, Wolf was shooting blanks, Detective. You know the same DNA that connected him to Tanya? Wolf had the mother and kid Ms Cooper is talking about come stay with him in the Silver Needle Hotel so he could get the child's DNA – off a soda bottle, no less – to prove he wasn't the father,' Hal said, wiping his hands against each other, as though he was brushing away crumbs. 'He shipped them off, back to wherever they came from. End of story.'

'Is that how he got rid of Tanya's mother?' I asked, repeating his ice-cold expression. '"Shipped her off"?'

'That's how he tried,' Hal Savage said. 'He gave her a fistful of cash and a one-way ticket to New Orleans. He never expected to see her pretty face again. I'm sure when he unloaded that one, he never imagined she was pregnant. Wolf wanted no more part of that woman, and no more part of her crazy Louisiana voodoo.'

Thirty-one

'Sorry I've offended you, Ms Cooper,' Hal Savage said.

'I'm not—'

'Your expression gives you away. Good thing Mr Chapman's only got five minutes before I show him to the door.'

I wasn't as appalled by his words and manner as I was speeding ahead and connecting the dots. Josie, the housekeeper in the Silver Needle who had done a disappearing act on us, was completely into voodoo. Could that be a link to Tanya Root's mother? And Mercer had talked to Wolf's fourth wife. She was also a former model, living in New Orleans, who remembered that another ex-girlfriend of Wolf's lived there. This gave us two more leads to follow.

Mike was on the same page as I was. 'There's this housekeeper at the hotel where your brother died. Her name is Josie. Do you know her at all?'

Hal thought about answering for a few seconds. 'Josie? Yeah, she's still hanging around.'

'Your brother recommended her for the job at the Silver Needle,' Mike said. 'What did she have on him?'

'You've really been digging in the dirt, Detective, haven't you?'

'You go where your victim leads you,' Mike said. 'This one feels like I'm in mud right up to my nostrils. Suits pigs better than it suits me, frankly.'

Hal clasped his fingers at the back of his head. 'Wolf might have liked you, Chapman. He liked attitude.'

'Haitian voodoo and Louisiana voodoo – what's the hook between them?' Mike asked abruptly.

'They're close enough,' Hal said, avoiding Mike's question. 'Tanya's mother dropped the news on Wolf that she was having a baby. It was months after she left New York,' Hal said. 'My brother sent her money and kept sending her money for years, until he got sick of sending her money.'

'What happened when he stopped?'

'Tanya showed up at the office one day. Seventeen years old, almost eighteen. Her mother put her on a bus all the way up here from New Orleans.'

'How'd that appearance go?' Mike asked.

'Not well, Detective. Scared the shit out of my brother, plain and simple.'

'What happened?'

'Tanya started out nice enough. Wolf told me they talked and talked for hours. After all,' Hal said, 'none of this was the kid's fault.'

'What was Tanya like?' I asked. I was thinking, too,

of her plastic surgery and whether she really could have been a model.

'I only met her twice. I'm getting to that part,' he said. 'Wolf thought she was a decent kid. Poor thing looked like Wolf, not her mother. He might have put her on a runway if she could have made that work, but she had a build more like her father's than like a model.'

'Did she ask him for money?' Mike said.

'You bet. But he had to stop somewhere, so he kept putting her off. I know he got her a room in a hotel.'

'The Silver Needle?'

'That first time? I don't think it even existed then. And he didn't want her around here, in the Garment District.'

'Don't you remember where it was?' I asked. Maybe it was a place she came back to on later trips, and even the one that ended with her death.

'She wanted to be uptown. That's all that comes to me. She knew a guy who moved up here from New Orleans to play in a jazz club in Harlem. Gentrified Harlem. Tanya wanted to hang out with him. So Hal put her up for a few weeks – had her taken care of.'

That could focus our search. If the hotel she stayed in then was still in the same hands, it could fit with the location where Tanya's body was found in the East River.

'She claimed her mother was dying and that she needed a bundle of money to care for her,' Hal said. 'The girl didn't want to stay in New York. So Wolf had his lawyer draw up papers. He told Tanya to come to our offices the day before she was leaving, and he'd give her a check to cover some of the medical expenses.'

'She showed up, of course,' Mike said.

'Yeah. That's when I met her. Tanya – I don't remember her last name, but it wasn't Root at the time. Wolf wanted me to witness the meeting, since he didn't trust anyone else with the family secret.'

'Did she take the check?'

Hal laughed. 'She wanted the check but she balked when it came to signing the document.'

'Why?' Mike said. 'What was it?'

'It was a release that neither she nor her mother would ever get another nickel from Wolf Savage after she turned eighteen.'

'But wasn't her mother dying?' I asked. It seemed like an awfully cold plan to me.

'I'm sure Wolf hired a private dick to find out about that. I really don't think it was the truth. I seem to recall it was all about the kid and what she wanted from him.'

'What did Tanya do?' Mike said.

'She tore the check in half,' Hal said. 'Cursed at both of us in some creole patois and stormed out of the offices.'

'That was the end of it?' Mike said.

'Hardly. Tanya called my brother the next morning. She asked if she could come by at the end of the day to apologize. She was willing to sign the release and take the check. I can't remember the amount, but it was at least twenty-five thousand dollars.'

'How'd that go?'

'I waited with Wolf till almost eight o'clock. I cut a new check and we started all over again,' Hal said. 'Tanya? Came in sweet as could be. Signed the release, pocketed the check – and then she went berserk. I mean you've-never-seen-anything-like-it berserk.'

He was on his feet, waving his arms around.

'Here comes the voodoo,' Mercer said.

'Right in this very office. The two of us – grown men – we were shaking in our boots, like we were made of jelly. A hex, Detective. Have you ever had anyone put a hex on you?'

'Not lately,' Mike said.

'Tanya had a bag with her. Like a cheap plastic tote that she sat on top of Wolf's desk. Here,' he said pointing. 'Right here.'

We all pushed our chairs back while he moved around, imitating her movements as he told his story. 'Then she pulled a hammer out of the tote, just an ordinary claw hammer, and she started whacking at the bag, cursing the whole time. Pounding at whatever was in the bag – we had no idea – until she pulverized it.'

He stopped to catch his breath. 'I tried to pick up the phone to call security in the lobby of the building, but she reached out and smashed the phone. She nearly nailed my hand to the desktop with the hammer.'

'Chicken bones,' Mercer said. 'Tanya was giving you the Bones of Anger hex.'

Hal Savage pointed at Mercer. 'How'd you know? How'd you know about it?'

'My wife has family in Baton Rouge. Let's leave it at that,' Mercer said. 'You want your hex to be potent, you make sure you've got dry chicken bones, and then you just work yourself up into a frenzy of anger and hatred.'

'I hope your people aren't as insane as this one was,' Hal said.

He took his imaginary tote bag and started circling the room, pretending to be sprinkling the contents of the bag all around on the floor.

He was chanting at the same time, trying to remember words from all those years ago. 'Bones of anger,' he said, 'and something about bones to dust. "With these bones your soul I crush, make my enemy turn to dust."'

He walked back to the desk. 'I picked up Tanya's hammer and ran out to my office. I figured my brother could handle the kid and the broken chicken bones. That's when I called security,' Hal said. 'Then I remembered about Josie.'

'Josie LaPorte?' I asked. 'The housekeeper at the Silver Needle?'

'Exactly. Only back then, she was on the janitorial staff of this building. Worked the night shift, cleaning offices. She used to make Wolf crazy, mumbling all kinds of things that had to do with voodoo and hexes and spells. I told security to find her – wherever she was and whatever she was doing – and get her to our offices stat.'

'Tanya was still there when security arrived?' Mike said.

'There was enough chicken dust in that tote bag to keep her busy sprinkling it all over the place for another hour,' Hal said. 'Fortunately, security came and, shall we say, restrained her. Wolf didn't want her locked up. We never called your department. He just wanted her on the first morning bus back home. He paid Josie to sit with her all night in one of the offices. That's when he bonded with Josie.'

'It didn't matter that Haitian voodoo and Louisiana voodoo aren't the same?'

'Trust me, those two communicated just fine. Josie went with the two security guards in the morning to the Port Authority Bus Terminal to see Tanya off – with her twenty-five-thousand-dollar check.'

'So she knows that Tanya was Wolf's daughter,' I said.

'Yeah. She even promised my brother she could reverse the hex. Something with a magic mirror and black salt and a photograph of Tanya. I didn't stick around for that ceremony, but Josie did it.'

'What did she get in exchange?' Mike asked.

'Night janitorial jobs in commercial offices? They're the worst. Cleaning up after everybody's crap, including all the stinking food that's left around. Plus, it's when the roaches and the mice come out to play. You don't want to be here at two A.M. Trust me. All Josie wanted was a housekeeping job in a fancy hotel. Daytime preferred. That's what she asked my brother to help her with, and he did. It was like going from being Cinderella to the Duchess of Windsor. First at some boutique hotel nearby that went out of business a few years ago, and then Wolf got her placed at the Silver Needle – working on his floor – which was empty most of the time anyway.'

'Did they stay in touch?' I asked.

'Oh, yeah,' Hal said. 'Every time my brother heard from Tanya, he asked Josie for help. I'd say there was an eight-year period when all was quiet. Then two or three years ago, Tanya started to call again.'

'Did she ever show up here, in the office?'

'No. At least, not that I know of. The first I learned she was anywhere near New York was from the medical examiner. If she was breathing down my brother's neck, he didn't tell me about it.'

'So Josie's the one to ask,' I said. 'If Tanya was bothering him.'

'That's a good idea,' Hal said. 'Josie was always telling Wolf that one of Tanya's revenge spells – that's what she calls those hexes – that one of those spells was going to bring him down. Be the end of him.'

'No wonder Josie wouldn't go into the room where he died,' Mercer said.

'No surprise there. She always thought evil spirits surrounded Wolf, despite her best efforts to cleanse him of them, because of what Tanya did. Josie would be a million miles away if she thought Tanya had anything to do with his death.'

We had to find Josie LaPorte. Two murders were enough.

'Now, gentlemen and Ms Cooper, maybe you can find a way to occupy the rest of your day and leave me and my team in peace,' Hal said, standing up and walking toward the door.

We all stood up, too.

'A couple more things,' Mike said. 'I'm going, but—'

'You're worse than Columbo,' Hal said, throwing up his arms. 'You've got two questions left, which means that one of them's a trick to make me confess to murder. I've seen every one of those TV shows. You think I'm a clown?'

He was mocking Mike now, never a good tactic.

'It would save us a hell of a lot of time if you confess, I'll give you that,' Mike said. 'Did your brother ever change his name? I mean go to court to have it legally changed?'

'Were you listening to me when we were with Dr Parker the other day, Detective? I'm Herschel Savitsky, like I told her. You got me, Chapman. Was that supposed to be a tough one for me? And my brother was born and died a Savitsky, just like I told the doc. Is that the best you can do?'

'I'll try my other one,' Mike said. 'Where's the money, Mr Savage? You're the company's CFO, why don't you tell me what happened to all the money?'

Hal Savage didn't like that question. 'Like I said, get a dirty old trench coat and you can give Columbo a run for his money.'

'It's not a trick question,' Mike said. 'I'm just trying to figure out who ran your brother's empire into the ground. Were you asleep at the wheel?'

Hal held up his left hand and began counting on each finger with his right hand. 'My brother spent a fortune on the ladies, Detective, in case you hadn't figured that one out yet. Then there was a period of his drug addiction. A very long, difficult period. If you didn't know about it,

I'm sure some snitch will bring it up. Cocaine and prescription drugs. He was running through money like sand through a sieve. What was I going to do? Let him kill himself that way?'

'No – but . . .'

'Look, the company gave him an expense account – at my direction – to cover all the food and wine he spent on broads. Then we paid for his rehab, 'cause we'd probably been covering the allowance for his drugs, too. And do you have any idea how many lawsuits I had to settle for sexual harassment over the years?' he said, raising his voice louder and louder. 'Do you understand how many millions went out the door to keep the stories about Wolf's harassment of women in the business from getting out? There's a guy around the corner who makes zippers for the industry. Understand that?'

'Yeah,' Mike said. 'Your nephew told us about him.'

'Only zippers. That's all the guy does. Well, even he couldn't make one that locked tight enough to keep my brother's penis in his pants. Do the math, Detective. Just try and do the math.'

Mike walked into the hallway. 'I get it, Mr Savage. First you blamed Reed for the missing corporate funds. Now you pile it on the dead man himself, putting the company he created in financial jeopardy.'

'Damn right. It sure as hell isn't *my* doing.'

'I'm certain your financial records will back all that up,' Mike said.

'Take a number, Chapman. The IRS and every other

agency concerned has had a shot at our records. In due time, why not you?'

'Thanks for this, Mr Savage,' I said. 'I was sort of hoping you'd blame all your problems on a dead man, even if he was a total sleaze when it came to women. It's so much cleaner and easier than admitting that as CFO, you took it on yourself to set up offshore accounts, creating off-the-books records to hide all the WolfWear losses.'

It was just a long shot, but this was the time to take it. Prosecutors had worked through corporate records to take on the Enron scandal, the Tyco disgrace, and the collapse and bankruptcy of Dewey Ballantine – a once distinguished white-shoe law firm.

'Why you—'

'Hold your tongue, Mr Savage,' Mike said. 'All Coop's suggesting is that maybe you cooked the books.'

'Don't you dare—'

'But you just go on ahead with next week's show. We've got plenty of time to look into that theory.'

'That's slanderous, Detective,' Hal Savage said. 'You better keep your mouth shut, accusing me of fraud. That's totally slanderous.'

'How long did you think you could hide all that from Wolf?' Mike asked. 'How far did you have to go when he realized that his global vision would be dead in the water if you'd been defrauding him for years?'

'Get out!'

'Happy to be leaving, sir. It seems to me Wolf's in the morgue and you're the one sitting in the catbird seat now.

We've got to figure out who that's good for. Is it you? Your nephew, Reed? The good folks at Kwan Enterprises? Or do I check the box that says all of the above?' Mike said. 'C'mon, Coop, let's see if we can stir us up a hex on mendacity.'

Thirty-two

We were back in the reception area of the WolfWear offices, where the flower arrangements were beginning to look as dead as the man they were meant to honor.

The receptionist – not the young woman who had greeted us on our first visit – was ferrying vases back and forth from the restroom to empty them, so we had a quiet place to talk.

'How'd you come up with all that financial fraud stuff, Coop?' Mike asked.

I had never worked in the white-collar crimes division of the DA's Office, but many of my good friends did. The time we spent together brainstorming on trial strategy and sitting in on one another's courtroom arguments kept me conversant with the case issues.

'Don't you remember Enron? I must have paid attention because it broke while I was in law school, so we had lectures about it back then.'

'It was an energy company, wasn't it?' Mercer said.

'Yes. One of the world's largest natural-gas and electricity businesses. You want to talk global? I guess that's what made me think of Enron. It was huge at the time,' I said, 'in building pipelines and power plants and things like that.'

'Then it began to lose money,' he said.

'Yes, its debt was tremendous. Even the sale of major operations – like what Hal Savage wants to do – would not have solved Enron's problems,' I said. 'So the chief financial guy set up a very creative accounting fraud – one of the best examples of willful corporate fraud and corruption ever.'

'Here all this time, Wolf gets credit for being the creative brother, when maybe Hal outdid him in original thinking,' Mike said. 'How did Enron manage it?'

'I'll have to pull out my law books. I know the financial guru set up offshore entities, and he put all the debts and losses into those accounts. As for assets, he greatly inflated them, and even made some up out of whole cloth.'

'They had fictional business accounts, right?' Mike asked. 'They just eliminated unprofitable entities from their books. But nobody got murdered.'

'No, no. But it was a public company, unlike WolfWear, so the top executives began selling off huge amounts of stock when they got wind of the hidden losses,' I said.

'Insider trading.'

'That's it. The stock plummeted from ninety dollars a share to less than a dollar, but not before the insiders and their families had sold off everything they had, knowing what was about to happen. How's twenty-five years in jail?'

'About what the sentence would be for murder. In Hal's case, twenty-five to life would be a death sentence,' Mike said. 'You like him for Wolf's murder?'

'I'm just keeping all our balls in the air,' I said as the receptionist returned with another empty vase and headed back to the bathroom sink with some drooping red roses.

'You're saying Wolf had his eye on the need to expand into other markets, and to the design end of the business,' Mercer said. 'That he left the financial health of the business in Hal's hands.'

'That's what it sounds like,' I said. 'I'm back to Chapman's Rules of Homicide Investigations. First is that there are no coincidences. We have a father and daughter both dead, and that fact can't be a coincidence. We all agree on that. On to rule two. There are four motives for murder: greed, jealousy, lust, and revenge. I'll throw in a pure hate crime, but that's not what we've got here.'

'Go on.'

'If Tanya Root was an isolated case, I'd start with lust, of course. But we have no evidence of that, and never will. With Wolf's death, I'd eliminate that completely.'

'Jealousy?' Mike said.

'Tanya might have been jealous of the two siblings who didn't seem to know she even existed, but that certainly doesn't explain why she wound up dead first.'

'You like revenge.'

'Whichever way you look at this,' I said, 'there's a strong element of greed involved. And maybe a twinge of revenge. Not the voodoo kind, just a straightforward settling of scores.'

'There are so many people we haven't talked to yet,' Mike said.

'George Kwan is one of them,' I said. 'What does he know about the WolfWear financials? How does Kwan Enterprises benefit if Hal Savage – or someone else there – is in command of the company?'

'Depends on who you cast your vote for as the weakest link. Hal? Reed? Take your best shot.'

'Let's find George Kwan. Do you know where his offices are?'

'I know they work out of a townhouse on the Upper East Side,' Mercer said. 'It's supposed to be loaded with security and harder to penetrate than Kim Jong Un's palace.'

The receptionist was back with another empty vase, heading for some gladioli that were emitting a foul odor from the corner of her desk.

'Excuse me,' I said. 'We were supposed to meet with George Kwan, but I didn't put his address in my contacts. Have you got a phone number for him?'

'Not for him personally,' she said. 'I can give you his office number.'

'Thanks. And the address, too. It's East Seventy-Fifth Street isn't it?' I asked as she pulled up her phone list on the desktop.

'Seventy-Eighth Street, actually. Mr Kwan is out of the

country for the weekend. I don't think we're going to see him until Monday night. You know, at the Met.'

'Of course,' I said, thanking her for the phone and street numbers as she went back about ditching the flowers.

Kwan Enterprises wouldn't put up the money for the big launch, but it made sense for George and his crew to be there in the front row to promote their planned venture.

'Ah, the inscrutable East,' Mike said. 'Where's George when we need him?'

'Stop with the political incorrectness,' I said. 'We're the only ones who can hear you, and we're over it.'

'Let's give the townhouse a shot. He can't be the only Kwan in the enterprise.'

Thirty-three

'What about lunch?' Mike asked.

We were on our way down in the elevator, to the lobby of 530 Seventh Avenue.

'Let's just grab sandwiches,' Mercer said, 'and power on through. It's already after one thirty.'

We reached the sidewalk outside the building. I recognized Reed Savage, approaching us with another man.

'Mr Savage,' I called out, waving to him, then speaking an aside to the guys. 'You'd be smart to talk to him out of his uncle's presence, Mike.'

We waited until the men crossed the street to our side.

'I – uh – I don't know what to say to the three of you,' Reed Savage began. 'I'm just sick at the thought of how close my uncle and I came to denying the medical examiner the chance to see if there's any evidence linking my father's death to a suspect.'

Reed was more humbled and apologetic than his uncle had been.

'Have you met David? David Kingsley,' Reed said,

introducing each of us to him. 'David is Lily's husband.'

'Good to know you,' David said, shaking hands with each of us and lingering a few seconds on me. 'Lily told me you grew up together, and how helpful you were in getting the NYPD to pay attention to Wolf's death.'

'Do you have a few minutes?' Mike asked both of them. 'Pop into a coffee shop around the corner, to get off the street?'

'Sure,' Reed said, 'if that's what you need.'

'I'll run along then,' David said.

'No, no. This is a good opportunity to talk with you both,' Mike said.

Mercer led us to a booth for six in the rear of the deli, which was emptying out after the lunch hour. The five of us were a snug fit.

'What did I interrupt?' Mike asked. 'Family reunion?'

'We're getting to know each other a little better,' Reed said. 'Making up for lost time.'

'My wife never had much of a family, Detective,' David said. 'Reed's been very welcoming.'

'I had enough trouble in grade school trying to keep straight the alliances in the Holy Roman Empire,' Mike said. 'You folks give them a good run for their money, excepting for the holy part.'

Reed broke a smile. 'David and Lily both have great business acumen. I think we need to find a place for them in the business.'

'I hope George Kwan is on board with that idea,' Mike

said. 'The way I heard him screaming at your uncle the other day, I'd be ready to duck and cover.'

David looked down at the Formica tabletop. Reed didn't respond.

Mercer flagged down a waiter and asked for menus. All five of us ordered coffee.

'How'd you two take the news about Tanya Root?' Mike asked.

'Poor Lily didn't know what to think. She was sorry to find out she had a sister she'd never known about – and was helpless to help when Tanya must have needed it most – and she was mortified that her father's dirty laundry is hanging out in public,' David said. 'For me, well, it's all a matter of being here to support Lily. It's not personal.'

I wanted to separate David from Reed, to question each out of the presence of the other. That was Mike's usual style, but he clearly wanted them to go head to head for some reason not yet obvious to me.

'But it is professional for you,' Mike said.

'You're very premature to say that, Detective.'

Reed was all ears.

'Wolf came to you more frequently for advice these last few months, didn't he?' Mike said.

'Look, I wanted my wife and our children to have a role in his life, and in this amazing business empire he built, too.'

'Will you be at the Met Monday night?'

David stammered a bit as he formed an answer. 'We

will be, Lily and I. Wolf invited us, and now there'll be a tribute to him of course.'

The waiter placed the coffee cups in front of each of us. Reed's attention was focused on his brother-in-law.

'Who's in charge of the big show, anyway?'

Both men were silent.

'For a couple of million dollars,' Mike said to David, 'I'd think you and Lily would want to brag about it.'

Reed didn't have to speak. It was obvious from the look on his face that he hadn't known until this moment who was paying for Monday night's extravaganza.

'Your father never told you?' Mike said to Reed. 'When Wolf made plans months ago to stage this launch at the Met, he must have thought that he had the dough to bankroll the show.'

'I'm sure he did,' Reed said, fidgeting with packets of sugar on the table. 'Things change, Detective.'

'I guess he left you out of the big money decisions at this point. So did your uncle Hal. And you probably didn't want any spoilers in case the Kwans were planning to keep you on board.'

David was discreet enough not to argue in front of us, but Reed was ready to leave the table. 'It's what I was trying to explain at lunch, Reed. I didn't quite get the whole story out, but I fully intended to tell you this afternoon.'

'It can wait, David,' he said, standing up. 'I've really got to get back. There's so much to do.'

'Hang on. I'll walk over with you.'

'No thanks, David. I've got a ton of stuff to organize,' Reed said, ready to turn his back on all of us. 'I've got the whole damn thing to run on Monday.'

He was attempting to regain some dignity in front of us by telling us how much was on his plate.

'I understand there's someone from the company putting the exhibition together at the Costume Institute,' Mike said, using the information I had given him about Tiziana Bolt without burning me in front of Reed and David. 'She used to work for your father, I think. Who does she report to now?'

'There's no one from WolfWear working over there,' Reed said.

'An old friend of your father's. Does that ring a bell?'

'Oh, Tiz. Of course,' he said, snapping his fingers. 'Tiziana Bolt, you mean. Yes, yes, an old friend of dad's. She's our liaison to the Met. I guess she'll be taking orders from me from this point on.'

'Good to know,' Mike said.

'Why do you ask?'

'Security at the museum can be pretty sticky. It must have been one of the workers there who told me to talk to Ms Bolt if we needed anything at the Met.'

Reed tapped two fingers on the table. 'You talk to me, Detective. I'm in charge.'

'I hear you,' Mike said.

'About Tanya Root,' I said to Reed. 'Did you know about her? Had you ever met her?'

Reed Savage paused, still tapping his fingertips. 'I'd

heard talk about her. Talk between my father and my uncle. I was aware of some off-the-charts crazy girl who'd made trouble for Wolf, but they never wanted me to mix with her. I never knew she was blood – not to him or to me.'

'Didn't it interest you – on a human level – to find out more?'

'Look, Ms Cooper. I live in London, so there's a lot of things that went down here that nobody talked to me about – especially my father's personal life – and it isn't my way to go looking for trouble.'

'How about if trouble came looking for you?' I asked.

'What do you mean?'

'That if Tanya wasn't making any headway with your father, she might have knocked on your door.'

'That's just it, Ms Cooper. I don't have a door here,' he said. 'Security at the front desk in the office building had strict orders not to let her in.'

I thought for a few seconds before I spoke. 'Exactly how did they do that if no one among you knew her last name?'

Reed Savage didn't flinch. 'She was always Tanya. That's the name she used, every time she showed up in New York. So it was the first trigger for security to stop her, once they entered it in their computer system,' he said. 'You'll have to ask my uncle whether they had a photograph, too, or not. Living and working abroad seems to have saved me from being confronted with Tanya's anger and acting out. RIP, dear sister.'

'Will you be around this weekend?' Mike asked.

'I don't mean to sound rude, but you don't seem to get the magnitude of Monday's event. The future of WolfWear is riding on it,' Reed said. 'I expect I'll be at the office part of the time. We don't have access to Dendur, for rehearsals, till after the museum closes. That's where I'll be in the evenings.'

'Thanks.'

'Are we done?' Reed asked. 'May I get back to work?'

He didn't wait for the answer, but just turned and walked to the front door.

'I guess I let the cat out of the bag,' Mike said to David Kingsley. 'It doesn't sound like there's been full disclosure between you and the Savages.'

'It's a business deal, Detective. Sometimes you need to hold things close to the vest till the handshake that seals it,' David said.

'I hear that you got more than a handshake from Wolf,' Mike said.

'Excuse me?'

'I'm not trying to hurt you, Mr Kingsley,' Mike said, stopping to take a few sips of his coffee. 'Otherwise I would have dropped this little bombshell in front of Reed.'

David fidgeted in his seat. His feet accidentally tangled with mine under the table. 'There's no bombshell.'

'Did you know we spoke with Lily this morning?' Mike said. 'Just over an hour ago?'

From the expression on his face, I'd guess he had no idea.

'You ponied up two mil for Wolf Savage,' Mike said, 'and in exchange for that, the man promised to revise his will.'

David pushed his cup away. 'That's not exactly how it went.'

'You mean that wasn't the deal – to cut Lily and your kids in for more money? Take some of the share away from Reed? Is that the part I got wrong?' Mike asked. 'Or was there something else you were holding close to the vest, like in any good business deal?'

'My plan wasn't to hurt Reed, Detective.'

'Who, then? The charities that will benefit from the estate – if your father-in-law still had any cash left? Or the loyal employees who served him over so many decades?'

'Or the people who'd squeezed Wolf for money all his adult life?' David Kingsley countered. 'Maybe some of them needed to get their fingers out of the pie. We're his family, for God's sake.'

'Did Wolf get the new will done?' I asked, softening the tone of the conversation.

David Kingsley glared at me. He was smart enough to know that we were looking not only for connections to Tanya and to Wolf, but for motives as well.

'Answer the lady,' Mike said.

'I'm not certain.'

'Well, that solves that,' Mike said, sarcasm practically dripping into his coffee cup. 'You can't be the killer because you wouldn't have offed Wolf if he'd gone ahead and made the fix, if he'd cut your family a larger piece of the pie. You'd have nothing to be unhappy about.'

Mercer stepped in with the flip side. 'Unless Wolf reneged on the deal. Maybe he gave you the handshake but then balked when the follow-up came for him to actually execute a new will.'

'Not guilty,' David Kingsley said, smiling at Mike. 'I can't believe you're even talking to me this way.'

'I have a lot of issues, Mr Kingsley. Manners is one of them,' Mike said. 'Deal with it.'

'Why?' Mercer asked. 'Have you got a copy of the will?'

'I'm quite confident that Wolf did just as he promised me he would. I was just giving Reed and Hal the chance to get through next week. I expect to be able to produce the new will shortly.'

'I'm so impressed with your confidence, Mr Kingsley,' Mike said. 'What's that based on?'

'Wolf Savage actually signed a letter for me,' David said, a bit too smugly for my taste. 'A testamentary letter to give to his lawyer – and to his son and brother – in the event of anything happened to him before his will was finalized.'

'You must have really leaned on the old man,' Mike said.

'I didn't have to lean at all. He wanted to do the right thing for Lily. I can show you a copy of it, of course.'

I leaned forward and cocked my head. 'Are you talking about a precatory letter, Mr Kingsley? Is that what you mean?'

'I'm a businessman, Ms Cooper. I'm not a lawyer,' he said. 'It's a letter to Hal and to Reed that tells them exactly what he'd like done for Lily and my kids.'

'In the law, Mr Kingsley, it's called a precatory letter. It's got language that says, "I'm writing to provide you some guidance about what to do upon my death."'

'Just like that. You're right.' He was excited I could acknowledge the formality of the document.

'It probably says something like, "It's my sincere hope that you will carry out my wishes about Lily and her children."'

'That's it, Ms Cooper.'

'I hate to tell you, Mr Kingsley. You might have kept this too close to your vest. You should have gotten some advice about this from a lawyer,' I said, sitting back.

'But – but that's the kind of thing they say.'

'Precatory letters are just that. Letters. Wolf Savage might have "hoped" for something that will never come to be,' I said, putting air quotes around the word 'hoped.' 'These letters are not legally binding documents at all.'

Thirty-four

'Savaged,' Mike said ten minutes later. David Kingsley was gone and Mike was biting into a ham and cheese sandwich. 'I'd say the kid was savaged by the old man.'

'He was savaged by Alex, too, from the sour face he dragged out of here,' Mercer said.

'Good catch, babe,' Mike said. 'How'd you know that predatory stuff?'

'Precatory, not predatory. Law school – basic trusts and estates. There are no formalities to it. It's just a letter, expressing someone's desires to his or her family,' I said. 'A valid will completely overrides something informal like this.'

'Whoa. That could make Kingsley predatory, too,' Mike said. 'I wish I could be there when he tells Lily he screwed up.'

'That's probably already happened by now,' Mercer said. 'These sands keep shifting under all the Savitsky-Savages, don't they?'

It was three o'clock by the time we finished lunch and rehashed what still needed to be done over the weekend.

I pulled a notebook out of my tote. I still liked paper better than an electronic device for my lists and memos.

'Who's looking for Josie LaPorte?' I asked.

'Lieutenant Peterson has a team dedicated to finding her, if she's still in the country.'

'Hotels in Harlem?'

'That's mine,' Mercer said. 'I've got the sketch of Tanya that was done at the morgue. I'll go back over to Hal Savage now to see if security at the office building has a photo of her that's of any value. I'm working tomorrow.'

'Me, too,' Mike said. 'But sneaking Sunday off if the lieutenant lets me – if there are no breaking developments. Jimmy North can cover me so I can take my mother to church.'

'What can I do?' I asked.

'Go back to your ballet class tomorrow morning,' Mike said. 'Hang out with one of your pals in the afternoon.'

'It's like I'm missing out on everything. Will you guys rethink Monday night? Can't I please come with you to the Met?'

'We'll be working, Coop. Don't whine about it anymore, okay?'

'But I'm so much more familiar with the museum than you are. I can get you through the Costume Institute and the area behind Dendur where they'll be staging the show,' I said. 'You should be grateful that I knew about precatory letters and found Tiziana Bolt to get so much good stuff from her and even tracked down the broken button from the hotel room. You guys owe me something.'

'And you'll get it when my night at the museum is over,' Mike said.

'Don't hold your breath.'

'The lieutenant would not be happy with me. It's a chance to see all the interactions, out in public where they can't too easily hide from each other. If we don't find George Kwan at his offices this afternoon, I can do a one-on-one right there.'

'Why don't we split up?' Mercer said. 'I'll double back and find out whether there's a photo and any record of the various surnames Tanya has used, and you try Kwan Enterprises. There aren't all that many hotels in Harlem, so I can jump on that. Talk to you two later.'

Mike and I walked to his car on one of the side streets. The foot traffic was slowing on Friday afternoon, and some of the shops were being closed early by the Sabbath observers who owned them.

We headed uptown on Tenth Avenue and crossed through Central Park on Sixty-Fifth Street.

For the entire ride, we batted around names and opportunities and, as Mike had wisely pointed out, the wavering alliances of the dysfunctional family members.

'Have we drawn the circle too tightly?' I asked.

'Maybe so. Wolf Savage was a man with a lot of enemies, going back decades.'

'Someone might want us to think it's all about the family, especially if the murder had to do with his business plans.'

'No question Tanya got pulled into it, one way or the

other,' Mike said. 'She was so vulnerable to anyone who knew of her existence.'

'Could be, then, she didn't come to New York on her own, but was invited here to be part of the problem, or at least a distraction to her father – and even to her siblings.'

'Here's your choice, Coop. I can drop you at home, or you can wait in the car at Kwan Enterprises.'

'But I can go in with—'

'Let me do this one alone.'

'I'll wait in the car.'

Mike stopped half a block away from the imposing double-wide townhouse that headquartered Kwan Enterprises, between Madison and Park Avenues. There were signs of tight security everywhere. Small cameras were mounted on the wall of the building itself and on light posts along the street. A large SUV with tinted windows was parked directly in front of the offices, and the driver standing at the ready next to it looked like a Bond villain – like Oddjob.

I watched as Mike walked up the front steps and rang the doorbell. I saw him speak into the brass intercom that was affixed to the brick wall.

When the door was opened by an employee, I noticed there was a full-length wrought-iron grate that still separated him from the interior of the building.

He was kept waiting at the entrance for three or four minutes, never once looking back in my direction. Finally, the gentleman behind the grating shook his head, and it was clear Mike was being denied admission to the townhouse.

He descended the steps and turned in the opposite direction from his car. I sat straight up and watched as he walked farther east, turning the corner onto Park Avenue. He was out of my sight.

My phone rang. 'What's this about?' I asked. 'You okay?'

'I'm fine. Just stay where you are, kind of slink down in the seat, and keep your eye on the door of the townhouse.'

'Why?'

'Why does everything have to be "why"? Can't it ever just be "Yes, Mike"?'

'Yes, Mike,' I said. 'I'm all slinked down and my head is covered by the baseball cap that you left on the backseat. Now, tell me what I'm looking for.'

'The security guard who answered the door told me to wait while he checked to see whether George Kwan would see me.'

'I thought the receptionist told us Kwan was out of the country.'

'She did. But I'm not banking on the fact that too many of the people we've talked to lately have told us the truth about anything,' Mike said. 'I could hear Kwan's voice – at least, it sounded just like the man who was screaming that first day we went to talk to people at WolfWear. He must have been in the hall, not far from the door. I heard him tell the security guard to get my name and shield number.'

'Friends in high places, no doubt,' I said. 'What's he going to do – call in a complaint to the commissioner? I know you didn't give him your name.'

'Right. I also didn't want the guy at the door to see me go back to the car and get a plate number off the cameras, so I walked the other way. Wait a good five minutes, then move over into the driver's seat and come pick me up.'

'Will do,' I said. 'Yes, Mike.'

The security guard had watched Mike walk away before closing the front door.

I slid over behind the wheel. The keys were in the ignition. I played two old Smokey Robinson songs on my iPad to make the minutes pass.

I was about to start the car when the townhouse door opened again. The security guard stepped out and looked up and down the street.

It wasn't George Kwan who emerged from the building. It was District Attorney Paul Battaglia.

Thirty-five

'I'm not only slouched down,' I said to Mike, from my cell. 'I'm practically stuffed under the steering wheel.'

'Is he coming your way or mine?'

'His driver picked him up right in front. He pulled up from somewhere behind this car, so unlikely he saw you.'

'Are they gone?'

'Gone. I'll be right there.'

I sat up and turned the key in the ignition, waited for traffic to pass, then drove around the corner to get Mike.

'I'm choosing the drop-me-at-home option,' I said, shimmying back over to the passenger seat to let Mike drive. 'I am so screwed. Curious but screwed.'

'I'll let you out at your apartment. I need to go up to the office and fill Lieutenant Peterson in on things. Stay off the telephone, Coop, and don't go near the bar, okay?'

'Who's the Wolf Savage homicide assigned to? Someone from the DA's Office must be on it with you by now,' I said. 'I've got to apologize for butting in. Tell them all I know.'

'You're safe,' Mike said. 'Trust me. Don't go calling around to all your buddies to find out who's on it.'

'Safe means it's one of my guys on the case.'

'That's why I was so pissed when you showed up this morning. Even with your damn button,' Mike said. 'You have a way of complicating things.'

'I meant to help.'

'It's Ryan Blackmer. More than you need to know, Coop, but maybe you can back off now and leave things to us.'

I let out a deep sigh of relief. Ryan and I worked together well and he distrusted Battaglia almost as much as I did.

'Let me brief Peterson and then I'll come home. We can stay in tonight. I'll pick up some pasta and salad from Primola on my way.'

'Why do you think Paul Battaglia was meeting with George Kwan?' I asked.

'Don't go there.'

'I bet they're huge contributors to his reelection campaign,' I said. 'I bet Kwan wants a favor from Battaglia – like keeping his name out of the murder investigation. Bad for business and all that crap.'

'Ryan and I will have all the answers for you next week. Give it a rest.'

'Ryan can't go up against the boss.'

'But you think you can?'

'I'm already on his shit list. Why put anyone else's job on the line?'

'You're way ahead of yourself, as always.'

'Do you know how much an individual can contribute to a candidate running for DA in New York?' I asked.

'Nope,' Mike said, turning into the driveway in front of my building.

'You can contribute twenty-seven hundred to someone in a presidential race,' I said. 'For Manhattan DA? The limit is forty-four thousand. Can you believe that?'

'That's absurd.'

'I'm sure there's a way – public filings and all that – to find out how much George Kwan has contributed to Battaglia,' I said. 'That could be useful to know.'

'You're going off-the-wall on me again, Coop. You mind your own business and I'll tell Ryan to check it out.'

'What other reason would Kwan and Battaglia have to be together, especially with a homicide investigation under way that has Kwan Enterprises smack in the middle of the players?'

Vinny opened the car door and greeted us. 'Going upstairs, Ms Cooper?'

'Yes, thanks.'

'Draw yourself a steaming hot bath, Coop,' Mike said. 'Gets out all those odd thoughts that bump around in your brain.'

'What is it I'm supposed to say?' I said, walking into the building. '"Yes, Mike." Right?'

'See you in a couple of hours.'

I got upstairs, threw off my coat, took out my notepad, and texted Ryan. 'Call me. Urgent. Home alone.'

'You're too toxic,' he replied five minutes later. He was smart and skilled, with a great sense of humor. 'Need hazmat gear to talk to you.'

'Suit up. Call.'

Ryan Blackmer phoned me ten minutes later. 'I forgive you,' he said.

'You don't even know.'

'Chapman and I just talked.'

'I do owe you an apology. I didn't mean to step all over your case, but there actually wasn't a case until we made it one,' I said. 'So I feel like I'm emotionally invested in this investigation, Ryan. And yes, I'm supposed to be staying chill till I'm back on my feet, but that seems impossible for me to do.'

'I ought to get you one of those exercise wheels – human size – like my gerbils have in their little habitat, Alex. They run off a lot of energy that way. Might be good for you,' he said. 'Good for Chapman, too.'

'Can I tell you everything I know?'

'Don't make me say what I want to say.'

'About this. About my impressions of the family members and the others—'

'Sure you can,' Ryan said. 'Your view is always helpful.'

We talked for about twenty minutes. I went through all the details I had jotted on my notepad.

'Have you seen the boss yet?' I asked.

'Six o'clock tonight. He wants me to come to his office to fill him in.'

'He knows that I was at the morgue with Mike and

Mercer,' I said. 'He's already confronted me about that. I don't want that to come as a surprise to you.'

'Thanks for telling me.'

'What he doesn't know is that I showed up unexpectedly at the Savage offices this morning. I mean that even Mike and Mercer had no idea I was coming. I was trying to catch up with them before they started doing reinterviews, because I thought I'd found an important evidentiary link—'

'The button? Chapman told me about the button.'

'But they had already started, Ryan. So I was there again today, after the boss told me to back off. I saw Lily and then Hal, and was still there when Reed Savage and David Kingsley came back from lunch,' I said. My instincts were to protect the detectives. 'I mean, Mike directed me to keep my mouth shut, but there were some legal issues that popped into the questioning – like offshore trading and precatory letters – so I have to admit I got more involved than I planned.'

'You might need two exercise wheels, kid. That's a pretty busy day,' Ryan said. 'And it was all before you saw the boss coming out of Kwan Enterprises.'

'I'm so glad Mike told you that, too. You're one of the guys who had my back when Battaglia and the Reverend Hal situation came to light – right before my – my . . .' I stuck on the word 'kidnapping.'

'I know what you're saying. I know when it was.'

'You don't need to fight *my* battles, Ryan. Just keep your eyes open so you don't walk into quicksand,' I said.

'And tonight, if Battaglia tells you to back off George Kwan for any reason, just promise you'll call me.'

'No can do, Alexandra Cooper.'

'But you have to.'

'I have strictest orders from Chapman,' Ryan Blackmer said. 'No further case communications with you.'

Thirty-six

I was still soaking in the tub when Mike got home.

'How cold is that water?' he asked. 'Because the food is piping hot.'

'I'll join you in a minute,' I said, getting out of the bath.

I dried off and wrapped a silk robe around me. Mike had turned on the TV in the den and plated our dinner. *Jeopardy!* was on, but he had muted it until the final answer was revealed.

'For once you followed instructions,' he said. 'No alcohol. Relaxing hot bath.'

'Yes, Mike.'

'Now I'm going to hear that – those two words – for the rest of my life?'

'That's what you asked for. You want me tepid, like my bathwater.'

'You sound hostile, babe. What happened since I left?'

'Not hostile. Just flat.'

'Let's have a drink,' Mike said. 'That'll unflatten you.'

I curled up in a corner of the sofa. Mike poured me a generous scotch, for a change, and sat beside me.

'You smell good,' he said, pressing his nose against the side of my head. He kissed me over and over again, working his way down my clean hair to nibble on my ear.

'Won't help,' I said.

'How about if I turn off the television and we go inside for a while. Will that help?'

'Could make things worse.'

'In the bedroom?' Mike asked, reaching beneath the silk panel and stroking my thigh. 'That would be worse than this?'

'I talked to Ryan,' I said.

'I begged you not to call anyone,' he said, removing his hand and slapping it against his chest. 'For your own good, babe.'

'I can't believe you told him not to talk to me,' I said, looking straight ahead and drinking some of my Dewar's.

'It's Ryan's case. You'd be livid if anyone put his or her nose into your business.'

'Tepid. That's all I am. Lacking enthusiasm, as the dictionary defines the word. I've been reduced to tepid. I couldn't be livid if I tried.'

'Then don't try,' Mike said. 'Besides, my chicken parm is getting cold.'

Mike unmuted the TV. Alex Trebek was about to introduce the final answer.

'Tonight's category is ASTRONOMY. It's astronomy,' Trebek said.

'We might as well pass,' Mike said. 'Too bad Mercer isn't here. It's his kind of subject.'

'Show me your twenty bucks.' I was pushing my Caesar salad around the plate. I was more interested in drinking than eating.

'I'm good for it.'

The contestants had written wagers on the electronic slates on their podia, and then the final answer flashed onto the screen.

SHE WAS THE FIRST WOMAN PROFESSIONAL ASTRONOMER

'I hate when this happens,' Mike said. 'Some blatantly feminist question disguised as a serious subject.'

'What's not serious about feminism? It wasn't all that long ago when women were not allowed to try felony cases in Manhattan's criminal courts. No lady prosecutors in the office,' I said. 'What would you have done for amusement back then?'

'I'd have found you somewhere.'

'I'm not sure our paths would ever have crossed,' I said, tousling his thick, dark hair. 'Want to double down on the answer?'

'Lady astronomer? Nope. Not Venus,' Mike said, 'not Pluto. I hate that you know the answer to this.'

None of the male contestants came up with it either.

'Who was Maria Mitchell?' I asked.

'Who?'

'She discovered a comet in the 1840s, not a planet. Miss Mitchell's Comet,' I said. 'First faculty member at Vassar College when it opened its doors. First woman astronomer. It's the kind of thing they drilled into us at Wellesley.'

'Here I thought you were just interested in black holes in the galaxy. Dark matter. All you've been lately is dark.'

'I'm trying to get back, Mike. There's nothing I'd like better.'

'I'll bet another twenty dollars I can change your mood.'

'Sometimes you do make me laugh, despite myself,' I said. 'I'll do the dishes and—'

'No dishes. I'll take care of that later,' he said, pulling me off the sofa and kissing me, long and deep. 'I need a shower. That Bolognese sauce is sticky.'

'I'm clean,' I said, ready to be romanced. 'Don't waste time when you could be cheering me up with some TLC, right in the bedroom.'

'You missed a spot behind your left ear,' Mike said, running his finger down my spine. 'And you didn't scrub your back. You'd be lost without me.'

He took me by the hand and led me into the master bath suite. I let him run the shower as hot as he could stand it, slipped out of my robe, and stepped in behind him.

He turned around, took my face in his hands and held it up toward the showerhead. 'I want you to feel safe again, babe. I want you to wash out all the toxins, all the poisonous venoms that have been coursing through your brain.'

'I feel safe when I'm here, Mike. I feel safe when I'm in your arms.' I tucked in against his chest and held him tight.

'This is where we'll be, then.'

'You think I've lost it, don't you?'

We both looked like we'd been caught in a torrential rainstorm, but neither of us moved from beneath the downpour.

Mike's answer to my question was another kiss.

'If you stay with me,' I said, 'I know I can make it back from this.'

'I'm in it for the long haul, kid. That's why I want you to see the shrink.'

I nodded. 'I'll leave a message for her tomorrow.'

Mike picked up the washcloth, soaped it, and ran it along my arms and body. I stepped out, toweled myself dry for the second time in an hour, and walked into my bed, pulling back the covers and snuggling between the sheets.

We made love, slowly and gently, for the next hour. I hadn't felt this secure, this calm, since before my abduction.

It was the beginning of the weekend, too, and it promised a sense of normalcy that helped to relax me.

We watched an old movie – a classic western called *Stagecoach* – instead of the murder mysteries that were our usual fare, and when it was over, Mike went into the den to refresh the ice in our drinks and let me finish the evening with a nightcap.

I slept well for the first time all week, and when morning came we braced ourselves for the cold and walked up to the corner for breakfast at PJ Bernstein. I was hungry for a change, and went whole hog with scrambled eggs, crisp bacon, and a toasted bagel.

I had packed a tote bag with my dance clothes in it. When we finished eating and I had worked most of the *Times* Saturday crossword, Mike put me in a taxi to send me over to the studio on the West Side where I'd taken lessons most Saturdays since I graduated from law school.

'What are you doing after class?' he asked, closing the cab door.

'I'm coming directly back here, tackling the paper mess that has grown in my home office over the last month, reading a novel – something dense and Victorian – and waiting for you.'

'I'm meeting Mercer. He didn't get very far on the hotel search yesterday. I'll be home in time for dinner.'

I had missed so many ballet classes while I was on the Vineyard that it felt especially good to stretch and bend and plié to the soothing music. Acquaintances expressed their concerns about me in the dressing room, but the nonverbal setting of the actual studio – the exercises at the barre and on the floor – made it a wonderful place for me to be.

I took my time dressing. I wasn't going out for coffee with any of my classmates, so I kind of lagged behind.

When I got home, I got right to work reading and filing the mail and bills that had piled up. It felt good to purge myself of paperwork I'd been avoiding and to clean my nest of some of its clutter.

I wasn't sure whether it was Mike's convincing display

of affection the night before or the prospect of having to engage with a psychiatrist in the upcoming week, but I was optimistic about reentering the kind of lifestyle that had seemed so foreign to me as I wallowed in my self-absorption.

I was able to concentrate on the plot line of a book, keeping an occasional eye on the crawl of the local news network. I hadn't lost my desire to know whether there were any developments in the two death investigations and how the Battaglia–Blackmer meeting went, but I had a stronger grip of control on my curiosity.

Mike was home by seven P.M. He told me that he had nothing to fill me in on. I told him about my healthily uneventful day and how much pleasure the peace and quiet had given me.

We braved a light flurry of snow to walk to the Beach Café for dinner. My intense morning workout had left me yearning for a tasty cheeseburger and fries. The neighborhood go-to for comfort food and friendly service never failed, and we even got through an entire dinner without any mention of crime.

I skipped hard liquor in favor of a nice bottle of Cabernet.

We took the long way around back to the apartment, strolling arm in arm and stopping to throw snowballs at each other on a patch of ground where the snow had stuck.

Mike took several phone calls out of my presence, in the den, but even that didn't set me on edge as it usually did.

I took an Ativan to ensure another good night's sleep, and closed my eyes while Mike was still watching a college football game.

On Sunday morning, we got up early and drove to Brooklyn so we could take Mike's mother – whom I adored – to church. It was only the second time since we'd been together that we did it, but it was obvious that she was happy to have us both beside her.

The Catholic service, rich in symbolism, was a reminder of how long it had been since I had gone to synagogue.

After Mass, we took Mrs Chapman for lunch at her favorite restaurant, hugged her while she implored both of us to 'stay safe' – her mantra – and came back to the apartment to spread out on the living-room floor with the Sunday *Times*.

My next-door neighbor had invited us over for dinner, as he often did. He loved to cook and it was so easy to pad down the hall and come back home without venturing into the cold.

I was still happy when Mike left in the morning. He understood me well enough to know what to tell me about his cases and when. I was still antsy about it, but I was trying to regain my balance. I told him I'd keep my plans for my quarterly dental cleaning at eleven and get back into working out at the gym.

I knew that he and Mercer were going to the Met that evening. I recognized that I had no business finding my own route to get in, but I remained jealous of their opportunity – not just to see the show in that setting, which would be lost on both of them, but to watch the interaction among all the Savage satellites.

I sat down at the table with a second cup of coffee and the morning papers. The Wolf Savage/Tanya Root stories were off the front pages, at last. That usually made the work of police and prosecutors much easier.

I had the television on in my bedroom as I dressed in jeans and a sweater for my hour in the dental chair. I was pulling on knee socks and boots, although the forecast was for an unseasonably warm and sunny day.

'At the Metropolitan Museum of Art,' the off-location reporter said, 'preparations are under way for a spectacular evening at the Temple of Dendur. You can see there, through the glass-enclosed northern wing of the Met, that thousands of dollars in flowers – flown in from Holland overnight – are being delivered for display as we speak. Ironically, the fashion extravaganza conceived by Wolf Savage is now a tribute to his life as well.'

The camera then focused in on the reporter herself.

'Meanwhile, I'm live in front of the Madison Avenue North, a small hotel on East 128th Street in Harlem, not far from the famed Apollo Theater.'

She gestured over her shoulder, where yellow crime-scene tape kept her on the sidewalk opposite the hotel, unable to get any closer.

'We got word this morning that NYPD detectives arrived here an hour ago with a search warrant. A longtime resident of the building next door claims that the police believe that Tanya Root – the estranged daughter of the legendary designer Wolf Savage – was staying here at the time of her murder. Police have asked for hotel records, access to the room the young woman occupied, and any other information that might be relevant to her disappearance and death. They're combing the neighborhood in case any locals had knowledge of Tanya and her companions.'

I speed-dialed Mike faster than the reporter could get off the air.

'Stay tuned for breaking news,' she said, signing off.

Of course the message went to his voicemail.

'I didn't think you'd pick up for me,' I said, pacing around my bedroom while I talked into the phone. 'I didn't think after all that coddling this weekend and even though I've agreed – at least I agreed on Friday morning – that I was going to see your shrink, that you'd think it important enough to take my call.'

I wasn't anywhere near as in control of myself as I had tried to convince myself that I was just the day before. Everything to do with solving this case, which seemed to me to be my path to an entry back into my old familiar self, put me on edge.

'Do you really think I deserve to get my updates from a rookie stringer on the street, Detective Chapman? Don't leave me hanging on this one, I beg of you. Don't turn your back on me now.'

Thirty-seven

The dental hygienist took my cell phone away from me while she scraped and cleaned my teeth. It wouldn't have mattered. There were no messages when I got out of the chair.

I walked home, fifteen blocks, knowing that if I kept a fast pace it would allow me to blow off some of the steam that was gathering inside me.

I called the office number of Mike's psychiatrist. She must have been in session. I told her that I wanted to see her and asked if she had any time today. I wasn't as tethered to reality as I needed to be.

I was home by one P.M. and eating a yogurt while I watched local news.

The same reporter had pushed herself close to the front of the pack. Her tenacity had paid off.

'An hour ago,' she said, 'detectives emerged from the hotel with several boxes that appeared to contain ledgers of some sort – perhaps a guest register.'

The footage showed Mike following two squad members

holding large boxes. He was gloved and carrying a green plastic garbage bag.

'Rumors are circulating that Tanya – who stayed here several times throughout the last three years – does not actually go by the last name "Root". We hope to have more for you on that by tomorrow.

'She was known to be a jazz aficionado, and liked the proximity of the Madison to the Apollo Theater.'

There was always a desk clerk to squeal, in every hotel in the world, if the price was right.

'Police are planning to release sketches of the three males – two African American and one white man – in whose company she was seen last month,' the reporter said.

This was the first mention of any male suspects of color since the case had come to my attention.

'The two are thought to be acquaintances of the white male, with whom she drove off around the time she was last seen at the hotel.'

An older man or a younger one, I wondered.

I called Vickee Eaton's number at headquarters. The press office would know as much as any of the detectives, and Vickee had no reason to shut me down.

'Sorry,' some nameless phone-answering police officer said. 'Detective Eaton's out in the field. May I have a callback name?'

I hung up the phone.

I tried Catherine Dashfer, who was keeping my seat warm at the DA's Office. She couldn't possibly avoid me by not taking the call – all of our phone numbers showed as UNKNOWN when incoming.

'Hello?'

'It's me. Don't hang up.'

'Alex? Are you all right?' Catherine was among my closest friends: wise, loyal, and tough as steel.

'Basically.'

''Cause what I'm hearing—'

'I'm seeing the NYPD's psychiatrist this week,' I said. 'I should be cleared to come back after the holidays. You can fly off to Tuscany for a vacation in January, I promise you. I'll be back at my desk by then.'

'Take your time, Alex. It's even nicer over there in the spring.'

'Any chance you can slip out for an hour this afternoon and meet me?'

'That would mean they'd be stuck looking for a permanent filler for me if I get spotted hanging out with you,' Catherine said. 'I'd be safer planning a rendezvous with Charles Manson.'

'Did Battaglia send out a memo about me? An AMBER Alert?'

'You know he's way too smart to do that,' she said. 'A few of us got called in, one by one. Nothing in writing. No paper trail. Just an understated comment or two about how you needed space to get your head together.'

'I don't want any more space,' I said. 'I want my life back. I want my friends, but most of the people I want to see are employed by the man who's making me persona non grata.'

'I tell you what,' Catherine said. 'I'll put something together for Friday night, okay? Come to my place and I'll cook, and I'll get as many of the gang together as I can.'

'Sweet,' I said. If I had to hold out until Friday, I'd do it. 'Will you throw Ryan in?'

'Alexandra Cooper! That'll be the last thing Ryan does, okay? Count on it,' she said. 'You can be sure Battaglia walked all over him with golf shoes on, in regard to Ryan's contact with you.'

I took a few deep breaths.

'Is everything okay with you and Mike?' Catherine asked.

'It's fine. I thought we had a great weekend,' I said. 'Next thing I see, he's on the news, carrying evidence out of a hotel that I know nothing about.'

'As it should be.'

'If anything changes – I mean, if you get a real itch to see me, Catherine – just call and come on up.'

'You know I miss you, Alex. If I get that particular itch, I'll need to buy a disguise to visit.'

'I didn't mean to put you in a bad spot. I'm going a little stir-crazy, and since all my buddies cut me off it's really hard.'

'Why not go back to the Vineyard?' Catherine asked. 'You love it there.'

'I probably will,' I said. 'Let you know before Friday.'

Things were so bad that my friends from the DA's Office thought they had to disguise themselves in order to visit the apartment. They must have been afraid that reports of their contact with me would get back to Paul Battaglia.

I fiddled with overdue correspondence to out-of-towners who'd heard about my ordeal, and thought about cleaning out one of my closets. That was too daunting a project.

I kept going back to Catherine and her offhanded comment about disguises.

I looked in my contacts for the telephone number of Joan's mother, who lived in an enormous duplex on the East River.

'Mrs Stafford?' I said quite cheerfully into my cell. 'It's Alexandra Cooper.'

'Darling, how are you?' she asked. 'My Joanie told me you might call.'

'I'm doing much better now, thank you.'

'I haven't seen you in ages.'

'My bad. But I hear you're doing very well,' I said. 'Did Joan tell you what I'm calling about?'

'She did. Will you come spend a little time with me this afternoon?'

'I'd be delighted.'

Someone who actually wanted to see me. How refreshing, I thought. And she happened to be in possession of part of the disguise I needed to get me into the Temple of Dendur.

'I've had that lovely dress taken out of its wrappings

and steamed for you,' Mrs Stafford said. 'You're still thinner than Joan, I'm sure. But you'll take up the difference in your height.'

I had abandoned all thoughts of crashing the Savage show at the Met that evening in the aftermath of Mike's tough-love talk with me. But now my paranoia overwhelmed me. It seemed that everyone had abandoned me to my own devices, and I was mad at the thought of being discarded by them all.

'I'll be over at five, Mrs Stafford. I'm trying to surprise some of my friends.'

'I love conspiracies, dear Alex. Your secret will be safe with me.'

Thirty-eight

I called Ty D'Auria, the owner of Citadel, a top-tier security firm built by a brilliant ex-detective who had cornered the business for the most important events in Manhattan at all the prime locations – specializing in events featuring art, antiques, jewels, and fashion.

Ty had promised to let Mike and Mercer in to pose as part of his staff tonight. I asked for the same privilege – I didn't want a ticket to sit on the edge of the runway – and the assurance that he wouldn't even tell them that I might be mingling with the ritzy crowd.

Done. I simply had to present my office ID at the basement service entrance and one of the guys from Citadel would walk me up to Dendur.

I never used much makeup, but I knew enough to put on a layer of instant bronzer to hide the pallor that the last month of my life had cast over my face. That suntan would fool anyone running into me. I put on rouge, dark eyeliner, and thick black mascara. I did a double-take in the mirror to make sure it was really me, and I smiled back at the woman who appeared to look so trashy.

Mike texted me midafternoon: *Tied up. Nothing to report.*

That was an oxymoronic message. Too busy to call me, but no news?

Everything seemed to fuel my instability. I could feel myself spinning out of control but also felt helpless to stop it.

I put on a baseball cap and my ski jacket, lowered my head on my way past the doormen so the makeup didn't freak them out, and walked out of my building carrying a sail bag with my high heels and pantyhose.

Mrs Stafford's co-op was ten blocks north and a few east of mine. There was a store along the way called Ricky's – part of a chain in the city – that carried every conceivable product related to skin, nails, and hair. I zigged and zagged on the avenues until I found the local branch.

'How may I help you?' the salesgirl asked.

'I'm looking for a wig.'

'Follow me. Could be your lucky day.'

'It hasn't felt like it until you said that.'

'Well, we've got a whole section in the back that's on sale. Half-price. All the leftover wigs and costumes from Halloween.'

'That's great,' I said. 'I love a bargain.'

'Tell me what you're looking for. Color? Style?'

'I was hoping you'd have something sort of flapperish, if you know what I mean? Like the really good-looking sister on *Downton Abbey*,' I said.

'That was huge this year. All that upstairs and downstairs stuff. The show is so popular I can't imagine what people are going to do now that it's over,' she said, looking back at me. 'You want a blond one? Like your own hair but shorter?'

'Black, actually. My dress is black.'

'You want the wavy look or a straight sort of bob?'

Once we reached the overstock area, the salesgirl reached into a huge cardboard box and came out with a handful of wigs.

'That one,' I said, pointing to a short black number. 'My hair is naturally curly. I want to get away from that look for a night.'

'I can understand,' she said. 'Ever done this before?'

'A wig? No, no. I haven't.'

'It's real quiet in here. If this is for tonight and you want me to help you get it on right, I'm happy to do that.'

'Very kind of you,' I said. 'I accept.'

'So with tax, half price off, the wig is twenty-seven dollars. Is that okay?'

'Couldn't be better,' I said.

My adrenaline was pumping. After all these weeks of being the new, confused, and always-nervous Alex Cooper, I was going to escape into a totally different identity.

'I'll take off the tags and we can go over to the mirror against the wall,' the salesgirl said. 'You okay if I sell you a tight net too? They're only a few bucks, and it will keep your own hair in place much better. Looks way more natural.'

We were both laughing as the twentysomething pulled all the wisps of my blond hair under the netting. I faced her and bent my head down, and after she fitted the wig in place I straightened up and turned back to the mirror.

'Awesome!' she said. 'You're not the same woman I was talking to a few minutes ago. I bet you could fool your own mother.'

'That's thanks to you.'

'You just need a headband. I swear I'm not trying to pad your bill, ma'am, but if you look at the photograph on the plastic bag, you'll see that with this kind of wig – this 1920s look – you really need a headband with it.'

By the time I walked out of the store, I had a completely new air about me. The cubic zirconia band that fit across my forehead and under my bob was temporarily tucked in with my shoes and pantyhose.

I was about to cross the avenue and approach Mrs Stafford's building. There was a fancy liquor store on the near corner, so I stopped in and bought a bottle of twelve-year-old Macallan. The single malt, served neat, was her favorite drink.

The doorman was my first test. He didn't recognize me and seemed startled even after I gave my name.

The door was open and I walked in. Mrs Stafford was in the library, catching the last of the afternoon sun in an armchair against the window.

'It can't be you, Alexandra!' she said. 'What's happened to all those golden ringlets?'

I leaned down to embrace her warmly. 'They're somewhere under here.'

'You know how I love drama, but I'm glad you warned me you were coming.'

We talked for half an hour, a bit about my recovery, but she had a keen sense of understanding, so mostly about Joan and her husband, and plans for Thanksgiving and the Christmas holidays.

'Do you mind if I get dressed now?' I asked, after a respectable period of time had passed.

'You'll find everything you need in the guest room,' she said. 'Leave that awful canvas bag here with your ski jacket. You can always pass by here tomorrow to pick them up.'

'Not to worry. I'll drop all my things with my doorman on my way to the museum. All I need is my ID and cab fare home. He'll hang on to my key and my bag and my cell,' I said, making my way upstairs to the guest room.

I'd have the entire security staff looking over things. I wouldn't even have need of the phone.

I had spent many nights in the guest room when Joan and I were much younger. It was easy to make myself at home.

I put on the underpinnings and then stepped in to the drop-waisted, low-cut straight dress. It was an elegant black chiffon fabric with a black silk bodice. The Savage Couture label was intact, and a small black wolf's head – the ubiquitous logo – was worked into the lavish design of bugle beads that covered the garment, front and back.

The skirt was short and the strips of cloth that shaped it gave it what designers called the 'car wash' effect – like the strips that smacked an automobile's surface to dry it as it passed through the machine.

I took a couple of twirls in front of the mirror. The dress was frisky and fun, and there was no sign of Alexandra Cooper anywhere in sight. It was a hell of a lot more chic – and easier to move around in – than the floor-length toga I had wasted my money on.

I went downstairs to the library, where Mrs Stafford was engrossed in the day's *Wall Street Journal*.

'What a hoot,' she said, standing up to turn me around. 'I'd love to come with you, Alexandra. You're going to have a grand evening.'

'From your mouth, Mrs Stafford.'

She walked over to her desk and picked up a large suede pouch. 'My Joanie was right,' she said, dumping the contents of the bag into her hand. 'You do need pearls with that number.'

'Don't be mad,' I said, holding my arms straight out and shaking my head. 'I'd never go anywhere with a piece of your jewelry. You can't do that.'

'Be still, Alex. It's my travel jewelry. No one needs to know,' she said. 'They're fakes, but good-looking fakes. The real pearls are in the vault.'

'I don't trust you entirely on that,' I said. 'I know how generous you are with all your things.'

'Well, you'll just have to trust me,' she said, walking over to me and doubling the long strand around my neck. 'You look naked without them.'

I kissed her on both cheeks.

'I can't have you being naked in public, can I?' she said, taking her seat again.

'Then we'll have to toast to my coming out – as whoever this is.'

'Oh, just be Joan. Joan Stafford. Everyone will be confused, but it's just one evening.'

I had brought the bottle of scotch downstairs with me. 'Still your favorite?' I asked, holding it up for her to see.

'Divine. Use those glasses on the shelf behind the desk.'

I opened the bottle and poured us each a healthy snort of Macallan. I carried her glass to her.

'Cheers, Mrs Stafford,' I said. 'You're the best.'

'Courage, Alexandra. That was always my father's toast,' she said. I knew that she was thinking of my current life circumstances, not about her father at all. 'You must always have courage.'

Thirty-nine

The yellow cab dropped me on Fifth Avenue at Eighty-First Street, to the left of the grand staircase and directly in front of the ground-level service entrance I'd been directed to use.

It was 6:35. Some of the three hundred invited guests had already started making their way up the red-carpeted steps into the museum for the cocktail hour in the Costume Institute that preceded the Savage fashion show.

Security must have been in place long before the doors opened. Mike had texted me while I was dressing at Mrs Stafford's, telling me that Citadel had supplied him and Mercer with rented tuxedos to take their places among the team.

I had replied, 'Nothing to report either. Visiting a friend. Bored to tears.' Two could play this game as well as one.

I glanced around but no one else was headed in the same direction. I shivered as I stood outside the entrance and phoned the head of the security team.

The door was opened by an ex-cop in a tux, who tried

to make the connection between the photo on my DA's ID and the look I presented in person. I recognized him from the courthouse, but my name didn't mean anything to him.

'If you say so, Ms Cooper,' he joked, handing me back my ID. 'Just don't make off with any of the van Goghs, okay?'

'You've got a deal.'

'Want me to take you over to the Costume Institute?'

'No, thanks,' I said. 'I know my way.'

'Take this, though,' he said, handing me a laminated Citadel ID card. 'I know you're not going to spoil that outfit by wearing it, but it gives you access to anyplace you want to go in the museum.'

'Thanks so much,' I said. 'Mind if I borrow your shoulder?'

I leaned on the cop while I slipped off my high-heeled shoe and stuck the Citadel card and my ID under the sole of my foot, where the twenty-dollar bill I carried for the cab ride home was already resting comfortably.

'Good to go.' I said, giving him a grin as I took off.

The last thing I wanted was to call attention to myself by showing up accompanied by a member of the security team.

The lower level of the museum was dead quiet. It had been cordoned off so that partygoers weren't free to roam through the vast galleries stocked with centuries of art treasures.

The route I had to take was circuitous. It led me up

one of the large interior staircases to the Greek and Roman wing, where I tiptoed through the collection of priceless classical art. It felt almost illegal to be let loose alone there. The lighting was low and the corridors were practically dark.

I had seen the black-figured Grecian vases and grave reliefs scores of times, as I had marveled at the bronze Roman portrait busts that had survived so many sackings and so much pillaging through ancient times.

I took a right turn at the two huge wall paintings that had been saved from villas on the slopes of Mount Vesuvius. From there it was a straight shot through gallery after gallery to the Great Hall.

I could hear lots of noise as I got closer to the main entrance. Tchaikovsky was being piped into the large space, which was dotted with six-foot-high antique urns loaded with flowers. At the moment, there seemed to be more coat-checkers, waiters, and waitresses than there were fashionistas and invitees.

Security was tight.

Tiz had told me that every ticket had to be scanned before the invitees were allowed to enter. There was a black market for fake tickets with bar codes that looked good to the customer but wouldn't get the holder past the front door.

I'd read stories about samples from upscale lines being taken by thieves who'd somehow gotten in and literally could steal a collection before the models ever stepped on the runway. Jewels from Tiffany and Harry Winston and

Van Cleef were on loan to make the shows sparkle, and they had a way of disappearing, too. In this setting, keeping trespassers from sneaking off into the rest of the museum was imperative.

I liked seeing security everywhere. It made me feel safe.

The stairs down to the Costume Institute were lined with waiters, each holding out a small silver tray. The choices seemed to be sparkling water and champagne. I still had a buzz on from the Macallan I'd sipped with Mrs Stafford, so I descended without a drink.

The installation of *Savage Style* had been completed sometime after my drop-in on Friday afternoon. Tiziana Bolt had gotten the job done, with whomever Reed Savage had assigned to help her. All of the mannequins had been posed in a different attitude, and each one, I noticed as I passed through the rooms, was dressed in clothes of a particular period, in chronological order.

Every woman I passed was wearing something Savage as well. It seemed to be obligatory to acknowledge outfits that were well known from a collection. One woman gave me a nod, asking, 'Twenty-twelve? Well done, young lady,' while another stopped me to say, 'I've got that one in emerald green. Mine shows the beading much better.'

I entered the last gallery, a cul-de-sac in which everyone who preceded me was making a U-turn to get out.

My hand flew to my mouth for an instant. My first test of the evening was directly ahead of me. Tiz was wrapping a long silk scarf, trimmed with fringe, around the neck of a mannequin whose scoop-necked gown left too much of her bare.

Standing beside her, whispering in her ear, was Hal Savage himself.

Tiz was striking. She was wearing black silk lounging pants that accentuated her long legs, and over them a bright geometrically patterned top – it must have been a season when Wolf Savage did his best to knock off Pucci – that clung to her flat chest. Her spiked hair had been gelled to hold it in place, and she was tastefully made up to fit in with the anticipated guests of this high-end fashion scene.

Like all the other men, Hal wore a tux. I could see the ruby-eyed wolf-head cufflinks peeking out from the end of his sleeve as he lifted a champagne flute while he talked to Tiz.

As I approached them – ready to try out my disguise in hopes of overhearing something useful – I studied the framed magazine clippings on the wall that curved around the gallery. They featured the collections at the time they'd been on the market. Hal stopped speaking.

He turned to engage me. 'I hope you're enjoying the exhibition, young lady.'

I was afraid to speak. So far, neither one of them showed a glimmer of recognition at my physical appearance. I had met Tiz only once, but I had been in Hal's presence three times in the last week.

I nodded at him and smiled, turning my back to them both to read the magazine copy describing the 2015 show.

'I see you've got your favorite Savage style on, luv,' Tiz said. 'Nice of you to be here.'

I was boxed into a corner with nothing to do but swivel and face them. She hadn't made me, I didn't think. She was just being polite.

'Brava,' I said, as softly as I could speak.

'Sorry?' Hal said, cupping his hand to his ear.

'She said, "brava", luv. Now, let her enjoy the evening.'

I kept walking until I reached the exit. On my way up the stairs I grabbed a glass of champagne. The flutes were only half-full, so I threw it back and left the empty with a waiter standing on the top step.

I had passed the first test, restoring my confidence and propelling me forward to the larger stage.

Young museum workers in black sheaths were pointing the way in to the northern wing of the Met. They had clipboards with names and seat numbers for each of the guests. The most valuable real estate was always in the front row on each side of the runway, and on the far end of it, so nothing obstructed the view of the models or the clothing.

The crowd was thickening as it got closer to show time.

I spotted more than a dozen celebrities, dressed by the Savage Couture team, no doubt, flawlessly coiffed and styled. Ladies who appeared regularly in the *New York Social Diary* were scattered throughout the perfectly lighted room like so many totems of Wolf Savage, emblems of his enduring style.

Some of the security guards had earpieces and seemed to

be receiving instructions about who to keep their eyes on. Others were obviously on their own, scanning the growing crowd and moving among the visitors from time to time.

Once I had taken a few steps into the glass-walled gallery that offered breathtaking views into Central Park, I heard the recording that had been created for the occasion. Chalk up another few hundred thousand dollars for the cost, as I immediately added in the fee for the recognizable voice of the actor speaking the lines.

'Welcome to the Temple of Dendur – and to an exhilarating evening showcasing the brilliant designs of Wolf Savage.'

Usually, the exhibits and even the narrations of the large shows were spoken by an anonymous voice – the VOG, or Voice of God, as programs announced it. This time, it was unmistakably Morgan Freeman, inviting me to join him in the spectacular space.

'You have just entered the largest exhibit in the Metropolitan Museum of Art,' Freeman's disembodied voice explained. 'This complete stone building, dismantled and removed from its endangered location within Egypt, was shipped here in more than six hundred crates, with an aggregate weight of eight hundred tons. It is surrounded by a reflecting pool, whose waters represent the Nile River.'

I stayed to the far right of the water – the wide moat that separated Dendur from the east side of the room.

'Egyptian temples represented, in their design and decoration, a variety of religious and mythological concepts,' Freeman went on. I listened as I walked the perimeter of the room, taking in all the faces, still wondering if there would be any frisson of dissension among the fractured branches of the Savage family.

'Above the temple entrance are images of the sun disk and outspread wings of Horus, the sky god. The two columns on the porch rise toward the sky like tall bundles of papyrus stalks, bound with lotus blossoms.'

I saw Calvin Klein, stopping to talk with two women who must once have been runway models, and thought it was very decent of him to show up to honor one of his competitors.

'We invite you to wander through the temple,' Freeman said in his seductive baritone, 'and note that the man depicted in the traditional regalia of a pharaoh is none other than Caesar Augustus of Rome. As ruler of Egypt in 15 BC, Augustus had many temples erected in Egyptian style, honoring their deities.'

I turned, and at the actor's suggestion, crossed over the water on the stone walkway that led into the temple. I was stopped by a guard – well muscled and well dressed, with a discreet *C* for Citadel button pin on his lapel. 'You can't come in right now,' he said. 'The principals are lining up for the show.'

I retraced my steps and continued around the outside of the grand room. I knew there had to be a larger staging area because of the number of models appearing on the runway. Despite the great size of this wing, not even a third of them could have fit in between the ancient structure and the thoroughly modern guests.

Halfway around the room and headed to the door through which I'd entered, I could see the ramp that had been created to give the team an adjacent space in which to prep for the show. The museum signs mounted on the wall were arrows that pointed out, from the back of Dendur to the American Art wing and to Arms and Armor.

When Morgan Freeman completed his audio tour of the surroundings, the tape looped over and started again. 'Welcome to the Temple of Dendur.'

I had a bird's-eye view of the runway – from the rear – as I stood against the window with my back to the park. The folding chairs were five rows deep.

Now that I had run into Hal Savage and Tiziana Bolt – although I had no idea what they had been discussing – I was scouring the floor for others I knew. I was most anxious to get a fix on Mike and Mercer before either of them got a fix on me.

In the fifth row, about fifty feet away from me, were two dark-skinned women, one much older than the other. It took me a few seconds to focus on who they were – one of them looked familiar to me – and then it struck me.

The younger one was Wanda Beston, the housekeeper at the Silver Needle who had found the body of Wolf Savage. I remembered that he had been fond of her – respectfully so – and that he had invited her to bring her mother, who was a seamstress, to the show.

I started to work my way toward the two women, fighting

the incoming flow of invitees who were being directed to take their seats. I got directly behind them before I leaned in and spoke.

'Ms Beston,' I said, looking her outfit over from top to bottom, 'there's something I need to ask you.'

She looked back at me questioningly. 'Who are you?'

'I met you at the Silver Needle,' I said. 'My name is Alex Cooper, and I'm the woman who was with the two detectives who were questioning you in Mr Savage's suite.'

'You don't look at all familiar,' she said, putting a protective hand on her mother's arm.

'I'm – I'm undercover,' I said. 'I can get my ID out for you.'

The announcer ordered everyone to sit down. I saw Anna Wintour walk in to take her seat in the center row, flanked by two security guards, one of whom was Mercer Wallace.

She had no handbag or evening purse. Only the cell phone with which she would snap photographs of any garments that won her approval.

Wanda Beston and I were both nervous. 'I was with that detective, see him? You talked about the Great Migration and how slave uniforms were the first things mass-produced in the Garment District.'

That factoid confirmed my ID better than a photograph could have. She exhaled and said that she remembered.

'I'm so glad Wolf Savage kept his promise to have you here,' I said to her, in a whisper. 'Is this your mother beside you?'

She held her forefinger up to her mouth to shush me as she said, 'Yes. Let's talk later.'

'I'll find you,' I said. 'I just need to know if the blouse you're wearing is your own.'

Wanda Beston was dressed in a silk blouse with a leopard-skin print. The buttons on it were the same as the one I'd purchased at Tender Buttons on Friday morning.

She nodded.

'You mean, you've had it for years?'

The man seated on Wanda's other side gave me the evil eye for talking as the music began to play.

'No, no,' she said. 'They gave it to me on Saturday, at the hotel, so my mother and I would each have something Savage to wear for tonight.'

'They?' I asked, ducking down. 'Who's "they"?'

'The garment bag was delivered to the hotel by a young man,' Wanda said. 'There was a note attached to it, and I assume it came right from the office. I think it was Reed Savage who returned the tickets to me and signed the note.'

Forty

The music stopped for a few seconds. I stepped away and flattened myself against the wall behind me. It was the only stone wall in this wing of the museum – the others were all glass from floor to high ceiling – and I needed something to support me.

My mind was spinning. There must have been hundreds of those animal-print blouses manufactured by WolfWear. Yet how many of them could have survived intact since – what had the woman in the button store told me – 1991?

I moved to my left, sweeping the room in search of the dead man's family, inching along toward the ramp that led to the staging area.

Why had Reed Savage – or anyone else in the company – given that particular garment to Wanda Beston? Had the fabric been damaged, in addition to the replaced button, or was it simply of no use in the exhibition downstairs or on the runway? I needed to speak to Wanda when the show ended.

I was almost at the dividing point that separated the

Dendur wing from the corridor to American Art. A security guard stood with his back to the rope.

I bent down and removed the Citadel ID card from my shoe.

A loud musical chord echoing through the sound system silenced the audience and stopped me in place. It was the familiar opening of the old Bangles hit song, followed by the lyrics: 'Walk like an Egyptian . . .'

Two stunning young women – dressed and wigged in identical fashion, wearing the same white toga that I'd bought at the charity show – emerged from the temple and struck a pose on either side of the runway. They had flat gold sandals on their feet, standing with one foot behind the other, and their arms were extended – one above and in front, the other low and behind. They could have been friezes from a pharaonic pyramid, except that the diamonds that hung from their earlobes and crowned their tiaras were way too glittery to have ever been entombed.

The guests roared with delight and applauded the human statuary. The two models held their positions for the three-minute ovation that followed.

The emcee must have been standing inside the ancient temple. The crowd had just stopped clapping for the surprise pair of Egyptian goddesses when he announced, 'Ladies and gentlemen, please welcome Hal Savage.'

The applause was deafening again, not because everyone there had even met Hal Savage, but out of respect for his late brother.

It was the perfect moment for me to duck out. I held up my Citadel pass to the guard at the rope and he nodded back at me, unclasping the hook and letting me slide behind him.

The corridor to the adjacent wing was about twenty feet long. The overhead lights had been turned up to their brightest to allow the models and workers easy access back and forth to the rear entrance of the temple.

The first two models waiting in the wings were clearly the opening faces and features of Savage style going global. I had no idea whether the Muslim upscale-clothing-market gurus would appreciate the debut of the line emerging from an Egyptian temple, but that's what the clientele was about to get.

Both women towered over me, made four inches taller by the strappy shoes they wore. They had taken their instructions to heart. Neither one cracked a smile as I passed them by. No eye contact. Stoical. The one in front was wearing a full-length abaya. The pale-pink fabric was covered from neck to hem in a swirling design of black silk. The hijab – the headscarf – reversed the colors but undulated in the same pattern. The sunglasses that hid most of the model's face were trimmed with pink stones, probably sapphires, and the alligator clutch she carried would have upped the cost of the entire outfit by another ten thousand dollars.

When I reached the closest gallery in the American Art wing, I could better understand the outrageous pricing of the museum rental for the night.

The current installation was the titanic ten-mural masterpiece of Thomas Hart Benton: *America Today: 1930–1931.* Its canvas panels covered the four walls of the room, depicting every section of the country from the dawn of the twentieth century: airplanes and dirigibles, locomotives and oil wells, and finally human images drawn during the Great Depression. Velvet ropes stretched in front of each one of the panels.

The center of the room had been taken over by the frenzied teams preparing the models for their runway moments. Racks of gowns from the new collection were everywhere. Spotlights had been set up so that the stylists could achieve perfection on the models' faces and on the details of their clothing. Small folding tables had been placed around the room, covered with makeup and hair product. Hairdryers were whizzing, each one connected by an extension cord to an outlet on the wall.

The walk-through was treacherous because of all the wires and other junk strewn about the floor. The elegant room looked more like a gymnasium after a track meet.

'I'd first like to thank you all for coming to celebrate our Savage style tonight,' Hal said. The sound system was wired in backstage, too, so models and show runners would get their proper cues. 'What was supposed to be a moment of great triumph for my dear brother here at the Metropolitan Museum of Art has become, instead, a spectacular send-off to him.'

Applause interrupted Hal Savage after every few phrases.

Taking care not to trip over cords or piles of jackets on

the floor, I made my way farther into the room. No one seemed to take notice of another gawker, so I simply kept walking, in search of familiar faces.

I wasn't that interested in the models or their stylists, so I looked beyond them.

In a far corner, seated on a bench below one of the murals, I finally saw Reed Savage. He was sitting with Lily Savitsky, and they seemed oblivious to the chaos all around them. I was hoping to move in close enough to eavesdrop.

Hal's voice boomed into the large space. 'But my brother refused to buy into the talk that this evening's venture, in this city's most spectacular venue, the Temple of Dendur, was a folly. Fortunately, we all agreed with him and with his vision that this glamorous site, in the center of Manhattan, was the perfect place to go global.'

I saw Tiziana Bolt's spiky hair, her height lifting her above most of the others, before I noticed the man who had engaged her in conversation. It was Mike.

'Which is why tonight you're going to see all these magnificent sheep,' Hal said, 'in Wolf's clothing.'

More laughter.

'And you know they're really not sheep,' he went on. 'They are the most beautiful women in the world, which is just as Wolf planned it. Savage beauties, all of them.'

Instinctively I turned my face to the wall, hoping not to make eye contact with Mike.

There was a description of the famed Benton work affixed to the wall and I pretended to be reading it. A guy in jeans and a sweatshirt, holding a makeup brush in his hand, walked up beside me.

'Mind if I give you just a touch-up? You could use some more color,' he said. 'Are you a handler for one of the girls?'

'Just security,' I said. 'No need to bother with me.'

'These paintings are amazing, aren't they?'

I was sideways to the wall now, talking to him so I could continue to watch the room. 'They really are.'

'Imagine,' the makeup artist said, pointing with the tip of his brush to the description of the murals. 'Benton didn't even get paid to do them, according to this description, for a boardroom at the New School, no less. He just got a year's worth of free eggs.'

'You're kidding,' I said, watching Tiz pick a hair off the lapel of Mike's tux. Watching his face, I almost laughed out loud at the idea that some might think it was tough work to do a security detail at a fashion show.

'Read it yourself. Benton used the yolks from the eggs to create the tempera he painted with,' the guy said, waving his brush in the air.

'So interesting,' I said to him. 'Excuse me. I've got to keep circulating.'

'Nice to talk to you,' he said.

I didn't know whether to disrupt the show by confronting Reed about the silk blouse Wanda Beston was wearing, or just wait till the event was over. There was no reason to give myself up to him or to Lily at this point. It was all the interactions, conducted in public, that I was interested in observing. Maybe the alliances would make themselves apparent.

I was getting closer to Reed and Lily when the matter was decided for me. Hal Savage finished his introduction, the familiar musical score from the movie *Lawrence of Arabia* soared in the space over the runway as well as in this gallery – another oxymoronic choice, it seemed to me – and Reed and Lily stood up to clear a path back to the main room. I assumed they were going to claim their seats.

I waited until some of the other dressers and stylists made their way after Reed and Lily, then took the same route they had.

I glanced over my shoulder again. A few more models seemed ready to queue up, and Mike was still talking to Tiz Bolt, holding a champagne flute as he engaged her in a lively conversation.

It was indeed standing room only as I squeezed into a place against the wall. The first model was rocking her abaya down the runway as the great music swelled. All it conjured up for me, though, was hours of watching Peter O'Toole on his camel, racing across the desert sands.

Mercer was standing now, too. Directly opposite me, outlined against the backlit glass, framing him against the bare trees in Central Park. He was as still as a statue, ignoring the figure on the runway but looking over the lineup of guests.

Lily Savitsky had taken her seat, I noticed, next to her husband, David. They were in the back row, the corner nearest the temple, so not actually in a position to see the models until they were a third of the way out on the runway.

That signaled to me that David Kingsley's two-million-dollar infusion of cash to Wolf Savage to allow the show to go on bought him whatever he wanted, but that he was discreet enough to avoid center stage at this point – smart enough to avoid questions from his adversaries.

Reed and Hal Savage had slipped into the room and chosen to stand with their backs to the glass wall, not far away from Mercer. They were not letting each out of the other's sight, is how I read it.

I kept looking around to see who Tiziana Bolt linked herself with, but she had still not joined the main action in Dendur. She must have been keeping Mike Chapman amused in the dressing area.

I couldn't make out who had replaced Mercer in the seat beside Anna Wintour. There still appeared to be a Citadel security guard on one side of her.

As the first model made her way back into the temple entrance, the second one – also in a black abaya, but this one sequined, like the headscarf, from head to toe – strutted out.

I took a few more steps to my right, much to the annoyance of the folks standing near me.

The man with the best seat in the house, next to Anna Wintour, was George Kwan. What possible connection could those two have? Then I noticed that Kwan's personal security agent, Oddjob's body double, was in the chair to his right.

The fashion industry was in fact, as Tiz had described it to me, a world of fantasy, of smoke and mirrors. That was so evident to me as I watched all the creatures preening backstage to perform before this crowd – magazine writers and clothing gurus who thought there was a place in the world for millions more dollars of haute couture to line the pockets of all the designers and vendors.

It was a business that now seemed to be as full of mystery to me as my own professional world. Thugs, thieves, and murderers – any combination of whom might be taking in this spectacle with me.

The music reached a crescendo as the second model stopped at the foot of the runway. She was unaffected – as directed to be – by the thunderous applause. She continued to stare straight ahead, not daring to turn until the clapping died down.

Reed Savage didn't wait for her runway return. Without a word to his uncle, he slipped through the crowd and headed for the dressing room in the adjacent gallery.

Forty-one

I took the same path back to the roped-off entrance to the American Art area, and the same guard waved me in without a show of my Citadel ID.

The next three or four models were lined up. The clothing theme was still designs for the Middle Eastern Muslim women, and the music continued to throb with the Arabian movie theme.

I could see the pod of stylists working on young women – white- and black-skinned, but no Asians – who represented couture from the other side of the globe. Traditional Chinese gowns appeared to be hand-painted, one with a tiger wrapping from around the back of the dress to the front. Its head was covered with crystal beads, which matched the beading of the frogs on the high-necked mandarin collar of the elegant dress.

Tiz Bolt and Mike Chapman were no longer in the room. I watched Reed Savage circle each of the tables, offering encouragement to the models who were primping for their turns.

Reed's eyes swept the room as well. I don't think he saw whomever he was looking for, but instead of returning to the Dendur wing, he crossed catty-corner, to an exit at the farthest end of the large gallery. The security guard there seemed to know who he was, opened the rope, and let him through.

I followed that route, staying a good distance behind so Reed didn't see me, and flashed my Citadel card to the guard. I was able to pick up the sound of Reed's footsteps as he walked ahead of me through the empty rooms in the American Art section of the museum.

The farther I got from Dendur, the darker the galleries became. They were unlighted and unguarded. All the security attention was, as expected, where the expensive clothing, priceless jewels, and fancy people were gathered.

The middle of the first floor, between American Art and the Great Hall, held the many rooms filled with medieval arms and armor. Even in the dark, I was comfortable in these halls, panels covered and cases packed with thousands of weapons from all over the world.

I had been dragged to this part of the museum on endless occasions – the reward to my two older brothers for indulging my mother's wish for a day of culture. They used to argue the merits of English versus French armor till I was blue in the face – Henry II's personal suit of armor when he was king of France versus those crafted in the Royal Workshops of England for Henry VIII.

Reed Savage's footsteps stopped abruptly. I froze, too,

somewhere between the wall-mounted Smith & Wesson revolvers decorated in silver by Tiffany, and the legendary Colts made in the 1870s and inlaid with eighteen-karat gold.

I heard voices ahead, and lighter footsteps than Reed's evening shoes had sounded. I tiptoed through the revolver gallery and past the display cabinet of helmets, fifteenth-century ones found in a Venetian fortress on a Greek Island.

If things continued to go badly with Battaglia, I figured I could always be a docent in the Arms and Armor Collection, I knew it so well.

I stood in the dark, hidden from view by a full coat of handsome Japanese armor that was standing on display at the open door of the gallery, shielding me from the people in the Great Hall.

I was close enough to hear voices.

'Thanks for the introduction, Tiz. I've already met Detective Chapman several times,' Reed Savage said. 'He's been terrifically helpful about uncovering the fact of my father's murder.'

'I hope you don't mind that—' Mike said.

'That you're here, Detective? It's a great evening. Enjoy the champagne,' Reed said. 'I'm glad you're not taking the on-duty thing too seriously.'

'How's it going with you and David Kingsley?' Mike asked.

'I see you've got one eye on me tonight while Detective Wallace is keeping tabs on George Kwan,' Reed said.

'Now, if only Alexandra Cooper were here, I'd say it would be the perfect storm. She could be trying to wrangle my uncle Hal.'

'What's that supposed to mean?' Tiz asked.

'Come with me for a minute,' Reed said to her. 'I need to check one of the displays downstairs in the Costume Institute.'

But Tiz Bolt seemed to be standing her ground. 'I met a woman named Alexandra Cooper last week,' she said. 'What's she got to do with you, Detective?'

'How do you know her?' Reed Savage asked.

'Well, I don't really know her, but she was here on Friday – at least, there was a woman who came in here and said that was her name, asking me a million questions,' Tiz said, nervously fingering the edge of her collar.

'Did she tell you she was a prosecutor?' Reed asked, sounding as though he was going to snap her head off.

'What's the difference? What does she have to do with tonight?'

'Nothing at all,' Mike said. 'Sometimes I work with her.'

I didn't know who had more of a right to be mad at Mike – Tiz Bolt or me. 'I work with her' was the best he could do for a description of me?

'Take a walk with me, Tiz,' Reed Savage said. 'Will you excuse us for a minute, Detective?'

Two sets of footsteps – Reed and Tiz – went in the opposite direction, farther away from my position. Mike Chapman paused for thirty seconds, then, as I peeked my head out from behind the Japanese warrior, walked away toward the Great Hall.

I was left alone to think, surrounded by a king's ransom of knights in shining armor.

Forty-two

I waited for more than five minutes, trying to think of a strategy for the rest of the night.

When I learned how to cross-examine trial witnesses, I was taught to figure out first what information it was I wanted to get from them. Only then I could structure a cross that would build to eliciting that critical piece of evidence, rather than a rambling and unsuccessful fishing expedition.

My thinking was too scattered. I wanted Wanda Beston to talk to me about her piece of clothing, and I wanted the chance to examine it to determine whether it had been damaged before this evening.

I wanted to know what Reed Savage had gone back to the Costume Institute to see just now – leaving the big show to do it – and I had to find out what Tiz Bolt had told him about my conversation with her.

What were Lily Savitsky and David Kingsley planning on for their business future, after sponsoring this show on behalf of the murdered man? And what was George

Kwan doing in the front row of a major event, next to the queen of the fashion world, when his relationship with all the Savages now seemed so tenuous?

I was still in the darkened armorial hall, trying to organize my thoughts, when I heard someone coming my way again.

I froze in place, expecting it could be Mike.

But it was Reed Savage, making a beeline back to the dressing area. He had not spent many minutes with Tiz Bolt.

Maybe it was nothing. Maybe there was some detail about the after party in the exhibition space that they had to clear up.

He passed the nook in which I'd hidden myself and kept walking. He was smoothing back his hair and wiping his nose with the back of his hand.

Something dropped from his other hand. It didn't make much noise – I thought it was a credit card, the sound of plastic hitting the museum floor. Then I noticed a second object besides the card – I could see its outline now. The flutter of the other object in the dark was eye-catching, especially the white trim on its edges.

Reed Savage stopped and turned around to pick them up.

He was only ten feet away from me and saw me – perhaps because of the shimmer of my stockings against the steel of the armor – and stood straight up.

I figured it was better to walk toward him than have him pin me in.

'Got them?' I asked, mustering my huskiest voice.

'Who are you?'

I could see what he was holding, the things that he was trying to put back in to the inner tuxedo pocket.

'No one you need to worry about,' I said.

It was a rolled-up bill – a hundred – that he had doubtless used to snort cocaine, cut into lines with his credit card, a few minutes ago. He was still sucking the white powder in, still wiping his nose, and as I stepped up to him I could see that his pupils were dilated.

'You a stylist?' he asked.

No one would confuse me with a model. 'Yeah.'

'Any problem with this?' Reed asked, wiping his nose again and throwing back his head.

'No.'

'Can you keep your mouth shut?'

'Sure.'

'Get in the dressing room and get back to work,' Reed said, pocketing the bill. 'There's plenty for everyone at the party later.'

It was very likely that there was cocaine everywhere, if all the stories the cops had always told me about the fashion industry were true. People in the business used cocaine like athletes used steroids – it was a performance-enhancing drug to get everyone from models to hairdressers to stressed-out businessmen through the long, competitive days and nights.

I waited until Reed Savage went into the dressing area.

Then I reversed direction, heading for the Great Hall

to look for Mike. This ten-second encounter with Reed Savage had shown me a side of the man that was different from the one we had met with last week.

He wasn't the supplicant looking to Mike and Mercer for help with his affairs, for understanding of his tenuous situation. He didn't seem insecure or indefinite. This Reed Savage was edgy and intoxicated in the middle of a high-profile crowd on this all-important night. There was an undertone in his voice, a hint of a threat, when he asked if I had a problem with his snorting cocaine. I was glad that I answered him with a no.

I walked all the way to the information desk in the center of the Great Hall. There were three Citadel guys – undoubtedly ex-cops – who were assigned to the front door.

'Any of you know Mike Chapman?' I asked. 'Have you seen him in the last few minutes?'

'We know him,' one man said. 'He was out this way just a bit ago, but I think I saw him go back into Dendur.'

'Thanks.' I jogged across the long, empty entrance hall and slowed down when I heard the applause for the latest design.

I tried to press my way through the people standing in the entrance, but no one was budging for me. I stood on tiptoe, scoping as much of the room as I could take in. I found Mercer in the distance, but Mike must have gone out by another path. There was no penetrating this group of onlookers, so I turned away.

I reversed myself to go to the dressing area, to reenter

the show. At the top of the staircase that led to the Costume Institute, I stopped.

Reed had separated Mike from Tiz Bolt just minutes earlier and taken her downstairs, saying he wanted to check one of the displays. I had heard that much from my hiding place. If she was still there, it was a good chance to talk with her. Maybe Mike had rejoined her after Reed took his snort. Together, he and I could try to sort things out.

I went down the steps, but the area seemed to be empty, at least in the front gallery.

The well-dressed mannequins looked poised for the opening of the exhibition, ready for their close-ups.

I made my way through the second and third rooms, but heard no voices.

In the fourth gallery, I saw Tiz. She was sitting on the floor with her back to me, legs stretched out in front of her, and earbuds in – listening to music, I expected – so she didn't hear my approach.

I got up close to her before she noticed me. She pulled one of the earphones out. 'You've got another hour to go, luv. Can't be in here until the show's over.'

'Tiz, I'd like to apologize to you,' I said. 'I'm Alex Cooper.'

She was on her feet in two seconds. 'You're what?'

'It's a wig,' I said. 'A wig, makeup, and one of Wolf's old dresses.'

'Damn. And what was that bullshit on Friday all about? That story about being a friend of Lily's and—'

'I'm apologizing because I never meant to mislead you.

I did grow up with Lily and she did come to me for help about her father. Those things are true.'

'You just left out everything else in between that might have interested me before I yapped away with you. Reed says you—' Tiz Bolt stopped short.

'What did he say about me?' I asked.

'Nothing. Nothing at all,' Tiz said. 'Where's your cop friend? Right behind you?'

'Close enough.' Truth was I had no idea where Mike had gone.

'Was I helpful to you, Alex?' she asked, growing madder by the second. 'All that stuff I told you about Velvel Savitsky, that you passed on to the cops? Me, thinking I'm talking to a brand-new friend who's all strung out, drinking her wine while I sipped my tea.'

'It's a murder investigation now, Tiz. Sooner or later they'd find out every single bit of detail about Wolf Savage. The women, the illegitimate children, the drugs—'

'Only now Reed's all pissed off because he thinks it came from me,' she said, jabbing her finger into her chest.

'I can make it straight with him. Right now,' I said. 'I can go upstairs and find Reed before the show ends. I can protect you in this.'

'Protect me? It's not him I need protection from.'

'Who then?'

Tiz Bolt wasn't moving. She looked like she had nothing more to say to me.

'You're frightened, aren't you?' I asked. 'Why don't you let me help?'

'You've already made things worse, Alex Cooper. Just get out of here.'

'Tell me who you're frightened of.'

Tiz Bolt was exasperated with me. She pulled off the earphones and knelt down to stuff them into her tote. 'Why don't you cozy up to your friend Lily's husband?' she asked.

'David Kingsley?'

'Yeah. He's the bastard who found out where Tanya was living and invited her to come up to New York.'

'Tanya Root? Lily's half-sister?' I said. 'It wasn't her own idea to show up here and try to get at Wolf's money again?'

'Thought you clear tapped me out of information the other day, didn't you? I guess you just didn't know what questions to ask,' she said. 'Do you think it's simply a coincidence that Tanya made another play for poor old Velly's dollars at the very same time Lily and David did? Total chance, that's how you figure it?'

Mike Chapman Homicide Investigation Rule Number One: There's no such thing as coincidence in murder cases.

'Did you just tell that fact to Detective Chapman when you were talking to him?'

'No, luv. We were having a much more personal-type conversation.'

Tiz threw that one at me like a sharply pointed dart.

'These are all things that are important for us to know,' I said. 'I mean, what you're saying about David Kingsley.'

Tiz was still on her knees, fidgeting with something in her bag.

I thought I might as well throw her a bit of news. Perhaps that would keep her in my corner. 'It's David who's paying for tonight's show, you know.'

She looked up at me, clearly surprised. 'Seriously? He put up the money?'

'He and his partners,' I said. 'You helped when you told me that George Kwan would never foot this kind of bill.'

'So I did,' Tiz said. 'That's a good piece of information you got. Have you told that to Reed? Have you seen him tonight?'

'Not to talk to,' I said. 'Just across the room.'

She pulled her lip gloss out of her bag and applied it.

'How close are you and Reed?' I asked.

'Business close, Alex,' she said, giving me a fake smile. 'Like you and that detective. You know how that goes.'

Tiz Bolt was getting icier by the minute. Was she guessing about Mike and me, or had he told her something?

'Nine years clean and sober,' I said. 'So why do you carry Reed's coke around in your bag for him? Why be the enabler?'

If Tiz was ready for hardball, then so was I.

'What would you know about coke, luv? Or about Reed Savage for that matter?' She was on her feet, smoking mad.

'A rendezvous down here alone with you, a credit card to cut the coke because he didn't have a spare razor blade, a Ben Franklin all rolled up to stick up his nose – kind of the rich boy's equivalent of a straw – and the telltale wipe of his nose,' I said. 'Backbone of the fashion industry. Pure blow.'

'You've got nothing, Alex,' Tiz said, holding her hands palms up. 'Now you see it, now you don't. As long as poor Reed has what it takes to get him through the night. All very emotional, you know. His dad and all that.'

'I'm not sure exactly what "heartbroken" looks like every time,' I said. 'But it's not a message, not a vibe I'm getting, from any of Wolf's relatives.'

'I'm so sick and tired of your—'

'Now, there's a line that sounds like it's straight out of your friend's mouth,' I said. '"I'm so sick and tired" – one of the man's favorite expressions, wasn't it? Or didn't you see his suicide note? It sort of looked to me like someone just chopped off the "and tired" part, Tiz, on a note that Wolf had written for some other reason. What's your best guess?'

I had to go upstairs to find Mike or Mercer before this conversation got any more out of control. I backed out of her sight and turned around to wind my way out among the mannequins.

'Done with me, are you?' Tiz called out. She was following me, almost overtaking me in her flat shoes as I started up the staircase. The bag was on her shoulder, although it didn't complement her formal outfit.

'I'm actually quite curious about one other thing,' I said.

'Go on.'

'I ran into Wanda Beston earlier tonight.'

'Who would that be?' Tiz asked.

'One of the housekeepers from the Silver Needle,' I said. 'The one who found Wolf's body.'

'A housekeeper? Here at the show? She's got friends in high places, doesn't she?'

'I think Mr Savage – Wolf Savage – liked her, respected her. He invited her and her mother before he was killed.'

'What's your problem, then?' Tiz asked.

'Wanda told me the office sent her over the outfit she's wearing tonight. It wasn't hers. She didn't own it.'

'Which one would that be?'

'It's a very dramatic print,' I said. 'Patterned like a leopard skin.'

'Ah, the Savage Big Cats,' Tiz said. 'Nineteen ninety-one.'

'There can't be many of those out in the world, can there?'

Tiz tensed. I could see her spine straighten. She was trying to second-guess what I was getting at.

'I'm not sure, actually.'

'Are there any others like it back in the office?'

'No. There wouldn't be any there. Even the collections that we archive are kept off-site,' Tiz said. 'There's no room for them, and they have to be maintained in the right kind of storage vaults.'

It looked to me like wheels were spinning in Tiz Bolt's brain. She continued up the staircase but then looked back down at me.

'This woman – this Wanda person – did she happen to say who gave her the blouse?' Tiz asked.

'She told me that it came to her from Reed,' I said. 'Does that tell you what you wanted to know?'

Tiz Bolt took the rest of the steps two at a time. I didn't know where she was going, but she seemed to be in a big hurry to get there.

Forty-three

By the time I reached the dressing area, it was so crowded I could barely see halfway across the room. The models who had finished their performances were sitting around – most of them just in underwear covered by a robe or kimono. Finishing touches were being put on the remaining crew.

'Do you know where Reed Savage is?' I asked one of the wranglers.

'No idea. He must be inside the show.'

I couldn't see any part of Dendur, but from the sound of the music I guessed the clothing on the runway was an appeal to the women of India. I half expected a cobra to rise up out of one of the makeup cases on the floor.

I asked for the nearest ladies' room. It was a pretty safe bet that Tiz Bolt would be dumping any drugs she had in her bag.

The guard directed me to the next gallery over in the American Art area, farther away from the Dendur wing.

Two young women were coming out of the bathroom

– a long, institutional-looking restroom with eight or ten stalls. They had finished their work for the evening and both had removed their makeup.

Three of the stalls were occupied. Some of the models seemed to be changing clothes. I didn't see Tiz's feet, from the look of the pairs of shoes under the stall doors. I exited, believing I had chosen the wrong spot.

I went back into the dressing area and began a careful walk around its perimeter.

People looked tired and their nerves seemed shot. No one offered to move out of my way. Expensive gowns had been rehung, but just about everything else wound up on the floor.

There was no reason to push my way into Dendur. David and Lily, Reed and Hal, Wanda and her mother, and probably even George Kwan would be available as soon as the klieg lights were unplugged. Then I would be able to get the attention of Mike and Mercer.

Just as I circled back to the door that led to the Great Hall, I spotted something bright on top of a pile of black clothes. It was the shocking-pink-and-cobalt-blue blouse that Tiz Bolt had been wearing. She had taken it off and discarded it, along with her bell-bottomed silk lounging pants.

I leaned over and rustled through the pile, hoping that her bag was still there. But it was not.

I picked up the blouse, thinking its distinctive colors might have caught someone's eye.

'Did you see the woman who was wearing this earlier?'

I ran from table to table, asking models and stylists and hairdressers. All I got were blank stares.

What had I said to Tiz Bolt to make her break out of her big night and leave the Costume Institute? Was it about the cocaine? Or the clothes that Wanda was wearing?

I ran out the door, through the next several galleries – each longer than the one before – toward the Great Hall. The only person ahead of me was a man, his back to me, starting down the narrow corridor that led to the main entrance. He wasn't in a tux, so I doubted he was either security or an important guest.

I was running in the same direction as he was walking, hoping to get to the guards at the door so I could describe Tiz Bolt to them, to ask them to hold her there till I could summon Mike or Mercer.

I stopped for a second to step out of my high heels, kicking them off to the side. It was impossible to sprint in them. I took Mrs Stafford's pearls and twisted them around so they fell down my back, instead of dangling in front of me as I ran.

The floor was slippery for my stocking feet, which I expected. I held my arms out to balance myself and sped up the pace. The man was tall, dressed in sneakers and a navy-blue parka, wearing a baseball cap. He didn't look back at me as I gained on him.

It was only when I passed him that I glanced over to see his face. 'Excuse me,' I said, 'I'm looking for security—'

But it wasn't a man at all. It was Tiziana Bolt. She had shed her elegant clothes, crushed her spiky hair under the cap, and used her slender, androgynous body to fool anyone looking for a one-time model on her way out of the museum.

'You've got to stop, Tiz!' I yelled at her.

'I don't have to do a damn thing to please you,' she said, breaking into a trot.

'Police!' I shouted, hoping to attract the attention of anyone in earshot.

Tiz grabbed at my wig and pulled it off my head in a single swipe. I caught hold of her sleeve and screamed even louder for the cops.

'Get your hands off me, Alex. You have no business touching me,' she said, swinging her bag at my face. 'Let me go.'

I fell to my knees, sliding on the polished floor of the hallway, and clutching on to Tiz Bolt by the open pocket of her ski jacket.

'Let it go,' she said again, cracking me on the head with her bag.

I fell backward, still hanging on to her jacket, ripping the pocket as I went down on the floor. Both of us heard the sound of the fabric tearing as she broke away from me. I propped myself up on one knee, trying to get back on my feet.

Not only had I torn her pocket completely open, but as I clutched the worn fabric in an effort to restrain Tiz, the pocket and the paper inside it came off in my hand.

'Police!' I yelled one more time as the sound of someone running toward us got louder. 'In the Great Hall!'

Tiz Bolt reached out for and swiped at the paper in my hand, but missed.

The expression on her face made it seem as though she wanted to crush my head with whatever was in her bag. She swung it wildly at me again. I had seen that kind of expression before, on people who meant to do me no good.

'Stop right there!' It was the voice of one of two men running toward us from the dark end of the corridor. 'Hold up!'

Tiz Bolt had no intention of stopping or holding up. Her sneakers had a better grip on the museum floor than the dress shoes of the cops in tuxedos who heard me scream and had given chase.

I had the piece of paper she wanted in my hand, but Tiz Bolt turned to glance at me once more before she ran out of the museum. She pointed her finger at me like it was a gun and flashed a look my way. This time, it was a killer look.

Forty-four

One of the guards helped me to my feet.

'I'm a prosecutor, sir. Manhattan DA's Office,' I said. 'You've got to hold on to that woman until I get the homicide detective who's inside the show at Dendur.'

The second officer was already through the front door, outside talking to other security men who must have been stationed on the front steps.

'What woman?' he asked me.

'The one – well, she's dressed like a guy but she's actually a woman – in the Red Sox cap and sneakers.'

'That tall guy who was on his way out when we got here?'

'That one,' I said. 'The one who tried to smack me on the head.'

His partner came back over to us. 'Sorry, ma'am. The guy took off. The guards said they didn't hear you yelling because these doors are so thick. Did he steal anything?'

'No. Not that I know of.'

'You want me to call this disturbance into the precinct?

I can't really leave my post here right now, but they could meet you and take a report.'

'No. I understand,' I said, wondering how and when we would get our hands on Tiziana Bolt. I didn't know quite what to report. 'But there's a Manhattan North Homicide detective inside the fashion show, sort of posing as part of the Citadel crew for tonight. I don't have a phone. I need you to call him for me.'

'You think I'm going to call inside that accumulated pantheon of who's who in New York society and break up the party? I got no interest in being on the cover of *Vogue*,' the cop said. 'Why don't you let me see some ID?'

'Sure. It's over there,' I said, pointing at my shoes, farther back down the hallway.

One of the guys was rolling his eyes at the other. 'Don't forget your wig, miss. You don't look ready for prime time with that net on your head.'

I pulled off the net and found my shoes. 'Here's my ID, officer, but you're just wasting time.'

'How about one of us goes into the room and presses flesh with the fashionistas?' he said. 'Is it Chapman you want? I'll dig him out for you.'

'Thanks,' I said. 'Tell him I'll meet him in the staging area right behind Dendur, where all the models are changing.'

'Roger that, lady,' he said. 'You okay? You look kind of shaky.'

'I'll be good, thanks. Just a dust-up that I wasn't expecting.'

I wanted to get back to that room and take off my pantyhose and trade someone for a pair of flat shoes. I'd even take overstock of the gold sandals before I'd dream of getting back in my heels.

'You need me,' the second cop said, 'or should I wait here in case your buddy comes back?'

'Waiting here is a great idea,' I said. 'Hold on to her if she shows back up. And if anyone else tries to leave before the show is over, hang on to them, too.'

'What's the offense?'

I hesitated. I didn't think I had a charge that could stick. 'Chapman will tell you.'

I paused in the corridor to see what was so important about the paper that Tiz Bolt had stuffed into her coat pocket. I unfolded it and read it.

What she hadn't wanted to me to get my hands on was an invoice with two boarding passes she had printed out earlier. Tiz Bolt and Reed Savitsky – not Savage, but with his birth name, Savitsky – were booked together on the six A.M. American Airlines flight from New York to London.

Forty-five

I was still in my stocking feet, shoes in hand, making my way back toward the large dressing area in the American Art wing.

I went the entire length of the Great Hall thinking about what it meant that Tiziana Bolt and Reed Savage had an intimate relationship. For how long had that been the case? Why had they concealed it? How did it play into the events of the last month?

I made the left turn to head to the dressing area. As I passed the top of the staircase that led down to the Costume Institute, Reed Savage was coming up. We practically collided with each other.

I lowered my head and kept walking, expecting he wouldn't recognize me, except as the person who encountered him after his snort of cocaine.

'Alex Cooper? That's you? You've got no damn business being here tonight, Ms Cooper,' Reed said. 'And trying to disguise yourself like that . . . what was that about? To catch me getting high? You'd have to arrest half the people here for that offense. What a joke.'

My free hand flew to my head. I was no longer disguised, but I had forgotten that in my scuffle with Tiz.

Reed stood in front of me, blocking my way. 'You want to do something useful, let me have your phone.'

'I haven't got one.'

'Did you spook Tiz? Is that why she's not downstairs?' he said. 'My phone's in her bag and I need to call her.'

'There's plenty of phones in the dressing area, I'm sure,' I said, trying to pass him by.

'You know where she is, don't you? Have you turned her over to the cops?'

'Why?' I asked. Reed Savage was totally in my face. 'For blow? She's your provider, I guess. Tiz told me her drug history last week. I'm sure she'd have no problem finding coke for you.'

'Let's go downstairs and have a talk.'

I wasn't going back to the Costume Institute. No one else was there. I wanted to stay close to all the people – security included – who were still working the show.

'You want to say something to me, Reed, say it right here.'

He stepped to the left, toward the opening of the gallery with all the knights on guard. I went with him.

'Tell me what you did with Tiz,' he demanded.

'I know your father – or Velly, as Tiz called him – used to have quite an addiction to Oxy,' I said. 'He went to all that trouble to commit himself to an inpatient facility to clean himself up. One time that I know of. Maybe other visits, too. We can check all that out.'

Reed was fuming now. He realized the information – and Tiz's nickname for his father – could only have come from her.

'Then somebody goes and undoes it all,' I said. 'I doubt that after working so hard to break the habit Wolf just fell back into it on his own. So I wondered, who was the temptress who could hook Wolf again on the drug? Who could reintroduce him to Oxy – the one substance that had been his weakness? Because that was an essential part of the plan, wasn't it?'

I would keep talking to him, feeding him tidbits, until Mike got the word to come looking for me or Reed made a break for the front door, where security was in place. Maybe I'd prod him into a response.

He gritted his teeth and spoke each word as angrily as I expected he would. 'There was no plan.'

'Sure there was,' I said. 'Getting him high on his favorite drug – just like old times – and then, when he passed out on the bed, you put the exit bag over his head and gave him a whiff of helium. That's all it would have taken, and you'd be rid of his control forever.'

Reed Savage slammed his fist into the wall, walking away from me into the darkened gallery. I looked behind me, but there was no sign of Mike yet.

'Painless. That's what Tiz told me,' I said. 'Really, Reed? You killed your own father, but tried to find a painless way to do it? He may have been a monster, but no more so than you.'

He was pacing the long room while I was standing still,

as though making a case to a jury – a jury made up of life-size hollow coats of armor, the legacy of men who once found the need to dress themselves completely in steel.

'Then there's the blouse,' I said. 'The one that you gave to Wanda Beston to wear tonight. That stymied me for a bit, but then it became so obvious.'

'What was obvious?' Reed asked. He was pacing back toward me.

'Like one of those Hitchcock plots where the murderer kills someone with a leg of lamb, then cooks the lamb and feeds it to the detective. The evidence was gone.'

'What?' He was banging on glass cabinets and doing everything but throwing down his gauntlet to challenge one of the knights to a duel.

'Tiz Bolt was wearing that blouse the night you two killed your father,' I said.

It never hurt to try out the theory of the crime on the killer. So many of them are anxious to show how much smarter than you they are.

'So you found the best possible way to get rid of it. When your father struggled with Tiz,' I said, 'which only goes to prove that murder is never painless, Reed, he ripped that button off the blouse.'

Reed Savage stood still, poised in the doorframe that led to the adjacent gallery. 'You've got nothing,' he said.

'Not so, Reed. Because a piece of the button that was damaged in the struggle was found by the cops in the carpet of—'

'That proves nothing.'

'Let me finish, please.' I could see how rattled he was – the cocaine? The truth? The missing accomplice? It calmed me to see him shakier than I had just been. 'The broken piece of the button was in the carpet of the room next to the one where your father was killed. You know, the one where you hid the hand truck with the helium canister while Tiz did her little dance of death with her old friend Velly.'

Reed had heard enough. He brushed past me and started out of the gallery toward the dressing area. 'I need a fucking phone.'

I kept talking. The men in armor seemed spellbound. 'Didn't Tiz tell you about the trail she left? Buying the replacement button last week to try to repair the blouse?'

It was all coming together in my own head. The hotel manager's description of the two men – Reed, no doubt, and Tiz in her boyish way of concealing herself – who wheeled in the hand truck on the day of the murder. The woman in the button store who described the tall, slim young man in a baseball cap and ski jacket, sunglasses hiding his face, who was in the shop a couple of days before I bought the button. The young man who delivered the damaged leopard-print blouse to Wanda Beston at her job. It was actually Tiz, who in describing herself to me on Friday had talked about her perfect androgynous appearance. The look of a prepubescent boy – great for the runway, and even better for concealing her identity when it was convenient.

'She did what?' Reed asked.

'Tried to replace the broken button so the blouse could take its place in this exhibition downstairs, as planned. One of Wolf Savage's classics. But the damage to the fabric the night the button was ripped off made that exercise useless,' I said. 'So how better to get it out of the company offices, out from under the detective's nose, than to give it to poor Wanda? To suggest, in case anyone was thinking it, that she might have been the killer.'

'Wanda *is* the one who found the body,' Reed said, raising his voice. 'How do you know what was going on between Wanda and my father? Maybe she's the one who struggled with him?'

'Stay with me, Reed. It's you who gave her the blouse – after the fact,' I said. 'After your father was dead. I've got Tiz so deep into this that she'll flip in a heartbeat.'

He tried to size me up for five seconds then turned his back on me.

'You don't really think you're getting on that morning flight to London, do you?' I asked. 'Not before we find out how you and Tiz killed Tanya?'

Now his rage was in full bloom. 'I wasn't even in the country when Tanya was killed. It's Lily's husband who lured that greedy bitch up here, so they could join forces to blackmail my father into changing his will. I wasn't anywhere near Manhattan.'

'We can prove that you were here, Reed. I've got the detectives working on that right now,' I said.

I was thinking as fast as I could. Of course the airline

ticket was in the Savitsky name, because Reed didn't believe we'd ever think to check the passenger manifest for that one. He'd be long gone by the time Mike showed up to interview him again.

'It's called dual citizenship, Reed. You've got an American passport in your birth name, and a British one when you turned full-on Savage, growing up in London,' I said. 'Isn't that right? You flew over here – under the radar, using your Savitsky ID – when you thought it was necessary, or just convenient, to dispose of Tanya Root. To hire some boys from the 'hood to club her over the head and dump her in the East River.'

He lunged toward me, missing me only by inches because I jumped back, right against the gallery wall.

I was tired of waiting for Mike Chapman to show up. I yelled 'Police!' as loud as I could.

But I also kept baiting Reed Savage. 'Did you watch them do it to Tanya? Kill her, I mean?' I asked. 'I know you're a devotee of painless, but it wasn't too painless for Tanya, cracking her head open, was it? And so much easier to pay for her murder with drugs than with cash.'

He charged at me again and pinned me to the wall of the gallery with one of his elbows pressed across my chest.

I squirmed to get myself free. 'Tiz is talking to the police now, Reed. Don't bother to call her, because she's giving it all up to the Homicide Squad. You'll go right to voicemail, and it will be the cops who download the message.'

He was going for my neck with both hands, but I grabbed his shoulders and pushed back hard. My feet slid on the floor and we both fell, taking down one of the knights with us.

I thought the crash of the armored figure would set off all the alarms in the museum, but the two of us were still alone fighting in the dark. The music from the sound system must have drowned out my repeated screams.

'You're dead,' Reed Savage said to me, up on one knee, his hand on my chest – probably trying to decide whether he was better off getting out of the museum or silencing me while he had the chance.

'Chapman!' I screamed. 'Murder!'

Reed Savage covered my mouth with his other hand, straining to keep it shut while I rolled back and forth on the floor, trying to catch his fingers between my teeth.

The fallen knight was beside me – the cold steel of his chest plate digging into my ribs as Reed tried to wedge me into a corner.

Something on the floor was glimmering. It wasn't my stocking, but it was next to my leg, long and shiny.

I screamed Mike's name again. Reed couldn't keep my mouth completely covered, so the sound was muffled but fierce. He grabbed at the two long strands of pearls that were doubled around my neck, pulling them tight under my chin to choke me while holding his clenched fist against my throat, blocking my airway.

I coughed and gagged, and my thrashing caused the strings of the necklace to break apart. Mrs Stafford's pearls bounced and rolled across the gallery floor like dozens of BBs exploding from the barrel of a gun.

Reed was looking around for something – something to hit me with, I thought. He rose up on one leg, his other knee deep in my stomach.

He spotted the antique helmet lying next to my head and tried to pry it loose from the stand that had anchored it to the rest of the body armor. I closed my eyes at the thought of it smashing into my face.

Reed needed both hands to wrest the helmet from whatever museum display device held it in place. He worked it and worked it, despite my twists and turns, till he got it free.

The long weapon with the sharp steel point that glittered on the floor in the dark room was beside me, close enough for me to reach. It too had been knocked loose by its fall.

I grabbed it by its shaft with my right hand and slid the handle back beside me so that the blade of it was just below my shoulder.

As Reed Savage hoisted the helmet above his head, aimed directly at my face, I lifted the bone handle of the deadly weapon three or four inches off the ground – as high as I had the strength to raise it while on my back – and thrust it forward.

I speared him in the fleshy portion of his thigh with every ounce of energy I had left.

The blade pierced Reed's leg. He fell over, off my body and onto the floor. His screams filled all the galleries around us, bringing half the museum's security team running to my side within seconds.

One of the cops called 911 to get an ambulance on the scene, while four others lifted the howling Savage son and carried him toward the front of the museum, unable to remove the thick blade without ripping open his leg.

A part of me was actually glad that the man who had killed his own sister and father was in so much pain.

I sat up, shattered and stunned, waiting for Mike Chapman. All I wanted was for him to take me home.

Forty-six

Security gave us an empty office not far from the dressing area. Mike and Mercer spent half an hour calming me while the show wrapped up on the runway.

The public rooms cleared pretty quickly, and most of the guests who had enjoyed the fashions on display in the Dendur wing moved downstairs to the Costume Institute without learning that Reed Savage and I had come within inches of taking each other's lives.

Mike got a sweatshirt from one of the hairdressers and leggings from a model, and I slipped into the restroom to change.

Mercer brought David Kingsley into the office first. David admitted that once Wolf Savage rebuffed his efforts to insert Lily into the business, David researched the whereabouts of Tanya Root. Her new surname had come from a short-lived marriage.

Tanya had been supporting herself by prostitution. The breast implants that ultimately identified her were an effort she hoped would increase her business, not an attempt at a modeling career. David had learned about Tanya's old hex on her father during his conversations with Wolf. He had the financial resources to hunt her down and was able to convince her that he could help get her fingers – and Lily's as well – on some of their father's fortune.

Lily was ignorant of David's plans, first hatched three years earlier, during their separation, and put in play after their child, named for Wolf, was born.

David talked to us because he was desperate to separate himself from a murder charge.

He'd been told that Reed was in police custody at the hospital – which would be obvious to Reed when he woke up from the anesthesia given to him for his surgery – and that every effort was being made to find Tiz Bolt, because Mike and Mercer believed that she and Reed had killed Wolf Savage together. She would never make her way onto a plane in the morning.

Mike would run down everything in the days that followed, but for the moment he wanted to know the broad strokes that had set two killings in motion.

David Kingsley folded his arms on the empty desk in front of him, put his head down on them, and cried for three or four minutes. That was all the time Mike was going to give him.

'Tell it to us first,' he said. 'It makes it that much easier when you spill it all out to your wife later on.'

David picked up his head. He appeared to be too emotionally exhausted to argue with Mike.

'I'm the one who encouraged Tanya to make another

run at her father,' David said. 'Lily didn't know. She didn't know anything about it. I figured that my new relationship with Wolf would bring him to rely on me to handle Tanya this time around.'

'Why you?' Mike asked.

'A couple of times at lunch – days when Wolf was drinking martinis and opening up to me – he told me the stories about Tanya,' David said. 'Things had changed between him and Hal – for the worse – so I convinced myself that if Wolf needed help with anything that had to do with family, he'd lean on me from that point on.'

'Why not on Reed? Why were you so confident that Wolf wouldn't bring his own son in?'

'I miscalculated, I guess,' David said. 'I was right here in town, and Reed was always an ocean away. Recently, Wolf had been on Reed's back because he'd failed to take the company global.'

That part of the story fit well with what we already knew. Reed had admitted it when we had our first one-on-one with him.

David Kingsley was rubbing his eyes. 'Maybe Wolf didn't like me any better than he liked his kids, but he was really into my success in business,' he said, and then, with hesitation, he added a line: 'That's what I was banking on. That and the fact that he was so vocal about calling Reed a loser.'

'And let Reed know that, too,' I said.

'You bet he did. Wolf let everyone know it.'

'So you were not only going to prop up your father-in-law's company,' Mike said. 'You also wanted to be the family fixer. Ingratiate yourself – and Lily – with the old man.'

'I guess you could say that.'

'Even at the cost of Reed's relationship with his father.'

David looked up at Mike. 'You could say that, too, Detective.'

'What happened when Tanya got in touch with her father?' I asked. 'Did she show up at the offices, like before?'

'I wasn't intending on her going that far,' David said. 'It just started with some phone calls. I mean, Tanya didn't need much prompting. She's much more unstable than I thought.'

'You set her in motion?' Mike said.

'Yeah, but then I lost control. Just lost her,' he said. 'Wolf never let me in on it – that's what's so ironic. He must have dumped the assignment on Reed after all, since he was already the king of hopeless causes.'

'Did Reed know you wanted a piece of the action?' Mike said. 'The family money?'

'Sure. Sure he did. Just my being around made him angry, especially since Wolf played us one against the other. Very much the Savage style.'

'That assignment to make Tanya go away gave Reed a chance to get back in his father's favor,' I said, 'by ridding him of Tanya and her bad juju.'

David threw up his hands. 'That's where it went dark for me,' he said. 'Tanya dropped me once I met with her briefly and gave her some cash – too much cash. We talked to each other a few times, I told her I'd back her if she wanted to get more money out of Wolf. But then, a couple of weeks later, it was quiet. Way too quiet.'

'What did you think?' I asked.

This was the most heartless group of people I'd encountered in ages.

'Well, just that she went back home. Took my money and left town,' David said. 'She was gone, and Wolf never opened his mouth to me about her. You have to believe me when I say I never thought she'd wind up dead. Never. This idea of mine was just about getting Lily and my kids – and even Tanya – money that I thought was rightfully theirs.'

Greed. Two people murdered. Two suspects, one already in custody. David's role would also be examined and re-examined in the days that followed.

David fell on his sword – the imagery seemed to fit the setting tonight – and admitted that throughout the period before and after Tanya arrived in town, he had been pressuring Wolf Savage to change his will.

'Did Reed know about that too?' Mike asked.

A motive for murder couldn't be clearer.

'He did,' David said. 'He even called me out on it.'

'Before Wolf died?'

David put his elbows on the table and his head in his hands. 'Yes, two or three weeks before.'

'Did you actually get anywhere with Wolf and a new will?' I asked. 'Anywhere beyond the testamentary letters?'

David wouldn't pick up his head. 'Does that make me guilty of something?'

'I think everything you had to do with Wolf Savage and the family makes you guilty of more things than I can enumerate for you right now, but most of them can't be prosecuted in a court of law.' I was short with him, sick of his self-serving whine. 'I want to know if there's another will.'

'Just an interim one,' he said. 'I got him to see my lawyer, but – but Wolf never had time to sign it. Time, or maybe interest in signing it. Look, are you charging me with anything?'

'Too close to call, like they say in politics. First thing we got on our plates is Reed,' Mike said. 'They're taking a splinter out of his thigh right now, but then I get to cuff him and take him away.'

I bit my lip. It would have been the first time I'd laughed all night. A steel 'splinter' embedded in the killer's thigh.

'Tiziana Bolt. What do you know about Tiz?' I asked David.

'Everything I know I learned way too late.'

'Like what?'

It was as though David Kingsley was getting a load off his chest. 'That Wolf had developed a habit, back in rehab, of putting his hands on her – all over her – and that recently he'd done it one time too many.'

'She told you that?'

'No. Wolf admitted it to me. He was complaining about her attitude recently. He was miserable about the fact that she had hooked up with Reed,' David said. 'Wolf was actually worried she was conniving with Reed to help him hold on to his share of the family fortune.'

'But he kept her on the payroll anyway?' I asked.

David looked up at me. 'She had put so much into the show, and into the exhibit at the Costume Institute. Wolf was going to get past this long week and then hang Tiz out to dry.'

Whether or not Reed talked in the next few days – to explain his relationship with Tiz in more detail, which he thought he'd kept secret from everyone at the company, to describe what had brought him to have Tanya killed, and to admit that he and Tiz had conspired to kill Wolf Savage and stage a suicide – Mike and Mercer were already planning ways to advance the case. There would be phone records, texts and emails, then airline tickets, hotel records, and witnesses to track down.

WolfWear and the entire Savage empire were at risk. The business was not likely to survive this week, despite the evening's dramatic launch.

Someone – perhaps a special prosecutor – would be assigned to see if there was any significance to the connection between District Attorney Paul Battaglia and George Kwan. Whether Kwan had any role in the decline of the Savage businesses would be an issue, too.

Hal Savage, the life of the party in the Costume Institute downstairs at the very moment we were meeting, was going to be the subject of a fraud investigation at the DA's Office. It seemed to me that he had not played any role in the murder of his brother, despite their falling-out over the financial state of the business, but too much money had disappeared, and the search to find it would start on his desk.

WolfWear, which had appeared to be such a worldwide success for so long, was teetering on the brink of failure. I had no doubt Battaglia's white-collar-crime team would be scouring the books and bank records to find the paper trail of its dwindling proceeds. The company seemed to be close to declaring bankruptcy, and this telescoping set of scandals was likely to topple the entire global enterprise – the lifelong dream of Velvel Savitsky.

Forty-seven

'Take me home,' I said to Mike when we'd finished talking to David Kingsley and Mercer escorted him out of the small office.

'You wanted to come to this party. I'm afraid you're here till the bitter end.'

'Please, Mike. I don't have the heart for this.'

'Commissioner Scully's on his way, babe,' he said, taking me in his arms. 'He's going to do a presser on the museum steps at midnight. You can't go anywhere before then.'

'I don't want to see Scully. Don't—'

'Hush. Come with me,' Mike said. 'It's all quiet in Dendur now. Mercer's gone to find a waiter to meet us over there. Let's have a drink.'

We started to walk through the hallways, the now-quiet galleries, toward the Dendur wing.

'I've got to go back for Mrs Stafford's pearls, Mike,' I said. 'Even though they're her fakes.'

'Mrs Stafford's pearls aren't real?'

'Her fakes are worth more than most people's real

necklaces,' I said. 'I was almost relieved when they rolled all over the floor. Real pearls have silk knots between every single bead so they can't break away like these did. She wasn't kidding when she told me they were her travel jewels – imitations of her great ones.'

'Not to worry, Coop. There are two janitors and four cops on their hands and knees chasing after the Stafford pearls. You can spend the next month stringing them back together – knots or no knots,' Mike said. 'It'll be the perfect therapy for you.'

'I should be picking them up myself.'

'No, you should be telling me what the hell got into you today. How come I didn't even make you in the crowd?'

'You're slipping, Detective. I thought you'd know me anywhere.'

We walked into the Dendur wing together. The cleanup crew had already removed the hundreds of folding chairs and stacked them outside the entrance. The spotlights had been shut off and the music had stopped.

The space was still and serene, a waxing moon hanging above the glass roof, illuminating the ancient temple and the shallow pool of water that surrounds it. It remained the most magnificent room in Manhattan.

I walked to the edge of the reflecting pool, stepped out of my purloined sandals, and sat down on the edge. I pulled up my leggings and put my feet in the water. My calves ached, but then so did all of me.

Mercer came in, too, followed by one of the waiters. The young man was carrying a silver tray, with a glass of scotch for me and drinks for both Mike and Mercer.

Mike rolled up the legs of his tuxedo pants, took off his shoes and socks, and sat down beside me.

'Don't get the tux wet,' I said, leaning my head against his shoulder.

'It's rented, babe. I can go for a swim if I want.'

Mercer stood over us, passing out the drinks from the waiter's tray.

'You won't be mad at me if I have a nightcap?' I asked Mike.

'You can have anything you want tonight.'

I sat up straight and lifted my glass.

Mike clinked me first. 'To Vlad! Here's to Vlad the Impaler. Head of the house of Dracula.'

Mercer tapped his glass against ours.

'I did get a bite or two in on Reed's hands, you know,' I said. 'Maybe there's something to the Dracula myth after all.'

'You got Reed with a glaive, Coop.'

'A what?'

'It's a single-ended blade on the end of a pole,' Mike said. 'First time I'll ever have one as evidence. You shafted the bastard.'

'He was trying to knock me out, Mike. Maybe worse.'

'I'm not being critical. I'm a little bit in awe,' he said. 'You nailed the sucker with the glaive of the bodyguard of the Duke of Mantua, 1580. That's what it says right on the wall of the museum. It will make for a great piece of evidence at the trial.'

The drink was as refreshing for my throat – and my spirits – as the cold water was on my legs. The setting was magical, even if the evening had almost been a catastrophe.

'Keith Scully is going to be so mad at me,' I said.

I was staring up at the moon, wishing I were thousands of miles away from the police commissioner and the district attorney.

'The commissioner? On a night you solved two homicides? For now, he'll be a prince, Coop. He won't tell you what he really thinks for another week or two.'

'Why? What did he say to you?' I asked. 'What does Scully really think?'

'That you're back in the game, Coop. That we've got you back in the game.'

Forty-eight

Keith Scully didn't need me standing on the steps of the Metropolitan Museum of Art with him when he announced the arrest of Reed Savage and asked for the public's help in finding Tiziana Bolt. He was flanked by Mike Chapman and Mercer Wallace.

I watched from within the Great Hall. Scully's announcement was short, because of the time of night, lack of notice, and need to put together a full package of facts. But it might have been the most elegant venue in which an NYPD press conference was ever held.

Mike came back inside after the commissioner left. We waited while crews took down the bank of microphones and all the cameras were carted off in reporters' vans.

The last of the security guards were waiting for Mike and me to leave.

Mike took off his jacket and put it around my shoulders. 'Time to go, babe.'

'Are you sure there are no photographers left out there?'

'Just pigeons, so far as I can tell,' he said. 'New York at night, Coop. Just pigeons and perps.'

'One fewer of those,' I said, walking through the revolving door behind Mike and taking his hand to go down the steps.

'We'll go to my place. That way we'll avoid anyone looking for you.'

'Makes good sense.'

We were halfway down before I heard footsteps. I picked up my head and saw a figure in a dark suit coming up the staircase, almost upon us.

'Mike—' I said, tensing up and dropping his arm.

'It's okay, Coop. It's your boss.'

'Alex,' Paul Battaglia said, calling out my name. 'Alex, we've got to talk.'

'This isn't the time, Mr B,' Mike said. 'I'm taking her home.'

'Keith Scully told me you were still here, Alex. I need five minutes with you.'

Battaglia was one step below me, practically face-to-face.

'Not tonight, Paul,' I said.

Not without my lawyer, I thought.

I saw a man leaning out of the passenger window of a car that had stopped at the curb. He reached out his arm in our direction.

I couldn't see because of the dark that he had an object in his hand, and didn't know it was a gun until he fired two shots.

Paul Battaglia fell forward. I caught him as he collapsed in my arms.

Mike ran down the museum staircase, but the car was already out of sight.

I lowered myself onto the steps, holding Battaglia all the while, repeating his name over and over but getting no response.

Blood pooled beneath us. I saw the hole in the back of his head.

Mike was on his cell, yelling at the 911 dispatcher for an ambulance and backup.

'It's too late, Mike,' I said. 'The district attorney is dead.'

ACKNOWLEDGEMENTS

'I don't design clothing,' Ralph Lauren once remarked. 'I design dreams.'

The business side of the fashion industry that is based on those creative dreams is now valued at close to four *trillion* dollars globally – about two percent of the world's gross domestic product. The seasonal visions showcased in glossy magazines and on designers' runways are elegant and chic, bold and original. They are meant to attract and entice women and men, to make us believe our lives could be altered if only we could own that particular look. And yet the process to get the products from the drawing board to the factory to the catwalk to the showroom to the retail outlet and into our closets is as tough to manage and to control as the most rough-and-tumble kind of enterprise.

New York's famed Garment District was long the capital of America's fashion industry. A neighborhood that once produced ninety-five percent of our clothing now makes only three percent. But it has a riveting history and is still the heart of a business that thrives on the illusions of its great masters.

My very dear friend Fern Mallis – a brilliant fashionista and former executive director of the Council of Fashion Designers of America – was one of my most important muses in this endeavor. I am grateful for her time spent with me, her unique insider's view of Seventh Avenue and its inhabitants, and for her fabulous book, *Fashion Lives: Fashion Icons.*

Jimmy West, formerly of the NYPD, has been a great friend and a lieutenant detective with unparalleled investigative skills. He gave me an unusual idea for a murder, for which only a crime writer – not a perp – can publicly acknowledge thanks.

As much as I love style, all my information about the business came from well-researched and written news articles. *The New York Times* is a favorite resource – especially stories by Vanessa Friedman, Jean Appleton, Ralph Blumenthal, Ben Schott, and so many others; Kirstie Clements in *The Guardian*; Nicholas Coleridge in *The Fashion Conspiracy*; and regular reads in *Women's Wear Daily.*

Once again, my heroes are the women and men of the NYPD and the New York County District Attorney's Office, always working on the side of the angels.

Thanks always to my Dutton team: Ben Sevier, editor and publisher; Stephanie Kelly; Carrie Swetonic; Christine Ball; Emily Brock; and Andrea Santoro. And to all who work with me at Little, Brown UK.

Laura Rossi Totten keeps me tweeting and Facebooking and linked in to the world of social media with grace and intelligence. Thankfully, she has Matt and Julia at her back.

Esther Newberg at ICM – about whom I have not much more to add after thirty years – remains *simply the best.* Thanks, Zoe Sandler, for all you do for me.

My family and friends are my greatest joy. I've said it before and it's still true. Lisa and Alex, Suzy and Marc – and all the 'Mighties' – this one is for you.

Justin Feldman, Bobbie and Bones Fairstein, and Karen Cooper – you are all always with me.

Michael Goldberg has my back, and more important, my heart. We are still swaying, which is a wonderfully happy thought whenever I am poised to pound the keyboard with Coop and Chapman.

The very first Alexandra Cooper

The days of Assistant DA Alexandra Cooper often start off badly, but she's never before had to face the morning by reading her own obituary.

It doesn't take long to sort out why it was printed: a woman's body has been found in a car rented in Alex's name in the driveway of her weekend home. It's not so easy to work out why her lodger – an acclaimed Hollywood star – was murdered, or to be sure that the killer had found the right victim.

As Alex's job is to send killers and rapists to jail there are plenty of suspects who might be seeking revenge, and whoever it is needs to be found before Alex's obituary gets reprinted . . .

*

'Final Jeopardy has it in spades . . . engaging characters, an intelligent story full of twists, terrific tension' *The Times*